Sweetbitter

Sweetbitter

A Novel

REGINALD GIBBONS

Broken Moon Press • Seattle

ISBN 0-913089-51-6
Library of Congress Catalog Card Number 94-71680

Cover image, "Floyd Burroughs' Working Shoes, Hale County, Alabama,
1936," by Walker Evans. Courtesy of the Harry Ransom Humanities
Research Center, University of Texas at Austin. Used by permission.
Author photo copyright © 1992 by Mary Hanlon. Used by permission.

Project editor: Lesley Link
Copy editor: Paula Ladenburg
Proofreader: Brandy K. Denisco
Text preparation by: Melissa Shaw

Broken Moon Press
Post Office Box 24585
Seattle, Washington 98124-0585 USA

For Reuben and Martha

Acknowledgments

With all my heart I thank Cornelia Spelman. And to Angela Jackson and Teresa Cader, my thanks.

For their encouragement and care and labor, their cheer and enthusiasm, I thank Lesley Link, Paula Ladenburg, and John Ellison at Broken Moon Press.

Contents

Contents

Part Three: Still 1910

Part Four: 1916

Contents

Sweetbitter

Prologue

Many generations ago Aba, the great spirit above, created many men, all *chahtah*, who spoke the language of the *chahtah*, and understood one another. They came from the heart of the earth and were made of yellow clay, and before them no men had ever lived.

One day they all gathered and looking upward wondered what the blue of the sky and the white of the clouds were made of. They determined to try to reach the sky by building a great mound. They piled up rocks to build a mound that would reach the sky but at night the wind blew from above so strong that the rocks fell down. The second day they worked again, building the mound but again that night the wind came while they slept and it pushed down their work. On the third day they began yet again. But that night the wind blew so hard it hurled the rocks of the mound down upon the builders themselves.

They were not killed, but when daylight came and they crawled out from beneath the rocks that had fallen on them and began to talk to one another, they discovered that they could no longer understand each other. They spoke many languages instead of one. Some of them spoke the original language, the *chahtah* language. Others, who no longer spoke this language, began to fight among themselves. Finally they separated. The *chahtah* remained, the original people, and lived near *nanih waya*, the mound they had not been able to build. And the others went north and east and west and were the different tribes.

In this way all the peoples of the earth were created, each from different substance and thus of different appearance, and at times struggling against each other.

Part One: 1896

1

Big House

When Reuben was about six years old his mother Molly Charles was leading him by the hand one early spring day, walking quickly to get down from the Big House, where she was working for the Negro cook in the garden. For days the cook had bossed several of Mr. Davis's Negro men and Molly about what she wanted planted and where and how. Only Molly, for her good hand with vegetables, for her being a woman among these men, had been treated with some regard; the others the vehement cook had called field nigger and sent to the devil. Rough men, they had laughed at her insults, but they had complied with her orders and had shot a glance from time to time at the barn or the back door of the Big House, in case Mr. Davis or the factor was watching them.

On her way home with Reuben, Molly was carrying a bit of cloth in which was wrapped her pay of a little meat and salt, some mealy stale flour, some seed potatoes and seed corn—she and her family had had to eat their own. Down behind their cabin her mother was planting their own vegetable plot, waiting with the younger children for Molly's help and whatever seed she might bring from the Big House. But when in her haste and her fatigue Molly cut off some of the distance by leading Reuben nearer than usual to the Big House, past the side window that looked out toward the river, Reuben wanted to see in. He'd never asked before. She said no, they must hurry down, to use the last twilight in their own garden, *ippokni* was waiting for them. But he slowed her,

7

stubbornly setting his small heels in the cold dirt and pulling her back by the folds and fall of her dress. She set down her little bundle and with a groan she lifted him up.

She herself had never been farther inside that house than the back steps to the kitchen, nor had she ever been in any such building. But she knew well what this room looked like. Since she herself was a girl, she had stopped secretly to stare in at this very window. On dark late winter afternoons after she had helped stir and wring the wash in two great kettles in the back yard, her hands chapped and cracking till she could grease them at home, she would stop a moment to see the candles and lanterns lit inside the Big House, and sometimes would quickly shrink back as Mr. Davis or his wife or one of their two children, the girl, the boy, would pass by. That family had to traverse a distance to get from one corner of their house to the other. Molly might imagine that somehow or other she would be invited to come in, that somehow she herself might have a little version of such a house; but she also thought that everyone inside such a house seemed separate and apart from everyone else. It was not really a house, but a great fantastic place in which only the little Davis family lived.

Now Reuben was standing on her knee, looking in at what she had already repeatedly studied; it had never been changed or rearranged. He would be seeing that the table in the center of the room was polished and that it reflected the image of the wall lanterns of the next room. And in the center of the table would be a great glass dish with early spring flowers standing up in it. Around the table would be eight chairs with striped cloth seats. The walls had more stripes running down and up. Against the walls he would notice a dark wooden chest with huge drawers, and a cabinet with glass fronts, filled with china dishes; he wouldn't know what those were. And more chairs. The room was more crowded with things than any place he'd have ever seen. On the wall he would see glass-covered pictures of things, like dark windows with black window frames around them; it had always been too dark when Molly looked, also, for her to have made out much of what they showed.

There was a fireplace, but he would not see it lit, for Molly never had.

A little rain began to fall, and Molly was in a hurry. But Reuben did not want to get down. He wanted to keep looking, he squirmed in her grip and stretched upward to see, when they were both frightened by a voice that struck them cold, calling sharply, "What the hell you doing?"

Molly dropped Reuben to the ground quickly, where he lost his feet and fell and looked up at her, frightened and hurt. She could not manage the struggle between the quick remorse she felt at letting him fall, the wound of that to both her son and herself, and the darting fear that made it hard for her even to look up at the tall young black man, the butler, dressed like a white man on Sunday, standing over her. Confused, in a panic, her head down, she looked to one side and then to the other, not answering him. She stared at his leather boots instead of looking up at him. He asked her what the hell her name was, and she whispered it. He asked her what the hell her son's name was and she said Reuben Charles. He wrinkled his nose and told her she was a filthy Chactaw and to get the hell away from there and if he saw her thieving around again by the house he would have her hauled off and whipped. Reuben, standing beside her, was shaking, but to witness his mother's humiliation made the air thicken in his lungs and throat, and perhaps it was in that moment that he first found how to make his eyes unreadable. A necessary skill, in later life. A little cautiously, he looked in a new way at his mother, too. (In after days, at play he mimed a whipping and shooting of invisible enemies.)

Not looking at the black man, Molly pulled her son up and then, as fast as he could go, together they ran off away from the Davis's house to their own cabin a quarter mile down the dirt road, saying nothing to each other, or to anyone else when they arrived, and in the half-dark planted the potatoes and corn.

2

The Doctor

By the time Reuben was about eleven years old, Molly had been ill and weakening for half a year, unable to work very much, going up less frequently to the Big House to help the cook. Every evening after the family had eaten—boiled meat when occasionally they had it, from Peter Hill's hunts or those of his sons, who were more active than he, but not much good as hunters, and thin corn mush cooked with it in the same big pot—she had pains in her stomach. When she stood up the pains made her feel faint; when she lay down in the corner on a blanket all day, they kept her from eating enough or sleeping. Peter Hill walked two days to ask the one doctor of whom they knew to come and cure his daughter. Waiting two more days for the doctor, Molly lay in misery at night, sometimes pulled half upright from her sleep by the knotted pain that pushed and tore at her and left her weak when after one hour or two it passed. The doctor arrived at last, and asked for his payment of a meal and dried meat and one dollar before he would begin. He was a foul-smelling and mean-looking old man with one cloudy eye turned upward and out, but he knew stories and rituals that he said were the old *chahtah* ways. The family listened and Peter Hill nodded and vocally assented now and again as the doctor chanted and recited. Pearl said nothing, only stared at her oldest daughter. The doctor pressed little rolled-up peas of cotton into Reuben's mother's bare belly, over where her pain lay. He lit them with a burning twig, and she winced. She was accumulating a swarm of blisters; but the pain did not abate. The doctor chanted. He bent over her body and put his mouth on her belly and seemed to suck at her flesh, with noises like a dog's; he raised his head and made an imaginary spitting into his own cupped hands, the one and then the other; and then he bent to her body again. Finally he stood up and went out of the cabin, with Molly's sisters and brothers following, while Pearl moved to her daughter's side; on the rough trunk of a scrubby pine growing to one side of the cabin the *chahtah* doctor wiped both his hands.

He prepared, for Molly, pine-root water, *tiaôksês shuwa*, and she took it in her tin cup that was so much her own, and she drank it down.

3

Resolution

The Davis's black cook had wanted to bring Molly to a black doctor. She said he knew cures better than the Indian doctor's. But Molly would not go. She was afraid. Lying abed, growing thinner, nevertheless she recovered somewhat again, as she had done before, and she determined to leave her home place entirely, as she had often said she would. She said it had become a poison place, and that when she left it she would get well. She did not listen to her younger sisters, who pleaded with her, or the cook, who warned her not to go but to stay. Her younger brothers said little, regarding her almost as if she were a stranger. To herself Molly argued that nothing would ever change for them, they were all hungry all the time, they would all have to make new lives somehow or die as their mother and father were dying, and for Reuben it must not be the same as for them.

It made no sense to travel when she was so soon and so precariously recovered, but she would not be held back. Secretly the cook gave her dried meat, cornbread and biscuits from the Big House, and talked to her about her road to The Nations, north and west, for the cook knew all about roads that led away. She brought Molly also some cucumber pickles wrapped in thick brown paper, some hard crackers, a big piece of cheese, and more food—more than Molly Charles could carry, and when she came home with it, the last time she would come home from that kitchen, her sisters looked so wretched that she divided the food and

13

gave half to her mother. Reuben would carry what was left, and although it would keep them only a few days, she said she would work here and there, as they needed more; and Reuben was big, now, it would be the two of them traveling and working together, he would help her. She was going.

It was in May, already the hot season. When she had gathered what few things were hers, among them the tin cup the cook had given her years before, and a small tin kettle with many dents, and the pair of unworn moccasins that Pearl had made, and two cotton blankets, and her provisions for the road, in two of her baskets, one small and one large, and had put on her clean dress, red and white checkers, and her bonnet, then with Reuben she had stood in the dooryard with her family and they had embraced each other and the women had wept, and her brothers had looked at her hard and uncomprehendingly, as if they couldn't even think of what to ask her, and her father had touched her shoulder and then walked around to the back of the house and out of sight. Molly's mother held Reuben to herself until he had to push against her to get free, then she turned to Molly and took her hands tightly in both of hers, and wouldn't let go. But Molly pulled free.

Sitting down, she took a moment away from them all, to gather her courage and quiet her feelings once more; then she stood up straight and took Reuben's hand and led him away, each of them carrying a basket she had made, and the two of them grew smaller walking away down toward the main road, which would take them to the bridge across the river.

Mr. Davis, the planter, who had not known of their existence, did not know of their departure.

4
—
The Grave

Molly pulled up the hem of her loose dress to mid-shin to try to cool her legs in the still air. Reuben was startled and stood back from her when he saw the stains of dried blood inside her dress. She saw his revulsion, and with her chin on her chest, silently wept.

He had worked harder and harder for her, to spare her. He had carried whatever they had had with them, for her. He had made more and more of their evening camp, and laid the fire and settled her near it and brought her whatever she had wanted that he could find. He did not ask her for anything anymore, but got it himself; nor even ask her for comfort, but tried to give it, although he did not know from where to draw it in himself, to have enough of it to give. He had learned to hold his shoulders differently, as if they were something he carried, as men carry themselves. But he did not know what to do now.

She lay down full on the ground, stifling her tears, and immediately she felt that, without intending to, she had irrevocably yielded to the pain; she felt her body loosen, and she knew of a certainty that her yielding was not a matter of resting an extra day. She tried to climb again into her resistance, her strength—she called to her son to help her stand up again and he lifted her easily but she could scarcely stay on her legs now, who had just walked more than a mile. He had to help her step away into the brush to relieve herself, and wait for her, and then carry her back because

15

after releasing her bowels she could not quite even rise. Then he understood that from her body blood was coming, bloody excrement, and that she could not live. He laid her down carefully, but then he dashed away and she had to call him weakly several times before he could overcome his new understanding for a moment and face her, help her spread the blankets just so, as if for the night, under the tree, so she could be (this last time) not on the undifferentiated ground like a dying doe but in a human space.

With no shelter for them if it had rained, he slept beside her on the pine straw. The next day, ravenous, he succeeded in killing a squirrel and ate it. She called him to her weakly, one time, and reaching up, she took his hand; with his hand in her feeble grasp, he bent down and then sat beside her, thinking she was going to speak to him, but she didn't. When she fell asleep, her grip loosened and his hand would have fallen out of hers, but he held on to her a while longer, till he laid her hand carefully down beside her. She had become very still, and he got up and roamed around restlessly. She would open her eyes from time to time, but she did not see him when he approached her. That night he lay not so close to her, and after he looked at her in the morning, he went back out to the road they had forsaken, and he waited there for fully half the day, till he stopped a white man on horseback, the first person to pass, and told him that his mother had died in the woods. Although he could easily have communicated this in English, he was speaking, perhaps without realizing it, only in his *chahtah* tongue, *chahtah imanumpa*, words of a *chahtah*.

The man couldn't understand him, but the grime-streaked Indian boy was insistent. The man overcame his suspicion and reluctance—the boy was scarcely a threat, himself—and let himself be drawn down off his horse and led back into the woods, where he found the small body of a miserable and filthy Indian woman. Then the white man told the boy loudly and slowly not to leave this place, and he tramped back to his horse and mounted, and showing a little more urgency, he rode on into the town, an extra errand added to those he had left home with.

Reuben waited by her till a late starving hour of the day when a white preacher dressed in black, as Reuben had seen before, back home, passing on the roads or driving up to the Big House, came in a buggy with two white men riding before him on horseback, one of them the man Reuben had first stopped. They all three got down and tied up the horses, and again Reuben led the way to his mother. The preacher bent stiffly at the waist to look at her and then he straightened again. He stared at her little basket and Reuben's big one, but he didn't touch them or look inside them. Then he stared at Reuben, but the boy could not know that the preacher's distaste came from the lightness of Reuben's skin, which he took as evidence of sin and transgression. He said in English to the boy, "What was her name, boy?"

The child seemed to be studying his face, but did not answer him. "Was she a baptized Christian?" the preacher said, and waited a moment, wanting to get through all this, but the boy remained silent. The man turned away from Reuben; perhaps he was almost but not quite drawn out of his accustomed self. He prayed briefly and without conviction over the woman's body, and the two men with him went back and fetched shovels from the preacher's buggy and dug a shallow trench alongside her where she lay. While her son watched, they covered her face with her bonnet that seemed to them would be a choking offense to her if she could still smell, and then they lowered her body into the grave and she said nothing, she did not move by herself at all, but hung like a small weight from their powerful hands. One of the men leaned down and tugged the hem of her dress where it had ridden up her leg. He pulled it down to cover her all the way to her ankles. Both men wiped their hands on the cloth of their trousers after they had touched her, and then they shoveled back over her, at first gently, the heap of sandy soil, even over her face under the bonnet.

"What's your name, boy?" the preacher said to the child. The two men who had dug the hole and filled it again had already made their way back to their horses, and the preacher remained, looking at the boy. Reuben looked away from him. "You come with me, can you understand what I'm sayin?" the man said to him, speaking more loudly. Out of the corner of his eye Reuben saw a little woods spider crawling on the white man's white shirtfront. The man looked around him at the thicket, and then in the direction of the road, which was too far to be seen. "Boy, I'm asking you," he said, "what's your name. You come along with me, now." He wasn't close to Reuben when he said this, but stood a little away from him. He didn't seem to want to touch Reuben, to take him by the arm or shoulder or hand, a boy's hand, dirty and damp, and lead him back to the buggy waiting in the road, his house waiting at the end of that road—a life different, possible, waiting in that house. Reuben had a thought, for an instant, of that huge polished room he had seen through the window one time, with his mother. He kept his eyes away from the preacher's. He looked into the woods in the direction opposite where the road was. He would not go with this man or any white man, or any man or woman. He was not ready to go. Not so suddenly, as if something were over now. It was not over.

The preacher looked around, at the blackened fire ashes, the hard, useless squirrel pelts, three of them on a thin dead branch, the pitiful few possessions. He put on his hat and, slowly at first, looking back, started away, stepping almost sideways, toward the road. The boy did not call him back or follow him. Then with a decisive squaring of his shoulders, the preacher began to stride faster, clattering and crashing authoritatively in his thick trousers and his bright shirt and sweaty black coat, through the brush and branches, impediments to his purpose, till he was gone and the boy was alone in the woods.

It grew dark and the night was especially hot. Mosquitoes thronged the air, tormenting him, and from time to time a small movement in the thicket would rustle or crackle. He did not want a fire, he did not want to be known of. He didn't want to lie down where he had lain beside her. He pushed together a pile of pine straw nearby, but could not sleep, trying to listen for movement in the thicket, while the trilling of the frogs and insects was deafening, and the infuriating mosquitoes hovered at his ears. Through the trees a little starlight gleamed, and the night was not so black as it might have been. In the darkness, under the light of a crescent moon, the palmetto leaves looked like fanned knives.

When he drank from his mother's tin cup he felt she was nearer, somewhere, moving above the ground, not in it. But even if somehow there was a way she was not in that hole, she was refusing to come close and be with him, and he was angry at her for hiding.

He sat for hours without moving; a tick came crawling up his leg; he watched it through the holes and rips in his tattered trousers and felt it tickling its way toward his center, and when it reached the middle of his thigh he picked it up and put it back on his toe and watched it start to climb the length of him again; then he knocked it away.

In the failing light he squatted in the dirt, drawing lines with a twig. He pushed two chestnuts with his stick and saw them as eyes, then to make a face he put a curling leaf for the mouth. But thus the mouth was open, crying out, and he stood up and dragged his foot through the face.

He sat across the little clearing, away from his mother's grave, staring toward it in the dark till he wasn't sure what he saw. He could imagine her suddenly getting up from under the sand, brushing herself off, saying, "That was rest that I needed, my son. We're going on, now, help me carry the baskets, my son, we have to keep on if we're going to see my two cousins of my mother, we have a long way to walk, yet, to The Nations, my son." That would happen now, if he kept looking at her grave; or, it would happen if he didn't look at her grave; or, if he looked up through the tree limbs above him in a certain way to the cloudy, black sky, and some spirit of the upper world came down to help him, it would happen.

The next morning, in a warm, heavy rain, the small figure

appeared on the road of dust and sand and mud. He was carrying a large basket with a little one inside it, and he struck off alone in the unknown direction in which he and his mother had been heading when their journey together had ended.

5

To the Afterworld

From the top of a smooth red pole, where a white flag lifts and falls listlessly, the spirit of the dead person leaps off to fly to the afterworld.

There, hemmed in on both sides by high rugged hills, a deep and rapid stream remains to be crossed, rushing and foaming, coiled and roaring, where folds and falls of water snake this way and that, and logs floating down snap and splinter against rocks and are tossed up like twigs and splash down again, caught in the torrents. Laid over the river for a bridge, between high banks, is one pine log, peeled of bark and slippery wet. Down from the other bank of the deep stream come two other spirits, guardians of the path, to block the way, thrashing and flailing, holding rocks in their fists. They will come out onto the log and throw the rocks at the spirit of the dead person. If the spirit of the dead person is bad or wicked, it will try to dodge the rocks and will fall off the log, fall far down into the rushing stream, and helpless in the currents it will be carried away to a whirlpool spinning with dead fish and toads and lizards and snakes, surrounded by dead trees, where the dead are always hungry, are always sick and cannot die, where the sun never shines on the cold desert around them, where if they succeed in climbing up the steep banks out of the whirlpool they can see far away the beautiful country where the good spirits are.

But the spirit of a good person pays the attacking guardian spirits no heed, and their rocks fly past the good spirit without harming it, and the good spirit walks across the slippery log calmly and steps onto the far shore. Then the spirits of all friends and relatives already dead, smiling with happiness at the full contentment of the farther world, where there is no pain or trouble, and people feast and dance and rejoice, greet the new spirit and lead her away with them.

Part Two: 1910

6

Street Scene, with Automobile

Weaving and careening in the dark, with feeble lamps unable to illuminate the road, a coughing motorcar came rushing through the street and chuffed past Reuben. Drunken male laughter blew from the automobile, and an imprecation against the vile nigger it had nearly struck.

Reuben corrected them in a mutter, as nighttime quiet recovered its domain. Crazy-mad, orphan part-Indian part-white part-just-a-man I hope, that can't even sleep nights, anymore.

And the night, around him as he walked in it, pulsating, eating and excreting, dying and living at furious pace under leaf, under rock, under water, under roof, was cosmographying itself. Eyes everywhere turned toward him as he passed talking to himself in his head. He looked up through the overarching tree branches that were silently, motionlessly trying to touch across the width of the dirt street. A gray sky, a muslin cover of cloud, lay between the dark figure Reuben made and the not quite infinite infinite.

Crazy, not just in your mind but in that thing between your legs, is what you are, over her. You know that's it, that's what's pulling you so far into this you better get out now, you better get out or they'll take your legs right out from under you, and that other thing, too.

A gunshot, distant, made him stop, listen more carefully, even though it had nothing to do with him. Then he was striding stealthily again to the hypnotic synchronization of throbbing and ticking and caterwauling around him, that beat like slow music under the quick pace of its callers and croakers and strident chirpers, that surrounded the dark houses and poured over them, wanting inside.

And from the ground a hissing and rustling in every weedy patch or bush, even near the houses Reuben was passing noiselessly. Bull snake and rattler, possum and raccoon and house cat, cricket and tick and flea.

But no. It's not just that. It's more than that. No, it's not much, it's just *everything,* is all it is. You're lost in her—not just in her body, you're lost in the whole world of her. Is there a white people's and black people's God, after all—like Francie always said—who brought this to me, brought her? No *person* did it.

At first, it had been perhaps only a kind of dangerous game—and he had escaped from danger many times and rarely had stood in need of help, as a man. He had played the game before, for the pleasure it gave. But that longing of women whose main hope was simply a moment's laughter and forgetfulness and being cherished, this he had every time felt pressing him at his chest, pushing him away as firmly as if a feeling were a real hand. He did not like to be with a woman for whom he felt sorry, a woman whose own need embarrassed him because he did not feel the same need she felt. He'd come to expect only transient pleasure; and had tried to be tempted by no hopes of any sort. That was his rule. He had looked around him carefully every day for all the years since he had begun to move alone through the world when he was eleven or twelve, since his mother had died of a terrific pain in her belly, lying in a patch of woods somewhere that he would never find again. He had looked around him and seen no encouragement for expectations. Not for him and not for others. He thought black people were wrong to believe in a God that hadn't done anything for *them*, unless you counted helping some of them survive the afflictions that He Himself must have let the whites bring down on them.

Reuben knew hard work, small wages, times of hunger. (But at least he had avoided, since the day he remembered tossing his mother's smelly little glass flask into the brush, the traps of alcohol. Although he'd gasped on several occasions at a full swallow and then stopped; or had sipped a small amount of warm homebrew and not liked the unpleasant tang and thick odor, not really liked the loosening of his limbs. He was not one to drink, as Drum had been.)

This intoxication, though, that was in his whole body, reached where nothing had reached, before. That he didn't cut and run from her, from the whole town, didn't mean he couldn't have. But he didn't. He was filled with a mood of awaiting, now, with a not-yet-knowing-but-I-will-know. I don't need her, he thought. I've lived my whole life without her. Without needing. But maybe his whole life wasn't what he had thought it was—which was just a simple thing: a boy, then a young man, on the move, carrying only secret memories of a family long ago, no home to invite or imprison him now. Not black folks and not white; not much of an Indian, either, for his skin was of some hue unclassified by the tireless classifiers. (They knew it wasn't their color, anyway.) And to confuse them further, he spoke well and he could read and figure and he liked showing that he could. He could talk any which way, white or black and shades between, depending on where he was— it didn't trouble his thinking but took care of itself by itself, his talking.

He counted off nine steps as he walked and multiplied by nine; then eight and multiplied by nine; and always had liked it that all the totals added up to nine if you added sideways. Then if you multiplied those totals by nine the new ones, so much larger, all added sideways to nine or eighteen. And on it went, that secret little dance of the nines. The white clerks in the stores must know of things like that, it wouldn't be news to them.

"*I* can *figure!*" he said to the night, loudly, as he walked straight on; said it with exaggeratedly correct white schoolmistress pronunciation.

"I can figure!" he said again, gutterally. And then, to himself,

Ah kin figgur. And what good's it done me? What good's it do me to've read through the whole entire Bible, Francie pushing me on? Does innybody care about that?

Snarling to the deaf night, echoing himself loudly: *"Keer 'bout dat?"*

Only the throbbing of the late late dark answered him. Most people were asleep.

Then there was some kind of noise and he stopped instantly in shadows and was invisible. A repeated rhythmical scraping sound, very near. He looked around. In the shadow of cloud-light a black dog was trying to vomit in the street and at last it did, and stood haggard and motionless over the phosphorescent puddle it had labored out of itself, and it raised its head toward Reuben, but it did not stir its legs. Man and dog looked at each other. Then the dog melted out of its exhausted rigid pose and walked slowly away, stiff-legged, into the darkness.

Reuben went on.

A young woman white woman not yet turned twenty! And he himself only a few years older than she. And was she entirely clear in her head? There were things odd about her, yes there were, *de-cidedly*. But maybe that was what young white women were all like, how was he to know? Or was it her, her own peculiar way? But it did not loom large against the sweetness of her, her scent, her limbs, her warm skin like some smoothness unknown on this earth, over which his hand moved smoothly.

Till again he was saying to himself, Crazy Indian, half-just-as-white-as-them—half crazy, for sure—they will kill you, boy. Or worse. In Texas.

He laughed. He lifted his chin up and laughed at the undersides of the leaves of the trees, at the undersides of the tattered night clouds rushing over the moon like fast water over a sunken stone, at Francie's God who was God to black people and to white people both. And he shook his head at himself, and his feet in boots were noiseless in the soft dirt of the street.

It had once been, long ago, that a white woman had touched his hair as he stood on a town street with his mother; and after he fled Francie's house, a white man had shaken Reuben's hand and congratulated himself for giving the well-spoken Indian boy a day's odd jobs and dirty work for nearly nothing in pay. But now Reuben was aware of eyes on his back, of a tenseness that came into the bodies of white people when he drew near them in towns, even though he kept the assigned distance between himself and them— just as black men did, unless in a flashing mood to annihilate and to be annihilated they embraced great danger. Such moods do come, and Reuben had felt them, too.

He had noted the relief he was to town people—in Three Rivers like everywhere else—when he moved past them and they let go of their fear of being accosted; sometimes the Negro women, too, even in Smithville. People seemed to expect his ways to be different from everyone else's. Just because he *looked* different from all the rest of them? If he spoke to them his ability to sound different from what they had expected put some of them—some of them— a little more at ease, and they could squint their mind's eyes shut on him or on who they had supposed or feared he was. Some of them. There were always others who looked shocked to hear Reuben talk, he was putting on unseemly airs, he was out of his place, usurping—mocking?—theirs. Anyway, he wasn't one to talk much to any but himself. And now despite all the warnings this world had given him, he was hiding here and there to be met by a white girl of good family, whose hands had played over his bare shoulders and face, whose naked breasts had pressed against his bare chest and fitted into the palms of his hands, whose body she wanted him to gaze at and touch, and hold, and enter. *Not* a "white girl," but Martha. His Martha.

He unbuttoned his shirt cuffs and pulled his shirttails out of his trousers. From neck to waist he unbuttoned and then flung the shirtfronts away from his chest like wings to each side, to feel the night air.

She smiled at him from below when he undressed over her.

That moment—their bodies naked to each other, and naked

29

together to the air, the unmeasured freedom of it, the anticipation, poured into his memory as freshly as when it had first happened a good many days before. And the times since. He walked faster. All around him Three Rivers slept. Now he was entering the zone between the white town and the black town, walking with a long stride, out in the open now, between a warehouse and a feed store, and then beyond, between fields. Heading to his room. His shirt blown back from him to each side as he walked. The unmeasurable freedom of it.

7

Why Doves Coo in Mourning

Long ago the people became very wicked and the Great Spirit decided to send a huge flood to drown all but Oklatabashih and his family, who were good. The Great Spirit told Oklatabashih to build a large boat and take into it the male and female of every animal upon the earth. This he did, and the rain fell until the earth was covered and all the people and animals who were not on Oklatabashih's boat perished. Then the rain stopped and there was only night.

In the north there appeared a streak of light, and the people thought that the sun had gotten lost and was rising in the north. But it was only the great wave of the flood, like mountains upon mountains, that rolled over the earth again and tossed the boat about.

When the boat had floated for many months, Oklatabashih sent out a dove, and when she returned with her beak full of grass, Oklatabashih rewarded her with a little salt in her food. Soon afterward the new sea that had covered the earth subsided, and the dry land appeared once more, and the people and animals went down from the boat to live on the land.

After her reward of salt, the dove had acquired a liking for it, and she visited saltlicks to get it. She passed this liking on to her children. One day when tending her grandchildren she forgot to eat a little salt, as was her habit. The Great Spirit was angry at her for forgetting her part in the saving of the men and animals, and he punished her and her descendants by forbidding her ever to eat salt again. Her grandchildren began to coo for their salt, but she could not give it to them.

From that day, in memory of their lost salt, the doves everywhere continue their cooing for it.

8

Martha Clarke

Slowly, after many months, after many conversations, after time stolen from time, and in places stolen from the view of any other person, because she was as white-skinned as the moon and he was something akin to the color of red clay, Martha Clarke drew out of Reuben S. Sweetbitter—the only other colored person (was that what he was, really?) she'd ever heard of who had a middle initial was the Negro doctor—some small part of the tale of his odd past and his solitary life. That he was reluctant to speak of it only made her want all the more to know who he was. He was so completely different from any other man she had ever met or was ever likely to meet. "I want to *know*," she'd say to him almost vehemently when he wouldn't answer some question she would have put to him about his own life.

Why did he, why, want to keep his secrets from her? It almost made her angry.

In particular, he did not seem to want to tell her any more about that moment, more than half his life ago, when with not even a bird voice from the upper world to guide him, he said, not even a powerless sparrow to keep him company, he had stood at the side of a muddy road with nothing behind or before him, orphaned by his mother's death in the backwoods, alone in a way Martha had never been and could not even imagine being. He said he remembered remembering at that moment what had gone before—in that rainy moment when even the birds were huddled for shelter on low limbs against tree trunks, and the morning sky was dark and overpoweringly huge, he remembered remembering, as he stood in that road, a little camp fire he and his mother had built one night, in some lost place marked by nobody else's passing. After they had eaten in the dusk, and she had told him a story in the dark, and on her blanket she had curled up on her side with her knees to her aching belly, he had lain awake looking at her, and then had turned his eyes to the dying fire. The green twigs hissed and sputtered, and a vein of sap would sing a note and then go out, and each popping of the wood tossed a few sparks into the air, where they would rise wavering into the darkness a little way and go out. And under the ground, under the waters, he had sensed the hungry and evil demons moving in the lower world. He said he had nightmares about those demons for a long while afterward. But that was a child's fear, he said—there was no lower nor upper world, he had decided, only this one in the middle.

Martha had carried notes from her mother to her mother's friends, sometimes in a basket with muffins or fresh bread; she had given her mother's name and where they lived to any adult who asked, when she was a child, who her mother was; behind her present mind there was some cavity, sealed by uneasiness, in which lay obscure memories that had made her mother a frightening power—to have had *no* mother, even one whom, deeply and dimly, she was not sure she trusted, was to her inconceivable. And whereas Martha's present sense of her mother had come along mostly unremarked in her own life, Reuben's life was scarred by that abrupt grief.

When she asked him, "What was your mama's name?" he still wouldn't say. She wondered when he *would* tell her, for she didn't want to ask again until she was sure he would answer, and she didn't even know when that would be, or in what relationship she and he would have to stand before he would answer such a question. She felt an avid appetite for him; for all there was to *know* about him.

Martha had just turned nineteen on July the fifth; she was

rounded and smooth. With strong legs, feet a little large, round hips, a waist much narrower than her hips, graceful arms and hands, small ears, very dark eyebrows, hair nearly black, full breasts. Her skin was very pale. In tightly wound braids her hair hung in kinked masses, ending in frizzy tails. She freed it and vigorously brushed it out and down every night, and again in the morning, before she braided it and coiled it into a bun and pinned its nearly ungovernable spring into close submission for the daylight hours.

She would sometimes sit hidden by the window of her room, mornings, where her mother had hung double curtains; Martha would tie back the heavy outer ones and look out through the lace inner ones. There, as if resting her body on the little boudoir chair while her thoughts flew so strenuously, she would remain motionless in the sound of a nearby turtledove repeating its melancholy call outside. Where her thoughts went was down the street to the square, and past it out the west side of town, past the sawmill, and into whatever it was that lay beyond. Which she had never seen.

She was very given to reading. Was often surreptitiously lost in pages of print, and had stolen down many books from her father's shelves in the wide alcove off the bedroom he shared with his wife, an alcove he called his "library." Martha had read the precise and fussy provisions of law, the florid historical accounts of European wars and American settlement, the cold descriptions of the diseases and afflictions of horses and cattle and chickens (as well as the several doctrines of their causes and the veterinary remedies to be tried). She had considered the ornate obfuscatory language of treaties, had read of American frontier wars and of the fiendish predations of both Mexicans and savages. She had pondered the orotundities and profusions of patriotic pride over Texas independence. She had puzzled over Confederate passion and theological dogma.

Her mother too had touched all those books, but only to take them down for dusting every six months; Martha had opened them. Nearly every heavy brown volume of his three hundred or so had been secreted in her bedroom one at a time, where even the Negro maid Pilgrim, more zealous at cleaning than she needed to be, would not find it. (Martha's mother had once turned away a Negro woman also named Martha, thoroughly unwilling to call any maid by the same name as her daughter. Peremptorily Mama had said to the woman, "That name won't do. In this house you will answer to Nellie." "No ma'am," the woman had said, "my name is Martha." She had been denied the job for her intolerable impertinence.) Then Martha would return each book to the shelves where she had earlier adjusted the others to disguise the gap. Hidden in her bedroom even more carefully were the novels she borrowed from Clara Simmons, whose mother went to Houston two or three times a year and each time brought back, among other purchases, novels and ladies' magazines. Houston was not so much more of a town as people there thought it was, but it was in touch with the world.

Martha's father, a man well-regarded for his legal practice in real estate, civil suits and business law, and a deacon of the First Methodist Church, had provided his family with a spacious house in which Martha, her younger brother, James, and the youngest child, Anne, each had a bedroom. But her father acted as if his responsibility to his family was almost exclusively material, and the more he invested ostentatiously in their house and furnishings, the more he seemed to resent any need of theirs, however seldom, for his attention. James, by virtue of having been frequently whipped with a belt when he was a boy, had perhaps received more attention than Martha or Anne. And in the town cemetery were the small graves of two more children who had died as infants. It seemed to Martha that on the annual family visits to their plots (her mother would go once a month) her father acted like a man to whom those graves were at most a passing curiosity. (But she thought it did occur to him once in a while that in one of those graves were the remains of another son.)

When he rumbled every half year or so that the times would eventually force him to the expense of a motor car, but that he was holding out a while longer, Martha's mother would mention how conveniently he and she could visit the cemetery if they had a motor car; he would glance at her with a sharp, surprised curiosity, as if she were a stranger to him, and her remark would seem to put him off the purchase even longer.

On evenings when parents and the two daughters sat on the porch, waiting, as often as not, for James to come home from ramblings that the parents willfully misconstrued as innocent, Martha would wonder what thoughts occupied her father, how she could be related to him, and then, pretending to busy herself with her crochet work or needlepoint, she might wonder how any one of them was related to her, she felt so different from them all. Was she a foundling they had taken in? Had they adopted her? She would never ask.

She studied the shapes of their hands, the length of their arms and legs, the configuration of eyes and nose and mouth. They could all seem strangers—plump Anne, an envious spy, not admiring Martha as Martha would have wished to have been admired by a sister five years younger; James, on whom Martha chose not to think; her mother; her father, a foreign person, always smelling strongly of tobacco and ink, who dressed and undressed—even thought and felt—so carefully shut away from the rest of them in his bedroom and "library" that he seemed actually to live in there and only to visit these outer rooms and spaces, these other persons of the family, on his way from his private domain into the world of his work, his office in town, in the morning, and on the way back into his retreat in the evening after pausing briefly for supper with them all. In there, he would read newspapers and write in his large journal-book of the satisfactions of his legal cases, and draft letters which only rarely he polished and copied out and mailed to the editors of newspapers in the region. Three Rivers' one paper had failed some years ago.

So thoroughly separate was Martha's father's realm that her mother would say of him simply that he was *in there*. Martha's mother had trouble sleeping (not least because of her husband's loud and incorrigible snoring) and was always the last person up at night, going round the house once more to check the lamps and doors, to check the windows if rain threatened during the night, looking in on her son and two daughters, each in a separate room. Martha would pretend, as did the others, no doubt, to be asleep rather than invite her in with wakefulness. They were not small children, after all. They wanted no embarrassing attentions at this late vulnerable hour; and such attentions, when they came—an attempt at affection that seemed intended as compensation for daylight chiding and sternness—were too late, unconvincing, off-key. It gave Martha a sudden shiver to think of all the nights when, having truly fallen asleep, unable to protect herself with her waking ruse of sleep, she had lain unknowing and vulnerable under that late-night maternal inspection; it was like a secret counting of hoarded silver. Even worse, in Mama's low sad moods.

Martha assumed that the other two, even James, felt somewhat as she did—she feigned sleep not only out of not wanting her mother to intrude on her in the privacy of her hidden thoughts as she was falling asleep, but also because this maternal solicitousness was an unwanted revelation of need in her mother, who played the role of self-sufficient woman during the day, when she was impatient with her daughters, always finding something lacking in them. She was forgiving only of James, in whom there was so much more to forgive, if only she knew, than in Anne and Martha.

Martha did not want to have to see that her mother was riven with anxiousness that the house not burn down from a lamp, that a thunderstorm not pour rain through open windows, that the children were all safe in bed, that niggers black as night, she said, not break into the house and murder them in their beds. (For what? *Why* would they murder *us?* Martha did not ask.)

Nighttime knowledge of her mother's weakness of spirit made it hard for Martha to shield herself from her mother's inflicted daytime damage. Anyway, it was no good for her mother to beg some absolution and yet never change her harshness.

But to think of Mama going round the house like that, every

night, with care for all of them, and then entering the bedroom she shared with Daddy, made Martha feel that all her mother's things in that room—her dressing table, her chiffonier and chest of drawers, her hat boxes, her boots, her sewing—were placed there only temporarily, were there on sufferance from him, it was his room, not hers, not theirs.

And James. James seemed no relation to either Martha or Anne. No more quick-witted than Anne or Mama, but far craftier. His pleasure with them was all in teasing and dismissing them. He was belligerent outside the house, compliant within it when their parents were present, often kissing Mama, but both girls could see it was a pretense and they resented their mother's willingness to accept his attentions with unquestioning gratefulness. Toward her James was nearly always cheerful, although as soon as Daddy called to him for some little errand he was all his father's son and became indifferent to his mother. Both Martha and Anne saw that James's attentiveness to their father was pretense, too, but this seemed only fitting, and only what Daddy deserved, especially after the years when he had routinely whipped the boy and then expected of him that he forgive the beating, afterward.

James had just finished the High School and was office boy now at the bank, and the favorite of men his father's age and older. They would stand beside him—these sermonizers on hard work often had leisure to do very little during the working day—and to anyone who passed or stopped to chat they would predict James's great future, putting an arm around his shoulders or clapping him on his back. As if they owned him. But he liked it. He had been a poor student but a great one to win people over. Somehow. They didn't really know him. Daddy seemed satisfied with James's new position. Martha looked at James and saw guile, energetic flattery. And a danger of which, in this family, only she knew.

There was a focus of concern on her at all times, now that, two years out of High School herself, she had not yet married, and seemed to lack interest in any of the young men who presented themselves.

They were all so awful.

In warm weather when the family was gathered on the porch after weekday supper or on Sunday afternoon, James would sometimes feign especially solicitous attention to Martha, offering to bring her a lemonade or cool tea from the kitchen. She would rebuff the unpleasant adolescent, who seemed about to burst his own taut body. James's presence resonated like a painful sound; she would hasten to escape him.

His eyes would follow Martha too fixedly, something unresolved in his face; then he would dismiss his older sister with a contemptuous shrug.

James was said by Anne—who was one to know, who had heard this at the High School and told it to Martha but not of course to their parents—to be a fighter and a cheat, even a bully. His older patrons, however, imagined he was only what they wanted to see in him; and through him they also flattered his father. In town, Martha had seen James treated thus, and she scarcely dared to look him in the eye because to have done so would have been unavoidably to share his hypocrisy and to have been obliged thus either to participate with him in it or suffer his retaliation for not helping him in his charade.

If, when they sat out on the porch on those early evenings, before the bugs swarmed, Martha's mother were to pass around a box of sweets—which she would buy for herself in town, and would introduce, as if they were a very rare event, with the words "These are my *only* indulgence, you all know that," smiling at them—then Martha would watch her father ignore the offer or fail even to hear it, would watch James take only one, they meant nothing to him but he would not miss an opportunity to thank Mama, and would watch her sister dip her fingers in and quickly take two or three, for Anne was a thieving and predatory eater of sweets. Martha would hold one piece in her mouth a long while, savoring it as her thoughts wandered—to that office where her father worked and she was not permitted to visit except very rarely, or to the bank in which James applied his pretended admiration to everyone above him, or to the houses of the town, where other people guarded their secrets, or to cities far larger than Three Rivers where a person would not be known by everyone, far beyond the west edge of town where the sawmill stood ceaselessly whining and screaming and smoking.

Martha's appetite was not bound within what she and Anne and James already knew. It would not be satisfied somewhere on the town square, where the two-story stone bank and Martha's father's small wooden office faced each other across the rectangle of parched grass and stood shoulder to shoulder with dry goods and doctor and dentist, on one side of the square, and feed store and livery and hotel and post office on the other. The buildings were of no interest to her: this was not a place of interest. What *was* there? Besides the mill: two warehouses, two lodge halls, the school, three churches, the tailor's shop, the wagon maker, the new "garage" for the sale and repair of motor cars, two taverns frequented by the unrighteous; and out past nigger town (they called it Smithville)—with its own houses and church and store and other small gray buildings—the tannery. The dust from the streets filled the air when a storm whipped through. A dust devil could blind one at any time, in storm winds or stillness, as one clattered up and down the low porch walks of the establishments. The hotel, where the businessmen and owners ate lunch, had a proper verandah. The summer heat was intolerable.

Martha's hunger was not to be satisfied, as Anne's was and clearly would be for all her life, by prying others in the family open to get at the soft sweet center of their nature and sucking at it—Anne was forever asking, and forever being told not to ask (her nature and her mother's could not have been more different), about Grandmother Brewster or Aunt Rose or the china flower vase from Germany that had traveled across the sea on a ship in Great-grandmother Catherine's trunk, or the old opal ring that would come down to her someday, or the necklace of pearls in Mama's jewelry box that would come down to Martha. Asking about *how* Uncle Briscoe had died, and what *exactly* was wrong with Cousin

Louise, and why was it, again, that Grandfather Clarke hadn't fought against the North in the War.

Martha shared Anne's curiosity—only she wanted to go farther. Her thoughts lingered on rumors she had heard of James's excursions into nigger town. It was said that he knew how to drive an automobile and had driven his friends or patrons there to make more of an impression on them, although of course there was no white man in the town who did not know where it was and what was to be looked for there. Martha pushed her imagination hard after him, but saw what she couldn't be sure of, which frightened and fascinated her.

Yet despite her remoteness from them all, and her somewhat calculated air of distraction—which vexed all of them till they had no patience with her over even slight things—Martha was in some ways the most coddled, the most hoped after, of the three living children. It was her moment, now. Every resource of the family seemed aligned to propel her toward a match. Even James would pour his attention over her when he could see that their father was noticing her on his way in or out. If there was anything to gain in her, in her choice of husband, James wanted a try at it, and welcomed a chance to remind her subtly of a vow to keep deadly silent a secret he shared with her. She was lovely and obedient and bright; she would marry well, they said. (Only that hair of hers, and her self-involved, sometimes sullen, manner, were against her.)

Her mother was making a new effort to fatten her, both physically and emotionally—to make her plump and sweet of character, so as to attract a nice young man of promise. "Someone like our own James," she would singsong, and Martha sickened at the misconceived comparison.

So she withheld herself; she refused or deflected what was offered. She was not entirely sure why this impulse ruled her, but she let it rule. She had come to feel uneasy about her own recalcitrance; yet she did not seek to change her mood.

Her father failed to see that she was smarter and more honest than James, but then she was already aware that he did not especially seek those qualities in a man, either, and was more admiring of a man's close mouth and cunning in a transaction, his knack at besting an adversary. In town with him, Martha had seen him forget her and come out of his apparent fogginess like a snake out of a hole, as hungry and alert for weakness in a man newly met about some legal matter or business possibility as the snake would be, having spotted a mouse. And no matter if the mouse was honest, earnest, or in the right; the snake looked only to strike.

Still, Martha could not help half-wanting to seek his approval: even now, after her lifelong failure to get it, she might find herself wanting to earn or capture his attention. All the more so because she knew she was as bright as he was, they were the two smart ones in the family, and it was only his acknowledgment that would do. Yet he, who would not cease his scheme to establish again a newspaper in Three Rivers, his obsession with it unrelenting but his success forever forestalled by the doubts and lack of capital among his cronies; he, who speechified regularly on the need for a rail line through Three Rivers, and on what an increase in commerce and manufacture it would bring and how the town needed *thinkers*— he did not consider it necessary or even advisable for a girl to read very much, and he would not have cared if she had quit school at fourteen, as she might have done, like some girls. So if talk turned to the matters she had read of in his library, she could not let him see how much she knew or he would want to know why she knew it.

She felt a longing to go out from him—partly just in pique, she would punish him—and from all of them, to someplace larger, wider. Or simply to follow a path that led, finally, definitively, past the edge of town to anywhere else. Yet she feared the world that lay beyond the town of her birth. Among thousands upon thousands of souls, she might not encounter even one who would know her, not even the trees would look the same, and no town or city would ever hold the same comfort, along with its imprisoning familiarity, as the square mile in which she had spent her life: going past hotel and livery and bank and lodge hall and school.

Then came Reuben. On him all her feelings suddenly, sharply focused like a beam of light.

He came from a place he scarcely seemed to remember; he had lived among both whites and coloreds and had made no enemies among either. He had no town, no family, no place to which he could return or wanted to return. His path was an unwinding one, going wherever he wanted or happened to go, although for now he was content to stay here. And his only close kin, his mother, was buried somewhere under a pine tree, or where a pine tree once had been, for who knew if that spot was not in the center of some field of corn, now?

Martha had heard stories of Indians ever since she was a little girl, and still heard them, because having killed off and driven away the Indians was a point of Texas pride. She had heard of the oil gusher that blew a stream of oil one hundred and sixty feet into the air for nine days before it was sealed off, down around Beaumont in oh-one, and that the oil people looking for oil in the Big Thicket still thought they should get rid of the few Coushatta on their little reservation. She had heard of Comanche and Kiowa Indians attacking settlers and soldiers in West Texas, and of Shawnee and Cherokee and Choctaw and Chickasaw living nearby in the old days, before her father was born, when they had massacred a big settler family somewhere farther south. Her Uncle James, her mother's older brother after whom James had been named, had visited twice from Jackson, Mississippi, and told the children Indian stories of old times, when the Choctaw stopped for a time in Texas on their trail to the Indian Territory and how when somebody important died, he'd said, the Choctaw would carry the dead person into the woods and cut trees and set up funeral poles around the grave. This uncle had fascinated the three children with the ghoulish tale, which he whispered and dramatized to shock them, of how it was said that before the white man arrived and outlawed and eradicated their savage ways the Choctaw had used to put their dead up on high platforms and the bodies lay in the open air six months till horrible long-fingernailed bone pickers came to scrape off the last flesh and hand down the bundle of bones to the mourning relatives and then, after climbing down, they set fire to the platform. Martha thought of all that, against the town cemetery where the two dead infants lay buried. (Only once in her life had she seen a burial, when with preaching and twelve pall-bearers they had buried her distant second cousin Phyllis and her husband who had died in the backwoods. Mama said of illness; but the other children at the funeral were whispering of murder.) Reuben's mother had been buried by strangers, had been covered over by only a few shovelings of sand and dirt, unmarked and forever unvisited in the woods, and dead and buried while her little boy stood by, much younger than Anne was now.

Reuben's mother's body lay there still, neither consecrated in the Christian way nor even mourned the way Uncle James had said the Choctaws had done.

Martha had also read of Indians in her father's library: the books described a people who seemed completely unlike the occasional Indian she heard spoken of in town or saw standing apart outside the dry goods store or drunk, sleeping in broad daylight and jeered at and abused by white boys. Reuben never spoke of Indians; she wanted to know about them. He didn't talk of his old life before his mother died; he talked about himself only if she pressed him.

He was the kind of large young man whose size and strength are not aggressive or hard (James, though small, was clear-cut in sharply drawn muscles). She had seen Reuben's body the very first day they had met, at the river. His muscle lay hidden under a smoothness of shape. His skin was darker than hers or than any-one's she herself knew personally except Pilgrim's. It wasn't nearly as dark as Pilgrim's; it had a burnished tint in it. It was of the sun. Forbidden to her, of course.

But nevertheless. She could see how, at the beginning, he certainly hadn't suspected how powerfully she felt drawn to him, till she had had to force him to see her, to acknowledge that she was not teasing or toying with him, but thinking about him fully as much as she had invited him to think about her.

45

There were things Martha was afraid she would not know, in that world beyond the town; he must know of them, and would tell her. There were things she didn't want to have to do, but wanted to see done, out there; he might do them.

When he sat at ease, alone, against a log pile, as she'd seen him one day at the mill at noon, his black hair with an almost iridescent ray of blue she couldn't quite catch sight of in it—when she saw him that time and he had closed his eyes and did not know he was being watched, then she could not help entertaining the thought of being with him. It had been a summer morning when she had prevailed on her mother to let her be driven in the carriage to get some air. Her mother said, as Martha had known she would, "Take Anne, too." As a ploy, Martha at first objected, in order to bring to the fore the question of Anne so as to push back and thereby win the question of the carriage. It was a carefully played scene, of Martha's devising and within her control, and although Anne did not know its motive she quickly understood what Martha wanted, and willingly she performed her role in it to perfection, just for the sake of the subtle contest. Till finally Mama had sent Pilgrim to Mr. Clarke at his office, and he had ordered the carriage brought from the livery, with Ned driving. And once away, Martha had directed Ned to take them at a walk in the direction of the mill, timing her arrival for the dinner break at noon. She held herself back in the covered buggy, unseen; but saw him. And Anne, seeing the great number of men there, was never the wiser about which one Martha had come to spy, and was excited enough that Martha was interested in any of them. "Who is it?" she asked greedily. But Martha only pretended Anne's question was far off the mark.

And later, by contrivances, Martha had arranged a series of apparently fortuitous encounters till Reuben understood, and, exciting her almost more than she could conceal from others, he had not been afraid.

In fact, at her father's sort of game Martha was besting her own father, putting into play the ambition and craft she had long owned but which she had been given no scope to employ. Then she and Reuben began to meet by conspiracy, her sense of danger charged by his sheer foolhardiness in being with her. Could it have been courage? Why, instead of looking the other way when first she spoke to him, and getting away from her, as any colored man or Indian would and should have done, since in speaking to him she broke all the rules, had he simply looked at her, and answered her mild small talk? Martha didn't know if a white woman had ever been known to talk to a colored man the way she spoke to Reuben. (Although for a white man the question was quite different: everyone knew that and seemed to accept it or at least never to speak of it openly.)

Wasn't it insanity for her even to think of him, and even a crime for him to think of her? Was it she who had placed him in mortal danger, was she responsible for it? For her the danger was lesser, although if she and he were ever found out it was not only of creating shock, of making herself unmarriageable, but also of living out her life, all her life, all of her whole long life, at home, as a result of this incomprehensible desire. Wouldn't she be locked away forever? Or would they cast her out? She was impatient with everybody. What they thought made no sense. She didn't want a life anyone else had already lived, anyway; she wanted her own. She felt cast out of some contentment all the others seemed to expect or to have, a contentment that for them made the days and nights of Three Rivers of sufficient interest. Theirs was a feeling which she could not attain; she scorned it.

She lay on the hard striped divan in the living room, much later than usual, her mother already beginning her nightly rounds with a visit to Anne, whom she had trapped into conversation which Martha could overhear—her mother forcing herself into Anne's thoughts with her almost pathetic late-night reversal into sweetness, and Anne scarcely answering the motherly questions. In the hot night, Martha was too tired to undress herself and then put on the constricting, stifling nightdress; she lay listening to the grandfather clock ticking more slowly than any clock in the world. She needed to get up and change and brush out her hair. She had an odd itching pain inside the heels of her hands, too deep to be scratched.

Her father had already gone *in there,* an hour before. At supper he said things like, "Dr. Garrison died." And when she and Anne glanced at each other quickly till Anne assumed the onus of asking the requisite "Who was Dr. Garrison?" then the heavy formal man who was their father had doled out a portion of his exaggerated and humorless irritation to his daughter: "Why, the man who single-handedly established the State Library last year! What *do* you children learn in school?" His evening retreat to his own room of books and papers, where he lavished disproportionate care on his collection and pondered new schemes of legal and financial advantage, freed them all from his alien, rigid manner. By this late hour he would certainly think that Martha was already in bed asleep—if he thought of her at all, and if he was not himself already asleep. Martha did not know what her father looked like asleep. She had never seen him asleep that she could remember; nor seen him half-unclothed; nor could she remember ever touching him—his face, his shoulder—except for his hand in church if she happened to be sitting next to him when the congregation joined hands at the benediction. (And his hands were surprisingly pleasant to hold and be held by—dry, warm, smooth.) She lay unmoving, a lamp near her still burning hotly at full wick. She felt like pages of an unused calendar of the year, from the stale dry goods store.

This afternoon she had kissed Reuben. And now whatever it was that had been set in motion—that she had set in motion; was he with her?—it seemed the one hard fact. It was the element in the center to which everything else must make an adjustment, shifting to a new position.

"Martha, kin that be you?" her mother said to her, having stopped suddenly as she was coming out the door from the kitchen. Martha had not yet roused herself to answer when her mother came to her, saying, "Martha. Are you feelin ill?" The mother took the daughter's limp hand in her own; the daughter's hand returned no affectionate pressure.

"I wonder have you got a fever, Martha," her mother said, "I don't remember you lookin so tired and drawn this afternoon." Still holding Martha's hand, she put the back of her other hand against Martha's forehead. Martha thought of when she was a little girl, and of her mother smoothing her hair from her forehead when she lay in bed, sleepy and hot in the hot summer night. "Martha, answer me," her mother said, withdrawing both hands from touching her daughter's body.

"Yes, Mama, I'm goin to bed now. I'm just tired." It was one of those moments when, despite the long-standing habits that have sealed up all the aspects of a relationship between mother and daughter into chambers from which they cannot break out, even though these are not the places either woman consciously wanted, one of them feels suddenly and only very subtly that it *would* be possible to speak with absolute honesty, from the deepest corner of the heart, as if all that habit had never existed, as if they were two intimate friends in a friendship beyond the closest either of them had ever known, as if now, in this moment of sudden access, they could change the way things were between them. If Martha could have said, simply and without fear of shocking her mother, there's something I want to tell you; if she could have spoken of being in love, and asked her mother to come with her into this feeling, to reassure her that despite its speed and danger she would be able to follow it without damage. If Martha had been able to speak, only for a moment, free of all the formed expectations between her and her mother, then everything would have been different between the two of them, life itself would have been different for both of them, and whether she would be permitted to love Reuben might not have been even as important as that in whatever she did, she would have this one companion who knew her, or could know her, better than any other woman.

"I cannot stand here waitin till your mood allows you to get ready for bed, young lady," her mother said, her body set in an admonitory posture, her voice thin and irritated.

Martha looked up at her quickly, feeling as fully betrayed as if she and her mother had really achieved the companionable intimacy she had only been able to think of, for an instant, and now her mother had shattered it. "I'm goin, now," she said, "I was waitin for somethin, too." And she rose and went out of the living room down the hall toward her own retreat, leaving her mother open-mouthed and saying out loud to the always listening walls and portraits, to the china cabinet that expected at some time to be smashed, to the chairs that worried about someday wobbling and collapsing, "I do not know what will become of that child," as she crossed the room to go *in there*.

9

Fala

Grandfather's best gift—even better than the ball-game sticks Reuben had never gotten to use—had been a fledgling crow he'd brought to Reuben, that he had found on the earth under the high nest. Unhurt but helpless. Reuben fed it worms and crushed seed of weeds and bugs and scraps of whatever he could find and it grew glossy black feathers and cawed at them almost speaking, and when it first began to fly it stayed near their cabin, roosting in a tree or on the roof. Reuben gave it its name—just *Fala*, he and Grandfather had decided—and when he called it it would come down to him with great wingbeats and land on the ground, fold its wings and take a few steps like a white preacher in his black coat and then it would look up, slantwise, at him—and to make the crow happy Reuben had to have in hand something for it to eat. Reuben's uncles laughed to see the crow come when Reuben called it, but Grandmother and his aunts hated it and stepped away from it when it came near them. It was completely tame and would alight and waddle up to any of them. The women warned Reuben that they would kill the crow if they found it in their beans and corn. (But that was never Reuben's crow that had to be scared off the garden that year; and they had nothing with which to kill a crow, all they could do was fling a stone.)

In the fall, Fala disappeared. In every flock scattered in a field or roosting in trees Reuben thought his crow must be one of the smart sentinels at the edge, watching the world of people which, better than other crows, it had known.

Once, with the crow following because he kept calling it softly—it walked behind him and then flew to catch up—Reuben went stealing into Mr. Davis's watermelon field, far from the Big House and screened by bushes and trees, on low sandy ground where nothing else would grow as well as the great green melons. It was a place where adults came only to fetch back a melon for the house.

Hatak lusa, one of the men with black flesh, had given Reuben his inspiration for a raid on the field. When Reuben had been hiding in bushes, at play by himself, this man had come out from the Big House one afternoon with the cook's angry curses darting after him still like pecking birds, and had bent down and looked at several melons, thumping them and listening, till one of them he picked up as high as his waist and then dropped very deliberately, and, the melon broken open, he scooped out handfuls of the heart of it that he lifted to his mouth and ate. When he had eaten enough, and the cook's words had flown beyond him completely and were gone out of sight, he chose another melon, a huge one, and hefted it to his shoulder and went casually back toward the Big House, his head bent to one side. Reuben, unnoticed and unmoving as a deer, watched him go.

After several more rambles past and through that melon field, on different days, picking his way through the hairy vines and around the hundreds of melons, thinking each time of what he had seen, Reuben came to be carried away by the liberating example of the *hatak lusa* to a plan and a project. He would steal into the melon field himself and drop one of the giants and eat its heart. He was hungry. Fala was hungry. They were always hungry.

Shuksi, Grandfather said for watermelons. They had their own small crop at home. *Shukshi nipi* for the seedless cool crisp sweet red flesh of it. But the white man also had *nipi—hatak nipi tohbi,* white-flesh-man. He was white inside, that was why he was white outside. While a man, *hatak,* or a black man, *hatak lusa,* were as they should be, inside.

Reuben did not know what the black man had been listening for when he had bent down and greeted the melons with a thumping finger. The day of his raid, Reuben patted the melons and to his ear they all sounded alike. He stood up, looked around him at the empty field, and then bent down to lift a great green melon streaked with yellow, but he could not manage the awkward weight of it. In his family, they told of when his oldest uncle was caught stealing from the Big House kitchen and white men tied his hands and feet and whipped him and he bled into the dust of the ground. That uncle was gone away now.

Reuben saw no one else in all the expanse of field and fields beyond. He kicked the melon with the ball of his small bare foot, his right foot. It did not break open. He aimed his heel at it and punched into its side. He shifted his weight and aimed a left-foot punch next to the first wound and at the impact a short jagged seam began to open up next to the hole and juice was dripping down the dark green side of the melon. He knelt next to it and put fingers of both hands in the seam and pulled. He no longer bothered to look out for himself. He stood up and kicked it again, knelt and pulled it apart, and with a deepening melody of splitting, as he pulled as mightily as his arms and shoulders could, the melon yielded, tearing and cracking, and fell open into unequal halves, a pale red light pouring up out of it. Reuben feasted till his belly was swollen with the sweetness of the melon. He called Fala, who was standing some distance away, but the crow remained there, and croaked at him, and then flew off.

10

Exile of Childhood

What he wanted was both to hide and yet to be found. But he could not hope to be found by anyone who would know him, so he could not be found, truly; a stranger could not find him, for only a person who already knew him could look for him now that he was lost.

How comforting it would have been now to be back again even in those lonely nights with his mother when they were in some unknown place with their little camp fire!

The rain stopped and the clouds curdled and broke apart here and there and the light came down more strongly, like true day-light, and the heat was wet and oppressive against him.

The dirt road lay alongside a small deep creek rushing with storm-water through eroded mud banks. Reuben came to a ford shallow enough for him to wade, even in the strong flood that pulled at him. The brown-green water climbed up his legs, trying to get hold of him to tumble him downstream. He strove against the spirits in the water grabbing him and holding him, and he crossed and climbed out.

The surrounding water oaks and sweet-gum trees wore beards of dripping gray moss. He intended to keep his bearings by his path from her grave, to know at any moment how to return to it. The mud on his feet dried and caked and fell away as he walked. His short cuffs, up around his lower calf, were soaked and filthy, and his shirt was still wet through.

He grew tired; it was not only physical fatigue but also the effect of the effort he was making to be alive while he was among the unending fields and woods on either side of the road, under the vastness of the sky that as far as he could see must be drifting over even more fields and even more woods in which he himself did not make even the smallest mark. He wondered how to count the leaves of the trees or the stems of all the weeds. His pace slowed; he dragged his feet, scuffing lines in the wet sandy road that was steaming under the renewed heat of the sun; and then he stopped and went off the road, drawn into the shade of the largest tree nearby. At first he stood beside it, looking back at the road; then he set the baskets down; absentmindedly he put the palm of his small hand on the wide trunk of the tree, as if to be companionable, or as if some friendly familiarity in the huge tree refreshed him. He was hungry, and had nothing, and was too tired to forage or hunt, too distracted by the emptiness of his prospects, by the grief in the gray moss that hung down from the trees and by the warnings of the jaybirds calling through the woods. He sat down and leaned back against the tree and half dozed, with a coiling empty ache in his stomach. A sparrow, clinging to the seed-head of a weedstem that bent and swayed with the bird's weight, was attacking the damp seeds with vigorous strokes of its beak. Then it let go and flew to a sturdier twig near Reuben, and stropped its beak, each side once, on the twig. Then flew straight up into the sky.

He woke, and picked up the nested baskets and went on. He saw only a few people, here and there; they were black, not white people. He was not as frightened of them as of white people, but he was wary, nonetheless. A memory of a black man yelling at him, at his mother, swooped past him.

Approaching a cluster of houses under pine trees, Reuben stepped off the road into the trees and crept into hiding behind the first house. Several children were playing in one yard. The three small houses he could see best all looked much alike—unpainted, gray, true houses of plank wood, with small back porches, and raised up, so as to have a wooden floor inside, as he had seen in his journey with his mother. In the dirt yards low lines of clothes hung limply and would have to dry of rainwater as well as wash-water. He could see meager stacks of firewood. Back in the trees nearer Reuben stood privies here and there, weathered gray like the houses. The house he had come to had a rickety chicken coop, as well, but the fence was torn and fallen, the chickens were rang-ing free; and a small backyard garden had tomato and pepper plants and beans and corn. The leaves and shapes of the garden plants were familiar to him and a jumble of memories spoke in his head at once. The children were playing a game; with a stick they were drawing a line in the dirt and then chanting together and jumping over it. The heat in the air was heavy. Overhead a band of jays arrived, riding a current of air, screeching angrily at Reuben for a fool, but the children did not know to listen to them; and then the jays rode another current of air away.

After a while, the three children, two girls and a boy, were called in to eat supper, and a trace of the scent of boiled vegetables and meat reached Reuben now and then. He didn't want to be seen by anyone. He wanted just one thing to eat.

The children came back out again and Reuben's spirits rose a lit-tle. Then he saw that there was a girl two houses down also watch-ing them across the empty intervening backyard. As soon as he saw her he felt a little different—no less alone but more secure in his own solitude. Yet she must have had someone in that house to whom she belonged. Reuben heard a flurry of clucking and alarm from the henhouse, then it was quiet again.

He settled down where he was, sitting on the ground with his baskets behind him, able to see, through the thin scattered scrub and the tree trunks, both the children playing together and, farther off, the girl not invited to play who was watching them from her own yard but, unlike him, exposed, unconcealed, her loneliness visible to him and everyone, while his was secret. The other chil-dren must have known that she was watching them and that she would have liked to play, but they didn't acknowledge her. Because they didn't know that he was watching them, Reuben felt almost a kind of power over them. He somewhat drove away his hunger.

The solitary girl wandered here and there in her yard, a few steps at a time. She picked up a stick and as though not even aware of what she was doing she mimicked the game the others were playing as she scribed a line in the dry gray dirt. She was diffident and moping, but he was now keen and almost distracted from himself.

For a few minutes more the children played, erupting into laughter or yelling at each other, then again in some concerted game quietly involved, till as the sky lost nearly all light, they broke up and went back into the near house, the little boy lingering to scratch more lines, wild frantic ones, on the ground and then, called in, going up the back step and inside where there was a woman's voice.

The girl was alone. She seemed freed somewhat by her solitude now, and could raise herself to a little resolve by her privilege of a later hour than the others, her sole dominion over the backyard nightfall. This was a happier moment for her, till the darkness grew too thick. She was standing very still, looking upward. She might have been holding her breath. He could follow the floating shape of her pale dress, but could scarcely see her dark limbs and face any longer in the night. Abruptly she had stopped moving, and was poised as if listening, as if alert to something.

His eyes were blearing, staring so hard at her. Then the pale dress fluttered and rushed away—she had suddenly sprinted into her house and was gone.

Barking dogs, to which he had not paid much attention as long as other persons were around, now seemed to him more numerous in the night. Perhaps they had scented him and were thinking of him and were going to come after him. He clung to one thing— that he knew how to get back to where his mother was buried.

He crept into the garden and groped through the plants. He found tomatoes; he took two great soft ones. Then he touched peas, and set down the tomatoes and harvested and ate the peas as fast as he could, peas and pods at once, chewing the sweet sharp green of them, swallowing the tough fibers. He did not like the raw taste. But he raided the whole row and then retreated with his tomatoes.

11

Of Memory

Till he met Martha, Reuben never encountered anyone to whom he had wished to tell what his life had been when he was a child, nor anyone who had wished to know. Now Martha was drawing memory out of him. Yet to speak every memory, as soon as it came back to him, or even after a time when it had steadied itself alongside him and stayed with him, felt like depleting himself somehow; he did not do that. He told of what happened here and there along his way; it seemed like she was as excited by his telling as she was by his touch. She amplified his narrative with questions and guesses, so he had to add more to what he told.

In his telling and her responding there was some third thing created, more of a tale than a truth, more than he could have told of himself if he had only thought it to himself, inside himself. Yet, given this almost love-making of talk, back and forth, item and question, memory and interpretation, was it not her story rather than his? Was it a story that belonged to either him or her? It was not the same as a true story such as he'd heard as a child from Grandfather and Grandmother—those that he remembered, he kept inside himself, safe—and from his mother, too. Those stories were of unchanging things that somehow, in the years of Reuben's life, had changed.

His own story was no story at all, he kept insisting to Martha, but only something that happened one time, to him, and of no matter to anyone else. Not even to himself. But sometimes she didn't seem to want him to think, she wanted to do the thinking, she wanted him to talk. She brushed aside his wanting to stop for a moment and think through what he was hearing himself say. It was inescapable that when they talked this way and every way they made something new out of each other's words as they bound themselves increasingly to each other, as much by talk as by touch, as much by the sounds of words as by the sensations of their bodies or the slowly forming intentions of their lives, the foggy problem that began to take shape ahead of them and which as yet they had not reached. And meanwhile she was asking him things like, "How did you learn to figure? Do you recall? (They taught me in primary school.) What are the Choctaw Indians like? Do you know how to follow wild animals?" She was toying with the fingers of his right hand; like she was counting them.

12

Decisive Recent Episodes in the Life of Martha's Informant

Between two towns, walking, maybe Reuben Sweetbitter would find some work. He walked under an oak whose limbs reached over the road to make one spot of shade, and he stood there a moment in the cooler air, but then he had to duck quickly because he felt a sharp rap on the top of his head and heard a fluttering of wings, and looking up saw the angry blackbird dropping down on him again. Reuben scampered a bit off, looking back at the tree, and the bird retreated to the limbs where its nest lay. Reuben laughed.

"I'm not comin to thieve your babies," he said out loud. He went on.

Not tall but a strong man, he wore his straight black hair cut short like a white man's, had worn it that way ever since Francie had first cut it. Had a little bit of soft beard which he shaved every so often. Owned two shirts. One, a blousey, long-sleeved white shirt with thin red stripes running up and down that he knew set off the gleam of his teeth and the handsome color—at least some women had thought, young black women—of his face. The other, which he was wearing, pale blue and patched where it rode over his right shoulder blade—and unfortunately with a hole in the sleeve where he had clumsily caught it on barbed wire while going through a fence, it irked him to think of it. He wore his shirt tucked into his trousers; his trouser cuffs fell over his bare feet. In the small bag he was carrying, containing the white shirt, he also kept a pair of plain moccasins and a thin winter jacket. He had his things. His old worn boots hung across it by their laces.

On another road somewhere between endless reaching jungles of green fields that would produce a mountainous heap of some-body else's corn, come August, he had once helped lift the side of a wagon filled with sacks of oats, when he had come upon two older white men who had not known how to get the loose wheel back solidly onto the axle, and were late to market. Wagons, whether stopped or rolling, were often being passed on the roads by auto-mobiles now, but this stretch of road had been long and empty, and Reuben had seen them ahead and known they would be watching him come down its length growing from a moving speck to their only unlikely hope. They were not bad men; they would not have paid him anything, but they'd have been willing to carry him along with them, back in the wagon bed on the oat sacks. One of them did give Reuben in thanks a clean white handkerchief from the pocket of his vest, and now Reuben kept that in his bag, too, al-though it was too good to be used.

Also he owned a straight razor with an ivory handle (the last half-inch of the blade was broken off; Reuben had found the razor behind a house in a town), a rolled-up blanket (he had carried everything in that, tied up with string, till he'd been given the cast-off carpet bag in payment for an odd job), his tin cup and six dollars.

He was pretty sure where she was buried; he had wandered back that way several times in his travels. Things had changed along that stretch of road, people had cleared a lot of the woods. He thought he would set out to find her again and once and for all someday, and put a little marker of wood on her grave, but he had not done it yet.

He had six bullets for a rifle, didn't know why he kept them, had no gun; he'd never owned a gun nor hunted with one. Had fired a gun but once, out in woods hunting for deer with a black friend, left behind now. When it was his one turn, he had missed his shot, and had shaken his head to clear it of ringing after the deafening report so near his ear.

He had a rolled-up newspaper he'd read several times already; a good pair of shoes too small for him that he figured to trade. He had four fish hooks, a good length of strong fine line, two lead sinkers and a cork from a bottle of wine.

He knew many towns in East Texas and across the river into Louisiana—white towns with banks and churches and town squares and paved walks and motor cars and high-stepping horses in polished tack and creaking harness drawing polished carriages on Sunday, and black villages with gray houses and mules drawing wagons and with one general store with a boardwalk out front over the mud or dust; and had seen the little Coushatta reservation, where the cabins and shacks scarcely kept out the weather, and the palmetto jungle lay thick across the soggy bottoms and the sunlight was as dim as the light of the moon. Must have walked enough roads to have gone all the way to California if only they had all been in a straight line.

He had left his last sizable town when it was still winter and he had finished helping to build a white church, working for day wages, till the whites had not needed him any longer and with a little money in his pocket he hadn't felt like staying. Since then, through spring and half the summer, he'd been wandering and working odd jobs.

Reuben had worked from the floor joists to the rooftree. He had laid the roof planks on the rafters and nailed them from above in the high cold, with two other men, both black. The boards had been whitewashed on one side before they were nailed in place across the rafters with that side down, so that from the pews the congregation would see the white, and against it, the blond rafters. The weather had been clear and very chilly, and the men roofing, like all the others working, smeared bear grease from a small dark tub of it over their hands to lessen the chapping cold. And kept their hands carefully off the white sides of the roof planks, except for inadvertent slips. Looking up from the inside when they had finished, Reuben saw only two handprints in the whole expanse of white. "Like angels' hands," Reuben had overheard a little white girl say, pointing. "But they *black*," her father corrected her, laughing at her, and she pouted and drew away from him and said no more. One of the handprints was Reuben's—and it would float above the congregation for as long as the building stood.

One other time he had helped build a church, in a black village, where he had left no handprint, for the carpentry had been simpler and on a smaller scale, and the ceiling wood had been left without whitewash. He had worked for the two good meals and the coffee, for the company of the young righteous women, and for the good provisions they paid him in kind at work's end.

In this town he was headed for again, Three Rivers, he had stopped perhaps three or four times in his working years. He'd stayed here or there—at the livery, in a shed behind the grocer's, or in summer in his own little camp in woods beyond the last houses—and white people had seemed as kind as he could expect them to be, as willing as he could hope they'd be to hire him for his strength and cleverness, so long as he didn't speak much to them.

Along the dirt road, through the white dust at leisurely pace he strode, a solitary figure in a hot landscape otherwise unpeopled, with insects clicking and buzzing over the whispering of the weeds. Bearded oaks, beech trees, sycamore trees with spiky balls at the ends of the branches, and pines, all stood leaning above the road on both sides. Upwind off beyond the woods to his left some fire of brush was burning, he could smell the smoke but it was too thin to be seen. If he had not been hungry he would have napped in shade till the sun moved lower in the sky. But he kept on, not slow, not fast.

He was pushing his feet through the thick deep pale dust, like flour, luxuriating in the cool feel of it under the baking surface. It came over his instep in the deepest wheel ruts. But he stubbed his right big toe on something and hopped one step and then re-covered his pace, grimacing. The pain, only a little sharp at first, grew stronger instead of fading. In only ten paces it didn't feel like it should, and he stopped and bent down and looked closely at his toe. He turned and went back, limping now. Where he thought it had happened he put down his bag, and with a long stick from the roadside he pushed the deep white dust this way and that and turned up a limp copperhead that could still writhe but was nearly dead from a broken back where a wheel or hoof had crushed it; half-alive nonetheless. Its venom was in his foot and leg. He clubbed it and looked around him. Under the heaps of high white cloud spread across the unattainable sky, he was alone.

He picked up his bag and headed on, limping stiff-legged but hurriedly, and in half an hour, with throbbing head and heaving chest, he came to a low-roofed cabin back among the trees on the left. A white man in worn faded overalls was sitting on the front step, watching Reuben approach cautiously through the dirt yard. The man's first word to him was "Snake-bit," and he waved Reuben forward. He took Reuben's carpet bag from him. "Lucky I jist come in. Was burnin off a field. I've got some turpentine right-chere," he said.

Reuben sat down on the porch floor, his feet on the bottom step, and watched while the man poured half a gallon of turpentine into a bucket and set it down clanking on the hard ground near the step. The man went into the shadowy cabin and came back out holding the blade of a pocket knife over a burning stove-match. He hustled down the three steps beside Reuben and dropped the match in the dirt. Reuben did not resist when the man picked up his foot as familiarly as if the two of them had been brothers. With no more hesitation than if it had been a hoof, the man carefully sliced the swollen flesh at the end of Reuben's toe.

Black blood spurted from it. Then the man put Reuben's foot back down, a little more cautiously, and set the bucket in front of Reuben on the ground. On his overalls the man wiped the little of Reuben's blood that had gotten on his hands. Reuben did not move, and blood was running off his foot into the dirt, clotting in the dust. The man nudged him and nodded at the bucket, and

when Reuben did not respond quickly, for the man was fuzzy and
mottled in his vision, the man picked up Reuben's foot, bent Reuben's knee, hiked up Reuben's trouser leg, and put Reuben's foot
into the bucket, and Reuben's blood swirled out and reached
through the swirling turpentine like streamers of deep red smoke.
"Thank you," Reuben said, his voice labored.

The man studied his face. "How far'd you come?" he said.

"I been walkin a ways," Reuben said slowly, looking down at his
foot. For an instant, he felt the coolness of a breeze on his sweating
face.

"Turpentine may not hep you, then," the man said, "but it
cain't do you no harm neither. He struck you good. But lucky you
got the hard skin that you got. Skin on my foot's like a baby's,
that's the truth. And your blood-line's some proof gainst the viper,
I always have b'lieved."

The man looked down, considering the bucket, the dusty cuff,
the heel resting halfway up the side, the foot flexed at the ball, and
the toes under the surface of the red liquid. "How big was it?"
he said. Reuben did not answer. The man took tobacco and paper
from a pocket in his overalls, sat down next to Reuben, and with
the tobacco-stained fingers of his right hand and the unstained but
equally work-worn fingers of his left he rolled a cigarette and approved of it, and then laid it very deliberately, very neatly, on his
knee. He rolled another and, even more satisfied with his effort
this time, handed it to Reuben.

But Reuben had leaned his head to one side against the splitting
gray porch post and closed his eyes. The white man carefully
tucked the best cigarette into his shirt pocket, and put the first one
in his mouth. He stood up and went into the cabin, and came back
with another match. He sat down again next to Reuben. He struck
the match against the step, lit his cigarette and tossed the match
into the dust. "What's your name?" he said. "You got a name?"
Reuben looked at the man. Smoke was curling out of the man's
mouth.

Reuben remembered a black-haired, long-haired man who drew

a mouthful of smoke from a pipe and then bent down and blew it over the wound of snakebite.

The next day Reuben woke lying in a low hammock made of canvas tarpaulin slung between two trees in the morning shade of the house. He was almost dragging the ground. His heavy right leg was hanging over the edge of the hammock and his swollen, purpled foot was in a beat-up baking pan filled with turpentine. His body was stiff and sore, and every movement rocked his head with reverberating pain that bounced inside his skull and only slowly subsided. He lay still and open-eyed, looking up through the sifting numberless pine needles toward the morning sky. There came down a scissortail and lit on a bare branch of the next tree over, a chestnut tree that was dead. The long tail-plumes trailing and wafting, it leapt up after insects and beat its wings fast to each catch and then turned in midair and fell back to the perch, time after time while he watched.

"Reuben S. Sweetbitter," he said. "Malcolm Mullaney," the man said, and extended his hand, which Reuben shook weakly.

A woman was standing next to Mullaney; she handed Reuben a dipper of cool water, and after he drank it he couldn't keep his eyes open. The scissortail would fly down and try to snip off his nose while he slept; he should wake and get away from it, but he couldn't wake.

When he did wake he was ravenous, but the woman gave him only water.

After a week of rest and her good food, he was walking again, although none too quickly, but he stayed with Malcolm Mullaney, whose ready welcome he had understood better when he'd seen Mullaney's wife, Adalia. She had skin about the same color as Reuben's own, and hair as black and straight as his, and a patient expression he thought he might be remembering from somewhere. Adalia had very little faith in Malcolm Mullaney's turpentine, and she applied her own remedy, a wet poultice of mashed leaves on the wound and many cups of a bitter infusion of black-eyed Susans. Whichever it was that healed Reuben, or neither, he healed, although the headaches remained a while longer than the swollenness and pain and discoloration in his leg.

Several miles up the road lay Three Rivers, into which Malcolm and Adalia did not venture much, together, but where they were tolerated without comment so long as they came individually. There Malcolm's carpentry and general handy knowledge, including horses and mules and buggies and wagons, was salable; at the mill, where he had friends, he said he would speak for Reuben. Reuben had not planned to stay; but now he didn't feel the need to wander any further, for a while. He'd worked once before at a sawmill.

Well, work at the mill was not a job, Malcolm said, that he himself would want. The mill was a very image of hell. But if Reuben wanted to work steady, then the mill would do for a man of uncertain breed who was young and evidently smart but was not trusted in the town and had no tools of his own. This was wages, and Reuben felt a desire to add it to his meager six dollars.

Still limping, he helped Malcolm turn the soil in his burned-off field with a mule and plough, and helped him sow it with long grass for grazing. They were generous people. They were lonely people, also. Malcolm taught him card games and liked to sit in the evening and smoke with Reuben and offer a drink of his own spirits, not talkative but appreciating the company. Adalia liked to see Reuben eat her food, and she showed him the wild herbs and weeds and leaves of trees to make a variety of cures. The pair of shoes Reuben had been thinking to trade were a tolerable fit for Malcolm, although they were better than he was likely to have occasion to need, and Reuben made him a gift of them. He did not choose to follow Malcolm down the long corridors of whiskey in the evening, and finally he left them, and he took Malcolm's name with him through Three Rivers and out the far side of the town to the mill.

Reuben was hired on and he took to the work quickly and just as quickly disliked it. Not because of what was done there—the pungent smell of the sawn wood pleased him, and the stacked lumber seemed an accomplishment—but because it was tiring work and aggravating on top of that to have to gauge one's place and role all day between the white men and the black. Yet within a few weeks he was put in charge of a yard crew when the man who had been bossing them suffered a crushed leg under a fall of loaded timber from a wagon. To make the quotas set daily by the mill foreman, Reuben had to work his crew hard and dangerously—a dispirited work gang of thin Negro men, some of them only boys.

All the timber came in and all the lumber went out on wagons drawn by teams of oxen or mules. Reuben's steady hand with the animals, and the mill's need, pushed him upward. The timber business was rushing forward so fast that Reuben thought he could almost hear the widening of its circle of felling and cutting, miles from the mill. There weren't enough wagons and teams to haul timber and lumber, and the mill owner was known to be festering sourly for the rail line to be brought to Three Rivers. There were trees to build a nation, and the owner couldn't get them cut and milled fast enough to deliver his share of lumber where the building was fastest and the money thickest. It was said, too, that he would replace the wagons with motor trucks.

Reuben, watching his men unloading logs and loading timber, maneuvering the wagons and the slow stupid teams of animals, stacking timber to dry in the yard, loading dried timber on wagons for delivery, remembered Francie's Eswold and Drum, their exhaustion and bitter impotent anger at the end of the day, and he did not hate their memory. The men of his crew gave him only as much attention and obedience as their work required of them, and they answered his friendly gestures, when he could make them, with a second of unmovingness—not of hesitation but of deliberate reserve, to mark a distance between themselves and him that they were not willing for him to pretend to close.

Reuben had never before found himself in the position of telling anyone else what to do. Pittance that his wages were, compared to the dollars that he could reckon those logs and planks made for the man who owned the mill, his pay was higher than it ever had been; fruit of the unanticipated luck of a snakebite. Odd how that lower world had helped him this time. But maybe it would take back what it had given. He understood well how his men felt around him, because he himself was treated the same way by the white crew bosses, who drove their mill crews at tasks even more dangerous and dirty than Reuben's hauling, or who were gone days at a time with their timber crews in the woods. Yet the timber crews, black and just as scorned as Reuben's own crew by whites, were proud of their status as fellers, and even they looked down on the men who worked within the confines of the yard and the mill.

After the first month, this was Reuben's longest experience of daily life working within the precisions of set hierarchy. There were different dangers, different tasks, different wages, depending on a man's skills and his skin and his nature. That the men didn't simply rise in rage and take over the mill struck Reuben one day as impossible to explain, even if the owner did have three white men with pistols and shotguns who stood patient bored guard all day.

Although he was of two minds about the mill, wanting the work and not wanting to keep doing it—thinking about going down the road again, west this time—he stayed at it two months, then three, becoming more accustomed to the tension of it, happy with his little savings, and content in living in his new room in the house of Mr. Corinthian Grooms, who lavished fatherly attention on him.

In September weather still hot, he went swimming one Saturday afternoon with two white workmates, Billy Simmons and Paul O'Connor, sawyers' helpers, who treated him decently enough, who talked with him at the noon dinner break, who seemed to like him, who were his age or perhaps a little younger than he, and who called him—he didn't object—Young Chief. They said they'd never met an Indian before; and Reuben allowed that he was Indian, although when he told them he just felt like any other man, they laughed. They welcomed him a little distance toward them, in a way they certainly would not have welcomed a black man. A white man who was older could have almost a kind of friendship with a black man, where each understood the terms. But young men were always testing, flaring.

Casually at the last minute Paul and Billy told Reuben to come swimming with them. When the three young men came to the swimming hole there were two young women already waiting, Clara Simmons, having come surreptitiously to see Paul, and Martha Clarke, having accompanied Clara to give her courage and to pass the time outside the stifling claustrophobia of home.

Martha had been somewhat plagued by attentions from the coarse, ill-mannered Billy, but there was a subterranean impulse in her, fired precisely by Billy's roughness and ignorance, to do more than be kind to him—to invite him. The fool had been coming around to seek her out—he would knock on the Clarkes' front door in the evening, washed and in changed clothes, his wavy brown hair pomaded slick and flat against his head. There was something almost good-looking about his buck teeth and narrow face. He would ask her out onto the porch and they would sit rather formally in two chairs and he would talk for a little while, thinking, she knew, about her pretty body; and she would mostly respond with politeness but distance, almost but not quite thinking about his callused hands—and then repulsed by him but hiding that from him.

Or, if her family were already sitting in their accustomed chairs, he would stand nearby on the ground, talking to them all for a few minutes. Then he would say good night and leave. These times he didn't have courage to ask for a chair; Martha had said to her mother that she must not offer him one, and her mother had agreed: Billy had no prospects at all, he was of an unpleasant family, and he had an audacious streak in him that was worrisome, he seemed to have no sense of what other people thought or felt.

It was laughably obvious how he tried to guess how to pursue his advantage with Martha's father. He was not half as clever as James.

"If it wadn't for jist a few thangs . . ." (he laughed nervously), "like the mosquitoes and the snakes and the heat, this is a magnificent country," he had said, more than once, to get Mr. Clarke's attention. He stressed the last two words, for he'd hung near conversations in the barbershop or in the bank lobby when he'd taken his mother's pension check, paid to her as widow of a soldier killed in the Philippines war, to cash, and he had heard men like Mr. Clarke speak that way. On the porch, this man of inaccessible status would nod down at Billy's words but scarcely look up from his out-of-town newspaper. Once, in the performance, for a bored audience, of his halting monologue, Billy had added, "There's enough timber here to last till the second comin a Christ—" and Martha's mother had jumped in her chair. "Billy!" she'd uttered sharply.

But Billy was not one to hold back. He would say, "The way we're goin now, there could be two or three mills in this town, if theruz men to work em. And we need that rayroad, don't we, Mr. Clarke?" Because Martha's father could leave no citizen unencouraged toward hard work and prosperity, even an unlikely and somewhat uncontrollable youth, he always agreed with this sentiment, uttering a word or two. Martha's mother would appear to fret; fretting was in her nature, like the scratchiness in wool.

And now here beside the small slow river was not only the familiar and repellent Billy but also this stranger, this beautiful young man, shabbily dressed, with his surprising skin—Martha glanced quickly at Clara to gauge her reaction—his eyes not like Billy's or Paul's, which might as well have been marbles for all the feeling they revealed. Here were eyes of a different character.

"Reuben S. Sweetbitter," he said, very formally, and he stood with his hands hanging at his sides.

"Call him Young Chief," Paul said grinning.

Clara made exaggerated but surreptitious signs of shock to Martha. How could she speak to Paul now? So typically, by bringing along this nigger, he had found a way to make it impossible for her to talk with him. From under her bonnet, she aimed at Martha a moue of disgust. From that moment, Clara did not acknowledge Reuben's existence; she willed him out of her recognition. But Martha was curious.

Martha did not like to go into the water. Anyway, while men and boys could swim, and very young children of either sex, women were mostly confined to wading in heavy bathing clothes or, more usually, in an old dress. The only place women could free their bodies to move and breathe and be open to the air, as men were everywhere free if they chose, was in the bath, or, if a woman was unafraid of the man she lay with, or did not feel more dislike or pity for him than love, in bed.

But at the water it was not the restriction of movement, the confinement of her body in the heavy wet clothes, that put Martha off. What troubled her was the half-immersion, the half-hiddenness of her body under the alien surface of the water; she was almost afraid that under it, the submerged part of her was—despite the cloth that covered her—exposed to hazard she could not see and did not want to guess. And sometimes, walking on the solid ground, she thought she sensed a movement following underneath her, under the surface of the earth as if it were no more solid than water; below her, moving swiftly now through the ground itself, more hazards swam or burrowed in search of prey. She could not help shuddering and quickening her step. She would hasten to climb into the carriage, or she would step down from it and walk briskly up the porch stairs into the safer house, not looking down or behind her. The mute motionless furnishings had mouths. Cabinets might open to swallow her and soundlessly she would fall down their black bottomless throats. Could the floor itself give way under her, a whole wall recede? She was sometimes a tiny figure in the diminishing frame of the mirror.

She shook herself and brought her thoughts back to the riverbank where she stood.

Reuben, aware now of the transgression that his mere being was, among them, withdrew into himself—his experimental camaraderie with Paul and Billy was over, his self-consciousness acute, his status again that of a kind of mascot for them. Although he himself had not intended it, he had overstepped. He saw the shock on the faces of the white women. Paul and Billy had evidently led him into a false ease just so they could enjoy discomfiting not only him but the women, as well. He could not take one step into anything, even with these two acquaintances, without risk.

Yet he had felt it was, for a change, quite natural to be invited by them as the men were leaving the mill at noon—he had accepted with pleasure and diminishing caution. He had enjoyed walking to the river with them, joking at the expense of the mill foremen and other characters, testing his status with them till it seemed they were all three good friends. Now he saw he should have trusted his first impulse and kept away from them after working hours. It was he who was responsible, if anyone came to blame, for stepping too close to the white people, no matter how close they had invited him to come.

Where white people swam was not a place Reuben would have wanted to go anyway. It was not much better a stretch of water than the weedier bend downstream where black people swam. Here the bend in the river was scoured a little differently by every big storm, and the sandbar snaking down the middle moved from week to week, but usually it made a place to stand; and inside it the water was always deeper, a darker green, not quite clear. A good deal of splashing at first would chase off the occasional water snakes, venomous or not, if any were about, but the currents and rains could sometimes bring a waterlogged dead tree to rest mostly under the surface, where you couldn't see all of it, and it might snag you. And when the water ran slow the persistent legend of a thick tangle of cottonmouth snakes under the surface could hold the first man in to a cautious pace.

On the inside curve of the bend, across the river from the low shore where Reuben and the others were standing, the bank rose fifteen feet to a sandy bluff on top of which stood a stout oak. Roots of the tree protruded from the raw sandbank like struggling fingers with knobby knuckles. From near the top of the tree somebody had long ago hung a thick rope with several large knots near the end. Swinging out on that, a man could drop straight down with a whoop and a splash into the deep water. Clara whispered to Martha that evidently Paul did not remember those nigger boys who had caught hell for playing at the rope one time when they thought no white people were around.

The three young men swam in their drawers, washing from their bodies the sawdust and sweat and smell of the mill. On the low outside bank of the river where it curved, the two young women, fully clothed, stood watching and talked about them, as young women will talk about young men, especially young men in whom they are disappointed, and at whom they may be angry. But that was of more moment to Clara than to Martha, who regarded all three men with only a little interest, but of the three, studied Reuben the most; till Clara, aware of the focus of her friend's gaze, felt she must chide her a little, felt the shock of such open looking at the irritating foreign presence. In the water, the men splashed; in the trees, above and beyond them, a jay clarioned and shrilled, the sound fading as the bird flew away.

Although Paul and Billy looked at ease, Reuben was not. He felt the danger; and his modesty was strained. They had undressed behind bushes, and last of the three young men he had pulled off his shoes, his shirt and trousers, his sleeveless buttoned undershirt. This had left him in a worn pair of once-full-length underpants cut off raggedly at his thighs. The other two, while not overly clean, had proper short underdrawers that at least looked more white than gray. They seemed not at all reluctant to be seen by the women thus. Reuben had thought the men would swim alone, would swim naked.

The young white men released their first high spirits, leaping into the cool slow-moving water off the rope, yelling at each other, engaged in shows of competitive strength in ducking each other, all this exaggerated. Now Billy and Paul felt vexed at Reuben for having come with them—was he so stupid he had to say yes when they asked?

Reuben stayed away from them so as not to be invited into their play; he had no trouble reading the turn in their mood now that their joke hadn't worked, or had.

Reuben had learned from Francie's children to paddle himself along and to swim underwater. He explored a little way upstream and down this river bend that the other two already knew well. He should have left as soon as he saw the women; he should have stopped short of even arriving. But he was hot and just as much in need of the river as they. After a few minutes, having gained in bravado, a sudden impulse struck him and without checking himself he followed it.

He climbed out dripping and running and quickly scaled the bluff. Billy and Paul only glanced at him. Martha and Clara were talking. He grabbed the rope and took a strong running leap off the edge and when his arc held him at the high standstill, higher than the other two had swung, he let go and fell slowly the slow distance down and hit the river with a huge splash.

After a long moment when the others became aware that he was not in sight, they stood silently looking up and down the banks, Billy looking into the water till dramatically he splashed deeper in and dove, his arms sweeping the murk for anything he might catch hold of.

On the far bank, Clara was standing with her head bowed; this was an embarrassment added to insult. Who wanted people to know you'd been there when that stupid Indian boy had drowned himself? Martha was looking up and down the river. Billy surfaced and got his feet under him and walked out, stood next to Paul on the sand bar, and they both looked at the current. "That ain't where the snag is," Billy said—puzzled, irritated, the whole excursion now deflected from its goal.

Paul called out loudly, almost humorously, "Ho, *Chief!* Young *Chief!*" And again, "Hey, Reuben!" with more urgency and once more, and when he did this, Martha also called once, how odd to say the young man's name, "Reuben?" Paul looked over his shoulder at her, startled. She did not call again.

Paul and Billy talked for a moment, too softly for the women to hear, and Billy walked back into the water on the shallow side of the channel and waded to where Martha and Clara stood. Martha might like him looking responsible by walking to town for help in finding the Indian's body.

Reuben rose into sight on the bluff opposite, grabbed the rope and swung out again with a whoop, grinning not at them but at the sky; and Billy stopped dead and he and Paul began to swear at him. Reuben had not known that young white women ever said such things as Clara yelled. Abashed, he did not drop off at the top of his arc but swung back, accelerating, to the bluff. He stopped himself with his feet, stumbling, and then looked down at them all. Billy and Paul were leaving the water, all of them had their backs to him.

It was still their world. He went down the bluff and entered the water and paddled across and got out, but not wanting to get out of it and be among them and apart from them. He would leave now. The four of them stood talking for a moment, they were between him and where he and the other two men had left their clothes. Reuben hung back, and then Paul and Billy drew away from Martha and Clara and with curtness Paul signaled Reuben, and he followed them back into the woods to peel off their underdrawers, wring them as dry as they could, hang them on some bushes for the moment, and put on the outer clothes they had left in three bundles in the low branches of trees.

Naked, Billy looked down at his own penis. "Nigger dicks are biggern ours," he whispered loudly, grinning. "Make Paul's look like a cutworm." And he flung out an arm to rap Paul in the privates with a backhanded slap but Paul dodged, chuckling. "I ain't seen a Injin dick before, Chief," Billy said, and he half leaned and cocked his head theatrically as he studied Reuben, who knew enough not to turn immediately away and disobey the superior power of the boy who took his own having of it for granted. But with an insisting slowness Reuben did turn and began pulling his trousers up over his bare legs. "No, lemme see it!" naked Billy said in full voice, and Paul laughed and looked over his shoulder through the trees and brush. Billy was putting a bare foot on the waistband of Reuben's trousers, which Reuben had only gotten up to just over his knees. Billy was holding them down, and Reuben backed away as much as he could, hobbled. It would not be permitted to bat at that foot, to strike it. Billy hopped after him on his other foot, keeping Reuben's trousers down, cocking his head this way and that as he made a show of studying Reuben's penis. Unlike them, Reuben had only sparse hair above it. Paul was laughing harder; Billy was pushing down with his foot now as if to stand on Reuben's trousers and his toenails scraped Reuben's knee, and Reuben was angry now, was worried his trousers would be torn, was about to speak. But abruptly Billy pulled his foot away and the force of Reuben's resistance jerked the pants to his thigh and he half stumbled getting them up the rest of the way. Billy giggled and danced buck naked, on one foot and then the other, lifting his knees high, rounding his back and hanging his head down to study his own penis bouncing against his thigh. Paul was dressed, waiting, laughing under his breath. When he turned to walk away, Reuben was ready, also, buttoning his shirt and remaining barefoot, carrying his shoes, leaving Billy to finish his dance and clothe himself and follow.

The four of them were going to eat and drink, although not as gaily as Clara, who had prepared the picnic, had hoped they would. Reuben started past them toward the road and found Martha staring at him. It was not an angry look, nor hostile. Her gaze seemed open. Not an invitation, certainly; but something like a recognition. Reuben stopped. He looked around—no one else had noticed. She turned back to the other three, but still looking at him over her shoulder.

He did not leave. He stood a way off from the rest of them, like a servant. Martha offered him food with a slight gesture; he shook his head and remained where he was. He did not know why he was staying. He did know he shouldn't be staying. They were all speaking in low voices, not to be overheard by him; and he did not listen. Billy looked over at him, shook his head with grinning contempt, snorted a laugh. Reuben met that gaze and kept his face calm.

He watched. He might as well have been invisible, not because he wanted to be, so that he could look at Martha Clarke, but because they chose not to see him and didn't care if he was there. He noticed that Billy, who had come the whole way from the mill speaking of Martha, now seemed unwilling to look at her, and she gave him only the briefest of opportunities to do so. Once in a while she darted her eyes quickly at Reuben. Somehow he knew that it was not for anything he had done—his foolish stunt—that she questioned him with her look.

Despite his hunger, he wouldn't ask them for anything.

At a moment when no one else was speaking, he felt a powerful impulse to call over to them, to say something, to explain that he had only wanted to surprise them, that he had thought they were . . . But what difference did it make to them what he thought they thought?

The instant he was under water he had gathered his body and stayed under, stroking downstream with half-open eyes through the murky water. He had found the big snag that they all had spotted at the downstream end of where the sand bar lay and the river turned again, and had pulled himself onward along the length of that—and it seemed to take hold of his foot with one branch to seize him, and he had to pull mightily to free himself, with a sudden memory of fear, of the *okwa naholo*, he'd forgotten about them, till the pressure he was holding in his lungs and throat almost exploded him. But by then he'd made it, just as he'd thought he could, around the bend to where he could come up out of sight of them. He had heard them calling for him.

Much later Reuben would tell Martha that when he was listening to Paul calling for him and then heard her, too, call his name, that one time, he had realized that he had not heard his name—"Reuben," not that stupid nickname Paul and Billy had given him—called that way since his childhood, and he had wanted to sit in hiding and rest, to listen to it for a while. But she had not called again. They all had stopped so soon. And hiding himself he had climbed up the bank and made his way quickly along the shore till, crouching out of sight, he'd got back to the bluff and looked down on them, and then they'd seen him, as he'd meant them to, and like a fool he had thought he could amuse them by diving in once more.

He was looking at her. Did she remember? Martha touched his brow lightly with the backs of her fingers, and poured her fragile smile into him. "That was very silly," she said.

Martha and Clara left. Billy walked with the two women a few steps, talking quietly to Martha; asking her something. Reuben could tell from the angle of his head that she didn't answer. She was walking with her eyes cast down, and with one hand at her neck, her fingers pulling a corner of the little collar of her blouse over her throat. Reuben would always remember that sight of her. She looked back at him, once, quickly, caught his eye a moment, and then with Clara she was gone around some trees; gone.

The three men retrieved their wet underdrawers and rolled them tightly into bundles. Billy and Paul talked to each other as they walked, bending to pick up an occasional stone and throw it hard at the trunk of a tree. They moved with an unconscious combative spring in their step, and with their shoulders as wide as they could hold them. Reuben glided softly behind. They were as hot again as when they had left the mill. There was only one road back to town. There, they parted with scarcely a word and Reuben went through Three Rivers and out the other side to the gray edge-of-town district of servants' and laborers' cabins where he lived with Mr. Grooms; the nigger town, white people called it.

The sound of the bubbling water in his ears, when he'd pulled himself downstream under the surface. . . . Bubbles had roared at his ears that time when he'd been dipped backwards into a little river, the Preacher's voice still sounding, but muffled. This time it had been hard to stay under water so long, till his lungs nearly burst; his body naturally wanted to float.

13

At the River

Hạshi, the Sun, is a blazing Eye, *nishkin*. It watches the *chahtah* and as long as the *nishkin* remains on the *chahtah* they are protected and blessed. But if the *nishkin* leaves them, if it loses sight of them, if it goes to watch others, the *chahtah* are doomed.

The River, *hạcha*, is the *sinti*, Long Snake. His head is in mountains so far away they cannot be seen, and his tail is in the lowlands. At a bend in the *sinti* where the *chahtah* can look upstream toward the rising of the Sun, every month at the time when the Moon is fully hidden, before it begins to grow again, the *chahtah* must jump into the water while a doctor sings and executes the rituals. Otherwise, the *chahtah* will live only a short time. Otherwise, offend the River.

The White People of the Water dwell in deep pools in rivers and bayous. These *okwa naholo* have a skin that is pale like a trout's. When the *chahtah* swim the *okwa naholo* may seize them by the foot and try to draw them down to their home at the bottom of the pool, and if they do, then the *chahtah* person they have captured turns in three days into another of the *okwa naholo;* his skin becomes like the white skin of a trout, and he eats and swims and lives like a trout.

If the friends of a person who was taken down under the river and became an *okwa naholo* go to the bank of the river and sing, he will rise to the surface and talk with them, and sometimes he will sing with them. But after he has become an *okwa naholo*, their old friend cannot leave the water again, for if he leaves the water, he will die like a trout that is taken from the river.

There was singing. There was chorusing and response to the Preacher's words called out to the people in good dress on the bank where the slow river made a bend and when the sun was rising over the treetops of the flat countryside.

White People of the Water lived under the river. And black people of the land, the middle world, had brought him to it as if to feed him to them.

While the Preacher was speaking to them, calling up to them all, and Francie there watching, and Frank and the girls, Reuben was being bent backwards into the water, in the Preacher's strong large hands, one under his shoulders and one on his chest, holding him helpless in their grasp. He was under the water, pushed under, just as at the last second he had gasped for more of a breath. His body floated nearly without weight, he lost his barefoot hold on the muddy river bottom. Francie had told him, told him, told him repeatedly, not to struggle, to let the Preacher hold him, to go down into the river when the Preacher let him down, and to rise up when the Preacher lifted him up. Then he was being raised, the water running off him, and he was struggling to regain his feet, and the Preacher was intoning some words over him, still, and he was up. And for the first time every face was smiling at him.

14

Their Assignations

Reuben and Martha: *certain*, both of them, that they must not think of each other, *certain* that they must not take any interest in each other or be curious about each other in any way, *certain* that they must never speak to each other, that they must never even see each other again. Both of them denied these certainties.

After their first meeting, at the bend in the green river, after never having noticed one another before in Three Rivers, now they saw each other several times unexpectedly and exchanged increasingly intense glances—beside the West Road when Reuben himself was delivering a wagon load of light planking because of another injury at the mill; out back of the livery when Martha was waiting in the family carriage while old Ned was conducting some business inside for her father; on a Sunday when Martha suddenly appeared going past Mr. Grooms's house—where Reuben was sitting on the porch—driven by Ned again to bring presents for the maid Pilgrim Hatley's daughter, who was so sick with fever that Pilgrim had not cooked or cleaned for the Clarkes for three days.

Despite himself Reuben began to keep an eye open for her; something was happening. But he did not know that she too found herself wondering where they might meet. And she had purloined some books of her father's, her intellectual excitement feeding a romantic fantasy so unthinkable she did not allow herself to dwell on it. For if, as she had heard, some people in New Orleans or perhaps in Houston, just perhaps, found themselves...what?

Something. With a colored person. But nothing of that sort could happen in small East Texas towns. Indian, for that was what he was; but, too, don't forget, part white. Her father had said, in her presence, to one of his business friends, *that he had nothing against good Indian people, but that even though Sam Houston himself was as much as Cherokee, there was none but degenerate and mongrelized Indian stock left now, that should be avoided even by clean-living niggers.*

Reuben thought: she was the only white woman he had ever met who had looked at him, and then, on the next occasion he saw her, had looked again. And again, till finally they had a moment's conversation, out of anyone else's earshot, and Martha was asking him to tell her who he was.

Anxiousness and desire, growing together, like twined vines. And grew, through her casual questions on their brief occasions, to a rendezvous when for a quarter of an hour they spoke.

The first time that they met not only by design but also with some sense of what was going to happen, acknowledging that it was their own will that was determining what they did, not chance, he approached the agreed place—which she had specified—with battering heart, walking as cautiously as if to escape a panther, till he found himself near her chosen bower, quite hidden, yet not even so far from her own house. He could not see her but she was waiting there, in a shelter of thick leaf where no one would pass, away from all the houses in the woods that belonged to the church nearby, empty at weekday twilight.

From within the brush she appeared and was extending her left hand to him, while remaining partly hidden. He looked around him quickly and ducked in with her, and she led him three steps to a thick, soft, dark red blanket spread on the ground. They sat, not speaking. For a while. But their hands touched, and remained together, while their breath came shallowly and in the heart of each was a skittering bird winging this way and that, trying to escape. After only a few whispers he left first, at her instruction.

But he hid himself when he was supposed to have gone away,

and he watched her come out. She looked around and set off for home at an easy pace. He followed the motion of her limbs with his eyes, with reverence, with desire.

And another meeting, of a full hour.

And she even wanted to conduct pencil-and-paper interviews— but she stopped after the second time: was she thinking this would be a kind of excuse, if anyone discovered them? He told her: No one's going to care about that little notebook. And onward, through all their stolen time, till they were unalive without thought of each other, till they were marked for each other, they weren't going to stop.

She had so many questions. She was a demon to know.

"Tell me about Francie," she'd said. And she'd prompted and prodded him to get stories out of him.

"Tell me about the white baby," she'd said, and he'd gone back, ever more shyly, to the day on a river where a white woman had stepped into deep water and he'd saved her infant from drowning.

"Tell me your real name," tenderly, carefully she said. "You told me Injin people have a secret name," she whispered. He smiled at her but kept silent.

Their talks grew longer and their stratagems for finding time together a little less careful. She took his callused hand and studied it; she looked into him as deeply as she had ever tried to look into another person, through his eyes and his whole face. He could dodge her probing gaze inside him, it was like a game, sometimes. Except that then it was he who was looking and wondering into her eyes and feeling like he was dodging this way and that through a night sky at dizzying speed, not knowing where he was headed.

Despite Martha's youth, she saw that for all his experience he was in some ways more innocent than she; she understood that for all her knowledge and position, compared to his, yet she was less formed than he.

She got foolish ideas, and he couldn't shake her from them, any more than he had been able to stop her pencil and paper till it ran its course. She wanted to take him in her father's carriage out on the east road to Malcolm Mullaney's cabin and go beyond to see where the snake had bit him. Reuben wouldn't do that, and she kept saying it was all right, and he kept telling her it was crazy.

The look with which she looked; the warmth of her thigh alongside his when they sat side by side in hiding like schoolchildren; the silences between them—this was not as when he'd been a boy, with quiet Sandra, the neighbor girl in Francie's village, or as with women since Sandra, for whom he'd had an appetite that, however powerful, he had satisfied readily enough in his body. What appetite this new one was, that ran through all of him, he had not felt before.

Till they drove each other past what they could abstain from, and they answered each other's thirst in a hot dark thicket, seized by their own bodies, bystanders almost at their own coupling who awoke from it abashed and amazed at what they had done. But at next meeting, and next, did it again, and everything else was mere pretense of interest that for each other's sake they kept up—for a quarter of an hour, perhaps, before their hands were playing over each other and against the pull of their clothing and they were floating without bodily weight against each other, joined together at mouth and hand and hip, pulsing like a double flame.

Then, apart from her, he not only agonized about their meetings and the secrecy they tried to maintain for safety despite their madness, but also—for the sake of holding on to her a little longer if he could, before he had to get out of town fast, he guessed—about his appearance, his way of speaking, his clothes. He, who through trials and sorrows had rarely felt unknown to himself, even when others had not known him, now had moments of surprise when he found himself odd, unprecedented. The most so when, coming out of hiding with her and walking away with feigned other purpose, his body was caught still in the spell of hers, and the taste of her was still in his mouth, the scent of her still in his nose, the shape of her still molded by hands that now grasped only the empty air.

All this in the space of five rushing, infinite weeks.

At the mill he worked only in order to distract himself, he exerted himself physically with the crew, who watched him but neither objected to nor welcomed him, who went on putting their backs to it as they had to do. Reuben felt he had already given something of himself to the mill, or allowed the mill, the bosses and hirelings, to take it, something he no longer had in himself; so now, having given yet another part of himself to another person, to Martha, who would he be? It was crazy even to think about her; daylong he thought about her.

He would put on one of the two shirts she had given him, and brush his hair back with water, and wash his face and hands, while Mr. Grooms, standing near, would cluck softly, sadly, and plead with him to cease the foolishness, to get away from terrible trouble that could cost him his life and hurt other people, too, black people. Reuben tried not answering these pleas, out of respect for his benefactor. But Mr. Grooms began to whine at him, to preach at him, till Reuben had to separate himself from the old man's concern.

"I'm not like you," Reuben said to him once. "They not goin to come after me the way they would after you. I'm not a nigger."

Mr. Grooms laughed bitterly and said, "Nigger ain't the color of you skin: Son, you doan know what nigger is. You *think* you do, because we done took you in, when you was little, like you tole me. You think you do, because you had a nigger girl here an there. You think you do, because at that mill they put you over the nigger crew, I know. Howsomever, you ain't really been at the other end of it yet. But now you *have* found a way to git to where we are, and *they* goan send you along right quick as soon as they know. Believe me. Believe a lifetime of nigger and then some. Nigger ain't what you is, it's what they make you. And believe me: they will." The old man shook his head and retreated to his Bible and his own steadfast cleanliness and orderliness of habit, which had long been his chosen defense.

And the fear that sometimes shook Reuben, the anxiousness, or something more powerful than these, had only partly to do with white people or anyone else. He was afraid, too, of what was only inside himself, or lacking there. And afraid he wouldn't want to be without her.

Feeling he was far more changed than anyone took him to be, he had come to be conscious of himself as he had never been—of how the mill boss regarded him, of how his black crew regarded him, of how the unsuspecting and not-to-be-trusted Billy and Paul thought of him, of how he thought of himself and regarded himself. What did they say? Did they say anything? Reuben did his work in a state of confusion; he would realize that he could not remember what he had just done or said, and he would look around wondering who had noticed. Every ordinary day he had lived was gone, and he could not think how he had lived, before, or how to plan to live, now. He simply let the days lead him. He did not know what anyone else knew. He felt watched, studied; he spoke only when spoken to. He said Yes sir and No sir, dully. He considered how he placed one foot in front of the other in order to walk.

He thought of her all day—of her hair, her face, her eyes, her mouth, her shoulders, her clothes, her naked back, the smell of her at her nape. At her waist. Her bare legs. Then when at last after his feverish waiting that distracted him from his work and held him more and more apart from every other living person, when at last he saw her and recognized her form from a distance, or when he crept to her in their hiding and did not see her at all till he was nearly beside her, his throat was constricted with such longing, such appetite for her, and such excitement that it felt nearly like dread. And she looked—every time—different from her as he had been remembering and imagining her. The same, of course; but different.

She had brought him those two shirts that had been her father's, but that the man had discarded because he didn't like them (his wife having bought them for him without asking his preferences, or rather, wordlessly insisting on her own). On Reuben they were a little long, but he looked fine and handsome, so that, even though an older part of him would not have cared about them, might have given them readily to someone else who needed them more than he, whom they would fit better, now he would put one on when he was going to meet her. Mr. Grooms would watch him do that, too, and shake his white-haired, close-cropped head. "You ought to *burry* them blouses in the groun, if you know what's good f'you," he said. Reuben looked in a piece of broken mirror the size of an egg and combed his wet hair to a part in the center.

"She wanted to go to The Nations," Reuben said. And explained that was what Indian people called the Indian Territory. Now Oklahoma. A Sunday evening. They were standing under a wide beech tree, in deep shadow; out beyond the protected underspace near the trunk of the tree it was dark and raining softly.

"Did you go there?"

"You mean after she died?"

Martha nodded.

"No. I never did go."

"You didn't want to see . . . your own people?" she asked.

As happened sometimes when she asked him something, he didn't answer.

She studied his face, from the side. She couldn't help but stare at him, sometimes, fascinated by his eyes, that were much darker than hers, by his nose, that was stronger than the miniature noses of her family, by his lips, that had kissed her, by his teeth.

But sometimes he would catch her staring and he would stare back at her, not looking into her eyes but just looking *at* her, the way she had looked at him, till she could not bear it, and was sorry if she had pressed him too hard with her looking. For his staring at her was indeed like a pressing against her sometimes when she was not ready for it, and she had to look away and draw her shoulders up, as if she were cold, in order to shield herself. From him. From his appetite—despite how much that very appetite had called her up into something different, had filled her and had made the days, and even the very minutes while the parlor pendulum clock tocked slowly through dead hours, a richer time than any she had ever lived through.

She spent hours and days in a luxury of expectation, awaiting their next meeting, constructing in her mind a thousand avenues of experience they might pursue in a life she was daydreaming for them. And when they were together all the thoughts she had already thought vanished and she lived only in the passing moment, unable to think, feeling different from herself, always different. Different from the people she knew, and eerily she sometimes could glimpse herself as she thought he saw her: a white girl. She had not known that "white" had such meaning, till now.

And the touching, the embraces, the pushing away of the obstacles between their bodies and fitting their bodies into one body. . . . She had to have it and she did not want it; she wanted it and she had to avoid it, sidestep it somehow. It carried her away and then she was frightened of the carrying even while she lay awake, alone in her bed, thinking about it and wanting him again. And the person that he was—she kept seeing him anew and trying to get more of him, to know all of him, but he kept opening up like a view from a train, and you could never see it all, and what you had succeeded in seeing was behind you and you couldn't go back to it anyway and what was there in front of you changed as you saw it from moving angles.

On a Sunday her father traveled to the county seat to argue a complicated case, and would be gone three days and three nights and Martha's mother with him for the excursion, and Martha was left in charge of the house and Anne and, nominally, of James.

They were in the back alley—right behind her house. She didn't just want to meet and wrestle with their clothes and then part.

They did kiss several times, and he brought his hands up and held her clothed shoulders, and felt the textures of her dress, and tentatively touched her dark, bound-up hair, looking into it and not at her eyes, which were pulling at him; and she took his hand and put his palm against her breast, through her dress.

But then she broke the spell of the moment and drew him toward the house.

Reuben was as loath to step inside—they were standing at the back door—as if it had been a steel trap with poison bait. But she had already assured him that her sister and brother would be out for hours; Pilgrim would not be coming on Sunday; the house was empty; no neighbors could see. She insisted he had to come in, he had to see where she lived, her room. In him a memory of some such house fluttered, the Big House into which he had surreptitiously looked through a window, and the black man who had frightened him and his mother. Had chased them like they were no better than stray dogs.

"No, 's not right," he said. "It's crazy-mad. No."

"It's not crazy-mad," she said, pulling him by the hand. "You have every much a right to come in as innyone else," she said. "You're my guest. I've had guests here before, and men callers, too, in the parlor."

"You don't mean men," he said. "You mean some boy." She looked to him as young as nineteen can look: beautiful and not to be denied. He felt much older than she.

She got him in the back door and into the kitchen, and she felt much safer to be inside—about the neighbors not seeing, she hadn't been entirely sure. With great pleading she got him to sit down on a kitchen chair, after she saw she could make him come no further, not even to look through the next door at the living room. For a few minutes she sat opposite him, waiting. He was as silent and pitched in tense readiness as a deer at woods' edge, about to bolt back into the trees.

He also kept to himself a small resentment he could scarcely recognize anyway that rose in him once he was in the house. He was not himself, here, but something half-changed by there being no place for him in such a house. He took no pleasure from being inside it, there was no reason or need for him to be there, while she was thinking it was a triumph of some kind. Into his mind's eye came the image of looking up at a strong young woman of his color. She was leading him, pulling him quickly by the hand. It struck him that this was his mother, and the image vanished from his mind, breaking apart or perhaps fleeing, not wanting to be seen. He felt like he had almost found out, in this image, something about her he had not known, or had forgotten; but the image had not stayed; had barely arrived when it had twitched out of sight again, gone; it did not wish to stay if he was going to be in this house. He did not know any more where any house had been that had been his or anyone's of his. He felt the chair pressing against his back.

She said to him, eagerly, "I have to show you just two thengs. Please?"

He let himself be pulled to his feet by her as she bent back from him, holding his hand. She dragged him through a swinging door across a dark parlor with huge pieces of dark furniture, as if crafted for giants, and pictures hung on the wall like windows, for they had glass laid over the scenes they portrayed, and also hanging on the wall a sword in a scabbard, and then through another door into a room where there was an enormous bed with black carved posts at each end and a high board of the same black wood at the head, carved along the top to look like grapes and leaves. Beyond that bed—he stared around the incomprehensible room— she pulled him into a kind of shallow side-room where there were dark shelves filled with books and a small polished desk of dark wood on which an ink bottle and a quill pen stood in isolated silence and readiness: sacred, it came to him, and an idea of a feather, and something else painted prettily, came to him also for a moment and then dispersed like blown smoke.

Martha was showing him a book, talking to him in an excited whisper, but he was trying to make that wisp of a picture in his mind come back, there was a voice to go with it that he knew was speaking but that he could not hear. He heard Martha's voice instead—he had told her how Francie had taught him to read in the Bible, and now Martha was wanting him to see these books, all these books, surely she didn't want him to look at every one? She was talking about Indians again, opening a book to show him. He tried to pay attention as she showed him this one and that, and laid a large one down on the desk and opened it to an illustration of three people, a nearly naked man holding upright a long straight stick with a large arrowhead on the tip and wearing six feathers on his head and beads around his neck and a ring in his nose and also carrying a tautly strung bow, standing in front of a kind of tree Reuben had never seen, like a feather duster stuck upside down into the earth; and next to him a woman also wearing beads, so many that they covered her little breasts, and a short skirt, and holding by the hand a little boy carrying a small bow and arrows, and behind them three other nearly naked men walking, and a little rectangular hut with round windows, and two more of the strange trees, that looked as if they too had feathers. "THE INDIANS Marching on a Visit or to a Feast," Martha read to him unnecessarily, and he stared at the page without seeing it, his mind elsewhere. She was racing; she closed the book and put it back on the shelf and was searching for another. He looked at the top of her father's clothes dresser, next to the desk. On it lay a shallow glass bowl on little feet, containing shirt and collar studs, and next to it a box in the shape of a cube with rounded corners, six inches on a side, covered with a bruised red pattern like wallpaper. A small brass clasp held the lid shut; the lid itself was shiny, a varnish of some specially smooth kind laid down over a painting of an Indian in tribal dress. Against a yellowish ground, the painting was of the upper body; the man had one feather in his hair, the long braids of which hung in front of his shoulders down his chest. He was holding a pipe, but his hands were hidden inside a blanket wrapped about him. Under the blanket his shirt was beaded and fringed. On his face was an almost melancholy expression, a look meant to be dignified, perhaps, but instead weak and biddable. Reuben could not quite grasp what it meant. (Here, to be admired, was the image that white people hated in the flesh.)

Martha was shuffling about. Reuben pulled the clasp loose with a fingernail, and cautiously lifted the lid, without any idea what could be kept in such a box. The lid had cloth hinges. Inside were a quantity of starched white collars, neatly piled up and nested in each other. These people had everything; everything was theirs to have. Martha knew what she wanted, and she could insist on getting it, it would come to her in her world, where he could never be more than a tolerated figure at the edge of a room or in a shed out back, or dressed in costume on the lid of a box.

"That's nothin—that's Daddy's old collar box, it doesn't mean innytheng," Martha said impatiently, trying to get his attention. "Isn't that silly." She took his arm. "Come on, I can't find what I was lookin for here," she said, and she pulled him away.

Hurriedly, from excitement, not apprehension, Martha led him out of that room again and across the dark parlor down a hall and to a door she opened saying, "My room." She pushed him in before her, and he stood in the pale light of the dim room, he looked at the bed, like a mound of feathers covered by a smooth pale fabric, and at the window, dark folds of cloth tied back with ribbons and a fall of thin white translucent cloth with designs in it, and still he did not quite hear what she was saying. Then some small sound from the front of the house, it might well have been nothing more than a squirrel across the porch roof, made him rise to the balls of his feet quickly and he was through the kitchen and out the back door, without even a cautionary glance around him, before she could catch up with him.

"You shouldn't have taken me to your house," he said. They were at one of their meeting places—out toward the Negro end of town, where if she could time it right she might chance on him walking home to his room in Mr. Grooms's house after work, at twilight. There were scarcely ever any whites on this road, either

in buggies or motor cars. She was driving her father's buggy herself now, excited to have just won that privilege after two years of
asking for it. She could harness Antonio herself.

"I told you I don't see why not." No one else was in sight. He
was walking beside the buggy.

"If you wouldn't take me when your mother and father're there,
you can see why not."

"There're places in this world where I am sure it wouldn't occasion any talk at all if we were seen together."

"We haven't been in one yet," he said.

"Drum told me one afternoon, when he was drunk, how he got
his name. Was a slave name." The spot all but best—closed in,
contained, entirely theirs, yet making them most anxious: in the
tiny hayloft of her own father's stable only twenty yards behind
the house, where he kept the old horse, Antonio, and the buggy
(the carriage and the two fine horses were at the town livery, but
Antonio was a kind of pet whom all the children had ridden when
they were young). The last of the light was nearly gone.

"But you haven't told me yours, yet—your true name, that you
said nobody knew but you," she said.

"My mama knew it, and people in my grandparents' house," he
said. He had been kissing her on the mouth, and she him, many
times. When he kissed her he felt like he was whispering something to her but not in words, because he couldn't say it in words,
and not to her ears, not—almost—*to* her, but *into* her, below her
hearing; he was speaking into her something she would keep for
him.

There seemed to be more to him than he himself had known, or
rather, more than anyone had ever before given him permission to
show. Maybe she would keep for him, in her recollection, some of
the things he hadn't known he knew about himself till she had
asked, and they would be safe in her, and he would be all right.

Despite the old blanket she kept in the loft now, a quantity of
hay was clinging to her dress, which in the light of the yard she

would have to take extraordinary care to get off before going into the house. She was trying to get her hair back into control, she brought a hairbrush with her when they met. She was a little apart from him, thinking ahead into seeing her mother, wondering ahead into what she could do. Running headlong and heedless toward the edge of a cliff. But hoping, almost praying, that some path would come suddenly into view down it, and she would follow it to new safety. He lay back in the hay, watching her as she sat next to him, her face away from him.

"You never tell me about *your* mama," he said.

She didn't want to.

"You don't get on at all well with *her*," he said.

She glared at him; but he was right, and she quenched her anger. She could not think it out, herself, so she could not tell him of it. She peered through a crack in the boards of the wall at her lamp-lit house up near the street.

"I have to go in now," she said. He could retreat unseen from the side of the stable away from the house, he could move into the trees and brush of the field that backed on their house, and never be seen by anyone. She was not ready to do whatever would come next in their lives; she could not imagine what it could be. She had come to count on that ability of his to disappear.

But it had begun to occur to him that her counting on it was only what others had always done to him. If he had to disappear from this, if there was no other way—and there was not—he would disappear this time, he would go away to a place where no one ever looked.

After he made love to her the first time, after he had kissed and as if eaten of her, a taste of muskmelon, persian melon, cantaloupe, in his mouth.

15
—

Progress

There has been such a march of progress in our State in these opening years of the new century as will grace the historical records for decades to come. History has never seen a braver struggle than that made by the people of Galveston since the great storm of 1900. Oil has been discovered and the oil industry has come to Texas to stay. The life-sized marble statues of General Houston and Stephen F. Austin, executed by the famous sculptress Elizabeth Ney, are the admiration of all who visit our renowned state capitol. The colleges have been increased and strengthened. The new colony for epileptics has opened in Abilene, and at the Austin Insane Asylum a Pasteur Institute has been established for treating persons bitten by rabid animals. The Daughters of the Republic of Texas have preserved the sacred Alamo and San Jacinto Battlefield. Irrigation is bringing untold agricultural prosperity and wealth to the formerly worthless portions of Texas which in the past bore no crops because of insufficient rainfall. The Department of Agriculture, the State Library Commission, the penitentiary reform, the school laws—these are the stepping stones of a great people in the march toward a world greatness.

When one looks backward over Texas history, he sees much for which we should be grateful to the Great Father above. Our wise and provident Government has over years of courageous effort removed the dangers of the frontier, given intelligent aid to the toiling agricultural masses, presided over the growth of our population, our industry and our commerce, safeguarded the wealth that has been poured into our coffers, and begun an enlightened state system of public education. We are uniting every portion of our state by railroad and uniting all the towns and cities of our state in a common campaign for improvement and progress. Let the boys and girls of this generation fit themselves to take up the duties that must soon fall upon their shoulders; let them learn to love their State; let them resolve that education shall be as free as the sunlight that floods our Mediterranean skies; let these things be done, and the Muse of History shall call for a golden pen and she shall write higher in the roll of fame that name we love so well—Texas!

16

Ethnography

Martha studied several books she took from her father's library, which now meant more to her than all his other books together. She could not guess how her father had even come to own those two volumes recently issued in Washington, D.C., with their gold-stamped spines displaying a torch of knowledge and lofty, serious, scientific titles.

But besides accounts of a few of the aspects of daily life, there was less to learn than she had thought there would be. She read: "Unfortunately, very little is known of the history of the people of whom this paper treats." And: "Unfortunately, comparatively few of the articles of food used by the primitive inhabitants are known to present members of the tribe of whom this paper treats." And: "They say there were no special designs of painting the face and that no combination of colors had any meaning." And: "The meaning of this word is not known to the Choctaw." And: "Comparatively few articles are now made, much of their ancient art having been forgotten." And: "They are excellent basket makers, although their work at the present time is greatly inferior to that of a generation ago." And: "They say they formerly had fish traps in the bayous, but seem not to remember how they were constructed." And: "Various other games and pastimes were undoubtedly known and practiced in former days, but these have been forgotten by the Choctaw of whom this paper treats." And: "There appears to have been very little lamenting or mourning on the occasion of a death or burial. The body was borne to the grave and the interment took place without ceremony of any sort." And: "The native method of reckoning the divisions of the year is no longer practiced, nor do the present inhabitants remember the names of all the moons." And: "Neither the men nor the women of this branch of the tribe appear to know of any special dances, although it is highly probable that in former years distinct ceremonies were enacted on particular occasions." And: "The tribe appears to be a quiet and peaceable people, and even now the few remaining inhabitants often refer to the fact that their tribe never took up arms against the Americans."

And this new young man, like a stranger from some remote place, or even some other time, Reuben, did not turn out to be the informant she would have wished, as she learned the very first time she tried talking to him. (And the talking, after all, was only a kind of pretext—she knew she knew this, but she pretended not to know it.)

"If you're aimin to teach me to read," Reuben said, "you know I can do that already."

"No—"

"But I haven't had much practice at writin," he added, his lower lip caught in his teeth, his eyebrows raised.

"No, of course *I'm* not going to teach *you!*" she said. "I'm goin to *collect* information *from* you," she said. "You're goin to teach *me.*"

He was doubtful. "I can't teach you innytheng—you already know more than I do. You had your schoolin."

"It's not about school," she said. He still looked skeptical.

"Don't be anxious about it," she said. "Just let me ask you questions."

He had not run the mortal risk of their assignation just to answer questions and wait and lose precious time while she wrote in an old school exercise book with a red cover.

But she did not write very much, after all. There was more to talk of than could be fitted into questions or answers, and, too, the spell was always wrapping itself more tightly around them.

The spell wrought certain effects on its victims. These included trembling, nervousness, deep gazes, sudden silences, tentative touching of hands, then of faces. And, as spells are intended to do, it carried them past their own individual wills and left them at the mercy of their fervor and in the grasp of their excitement. The spell was a power of the breathing body and the living spirit, not of the thinking mind that had concluded by cogitation and reflection that the world was as it was. The world was not as it was, after all; it was another way that neither Martha nor Reuben had known of firsthand, before, although she had talked of it with friends, and read of it, and understood what she might call it, to herself; while he had only heard of it occasionally, and had thought it did not or would not apply to him.

Till by the third meeting he found it the most natural thing to do, and she too, that as they stood facing each other he put his hands on either side of her claspable waist and pulled her slowly to him, their bellies and hips pressed gently to each other; and he looked at her with a quizzical expression when she said very seriously, holding her pencil at the ready, leaning back away from the heat of their touching of bodies, that she really wanted to go through her questions and his answers. "I'll give you kisses afterward," she said, her voice deepening. "Not now, not this time."

He let go of her. Agreeing, smiling resignedly.

Sitting on the ground, hidden with him in deep shade and muffled by the rattling of leaves and the whispering of weeds in the hot wind, with her legs tucked properly under her capacious skirts, she tried to begin what she imagined would be a proper interview.

"I don't know" or "I'm not sure," he said, any number of times.

"Did you ever wear your hair long?" she asked, persisting in her formality. And in a softer voice the tone of which asked his pardon for the game of formality—"like" (she was beginning to pronounce the word carefully) "an Indian?"

"Remember Francie cuttin my hair for me, and talkin about it."

"What did she say?"

"Oh, I don't know. Her children were pickin it up off the floor and lookin at it as she cut it. Must have been long when she cut it the first time."

He was sitting by her side patiently, his hands folded in his lap, away from her body.

"Did your daddy wear his hair long?"

"I didn't know him," he said. "I told you that."

"Oh yes. He must've bin white, anyway. Did your grand-daddy?"

He looked up at the thickness of branches and leaves, and past the branches and leaves at the sky. She waited. Before her own eyes he could become opaque to her, if he wanted. She didn't know him very well. Yet.

She could tell he was looking inward, not at the sky. And when he said, "I'm not sure," she felt he *was* sure, and she wondered why he wouldn't just *say*.

As yet she had written almost nothing. In three attempts on three different afternoons. "I remember him almost, pretty good," Reuben said.

"You don't want to tell me, do you?"

"Sure, I'll tell you. Ask me what you want." Grinning.

"All right. Did he paint his face?"

"What?"

"Did he put colored paint on his face—for example, for *Indian* dances."

"We didn't dance. There was no one to dance. Jest us, our family. We didn't paint our faces!"

He bowed his head. He saw, in the ground of himself, his own track leading backward.

"I heard the Coushatta on the reservation paint their faces and dance with a drum. Men told my father that," Martha said.

"I bin there," Reuben said, without looking up. "I didn't see that. Jest some pore people with nothin."

"Oh," she said. The wind sang a breathy tune, gusting hot from the southwest.

She wrote briefly in her exercise book, and he looked over at her writing.

"Did innybody in your family have tattoos—on their face, for example?"

"I sure don't think so. Another woman, she was friendly to my mama, had a tattoo on her cheeks. Or more like a kind of scar in little rows."

"Who was she?"

"A black woman, that worked at the Big House, I b'lieve." An instant's trace of a back door up some wide painted steps; then a window.

"Oh. That doesn't count."

"No?"

"No—not if she was a nigra."

"Well, she didn't seem inny worse from us. And she lived better than we did."

He looked over at her exercise book; he wasn't sure he remembered ever having seen clean paper before, that had never been used for anything. "Can I look at your handwritin?" he said.

"What? But I haven't put innytheng down yet, you haven't told me innytheng yet."

"I jest want to see what it looks like, your writin."

She showed him, but didn't let him take the exercise book from her hands. His hands over her hands.

He couldn't make out the words of her cursive script. The letters, all connected in a continuous line, were not at all like the printed script Francie had taught him, that he could write well enough from imitating the look of the letters printed in the Bible. Martha studied him as he looked at her two little sentences; he made no comment, but glanced up at her quickly, and then was looking down at her writing again.

He shifted his body, and when he lifted his eyes—hers never having left his face—his expression was simpler than before, but not exactly guileless. He might have withdrawn a little into himself, to hide from her. He was certainly not the cooperative informant of her father's books, filled with tales he would give only to her. She had missed or muffed her chance. The relationship *she* had wanted—perhaps it was to control that other thing that had already bound them and which was frightening because in it they were equally bound and equally vulnerable to each other—was over before she could even get it started. She saw this.

She shrugged at him, smiling. He smiled back. And took her hand, pencil and all, and toyed with it. She would go ahead and ask her questions; but she knew the answers would not be of value, that her little project would come to nothing; and she felt a small flicker of superiority to him.

"Did you have inny jewelry?" she asked.

He pondered that, or pretended to. "I b'lieve my grannie—"

"What did you call her?"

"Well—Grannie," he said, a little slowly.

"You did?" She wrote that down.

"Grannie Mary," he said.

"Mary?" She brightened.

He frowned; he couldn't deceive her. "No," he said.

She cleared her throat. "What about her jewelry?"

"That was her name, a jewel—Pearl."

"Wonderful!" she said, and wrote it down.

He felt a kind of tender pity for Martha. What she was doing, it was almost touching. And she was looking at and into him, which excited him. He did not take hold of her, as he wanted to do.

"Pearl what?"

"I couldn't tell you," he said.

"Didn't she have an Indian name?"

"That would've been different—not a name like that but in . . . our language. Language we spoke then."

She questioned him with a look.

"Our words," he said. "I couldn't tell you inny more." And he lifted his eyebrows, asking with that gesture if she still wished to continue.

"Jewelry?" she said firmly, her pencil poised.

"Well," he said. "I do recall that Grannie had a little pin she wore on her dress, wore it at her throat, made of a silver dime that was hammered out flat—little pin that she never would sell nor trade no matter what. And we used to talk about it. About her sellin it to get—whatever. I remember everbody used to ask her to sell it."

"Why wouldn't she?"

"Wouldn't've brought that much. And then it would've bin gone for good. Guess she knew that better than we did. Like as not, it was made for her by someone ahead of her, maybe when she was young. But I don't remember ever seein innytheng else of jewelry." How could Martha think his family would have jewelry?

She laid the pencil in the center crease of the exercise book and her hand went to her throat, covering it. "No beads?" she said, less firmly.

"No."

"Or earbobs?"

"No."

She picked up her pencil again. At this rate the point would last forever.

"I sure don't think so."

"What about things people *made*? Like tools. For farmin. Or weapons?"

He smiled at that. "Granddad had an old rifle. I used to hope I'd git that rifle someday. (He didn't make *that*.)" He paused. "Workin, everbody used the same short hoe they use now, nothin diffrunt. Had knives made of steel. Mama had a cup that was hers, don't know why it was important to her—it was tin, I've got it still, all beat up, but was hers." He smiled at her: "And when we were walkin from Miss'ippi to Texas, Mama and me, had her two baskets that she'd made at home, were what we carried our food in—and whatever else we had. I don't remember what else was in em, but remember carryin that basket."

"What'd it look like?"

"Wasn't too big, really, and had a handle. Well, we had two.

They had a handle, and the bottom was kinely pointed, worked to a point, so you couldn't rest it on the ground straight up, you had to lay it down on its side, like." He picked up a twig and drew in the dust a triangle standing on its point, with a semicircle attached to the broad top of it, a handle.

Martha copied his design. She forgot for a moment that he was only humoring her; and for a moment he forgot it, too.

And so for a while longer she catalogued the paltry few items he would vouchsafe to her from his inventory of knowing and unknowing—he didn't have anything to tell her about pottery or games, medicines or foods, or even stories.

He liked to please her but was tired of her questions. He intervened and won a change of mood in her by stopping her writing hand, this time holding it firmly, and asking her with his eyes to see him instead of scrutinizing him. That led back to the life of the body and the spirit, and her thinking lay off to one side with the pencil and the paper on the ground, like a wasp caught in a jar, that couldn't bother them for a time.

17

Remembered Life

Inside her house, where he'd let himself be led, Francie asked him, "Boy, what's your name?"

He said nothing.

"You got a daddy? What's *his* name?" she asked, but he said nothing.

"You got a mama?" she asked. And he looked away from her, not at anything. But did not try to get out of her grasp.

"All right, you got a mama, most people do," Francie said. "Where she at, your mama?" He had not looked back at her yet. "You did have a mama, no child that don't have," Francie said, "but clear as day somethin took her from you. Or took you from her." She turned to her family, waiting silently around her and the boy. "This is a orphan child," she said. "He look like a lil Injin boy, y'all understand? This child ain't got no mama."

Francie's children were staring. The children he had spied on, as they played, the night before.

Francie shook her head at the sorry state of his clothes—she was accustomed to patched and worn clothing, but not to clothing so dirty—and to such dirt on the body.

"God left the lil Injin boy here, God led him to us. White people not going to care nothin about this lil orphan Injin boy, even if he have their blood in him, which certainly he look like he do. Lord, who ain't got their blood? So it has to be us that take him in." It was an entire speech to her family. But they looked dubious.

111

He would not at first tell them his name or say anything at all, and yet he seemed not to want to run away from them, so Francie dubbed him Saved, for he'd been found in the woods by her and saved from the wild, and also saved for God. Francie would have him baptized the next Sunday. But then he mumbled his name was Reuben.

"Thass a *Bible* name!" Francie said. "Thass *good*. Listen y'all, you know how Preacher has told of Joseph sold into slavery? And was his good brother, Reuben, tried to hep him, to save him from his evil brothers. I have read it over in the Bible many times," she said.

"You got a last name?" she said. But he didn't answer.

She said, "Um-hum. Well, all right. Now, you have to take 'Saved' for a middle name. And for a last name, same's ours, is that all right, honey? So—listen now—so now you Reuben... Saved... Sweetbitter. You say that?"

He didn't. And because among the paltry and desperately tiny hoard of possessions in his baskets, was one thing which above all he guarded as fiercely as if it had been hammered of gold in heaven, the children called him Cup. The beaded moccasins, a woman's, far finer than the cup, and covetously regarded by everyone who saw them, he also held to himself firmly, but it was the cup that he seemed most defiantly to protect from their curiosity and their grasp.

The first side room was Francie's bedroom, where the girls slept, too. The back room, where all of them were standing, was the kitchen—filled, it seemed to him that day, with food. (Later he would see it as being scarcely supplied for their number.) Francie guided him to a proper chair. It was the first he had ever sat in, and to him it felt like someone was holding a hard hand against his back all the time he sat in it, so he kept leaning forward to get away from that hand. She stoked the fire in the cookstove and soon gave him a heaped plate of warm potatoes and green beans and beets and a little fried bacon, and bread. He wolfed it all with terrific hunger, eating with his fingers, and the other children laughed at him but were jealous. Their own food hadn't seemed so precious to them till they saw someone else eating it up.

Reuben scarcely looked at the food; with his face down close to the plate as he chewed and swallowed and kept bringing food to his mouth, he looked around the room at them, and his eyes watered. He said nothing, he had gone back to remaining silent.

"Drum!" she called to her husband, who was dressing in his room, the small front room. Drum came slowly back. "Where this boy goan sleep—with you in your bed? You got the bigges bed."

"What?" he said. His eyes narrowed. Her good humor, her hope, continually offended him, who allowed no hope nor cheer, having never been allowed any by those with the power to give it. "With me?" he said. "No, woman. No. You be askin me to take a *white* boy in with me, might as well."

Testing him, as she did always, was the only way she had left, after their years together, of bringing him into talk. Children were clamoring around her, "Not with *me!* He not sleepin in *my* bed!" They owned only three beds, and now, counting Reuben, they were seven.

"Eswold," she said. "Eswold?" A boy of about fourteen was looking in through the doorway behind Drum. "With you and Frank?" she asked him.

Eswold retreated into the dim room without answering. "All right," she said, "won't go drivin Eswold out of dis house, after all we bin through with *him*." Perhaps she was only confirming for herself that they would fail her in this. And she had to leave now to get to work in town.

Eswold hadn't gone away entirely. From within that room his voice came to punctuate the discussion with finality: "He not touchin me or my bed."

"Lord God, already you trouble to my family," Francie said to Reuben. She put a hand on his dirty straight hair, feeling it. "But if the Lord brought you to my house, then may He also deliver goodness to them that worships Him, so hep me I'm goan provide for you in a Christian way." Reuben was sitting forward in the

113

chair, his plate clean, thirsting for water, gauging the distance to the door, wanting his things.

"Now I'm goan go late to Miz Stephens, we goan get you a bath. I ain't worked tin years for her without earnin some late mornin once in a while." Frank and the two girls began to laugh with delight.

"Y'all *hush!*" she yelled at them, and they backed away, still smiling.

She took Reuben completely by surprise when she held shears up to his nape and snipped off his long hair. He couldn't comprehend it and he bolted to his feet. She put her free hand on his shoulder and waited, and after the trembling in his body had run up into her heavy arm and ceased, he sat down slowly again. And she finished the job neatly.

Eswold came into the kitchen and found Reuben alone. He stepped up to the smaller boy and hit him once with his fist, in the chest. Reuben sprawled backwards and fell to the floor, his head missing the stove. "Ain't suppose to bruise yo face, I figger," Eswold said. "It might show kinda bad on *you*. But you do what I say, don't matter what that woman tell you," Eswold said. Reuben only looked at him, and Eswold walked out and was gone for the day.

Drum slept on a bed of his own, and Eswold and little Frank shared a bed. In a corner of this room, Francie made up a pallet of two old blankets over a thick layer of pine straw she had ordered the children to gather after supper. Francie had a large cast-off mattress and true bedstead from town in her room where the two small girls, Therese and Mary, slept with her.

Drum came in looking tired and angry, and without speaking to anyone he went to his bed. Later, after all the others were asleep but Reuben, who lay awake listening, Eswold came in quietly and lay down with a groan that startled Reuben because it sounded like his own mother, and then images of her came to his mind, and he fell asleep thinking of her sitting on the ground, leaning against the tree in that clearing. Where she had died. She was dead. She wasn't going to come fetch him from these people. Ever.

To keep the tin cup from making any sound if it moved or even shifted, to keep anyone from finding it ever again, the boy stole a clean rag from Francie's kitchen which he stuffed into the cup, and this he hid up high at the corner of the room where the bare rafters met the wall. He stood on a chair from the kitchen. He kept the baskets, with the smaller inside the larger and the moccasins inside that, between his pallet and the wall. The safety of his private things much preoccupied him. But in the woods, where he could have hidden them better, they would have been exposed to rain and wind and rust.

Only once did Reuben go to the school. The class was held three afternoons a week. Stooping gray-headed Mr. Pogue, whose skin was as pale as Reuben's but of a different hue, made them sit in rows and study writing and numerals that he wrote on a slate with a lump of chalky stone and held up in front of them. Everyone stared at Reuben, and then frowned as, in this one afternoon, he caught on quickly to the numbers. Mr. Pogue, however, ridiculed him and Reuben refused to go again to the class. Francie, studying the problem momentarily, determined that she would teach him some Bible verses herself—she had never been able to make Eswold learn them—and these would be sufficient for an orphan Indian boy's learning.

The children spoke evil of Mr. Pogue when they were where Francie could not hear them; he was mean and made his least favorite students bend over before the class and he whipped their behinds through their trousers or thin sack dresses with a switch; this was for anyone—boy or girl—who did not do as he said, and after he had whipped a girl he might quickly, like it meant nothing, touch where he had whipped her. If Reuben had been one to tell anything more of himself, he would have told Francie of Mr. Pogue calling him to the front of the class and making him turn around and around slowly while Mr. Pogue had pushed at him with the point of his switch. And then Mr. Pogue had grabbed Reuben's arm and yelled in his ear that he was a heathen no matter his coming baptism, and of an evil heathen race, filthy scalpers and slave-owners worse than whites, and incapable of learning to read or even to talk properly. And Mr. Pogue had pushed him down with the children only six years old, who stared at him with the fright the man had put in them, while the older children laughed at him. And Mr. Pogue had silenced the class and gone on with his lessons, screaming needlessly at them.

And yet the game with the slate had been interesting. When Francie began, one evening, with the cracked, open Bible, and started him on letters and small words, he fixed the curious humped and spindly letter-creatures in his mind quickly enough, and learned the inflexible order in which they were to be marshalled in memory. He learned what a word was, and the fluctuating rush of talking broke into hundreds of separate pieces like new toys where before he had not thought there was anything but a kind of current, like a stream. Now he began to think not of what to say, when Francie spoke to him, but of what words to say. And words, like a descending flock of birds, attached themselves to everything, perching on every object in sight and in mind.

"You arrive talkin half-white already," Francie said. "Like you already bin to school. You bin?"

He said no.

"You got a talent, though," she said to him, quietly. "I ain't one to hide talent under a bushel, neither. So we'll put a little polish on yo lamp, you and me." She looked very satisfied. "Now look at thisyere verse, book of Matthew, where it say"—and she read it out slowly for him, touching each word, as she spoke it, with the tip of her chapped index finger, marking her accustomed rhetorical emphases with her voice: "That *ye* may be the chirren of yo *Father* which is in *heaven:* fo he *maketh* his sun to rise on the evil *an* on de good, and *sendeth* rain on the just *an* on the unjust."

"Say it wit me, now?" she asked.

And so he began learning.

Only, he did not let Francie know that when she was away he would look through the newspapers that he and Frank were delegated to collect in town, and he began to find in them another sort of story that fascinated him fully as much as those in the Bible. As he made more and more out, learning more and more words, he understood less and less of what he read—in most of the newspapers the persons, events, and places that were written of he could not quite conceive: banks, ships, New York, a president, an army, and more, these were words that remained empty, that did not attach themselves to anything he knew. But if he worked steadfastly down the columns of fine print, he would find something that leapt out at him: a storm, a strange calf with an extra leg sticking out of its side, a fire in which people died, a crop harvested, a rattlesnake found in someone's bed, a white man and woman married, a runaway buggy, a black man burned to death by a mob of white people.

Reuben could bring in a killed squirrel nearly every day, if he took the time to hunt, and Francie came to depend on him for that. Drum begrudged Reuben both his ability to get this tiny bit of meat, and, because Reuben was still a boy under Francie's protection, his time to hunt. Drum asked Reuben his age several times, but Reuben did not know he was eleven. Drum said to him, "You thutteen, you as strong as Eswold but he's taller dan you, always goan be taller dan you. You ought be workin for wages if you could make but thutty cent a day." Reuben never replied to these assaults. He looked to Francie to answer the questions Drum raised, but she would not answer him either.

Always in the evening, after Francie had eaten and was resting, and again on Sundays, she would take a little while to go over Bible verses with Reuben, not only to keep him reading but also to interpret the meaning of the verses to him, as she understood them from instruction and her own weighing of them. He learned fast, and kept learning more. Francie took him through the Gospels, and through the tales of Moses, and then let him wander as he wished. And often under a lamp that Francie turned low to save the coal oil, but kept lit, just for Reuben, he followed passages through the labyrinth of stories. He remembered, like a sudden talking vision one evening when he was sitting over the Bible puzzling out alone a story he could follow but not understand, the cook saying to him very sternly, by the Big House, "You learn to read you won't remember nothin." She was teaching him plants to pick and use against sickness. She had scared him and he'd run.

The children paid Drum little attention, he was Eswold's father, and then had been gone a long while, and come back, and was Frank's, too, but not father of the girls, who had been born in the meantime. After Frank was born Francie had ceased to have any relations with men.

Reuben overheard, from outside, a Sunday afternoon argument between Francie and Drum when Drum flung down onto the warped wooden floor a few coins and Francie yelled they were hers, she had earned them, and Reuben heard her fall to her knees to gather them before any slipped through to the ground below. But one must have rolled on edge across the boards to a crack and dropped through for she began to sob and she cried out miserably, Ruby, Ruby, as she called him. Why was it his name she called first? He waited a moment to make it seem that he had come from farther away and then he went in the back door feigning a little breathlessness from his fictional exertion of having come fast. Drum was not in the room.

"Go down under the house, Ruby, quick, crawl under like when you kids have to git after one of them sorry hens and fine where she's layin." She held a little shining silver coin up to him. "There's one a these right under thisyere floor, it fell thoo the floor, you got to fine it for me, quick. And doan lose it in de dust down there. Now run, quick, and git it!" She held the coin right in front of his eyes. Drum was complaining from his room. The children were away, somewhere, out.

Where the gap between the earth and the floor joists was highest, beside the back step, Reuben got down on all fours and looked underneath. He would have to go at least the length of his own body under the floor, and then reach as far as he could, to get to the coin, if he could find it. On hot days it was cool under the floor—that was why the chickens left the rickety open coop and set under the house and laid eggs there.

But just over his head and his neck, his back and his legs, as he inched forward, pulling himself with his elbows, the angles of old wood were thick with horrible spider nests and long crawling bugs, and in the dust there might well be a snake. He went slow, breathing shallowly the damp, musty odor of the fine dirt and the aged wood, while Francie stood over him, creaking the floor with her anxious weight and calling to him.

"It's right where I'm standin," she called, louder than she needed to, for, right underneath her, he could hear even her breathing. "You hear me, Ruby? Right here, I'm callin down to you where you can find it. Do you see it? Jesus will guide you to it! Keep lookin! Lord if one a them hens'z down there and saw that dime it might peck it right up. Do ya see it?"

He could not see anything much in that alien under-place, the dark lower world. Her footsteps would make some creature fall on his neck. From around the edges of the house, except on the south side where thick weeds grew, the light came in sideways across the clods and gray dirt and made it hard to see what was right before him. He felt ahead very gingerly and identified by his touch a piece of broken glass, a round stone, a calcified turd, and finally the coin.

"I got it!" he called to her and he began shoving himself backwards to get out as quickly as he could. A chill raced down his spine when he caught his behind against a floor joist and wondered what he had jarred loose to fall on him as yet unfelt. Once out, he scrambled to his feet and shook himself and shook his hair; rubbed his back against the side of the house, and then Francie was in front of him taking the coin from his hand and making a tight fist around it, and with her other hand—her hands were always swollen from work—she was brushing his chest and his back and his hair and crying and saying, "Oh Reuben, thank you, son, thank you, saved child, you a good boy and I'll find you somethin special and bring it to you tomorra, you wait and see, you practice readin you Bible verse and read it to me tomorra night and I'll give you somethin special."

She went heavily up the three back steps into the house, saying to herself that the rent money was saved, the burial society money was saved, praise Jesus, and clasping the coin.

Bible verses were easy for him. Fluently he read her some of her favorite ones as she sat beside him, her eyes closed in pride at the work she had accomplished for God in teaching this child. She was holding her gift for him in one hand, he had already seen it—one piece of hard candy, not as pretty as the candy some mothers often brought home from their white ladies, and dull-looking. Francie opened her eyes wide and smiled as she handed it to him. "I'm goan to git a Bible for you, you own Bible, goan put you name in it," she said to him. "Saved." She was waiting to see him like the candy, so he put it in his mouth. It was stale. He smiled at her.

When it was the hour to sleep, he went in to his pallet and took off his pants and shirt and beat them with his hand, knocking out the dirt, trembling a little. Then he put them back on. All the children, and Drum and Eswold too, slept in their clothes except in hot weather, when the boys and men wore their underdrawers to bed and the girls had some soft thin gowns of sacking that Francie had made. At the head of Reuben's bed were the two baskets, the smaller inside the larger, and the tin kettle inside the smaller. The cup, safe up above. Nothing else of the little he had had in the baskets remained. His mother, in her dress and bonnet, was lying under the dirt, down inside the dirt, underneath the weight of it, down there.

Drum came home drunk one cool evening, after Francie, unusually cross and acting more like Drum than herself, had chased all the children away for their noise, and had collapsed, asleep, on her bed. Therese and Mary and Frank were out among the houses somewhere despite the dark; they were running and playing late to stay warm. Their voices came back unintelligible but recognizably theirs as they yelled. Reuben was lying on his back on his pallet in the unlit room, feeling the chill, avoiding their slights, preferring the company of his own thoughts. Drum plodded into the room and noticed him and grunted, and let himself fall back sitting onto his bed, which made the ropes creak, and he pulled his shoes off and let them fall thudding to the floor.

Drum's bed was in the interior corner of the small room, airless in summer, but the warmest spot in cold weather. He began talking under his breath as if to himself, and Reuben could only make out a few words, but Drum's voice rose gradually, as he sat with his right ankle across his left knee, massaging his right foot. Smelly feet. "You a quiet little Injin man, ain't you," he said. "*Saved* from what? Saved *fo* what?"

Reuben did not answer him.

"Cain't you talk?" Drum asked him loudly.

"I kin talk," Reuben said at last.

Drum lowered his voice again. "And you got my name, too, now, though you ain't mine," Drum said. "*Mr.* Reuben Saved Sweetbitter yo name. Ain't it?"

Reuben did not answer him.

"Well we all know you ain't saved fo *nothin.*" He looked up at the dingy ceiling. "I ought tell you how I got called Drum, you wanna hear a story bout a name," Drum said. Slowly he reversed the position of his legs, and took a little bottle out of the pocket of his trousers and drank from it, tipping it almost all the way up, and then set it carefully on the floor and massaged his left foot. The smell of Drum, sour and harsh, was familiar to Reuben. Into the boy came a faint memory of such a smell, leading him toward a recognition: it was his grandfather, silent among his family, leaving the house and going eternally around to the back, to be alone, not stumbling from feebleness but from drink. No one had ever spoken of it, and only now did Reuben understand it. But there was no time to think about it now, for Drum was speaking to him.

"Done had my name *drummed* into me, dat what," Drum said emphatically. "Din't want it, but thass what anybody *call* me, after dat." The man put his foot back on the floor and picked up the little bottle. He swung his legs up onto the mattress as if they were heavy objects he was straining to lift, and he leaned back against the wall at the head of the bed.

"You a *kind* of cullud. But you doan know, you a chile," Drum said. "You doan know whass the diffunce tween white and black, cash money and a share a crop. Between a heap a things." He shifted his weight on the bed, and groaned. "I know you ain't got nothin, just like us," he went on. "But you ain't even *seen* nothin, so you don't even know what you ain't got."

Drum half-rose to take the last sip from the bottle and then capped it and put it back in his pocket. He rolled onto his side, facing the wall, and spoke from there, his voice muffled. "The tin pans was our drum. You a child, but you people had the slaves just like the white folks did, you probly doan know bout dat." He was silent a moment. "You bout thutteen years old, I'z only eight or maybe nine, my mammy and pappy was dancin with all the rest a the niggers, Marse'z gone away somewhere, a Sadday night. But he come back early and din't like dat, not one lil bit he din't, and he whupped ever nigger dat was there. Starting with old Charley what played the fiddle—and *his* hair was *all white,* he was so old. Down the line, ever one. Whupped my pappy, my pappy stood and took the licks, din't say nothin. But dat wadn't'z hard fo him as what come nex. Marse *whipped* my *mam!* . . . Whipped my mam. My pappy'z sold off after dat. Never heard what happen to *him.*"

Silent on his pallet, Reuben withstood a chill. Drum's voice was eerie, sounding out of the corner like a spirit-voice. The hair rose on Reuben's arms and on the back of his neck.

"Down the line! Ever one," Drum said. "Marse whupped my

mammy. And Sawyer the strongges fiel nigger on the Place wrapped my pappy up in his big arms, had arms like legs on other peoples, and held a han over'z mout so he wouldn't rush in and get hisself killed. No way a chile like you could know what dat felt like fo my pappy. No way. To see her whupped. . . . Nobody holt onto me, though. I watched Marse whup my mam with a whup, I seen it too."

Drum was quiet, breathing heavily. Reuben thought Drum was falling asleep, but the voice started again.

"Down the line." And then, suddenly loud, "To me!—what was the littlest one, I'z only there cuz I was so good at drummin on dat tin *pan*. My mam love to see me drum on dat tin pan when the niggers was dancin. Everbody'd laugh, dat'z one of the *few* times they'z happy. My pap had the bigges laugh a any man. Oh he had a wondrous laugh. He did.

"But Marse put dat whup on my back same as on ever other back in dat line, and says, 'You ain't gone drum no more, *I'm* drum you dis time, *I'm* drum you!'" Drum said it several more times, his voice growing softer again. Then his voice came a last time: "An if you took dis ole shirt off dis ole body, you'd see right now *today* a mark of dat whup, dat drummer done beat dis drum till it ain't got no more music lef in it, not dat time, and fo a long time after."

Then he was quiet.

Reuben felt exalted. With the charge of sorrow that Drum had entrusted to him. He wanted to speak, now, to ask Drum what other things had happened back then. But Drum was asleep, or lying awake in anger. And Reuben lay awake with him.

18

Reuben

And they said one to another, Behold, this dreamer comest.

Come now therefore, and let us slay him, and cast him into some pit, and we will say, Some evil beast hath devoured him: and we shall see what will become of his dreams.

And Reuben heard it, and he delivered him out of their hands; and said, Let us not kill him.

And Reuben said unto them, Shed no blood, but cast him into this pit that is in the wilderness, and lay no hand upon him; that he might rid him out of their hands, to deliver him to his father again.

And it came to pass, when Joseph was come unto his brethren, that they stript Joseph out of his coat, his coat of many colours that was on him;

And they took him, and cast him into a pit; and the pit was empty, there was no water in it.

And they sat down to eat bread: and they lifted up their eyes and looked, and, behold, a company of Ishmeelites came from Gilead with their camels bearing spicery and balm and myrrh, going to carry it down to Egypt.

And Judah said unto his brethren, What profit is it if we slay our brother, and conceal his blood?

Come, and let us sell him to the Ishmeelites, and let not our hand be upon him; for he is our brother and our flesh. And his brethren were content.

Then there passed by Midianites merchantmen; and they drew

125

and lifted up Joseph out of the pit, and sold Joseph to the Ishmeelites for twenty pieces of silver: and they brought Joseph into Egypt.

And Reuben returned unto the pit; and behold, Joseph was not in the pit; and he rent his clothes.

And he returned unto his brethren and said, The child is not; and I, whither shall I go?

Having found by chance his own name in the Bible, Reuben looked up from the dim lamplight. Francie had been sewing, more by feel than by sight; but she was asleep in her chair, her coat in her lap. Needle and thread still in her hand. Her breathing was labored, her head fallen to one side in exhausted sleep. On the floor, at an odd angle, her bad foot was unbound and released from her shoe, but it lay inert, not to be refreshed by rest. The house was silent; outside, the night was silent. Drum, Eswold, the children, had all gone into their rooms, were asleep, most probably.

Reuben read on, but found no more of this first Reuben, who had loved his younger brother.

Hadn't Joseph objected or fought against them or sworn at them when they threw him down into the hole in the ground? Why hadn't he?

19

The Undisclosed

As for true names, Reuben's true name had been bestowed on him only for him to know, and his mother and his grandparents, not for other people, not for whites and blacks. If anyone outside the family had asked Reuben his name, he would have known only to say "Reuben"; he did not know that he had a surname.

Reuben Charles spoke two languages—in his grandparents' home was one, used from time to time, not lingered over, mixed in with other kinds of words like an occasional taste in the mouth; and outside that home was the other language, that filled their mouths most of the time: the language of the Big House, of the store and the trader, of people passing by, white and black and sometimes even red, although whites and blacks spoke it differently. Like his mother he spoke it somewhere in between. Molly knew it too as the white people spoke it, from her childhood schooling, but she did not speak to Reuben in their way, with their phrases and tones. If Reuben heard a story, once in a while, from her or from Grandmother, it was like two tastes in the mouth at once, the ordinary everyday taste with bursts of that other taste, like berries, when a word or a phrase flew out of the story in that language which neither whites nor blacks knew.

20

It Is Not Known How This Was Reported from Three Rivers to the Major Cities

A sound something like the wind, but higher and more intense, came into Reuben's consciousness as he sat on Mr. Grooms's porch. It was well after dark; there were few windows alight in the shacks and small houses nearby. The sound was coming down the road, getting closer. It became a yelling. Excited human yelling—many voices—of a sort he had not heard before. Mr. Grooms appeared beside Reuben, agitated and still holding the Bible from which he had been reading. He rushed back inside and doused the lamp and called to Reuben, "Git in here, quick." Reuben stood and went in, looking back over his shoulder. Mr. Grooms closed the door quickly and silently and threw the bolt shut and stood beside but not at the window, looking out. Reuben behind him.

It was a dozen white men on horses, carrying torches, followed by two slow-rolling automobiles with headlights blazing and wobbling like thick wands sweeping through the dust thrown up by the horses' hooves. The automobiles were crammed with men. Then came at least fifty more on foot behind and beside the cars, some of them carrying torches also. All the men on horseback and some, though not all, of the men on foot wore white pointed hoods. The men on horseback were silent, those on foot and in the cars were howling and yelling. Tied to the back of the first car by a rope around his neck, and with his hands bound behind him, a young Negro man of no more than twenty was stumbling and trying to keep from falling, as white men came up to him and struck at him with sticks and fists and guns and he staggered.

"Ray Newsome," Mr. Grooms whispered to himself. "My Lord," he said. "We ain't seen this kind a thing for a good long time and I thought twas over, O my Jesus I hoped we'd never have to see this one mo time." The caravan was directly in front now, passing Mr. Grooms's house before reaching the center of the village. Reuben and Mr. Grooms hung back in the shadow of the room.

"O my Lord, Ray Newsome," Mr. Grooms said softly. "A good boy, whass he done, *why* they come to do this to him. He suppose to marry Althea Green nex week."

One of the men on horseback was shouting to the houses, shouting a short speech to them, and the mob stopped and was milling around the young man, who sank out of sight. Fallen to the ground.

It was hard for Reuben to hear if there was any sound coming from the houses. All the house lamps were out, now. In one of those houses, Reuben did not remember which, Ray Newsome's mother would be shaking with the fear and horror of seeing her son in their hands; and maybe she had come out. He listened carefully, trying to sort out the sounds, and it did seem to him he could hear the crying of women over the sound of the white men.

There was a sound of breaking glass, and then again; and the sound of cracking, snapping wood, of fists hammering on doors, now here, now there, that did not open to them. Feverish hatred emanated from the white men like a smell.

Like a huge ungainly bug half on its back the mob began turning itself around to come back, and there was a sharp rising of the sound, inhuman and human, of the mob screaming curses at the shacks and small houses, and some pistols went off, perhaps fired into the air. Mr. Grooms stepped back from the window and squatted down on the floor, and pulled at Reuben to get down with him, but Reuben kept one wide eye at the lower corner of the window. The bug got back on its feet fully and began to return toward where it had come from. The boy must be up again, now, trying to keep from being dragged by the car. White men were blocking Reuben's view. He saw one man on foot, wearing a hood, whirling in a hunched-over one-man dance, and he knew who that was. He sat down with his back to the wall, not trying to look any more.

The mob kept going by, the rumble and coughing of the automobiles, the footsteps hissing in the dirt, the voices enraged and drunken-sounding. The convenience of having a front porch nearly at the road had never seemed such a mistake as now to the old man.

One of the cars raced its engine like a threat, and a horse whinnied in fright at the sound, and the men kept yelling. They might be going all the way back to town, perhaps to the square, or perhaps only halfway, to a tree where they would bind the boy and strip off his clothes and unsheathe their knives and heat their irons and begin their tortures; and then pile up dry wood around him and pour gasoline on it and reload their pistols and invite all eyes to Ray Newsome's final moments of human life.

The last of the white men, with last cold threats in their mouths, were just passing Mr. Grooms's house now. Reuben shifted his weight. He felt heavier. Now indeed he could hear the crying and hushing in the other houses, as the mob moved off to do its advertised deed, leaving behind it the sickened air it had exhaled. Reuben leapt within himself when with a heart-stopping thud heavy boots stomped up onto the porch and the wall against which he was leaning was hit by something right at his back—a club, a stone—and then a stone came crashing through the window, shattering the glass and skidding across the floor under Mr. Grooms's empty chair, and immediately the sounds of the mob were crisper and came in with a razor's edge as the footsteps left the porch and were gone. Neither man had moved; they were looking at each other as the guttering torches played a final eerie pulsation of light into the room.

"I doan have to tell you what *this* means, do I," Mr. Grooms whispered to Reuben.

It could be for such as suspicion of murder that they had caught Ray Newsome; but it could just as well be for an angry remark to a white man. It could be because Ray Newsome's brother was a troublemaker and they couldn't find *him*. There were any number of pretexts. Especially assault, or near-assault, or the idea of assault, or somebody else's opinion of the possibility of there having been an intention of assault, on a white woman.

Reuben leapt up so suddenly Mr. Grooms cowered, afraid the door was about to burst open. But Reuben only wanted to see out the shattered window. Watching the mob's trailing denizens, evidently most intoxicated, move away.

21

Hypothetical Meditation

Differently formed than THEY. Differently governed than THEY. For anything I might do to THEM outside of the Law, or even outside THEIR custom, I would be severely punished; but for everything THEY do to ME outside of the Law they escape punishment.

Because only THEY can punish; and THEY do not punish THEMSELVES for what THEY do to ME.

To US.

But there is no US.

Who are WE? There is no WE.

Evidently there was a WE but WE are gone. Gone in death, gone from here, gone to what were The Nations but I do not know what were The Nations.

In this place, in all places I have been, there is only I, and two different THEYS—the white THEY ruling the black THEM, or I can say the black THEY ruled by the white THEM. And for anything that the black THEY might do to the white THEM outside of the Law or even the white custom, the black THEY are severely punished; but for everything the white THEY do to the black THEM outside of the Law (or within it, for the Law and the white custom that made the Law form a spacious realm for the white THEM, but only a narrow confine, smaller than a coffin, for the black THEM), the white THEY will always, do always, escape punishment.

THEY and THEY and more THEYS, the world must be full of THEM. And for someone, at some time, perhaps WE (there is no WE any longer) were THEY, and THEY were WE. But there must always have been, there must always be the difference that divides—divides one way, divides two ways or a dozen ways.

There is the Upper World and the Lower World, and this world in the middle, This World.

There is Day and there is Night, and this time in between, when the birds grow quiet and the deer rouse.

There is Warmth and there is Cold, and this time in between that is mild.

There is Hunger and there is Feast, and in between, the feeling of not wanting or needing.

There is Thirst and there is Drink, and in between, a readiness to go on.

There is Wild Country and there is Town and between them a place where one's steps are uncertain.

There is Field and there is Wood, and a secret place between them from which to observe, as a buck watches, ready, uncertain.

There is Bird and there is Snake and walking between them a man, uncertain.

There is Woman and there is Man and between them a child, uncertain.

There is River and there is Land and between them a zone of Shore where escape is not certain.

There is Black and there is White and between or beside them some others.

There is always some other.

Differently governed.

Differently formed and observed and regarded.

Of a different mind, yes, surely.

But of different bones and blood? Different hearts and different tears?

22

Worship

At the dull clanging of the church bell of the First Methodist Church of Three Rivers in the cool morning air, in a thin fog
almost pink that was clouding the sight of anything beyond fifty
paces, the straggling dozen male worshippers who were still outside the white frame building tossed their cigarette and cigar butts
into the dirt and started in—those who were late, hastening; and
others, reluctant, speaking a last worldly word to a companion,
and with head down, as against an unpleasant wind, entering the
precinct of the holy. The officious head usher, not unhappy in the
exercise of his simple but very visible duties, pulled the double
doors shut on the self-sufficiency of the Methodist service, and
soon the voices inside rose in unison to the tune of a familiar
hymn, accompanied by a piano whose strings had irregularly
slackened a little into mild dissonance.

Many had walked, but carriages, wagons and automobiles stood
parked beside the church. In one of the latter sat an idle chauffeur,
black and ostentatiously uniformed, as foreign to the scene as
if he had been Austro-Hungarian. Unlike the motor cars, the out-
moded conveyances jerked and rolled this way and that, as if with
life—the horses harnessed to the ranked buggies stood stamping
and switching their tails, attended by black groom or family servant, or the occasional white husband or uncle whose righteousness extended to observance of the Sabbath in dress and routine,
but not in worship.

Inside, greetings and welcome and hymn and announcements were followed by a performance of the small choir, in uniform robes of reddish purple, and by readings from the Gospel and responsive readings and another hymn and the collection of offerings in flat wicker baskets passed along the hard pews hand to hand and from row to row by the four ushers, men whose exaggerated consciousness of their position gave their faces not a worshipful but a grim expression. As the pianist ended her solo, the ushers carried the wicker baskets forward from the last pew and placed them as an offering on the altar, while the seated preacher frowned and studied the toes of his shoes, before his performance.

Then, dramatically, he rose. Smiling at them. As if to reassure them that his enormous power would not be used against them, that he was their friend, their advocate to God, above all else.

For the most part passive and enduring the rituals of the service, the congregation sat still with eyes raised to the pulpit, unable to relax their attention with a clear conscience, unable even to shift for comfort in their pews, until the moment when the preacher would attain in his sermon the safe ground of the first Anecdote. Beginning with his welcoming smile of patently forced breadth, which signaled them to be grateful for this effort on his part to palliate the stern and vigorous righteousness of his true thoughts, the preacher began quietly, informally, then eased toward a deeper seriousness of tone, and recalled to them the lessons already rehearsed many times of their evil and sinful nature, which they were powerless *by nature*—powerless!—to reform by will or thought. Patiently, he instructed them again in their heritage of faithlessness and worldliness, which had caused God Almighty from time immemorial to feel not contempt for them—which he might well have felt and with full justification—not contempt, not rage only, not indifference but rather tender *love* that issued in the creation of a Son of God—a *Son!*—whom God, baffling our comprehension with his infinite mercy, had given over to men to be sacrificed—*sacrificed!*—as if he were a mute small defenseless beast—a lamb. To be betrayed by the *Jews* and tormented and murdered by the *faithless;* and despite the multitudes whom he had blessed and even cured, to be followed and recognized at first by only a tiny *handful* of men and women of great and abiding faith, to whom he had given the open secrets of a universal forgiveness, a message of hope, and a life eternal. And who were rewarded by the presence of this same Jesus among them, a living being again after his cruel death and naked entombment.

The preacher withdrew a brilliant starched white handkerchief from under his robe, and patted the holy sweat from his brow. There was immorality abroad in the land, a terrible immorality. Drink, and gambling. Dancing, and lewd behavior. Especially in young women who had not the strength of love of God, of faith in Jesus Christ our Lord, to conduct themselves righteously. Sins that would bring God's wrath down in punishment. Foolish, and doomed to eternal torment, and evil, were they who turned away from Him to indulge themselves in pleasure, even unto sin and rank fornication. And yet, and yet—God would forgive. *Believe* in Jesus, confess to Him and beg Him for forgiveness, and a new life would begin! Not only a treasure stored up in Heaven, but a new life, right here in this world, right now!

And then came the first Anecdote, and the tense uncomfortable congregation in the pews relaxed a bit, settled themselves anew, the pews creaking, and they shot quick glances at their restive children, and were thankful not to have been accused, there and then in front of all, of their own proven sins both private and public that would stand in evidence against them for a sentence of eternal hell were it not for the mercy of God on which all had been taught to count. And hoped that having come this far without mentioning the awful event of the night before, the Preacher would withhold any comment upon it at all. And this worshipper or that was mulling over her disappointing husband, her unfinished sewing, her sick mother, her son who was drinking, her listless daughter, her baking, her maid or her mother-in-law, and here and there another was lost in a reverie over his business problems, his impatience with the slow passage of days before the hot weather would break, his crops, his workers or his own aching body, his bank account, the legs and ankles of the young woman in the long navy blue dress, Clarke's daughter, across the aisle at the near end of the pew ahead.

And the Preacher, towering in his role as God's Agent, abruptly relaxed and spoke more intimately. It Seems That There Was a Farmer Who for Three Years Running Had Had the Misfortune to Make a Poor Crop While His Neighbors on Both Sides Were Prospering Mightily. . . .

And the pleasant tale was drawn out and resolved, although as usual the resolution resembled the end of a lame joke more than the mystery and point of Biblical parable from God's Own Word. (Well, he was but God's Agent.)

And then a second time the preacher built out of words a tremendous structure—overheated because it was built directly over the furnace of hell—of futile human striving, of the threat of unending punishment (as if they were all bad children, all with the one Father), of Godly forgiveness, and of the great condition of reward, Belief. Faith in God and in Jesus. Repentance and prayer.

And *why* was God willing to see his own Son slaughtered, and *why* did the Son of God undertake to endure the torment of the crucifixion voluntarily? Because of His love. In order to *save* men. To *save* them from eternal punishment and misery. To *save* them for the day of Resurrection when the faithful would be called by the Holy to join Them in God's Heaven. To *save* men from the pains and sorrows of this earthly existence that grieves and burdens us. Therefore, to spurn the offered *salvation* of God, and not *want* to be *saved*, was not only a sin in itself, and a mortal one that would be punished by eternal damnation, but it was pure madness! *This* was why God had saved Noah from the flood, it was for *this* that God had sacrificed His only begotten Son—to save man from his own sinful nature!

Then the second and final Anecdote blew through the hot suffocating house of words like a breeze, and again everyone could breathe more easily again. The end of the hour was approaching;

surreptitiously the pianist had prepared to strike her introductory chords for a hymn that would begin the very instant after the preacher concluded his theatrical prayer.

Which he did, drenched in his perspiration, having exhausted himself physically and morally for their sake, for all their sakes, and calling them to rise and sing, and leading the singing with his voice and his exhorting smile.

And opening their mouths and breathing out the stale taste of their own passive silence, they began to sing, shakily at first but, after a few bars, with more force.

And then the rest of the ritual ran rapidly to the grateful end. The ushers unnoticed had opened the double doors of the simple narthex. The preacher, having uttered the benediction, was sweeping down the side aisle in his immaculate black robe to reach the front door quickly, ever mindful of the punctilio of his calling. Outside, the small number of subservient or unrepentant waiting men—likely to be diffident and at ease if white, whatever their crimes or sins, and susceptible to being nervous and watchful if black, however upright—were standing here and there at the ready as to the triumphal pounding of the pianist the congregation rose and left their pews and came out blinking in the sharp brightness of the true light of a day that had cleared somewhat and lay very still under a sky nearly white.

There was a chattering of voices, and children louder than the adults; horses stirred; tack creaked and clanked; motor car engines began to clatter and spew and smoke. And here were the Clarkes, and their three big children, Martha fully grown and James not far behind, quickly shaking the preacher's hand and moving on, and Anne their youngest giggling with her friends, and Mrs. Clarke smiling with pride in the entire race of man, while Mr. Clarke lingered a moment and he and the preacher made noises of importance to each other, satisfying each other quickly and efficiently in this sub-ritual of the end of the Sunday morning.

And there among the teams and buggies, given an unwelcome obligation to wait, to be ranked among the serving, but also to watch the Clarkes unseen, was Reuben, who for his suitable hard work and presentable appearance had been commandeered, unexpectedly early that very morning, to serve as temporary substitute groom for the owner of the mill, Thomas Reedy, rapacious of woods, avid of railroads, the thin stooped cantankerous donor to the church who in memory of his long-suffering, supposedly much-loved wife had donated the cost of the cheaply cast bell now clanging in exultation.

One did not refuse such a message as was brought at dawn to Reuben by a black maid out of breath. The shock was that Reuben had been so noticed in the mill that the foreman would have recommended him to Mr. Reedy. Whose groom, Lloyd, was one of those black men who had now left town without a good-bye after the death of Ray Newsome, in search of some better place—as had Ray Newsome's soul, without doubt.

Reuben held the horse steady and still as Mr. Reedy pulled himself up into the closed carriage, in which he rode alone. Then Reuben climbed to the box and clucked at the horse and they wheeled out of the churchyard at a dignified pace.

23

Intelligence of Recent Events in the Region

Often from travelers—salesman or buyer or land specula-
tor or someone stopping over on the way west—Mr. Clarke obtained newspapers from as far away as Chicago or New York City,
and although he read them with seeming care, he rarely spoke of
their contents to anyone in the house, and he kept the newspapers
to himself without letting his children or wife read them. He was
keenly interested not only in what went on in the other parts of the
nation, but also in how his part was perceived by those other parts,
especially the great metropolitan centers whose stature in industry
and commerce he believed his native state could outshine during
his own lifetime.

He noted, on a typical but, as it turned out, ominous late
afternoon in the middle of the week, the following items in the
weekend papers from New York and Chicago, which owing to a
concern much like his own over recent incidents, Phin Fletcher
had collected at the hotel and then passed on to him: A great increase in automobile accidents is being reported, especially involv-
ing automobiles running fast and in accidents, either alone or with
other automobiles or stationary objects—turning turtle and
crushing their occupants.

An infamous recent murder case involves Doctor Crippen, accused of killing his wife. A man believed to be Crippen, having
gone to Europe, is returning with his mistress and his son, this
time for a Canadian port, without knowing that the ship's officers

141

and all the world know that he is on board and will be arrested as soon as the ship docks. This is because of the amazing power of the wireless.

The Belgian aviator M. Olienagers achieved a new world record height for monoplanes of 4,712 feet.

The sad case of a young woman's death is reported in Chicago: using gasoline to clean draperies in a room of the hotel in which her father was manager, she ignited the substance accidentally and her clothes immediately caught fire. She ran down the hallway calling desperately for her father as the flames grew but she fell to the floor terribly burnt before he heard her shouts of terror and cries for help. She died soon afterward.

The crew of the small cargo sloop Sunlight, under sail power only, were found two days out from Barbados unconscious and dying of hunger and thirst on their capsized boat. They had been living for thirteen days on sugar and vinegar after they lost their bearings in a fog and a storm carried away their compass and provisions.

The former Secretary of the Treasury John G. Carlisle suffered a sinking spell in New York and may succumb at any moment.

Several thousand acres of tobacco, wheat and corn were destroyed by a cloudburst in Kentucky, and a number of buildings and a flock of sheep were washed away. Several farmers and their families barely escaped death.

Wendling, the alleged slayer of the Kellner child, was found in San Francisco hiding under the sink in a rooming house. Police have arrested him but he denies he killed the girl.

The Chicago Chief of Police ordered a ban on screeching automobiles, which are being driven through the downtown district, disturbing businesses with piercing blasts pouring from open exhaust pipes. Henceforth offenders will be arrested.

According to the front page of the *Chicago Daily News* of Saturday, July 30, reports of the unfortunate disturbance in Palestine had reached northern ears. They were only too eager to hear of such things:

MANY SLAIN IN TEXAS RACE RIOT
Negroes and White Men Battle
in Texas—Militia May Be Called
[*By the Associated Press*]

HOUSTON, Tex. July 30—More than a dozen negroes were killed and several white men badly wounded in a race riot which began late yesterday at Slocum, Anderson county, a small town fifteen miles south of Palestine, according to special dispatches from Palestine to-day.

The trouble was precipitated by a controversy over a note which James Alford, a white man, indorsed for a negro. The negro, when questioned as to the reason for not paying the note, is said to have cursed Alford and said no white man could "do" him. Fighting between them began at once and others being drawn into the affair, the trouble continued throughout Friday night.

Sheriff Black and a large posse of citizens heavily armed, have gone to Slocum. Many citizens not included in the posse left Palestine to-day and will aid the whites.

Austin advices are that four rangers have been hastened to the scene of the trouble and a company of militia has been placed under orders for prompt movement.

Two hundred negroes are surrounded at Benson Springs, and the whites are awaiting the arrival of re-enforcements before opening fire or forcing them to surrender.

The *New York Times* had its own reporter for its Sunday paper:

SCORES OF NEGROES
KILLED BY WHITES

—

Eighteen Bodies Already Found in
Woods After Outbreak Near
Palestine, Texas

—

MILITIA MOVES ON PLACE

—

Trouble Started Over Non-Payment of
a Negro's Note, Indorsed
by White Man

—

[Special to the New York Times]

PALESTINE, Texas, July 30—As the result of a race war at Slocum, fourteen miles south of here, eighteen negroes are known to be dead and the total will reach twenty or more, as dead bodies are scattered over a large area.

The trouble originated between a white farmer, Redin Alford, and a negro, whose note Alford had indorsed some time ago. The negro left town and Alford was obliged to pay the note at one of the local banks.

A few days ago the negro returned, when Alford called on him to account for his conduct. The negro grew insulting and trouble followed.

It was reported to-day that some two hundred negroes had armed themselves and congregated at Denison Springs, twenty miles south of here, and were ready for trouble.

The white people of the little communities in that neighborhood were without arms and were uneasy over the situation, and this morning, following the killing of the negro at Slocum, the trouble started.

Messages were sent to Palestine and other places in the vicinity asking that white men with arms and ammunition be sent to Slocum at once, as the negroes were advancing on that place and trouble would follow. Sheriff Black also received an urgent appeal to come to Slocum, and left early this morning with a large posse.

The news spread like wildfire over Palestine that a race war was on at Slocum and that the people of that place wanted help immediately. By noon over 200 men, armed to the teeth, had left for the scene, and all day long groups of men with arms departed for that place.

District Judge Gardner appointed Capt. Godfrey Reese Fowler, who figured recently in the Nicaraguan revolution, as a special deputy to go to the scene and appeal to the people to avoid bloodshed, and also to summon witnesses to appear before the Grand Jury, which will reconvene Monday afternoon especially to probe the killing of the negroes.

All saloons in Palestine were closed this morning, and orders were given to dealers in firearms and ammunition not to sell or rent them. Messages were also sent to Gov. Campbell urging him to send troops and State Rangers here as soon as possible as further trouble was feared.

Not one white man was hurt, and at a late hour this evening everything is quiet and no further trouble is feared by the officers.

Large posses of men from Elkhart, Denison Springs, Crockett, Grapeland, and other places arrived at Slocum in the afternoon, and several hundred men have returned here, but others remain at the scene of trouble, as people of that section of the country are terrorized and fear another outbreak.

The negroes of Palestine have been very quiet to-day, and this evening scarcely any can be seen on the streets, which are crowded with groups of men discussing the many killings, but no further trouble is anticipated by the officers.

Several State Rangers arrived in the city at 7 o'clock from Austin and a company of State militia arrived from Marshall at 7:30. They will patrol the city to-night.

No names of the negroes killed could be secured at this hour, owing to the intense excitement, but eighteen bodies have so far been found in the woods.

And this, also from the front page, middle column, of the *Chicago Sunday Tribune* of July 31, 1910, amply demonstrated that newspaper's exaggerations, which, in Mr. Clarke's opinion, gave a terribly false and unfair impression to northerners:

TEXAS RACE WAR
COSTS 25 LIVES

—

Whites and Negroes Fall in Pitched
Battle; Troops Are Called to the Scene.

—

WOMEN ARE GIVEN ARMS

—

More Bloodshed and Raids on
Unprotected Homes by Blacks Are
Feared.

PALESTINE, Texas, July 30—[Special]—Twenty-one negroes and four white men have been killed so far in a pitched race battle which has been waged for twenty-four hours between Elkhart and Slocum, fifteen miles south of here.

Two companies of militia are rushing to the scene and a full company of state rangers has been ordered to follow them, while more than half the white men of Palestine have formed in different posses and gone to join in overpowering the blacks.

Five hundred white men are reported to have given battle to 1,000 or more negroes generaled by a giant fanatic of their own race who rides back and forth along their battle line, shouting encouragement to his men and defying the concentrated fire of the entire force of whites.

WOMEN ARMED WITHOUT COST

Although the hardware stores of Palestine have been ordered not to sell any arms or ammunition, rifles, shotguns and revolvers, with ample cartridges, have been dealt out without cost to the women and older children in every home in the city, with instructions for their use in self-defense. This precaution has been taken because a large number of negroes have remained in the city, while most of the white husbands, fathers and brothers have gone to the battlefield.

Palestine is under martial law and all saloons have been closed, but the negroes are muttering angry threats and it is feared the night will see sporadic attacks upon isolated white homes. Fear is even expressed that the negroes here, emboldened by the absence of white men, may enter upon a general raid against the women and children, ignorant of the fact that the latter are armed.

QUARREL STARTS THE WAR

The race war started yesterday afternoon when a white man, James Alvord, killed a negro, following a quarrel over a disputed debt. Both were farmers. Men of both races obtained arms and rushed to the scene of the killing. It is reported that a deputy sheriff of Houston county is among the dead and it is known that a deputy sheriff of Anderson county was killed.

The battle took place in a belt of thick woods between Elkhart and Slocum. There is poor wire communication to these points, and even this was cut off this afternoon. Immediately upon the receipt here of news of the battle the citizens rushed to the scene. Palestine is in the midst of the Texas black belt, and there is much enmity between the two races. Scores of citizens were disarmed on the streets today.

Parties from Jacksonville, Byron, Crockett, Cronin, Stark, and other towns organized and went to the scene of riot in automobiles, heavily armed.

ONE REPORT SAYS FIFTY DEAD

An unconfirmed report says fifty negroes have been killed. Capt. Reed Fowler has assumed charge of the largest posse from here. Another posse is headed by Sheriff Black of Anderson county. Capt. Fowler won fame serving under Estrada in the Nicaraguan revolution. His home is in Palestine.

There are 7,000 negroes residing in Anderson county, and there are more than 1,000 now gathered between Elkhart and Slocum. Elkhart is on the International and Great Northern railroad and Slocum is a small interior town, the section between being occupied thickly by farmers. It is reported that more than one hundred negroes have been driven into a gully ten miles from Elkhart and ordered to lay down their arms and surrender.

The negroes at Bensen Springs, 300 in number, have armed and threaten to clean out the whites. Unless they are overawed by the state troops and posses, fear is expressed that there will be a general attack. The whites are determined to make no mistake and are waiting for reinforcements before leading an attack. They declare that they will force all negroes to leave Anderson county at the point of guns or will commence a general fire.

MORE MILITIA IN READINESS

The arrival of the troops with Adjt. Gen. Newton at their head will calm the whites, it is hoped, and avert a second and bloodier battle.

Messages from Austin say more rangers and companies of National Guard will be sent promptly if needed. Many companies throughout the state have been advised to make preparations for the trip here.

The majority of negroes are armed with shotguns, rifles, and revolvers, but more than 100 are carrying scythes and pitchforks.

Palestine is the home of Gov. Campbell, and advices from Austin say he will probably come here tonight or tomorrow to direct the movement of the citizens and troops.

Two white men were killed in this morning's fight and the other two fell in a conflict at 3 o'-clock this afternoon. A party of 200 men left Jacksonville tonight to aid Fowler's posse.

TWO BLACKS LYNCHED IN FLORIDA
BONIFACE, Fla., July 30. After having confessed to the murder of Bessie Morrison, a 12 year old daughter of Mrs. Mary Morrison, near Dady in the northwestern part of Holmes county, two negroes were taken from the sheriff and lynched by a mob of infuriated citizens late this afternoon

—

SNAKE IN TEMPERANCE DRINK
Real Reptile Wiggles Out of Faucet
In Oak Park Man's Residence

The snake of "red eye" fame may take a rear seat. The water wagon snake has come to Chicago. Charles Greenburg, 426 Marion Street, Oak Park, discovered it yesterday. . . .

The newspapers of Mr. Clarke's region, it was true, had not done as they should have and played down the entire affair, which was enormously bad for the local reputation and of no help to business. The Palestine *Daily Herald* was far from sober, reporting a "race war" when all they had to go on was telephone messages from Slocum.

There was a note of seemliness, at least, in that "Major G. R. Fowler left this city just before noon in an auto tendered him for the purpose, and was accompanied by a number of other gentlemen, who will assist the officers in restoring peace." And a company of the state militia arriving by train from Marshall. But the newspaper had reported also that four white men had been arrested and locked up on a charge of murder, and a grand jury convened! Demoralizing the community with reports that all but two or three of the dead blacks were shot from behind. If they had anything right in Palestine it was certain, at least, that the newspapers from New York and Chicago had gotten everything wrong— wrong names, wrong accounts of the conflict, wrong about what had started it all, for here was the *Herald* reporting that the black who had supposedly been killed at the beginning was named Marsh Holley and was actually in jail, where sensibly enough he had gone to ask for protection. And it was reported that many negroes had fled Palestine and were heading north.

Why could not there be more positive sentiment in the newspapers? Why could not there be more editorials like this one, which made him breathe out heavily with pleasure:

"The population of Texas has increased nearly 100 per cent within the past ten years, and still the state has hardly begun to settle up. Eventually this state will be home to 15,000,000 or 20,000,000 citizens. People are just beginning to learn of the greatness of East Texas, and we may expect a great rush to this section within the next year or two.

"East Texas is wonderful, West Texas is wonderful and South Texas is wonderful. The whole state is the nearest approach out of doors to the garden of Eden. No need to worry about its settling. Sooner or later it will be carrying its limit of population and every one of them will be accounted fortunate."

But then his eye came on the next page to more of the irresponsibility that so troubled him: "The two wounded darkies are in the home of their mother, Ava Wilson," he read. "Their injuries are quite serious, but they are not complaining of the effect of the wounds and their mother says that they have not had medical attention since their wounds were first dressed." For the newspaper to found its reporting on rumor was irresponsible, all the more so since its own columns reported that the primary cause of the conflagration was "the exaggerated rumors which had gained circulation."

People over the state and over the country generally should not be misled or misinformed as to the actual conditions in East Texas regarding the community trouble at Slocum. In fact, newspaper reporters should be very careful to give only what was justified by actual facts and let it go at that. Any attempt to make a sensation for the sake of sales for the yellow journals should be frowned upon and disapproved. It was clear to see in the newspapers from afar that many of the dispatches sent over the country are untrue in many particulars. Exaggerated reports of the trouble are not calculated to do Anderson county or Texas any good and every law-abiding, loyal citizen should use his best efforts to see that only the truth is told. Mr. Clarke polished his formulations in his mind before sitting down at his desk to pen them and send them by mail to the *Herald*. Why here, in the very same newspaper, was proof of the *Herald*'s own mistakes, to say nothing of those of the other newspapers: "The report that a large body of armed negroes is congregated near Slocum to do combat with the whites is now conceded to be unfounded, and it is a difficult matter to locate a negro within miles of that point." Now troops were standing guard outside the Palestine jail and Rangers inside, to hold the white men who had been arrested for murder against any mob that might try to break in and free them.

The *Houston Post* reported that Deputy Sheriff Riley Reeves was the first officer on the ground after the news of the trouble had spread. He said that there was no congregation of negroes whatever, that the only negroes he saw were at houses and that these welcomed his coming as their protector. He stated that he found but few arms; that a few single-barreled shotguns were found in the negro houses. Deputy Reeves found in one house where four negroes were killed a rusted single-barreled shotgun and no shells. In this house one of the negroes killed was an old negro 80 years old, who was shot while seated in his chair.

Trouble is anticipated on account of the arrest of the white men and, though definite information is meager, it appears that the situation with the whites has gotten beyond control of the officers. Further trouble with the negroes is not anticipated, the serious feature now being that of dealing with the white men who have participated in the trouble. The usual uncertainty enshrouds this.

While it is the consensus of opinion both in the surrounding towns and about the scene that there were a few negroes in the community who deserved punishment for recent minor misdeeds, it is also the opinion that a very grave mistake has been made and that innocent people have been made to suffer thereby. While it was reported that negroes were heavily armed and were shooting at the whites whenever opportunity presented itself, it is a fact that no deadly weapon of any kind has been found on or about the person or clothing of any of the negroes found dead. Near the bodies of several were found grips, suitcases and handbags, indicating that the owner was about to quit the country.

At noon Sunday thirty negro women and children applied to the Rangers for assistance and were assured that they would be given it. They are encamped in one house some four miles from Slocum, in destitute circumstances, many of them having lost husbands and brothers. Other families who live further back in the woods have stayed indoors since last Friday morning without food and those people are being cared for by the farmers of the community. A particularly pathetic scene was found by one party of searchers during the late afternoon. Advancing upon a negro cabin situated some three miles from the road, they were startled when two grown negroes darted out a back door and into the nearby woods. Going on into the house the searchers discovered an old negro and his wife, upwards of 75 years of age; about their feet were five small children while on the bed—the only one in the room—lay a negro man about 25 years of age dead from a buckshot wound in his side. They had found him on the hillside the night before and dragged him in. Not a member of the family had touched food for two days and nights and had no idea of the nature or extent of the trouble about them.

Quietude again reigns and the planters and their families will not speak of the matter except to their friends. When asked who, in their opinion, killed the negroes, they invariably answered that it was officers. Wives and daughters, even the babies of the family, have been carefully instructed not to talk.

Somewhere between ten and forty negroes have been killed, but it is impossible to secure a full list of the dead. It is now definitely known that no white men were killed or injured.

Reuben made a neat stack again of the several newspapers, which he had read more than once. Had studied, really. He rose, stretching his arms before him, and called to Mr. Grooms and went out the back door. He went walking out in the drizzling rain, thinking.

24

Episode at the Mill

Among the whites at the mill there was plenty of talk of the lynching in the days following. One man was showing around one of Ray Newsome's fingers. It was drained of blood and stiff, and he provoked considerable laughter by unbuttoning his pants and with his hand inside them poking Ray Newsome's finger out through his fly like a little dark penis with a fingernail. Then he put it back in his pocket. Reuben's crew—and all the other black men at the mill—labored nervously and hastily and Reuben saw them make dangerous mistakes and he called out to them repeatedly, and always too late to do any good, to watch their work; no one was hurt. They had all gone to the funeral on Sunday, Ray Newsome's charred body having been removed from a field near town by the Negro undertaker. Several black men had left town.

By Wednesday three of the Negro workers at the mill, evidently having tried to stay at their jobs, had finally decided against such bravado and they quit and collected their pay; taunts came at them from some of the whites. The moment could have snarled and turned on itself violently.

The rest of that day the foreman John Rome poked into everyone's face and told those blacks who stayed, even as they were shifting timber in the yard, how worthless they were and that they could live clean if they took this example to heart.

What had been the offense? Whites were talking about a remark to a white woman. Blacks spoke of a little money owed and of bad

155

blood between Ray Newsome and the man he worked for. Each day when the last whistle blew and the saws whined down to a stop—at the last light in which it was at all safe to work—the exhausted black men left the mill fast and stayed together on the way back to their village. There were night services in the two black churches every night, and the funeral had drawn nearly everyone whose skin was not white. Not Reuben, but yes Mr. Grooms, yes.

Reuben, as invisible as he knew how to be, would not look even once in the direction in which Martha's house lay as he too walked home. But he didn't leave town, he didn't give her up. He watched every man around him more carefully. He waited for things to calm down. Then everybody was talking about the race war in Palestine. Only he knew there had been no such war; but said nothing.

Men did work hard, and at dangerous things, often out of brute necessity, but sometimes in the case of those white men who could have sought work of less danger it was also as though that sense of play, of adventure, which they had had as boys, they must sustain, to carry them through the killing strain and the humiliation of labor; and they could only sustain it if they made the stakes of their play their very limbs, their futures, their lives. When they craved power over another, they sought it in the customs of hatred and bravado. Anything that threatened this attitude, that tugged at any corner of the web of their related illusions, must be attacked vigorously. The web must be defended. And the web was large and anchored at many points; it stretched from their mothers to their drink, from their work to their women. Thus they protected themselves from an understanding of their own suffering, their own condition, their own nature. And when this ritual of protection gave them the opportunity to laze in satisfied acquiescence on the side of their own power, they drew sustenance from it as from food.

The foreman at the sawmill, the heavy John Rome, walking with his fat man's feet pointed outward, would often say that he had been bossing all his life and knew how to do it better than anyone. For his employees this was the spoken refrain that served him as his jurisdiction over them and his justification for driving men to the edge of collapse and accident, and from time to time, as if with the cold curiosity of an experimenter, over it.

He was nearly sixty, stout and strong, a big drinker in the evenings, yet he could rise early to crack the whip. He had bossed crews of ex-slaves, still bearing their slave-days title of timber-niggers. The clearing of the forests had been moving west, and he'd followed it, like many others white and black, into virgin timberland in East Texas.

To log and to haul logs and lumber in and out of the Three Rivers mill John Rome had four white woods and yard bosses and Reuben; under two of the white men were mixed white and black gangs, and under each of the others a team of Negro men and boys worked: fellers and buckers, skidders, loaders, drivers. Crews went out into the diminishing woods and felled the trees and trimmed them, loaded the logs and brought them in. The yard crews sorted and stacked the milled lumber, pushed the dollies, stoked the drying kilns and the waste burners that heated the boilers, sometimes even carted lumber to buyers, and swept out. Over the mill white steam and black smoke billowed and spoiled. A whistle let all the men off at noon for half an hour, but the woods crews that happened to have come in with logs would stay apart from the sawmill workers; they considered themselves superior to the slaves of the mechanized din and repetitive dangers of the mill. One of Reuben's men was missing his right hand but was good with the mules; others had lost fingers or gained a limp from accidents. The worst-injured were gone, heard of no more.

The quitting hour depended on the season and the light. It was said that Reedy was going to bring electricity to the mill soon, and the saws would spin and scream all day and all night with lights blazing down on them as bright as the sun.

At noon John Rome would come smiling among the men and

chaff them with his false air of friendliness. The men sat and ate and reclined on the piles of logs in two groups, white and black, in the thick scent of wood and sap and wood smoke and sawdust and often the under-scent of putrefaction, from wood rats caught and killed in the shifting of timber and lumber and from the stagnant oily green water in the two-acre mill-pond. Reuben was pulled as if by an unavoidable but unspoken imperative to sit with the whites, beside Billy and Paul, and silently he ate his lunch, which was wrapped in one of the old linen napkins that had belonged to Mrs. Grooms. To some of the men their lunches were delivered by their own children.

At noon, the group of white men included the junior clerks from the office, their starched white shirts the badge of their freedom from soot and sawdust—that is, from sweat and physical danger. The talk would turn on feats of physical strength, episodes of gruesome laughable harm to others, or sexual forays, among women both white and black. All such talk was by intention almost but not quite out of earshot of the Negro workers. They in their group talked also but the whites did not bother to listen.

On Thursday the white men were talking. Reuben's secret of having Martha, his secret of her, filled him at the noon hour till his skin was as taut with protected pressures as the membrane of a balloon.

Billy was a friendly, grinning left-handed boy. He liked to talk and put on an air of authority about whatever he said. He could throw a stone farther than any man at the mill, although he could not lift as much as some others. Among his work-mates he was also known to be able to piss an arc over a pile of sawmill logs ten feet high if he held his water long enough during the day, drinking often till he was ready to shoot, as he said. Beer did it best for him, he said. He had often loudly challenged anyone to beat him at it, especially black workers, who tried not to have to say No sir to him, but sometimes were forced to reply to his taunts. No one, not even the white men, bothered to try. Billy seemed to think Reuben a most amusing addition to the mill.

Paul was quiet and by comparison peaceable. His hair was a dusty pale brown and would never lie as combed. He lived with religious parents, the youngest of a brood of similarly pale and mostly over-disciplined children. He offered no great warmth to Reuben, only a passive toleration.

Martha had decided she must mislead any eye that might perceive her interest in the mill, and she had even allowed a young clerk of her father's to call on her once, so her earlier false welcome of Billy had now led to an exasperation of his puny understanding of her, and he was angry. She hadn't told Billy not to call anymore, so he had continued to appear at the Clarkes' house but she had taken to going inside and leaving him alone with her family. He had been thus humiliated two times by her already. But at the noon hour, no one spoke rudely of women like Martha.

Billy was joking, however, of young James Clarke. He delivered himself of a veritable performance as his anger at Martha fueled his vindictive fancy and he imagined out loud James's sordid exploits. Billy stood before the men as they ranged on a pile of logs; he had a natural theater. He raised his voice, aiming to disconcert the blacks as much as he could with his descriptions of some black girl he knew of or had made up, a girl on whom he described the absent, heroically bestial James Clarke romping. John Rome left his own baiting and threatening of the Negro crews; he approached and approved. His sweat had drenched his shirt.

Reuben could have tolerated Billy's performance without undue unease, as it was what he had come to expect, had it not been Martha's own brother the men were laughing at, had it not been for what had happened to Ray Newsome. As the week had proven, it was the code and gospel of the white world that the opposite case was not a joke but the most intolerable rent in that web of illusion by which they lived. Reuben had already felt for weeks, as he lived on without being able to answer the question of what to do, that the whites were looking at him, every day, with lazy, deepening, accustomed suspicion. As Billy went on, Reuben began to feel that he himself was being appraised, with a quick glance or a bold stare. He gathered he was supposed to feel as they did, supposed to feel himself, against himself, a part of their web. But as soon as he joined them, if he did, then he would be an arrogant bastard son of an Indian whore who thought he was as good as a white man.

It seemed that Paul, most of all, was holding Reuben in his eye. There had been enough uneasiness in their relations since the swimming day. Paul had his quiet, almost diffident way of signaling his resentment or worse. Now there was something in this performance of Billy's that was coming toward Reuben as if to catch him out. Like Reuben was being crowded to the edge of a roof and must leap down and Paul was watching to see how he might fall.

"So he gits up on er, this time, she's on er belly, she don't like that, she don't like it thataway, she's asayin, '*No,* Jimmy, *Lord* no, you white debbil!'"—Billy's voice a high-pitched exaggerated woman's shriek with parodied intonations—"but then he starts awhalin away on her—." Here even Billy's self-intoxication could not carry him to say more, he was so out of breath, although several of the white men were whooping with hostile delight, and John Rome's deeper voice was saying repeatedly, "He give it to er, he give it to er all right."

"*Raise* yo ass up here, *higher,*" Billy was saying, playing the role of the obstreperous James, whose very youth—he was younger than any of the white men—added to the shock of triumph over the woman that so excited the men, and Billy was cupping his own crotch, his legs half bent, his shoulders rounded. That dance of his, again. The men yelped, and John Rome laughed softly, his big belly heaving. He wiped his face with a wet bandanna. Billy collapsed with feigned helplessness and exhaustion. He lay on his back kicking his legs like a bug, giggling. Paul shot a soft call at Reuben, "You fucked nigger women, ain't you Reuben? Tell how they like it. Was a Injin dick big enough for em? *Hey!*"—he shouted at the black workers—"you boys listen, now." The smoke of Ray Newsome's body still hanging in their minds.

And Reuben, quiet even on an ordinary day, only stared at him.

"C'mon, Reuben. You got some idea in dat black-haired head a yours," John Rome added, looking at the others with a great smile on his face. "You ain't fucked no other kine a pussy, have yeh?"

Somehow they knew; they were toying with him.

Billy got up. He was filthy. Sawdust and dirt were stuck to his wet clothes like flour on a raw biscuit.

But if they did already know something, he would already have been in greater trouble than this. So why were they coming at him?

"We *waitin* on you, boy! Don't let it *die*, now, give us a laugh!" John Rome called. They were passing the performance to Reuben; forcing it on him. The obscene rollicking. The white men were all looking at him. And behind him, the black men were quiet.

"No, I ain't," he lied.

"Ain't *what*," Paul said.

"What he ast me."

"What'd he ast you?"

John Rome said, from one side, "No, no, no, I got de feelin you been in de bushes wid a nigger girl mo dan once," John Rome said. "Don'ch'all?"

"I don't know do Injins fuck that much," one man said. "Maybe he kin tell us."

"They too drunk to do it, mosely," another man said, "when you do see one. Except for our half-breed here, that we got. He don't drink nearly *enough*."

There were beads of pine pitch glistening in the sun on the cut logs.

"You ain't a man if you ain't bin with a nigger girl," Paul said, to everyone. Proverb of the white man's Texas.

Billy was breathing out the laughter of his being pleased with himself, and brushing himself off. Another white man slapped his back repeatedly, tenderly, to knock the sawdust off him. Billy turned his attention to the symposium. "Thass right, Reuben," he said.

They were offering Reuben a ride in a wagon in a comradely

way just so that when he stood up in the bed of it they could lash the horse and roll it out from under him.

He did not want to be them or anyone. He did not want to be. He didn't know whether they were about ready to laugh at him and let it go, or pursue his humiliation till he rebelled, or kill him, nail him to a log, castrate him with a knife, saw him in two in the mill, or what.

Having surrounded him mentally, like a pack, the white men, or at least most of them, were waiting for Reuben's acknowledgment of their belief, his admiration of their ways, his honoring of them as the only ones. They were not offering him membership—he was not worthy of that. But even so, they were requiring him to ape its conditions. They were not asking him to ally himself to anything more than what they had pledged themselves to, nor to betray anything more than what they had betrayed. But not knowing what they had betrayed, they were self-betrayers; they had no reluctance to betray others. Unwittingly, they were self-abased by their allegiances and adherences to the ideas they had received from their fathers and uncles and older brothers, and from their mothers as well. Eventually almost all men came in from their doubts to the safety of belief. Even some of those like Reuben with mixed blood had joined them; others as black as the blackest man in Africa itself had learned to agree with their illusions in order to survive the ever-present physical threat and then had suffered the madness of self-hatred. But there had to be some other path, somebody must have found it.

Reuben did not move from where he was sitting on one of the piles of logs. But Billy stepped near him and leaned so close to him that his chin was almost touching Reuben's, his bread-and-cheese breath in Reuben's nose, his marble-hard eyes yielding nothing, but piercing into Reuben's own thoughts and confusing them. There was dead silence. Reuben could hear the sweat dropping from the men's faces; he could hear wood beetles inside the logs; he could hear the heartbeat of a redbird in the scraggly bushes outside the yard.

Billy straightened his back, still looking at Reuben, and said loudly, "All right, then. As of today—listen everybody!—we're making you an honorary nigger, Chief, you yoursef an honorary nigger, thass right. But wait a minute—mebbe we cain't *do* that, mebbe only you boys can"—looking at the black men. He stood up as tall as he could and yelled, "Y'all c'mere, one a you boys, and hep us out a little!" And to his pals, "We could have a little ceremony."

Reuben stood up from under Billy and looked down on all of them just for an instant then tensed his body and leapt over two men half reclining below him on the logs, and landed heavily on the ground. He pitched forward and caught himself before he collided with anyone. "Whoa!" Paul said.

No one spoke—least of all the black men, whose gaze was as distant and cool as the white men's was close and hot. If Reuben opened his mouth to say even one word he would be like a man who voluntarily appeared before a court and confessed to a crime of which no one had openly accused him, the proof of which only he could have brought against himself.

He started walking away from them. A round of surprised calls flew after him; and now their irritation would resolve their mixture of feelings and turn them toward clear dislike or even hate because he had not braved it out, acted the part, come in with them. There was something up with a man, even a colored man, who would not do that; he wasn't to be trusted, and if he wasn't to be trusted then he was to be put in his place. Did a fucking half-breed think he was too good for their company?

"Hey, boy!" Rome called after him.

White eyes and suspicion were following Reuben's back as he walked away from them toward the men of his crew, who did not move, who watched him come. He had been crazy. Crazy even to think of her, even crazier than that to look at her. Much less to touch her. Much less to become so entangled in her.

The for-once merciful whistle blew and all the men rose slowly, the order of work superseded all other claims and customs and

163

rituals, the whistle spared none, and Reuben's gang turned their bent backs to him and set to work, speaking neither to him nor to each other. The whites walked away from their mortal sport unsatisfied and dispersed toward their separate powers, their balls aching but their thoughts on the next chance, which would be even more interesting.

25

The Modern State of Texas

In 1860 east of the Trinity River there were about eighty thousand black slaves, comprising 31 percent of the total population. This East Texas was distinctly southern.

The greater part of the tribe of the Alabama finally drifted to Texas, where they settled in what is now Polk County between Livingston and Woodville.

Those of the Koasati who went to Louisiana occupied several different places, the name of one of which is preserved by the present Coushatta. Some lived for a time in the Opelousas district and then went to the Sabine. Later we find Koasati on the Neches River, Tex., and others on the Trinity. Those who moved to Texas suffered severely from pestilence and the remainder collected in one village, which united with the Alabama Indians. In 1882 the United States Indian Office estimated that there were 290 Alabama, Koasati, and Muskogee in Texas, and this figure was repeated through 1900. The census of the latter year, however, returned 470 of the allied tribes and the Indian Office repeated this till 1911. In 1910 a special agent was sent to Texas, who omitted the Koasati from his report, but the United States Census of 1910 returned 85 in Louisiana, 11 in Texas, and 2 in Nebraska, a total of 98.

By 1906 the Choctaw Nation in Indian Territory was dissolved by the federal government (and in 1907 Oklahoma was admitted as a state to the Union).

By 1900 the timber harvest of Texas, consisting almost entirely of yellow pine, was valued at $16,296,473.

By 1910 the population of Texas was 3,896,542, of whom 401,720 were Baptists.

By 1910 there were 13,819 miles of railroad in Texas.

Cottontail rabbits, raccoons and squirrels are common in the forests. A few otters, beavers and minks are still found in eastern Texas. There are opossums, skunks, the Texas lynx (*Lynx rufus texensis*), several species of mice and rats; the green lizard, the fence lizard, and the whip-tailed lizard; the blow snake, or spreading adder, the black snake, coach whip, the diamond water snake, the king snake, the pilot snake. Of venomous snakes, the harlequin, or coral snake, is common along the coast; the copperhead along the wooded banks of creeks and rivers; the cottonmouth in all parts of the state, and several species of rattlesnake. The long-leaf pine is the dominant forest tree on the uplands of the Coastal Plain, giving way farther inland to the short-leaf pine. Between the rising swells of long-leaf pine lands are impenetrable thickets of hawthorn, holly, privet, plane trees and magnolias. Loblolly pine, cypress, oaks, hickory, ash, pecan, maple, beech and a few other deciduous trees are interspersed among both the long-leaf and the short-leaf pines, and the proportion of deciduous trees increases to westward. Since the blight of 1905 the chestnut is uncommon.

By 1900 the total farm acreage was 125,807,017 acres, the total number of farms being 351,085 (not including farms of less than three acres), their average acreage 358.3 acres, 84.9 per cent being operated by white farmers.

The value of all domestic animals on farms and ranges in 1900 was $236,227,934. By 1910 there were 8,308,000 cattle including 1,137,000 milch cows. In the number of mules the state ranks first by a wide margin in 1910, with 702,000 head. Of the population in 1900, 94.1 per cent was native born, 79.6 per cent was white and 20.4 per cent (or 620,722) was Negro, or of Negro descent. There were in 1900, 2,249,088 native whites, 179,357 persons of foreign birth, 836 Chinese, 470 Indians and 13 Japanese.

26

That Moment

She did not think till it was over, every time. In those moments of not-thinking she had such an appetite to hold his shoulders, his back, his face, his hands, his thighs, in her hands. Rapidly she drew the palms of her hands over his smooth dark skin, up and down his body. She wanted somehow to have him, to draw from his skin, from his muscles, from his body, something she was desperately hungry for, and his beauty. And his hands were on her body, moving the same way. She felt held, known, contained, completely inside his protecting sheltering attention. Attention that was like water to the thirsty plant of her. She almost felt she was a different person. His hands sliding down her back, his hands at her waist, on her breasts. How did he know to touch her just so, she couldn't bear to think he had learned from some other woman, she did not believe he had learned that way, he just knew, he was just a man who without thinking drew her against him and shaped her, created her over again, with his hands. Till she had to be as close to him, as tightly clasped to him, as she could bear. As much in him, somehow, as he was in her. Which made her draw her breath in quickly, every time he entered her body. And wrap her arms around his shoulders and hold him as tightly as she had strength. That moment. And then the moments that began with that moment. Till he climbed a pine tree and leapt upward off the top of it to someplace else. Till she made her way into a consuming expectant tenseness, trembling, her body trembling, her spirit floating somehow holding him to her, to her, to her and then that wave that finally came in and lifted her up like the waves at Galveston when she was a little girl, lifted her off her feet where she had been standing on the muddy-sandy bottom, carried her up and then swung her down again, this wave too was going to swing her down again, down again, and his hands had stopped moving and he was arching up away from her and he had stopped moving and she was moving still, floating, there was more, there was yet more, she would swing down and then up again, like another wave and another, she wanted them to arrive, she could feel them there, approaching, on their way to her. And each time she thought *this time*.

A tenseness in her, which he touched and calmed; an expectation in her, which he excited and intensified; a fear in her, and he assuaged it; an appetite in her that he fed; a tightness in her, which he entered and she loosened; a power in her which she took for her own.

She looked into his eyes, into his face, and she saw a part of who she was.

And afterward she began to think. While they were tangled in each other's bodies, she had been free of thinking, she was just herself, or some creature she had never been before, that didn't know or think and didn't have to, and then she was herself almost just as she had always been, and she began to feel empty, it was unpleasant how she felt, she felt something was lost, she was lost from something, now, someplace she hadn't even liked but it was the place she had known, now she was lost from it and marked as lost. No one else knew, but she knew. No one else could look at her and see any difference (could they?) but she was different. She looked at the faces of her family and she felt the cold shock of knowing that they did not know her. Once before, she had felt this and gradually, gradually she had come to feel again that she was who she was, and not some other person, some person unknown to anyone. For if they did not know her, with whom she had lived her entire life, who was she? But here again was that dizzying not-knowing, that question of "Martha." Who was "Martha"? "Martha" was what?

Once already she had tried to forget what she hated about herself and had succeeded, somehow, but here it was again, stronger than ever, and she loved this man, she didn't hate him, she wanted to be with him, she didn't fear him, she wanted to see him and touch him, and be seen and touched by him, she wasn't repulsed by him. Yet that didn't matter. This was bad, was irrevocable, was dirty, how could it be those things, how could that moment with him be what she had been made to feel it was? Didn't anyone else in the world feel what they felt, was it supposed to be good when the man was white and you were married to him and bad, evil, horrible, if he wasn't and you weren't? Was it supposed to be heaven in the one case and hell in the other? The same thing? (If anyone in the world felt what she and Reuben felt.)

She changed clothes more often; she bathed more often; she looked at herself in her dressing-table mirror more closely; with quick secret glances she spied on her mother and father and sister to see how they were looking at her. She thought and thought.

27

Attitudes

Some black women and men knew of Martha and Reuben, and had shaken their heads, even though it was the half-Indian, not one of their own, who had done the unthinkably insane. For their own were already at risk, the madness of the white mob's recreational hatred rising again. Only a few, who would abase themselves to gain the abasement of condescending favor, spoke of it obliquely to their own whites. Whether then they were believed was not in their control. Yet they too were heedless in their way, for any such incident filled Smithville with danger for all.

Reuben's thoughts, his ideas, the expectations he had not even realized he had formed, had become as suddenly clear as the shape of the mill against the hard sky, and then had tumbled to the ground in ruin. He felt he had awakened from a stuporous sleep. He knew what he wanted to do.

The evening of the episode at the mill, secretly and with monstrous apprehension that half-destroyed his desire for her, he went to meet her, as he and Martha had already arranged days ago, at their first brief meeting since Ray Newsome was killed. He could see with some clarity, now. He felt also a kind of excitement of dread at being able to tell her that he thought he and she were suspected. (Or almost suspected—since suspicion alone would be cause enough for that hate-dancing mob to form once again. Only *this time*, what would they do when white Martha would not accuse, or repent?) He almost felt glad to hold the power of bringing bad news, for it seemed to him she had held all the power in what happened to him, and what had happened to them both. Every meeting had included its moment of panic, in which whether they said it aloud or not each of them had thought, But what now? What can we do? What are we going to do? He was going to leave, leave her and leave Three Rivers—no matter how much the thought of not seeing her ever again made him feel hollow and sick, no matter what she said. He would not even touch her this time.

But this time, while they spoke, they were indeed seen, and it was only this watching that accomplished the very revelation that Reuben was afraid had been already given to others; it was his failure to see he must stay away from her *this time* that delivered them into the sight of others, finally.

Billy, excited by the noon hour's sport, and following an intuition he did not even realize he had, came also, washed and in clean clothes, late and unannounced, to call on Martha yet once more. Before he reached the Clarkes' house, approaching from the back so as to arrive with the advantage of surprise, he caught sight of two people hiding together, not touching but standing very near each other in the dusk-shadow of low trees where the Clarkes' property met the back alley on which stood their little stable. To Billy's astonishment, Martha was talking to Reuben Sweetbitter. She was standing close to him, looking into his face. And then she reached out both her hands and took his hand. Billy had never guessed, nor had Paul, that Reuben had even dared to notice Martha, or, if he had, that anything whatever could come into his ignorant mind about her. Now Billy shivered with repulsed and exultant triumph at his discovery. He would repay Martha for putting her precious nose in the air; he would destroy the filthy Indian he should never have even spoken to at the mill except to hold in his place. The deceitful whore—on her front porch she had pretended to laugh with him at the memory of the fool Reuben at the swimming hole! As he stood in hiding, spying on their hiddenness,

Billy's mind began to fill with impossible images that shook him but which he relished, multiplying them, repeating them, in his mind's eye, till they were a kind of howling dance.

Martha was in a panic. But she could see that Reuben was stricken, he was chilled. Tentatively she reached for his hand, to prove to herself that he still existed in the flesh, there before her, to take a lingering touch of hand to hand in hope of stopping what was happening. He said he was not going back to the mill at all; there might be someone who knew of them, had she heard anything? He would leave. He would leave early tomorrow. He couldn't stay. He was sorry, he was sorry. Slowly he pulled his hand away from hers. They were both weeping tears of panic, not touching each other.

Billy crept away. His mouth was dry and of a bitter taste. He shivered. Not hearing but seeing, unseen and unheard, carefully he crept away and carried his knowledge with him like a gold piece he would invest for enormous return.

28

Useful Practice

Down by the little river, in the cane and willows that grew taller than he, Reuben knew a place of hiding, and played games of stalking and killing the bear and deer that his grandfather told of hunting. He spoke to imaginary enemies, to the bear and the deer he hunted in mime, to the turtles and frogs he caught, to himself in order to sort out what he thought. (But not to snakes, from whom he ran away in the direction of home.)

Once in a while in his solitary play he came on Grandfather, standing silently as if he didn't walk on the ground but could appear like a vision. Reuben felt that Grandfather glanced at him very meaningfully, but the meaning was not clear. If Reuben approached, and said *qmafo,* the old man would signal him to be silent, and would look out again as if expecting Reuben to follow his gaze. But Reuben had never figured out what Grandfather was looking at in such moments. Reuben would grow restless and would retreat, and something like a pressure against his chest would lighten. After moving quietly till out of sight around a bush or tree, Reuben would hasten, then, away, in search of a new place where again he could feel free.

And Reuben was good at hiding. At hiding and following without being seen. His love of sneaking up on his aunts was a family joke. His skill at disappearing, when his uncles intended to tease or torment him, was a cause for family wonder.

29

Mr. Corinthian Grooms

Just leave. Leave Martha. Leave all of it, all of them, start again somewhere.

The evening had cooled considerably. Reuben sat in his tiny room. He owned little. His packing would take but a moment.

He had touched her hair, had put his hands over the bare soft skin of her breasts, had held in both hands that waist of hers that made him almost dizzy when he looked at her. He carefully folded the two white shirts she had given him, unfolded them, folded them again. He laid them to one side for Mr. Grooms. He looked at his collection of yellowed newspapers, that he had picked up from streets and trash barrels and back doors and had read every word of, and had kept folded and stacked neatly in a pile on the top of his pine bureau. Mr. Grooms did not read them, and would take them to the privy after Reuben had gone.

The same was true of Reuben's exercise books—although of these Mr. Grooms had approved when he saw Reuben endeavoring to better himself, sitting at the kitchen table, the lamp lit, and copying out the newspapers or the Bible in his exercise book, clarifying his handwriting. Reuben had not told Martha of this. He had bought and filled six exercise books. Now he left them beside the newspapers.

On top of the pile of newspapers lay the edition Reuben had only just recently picked up from the street, that gave the white account of what had happened near Palestine. Word had reached

Smithville in other ways. What black folks heard was not what Reuben read blazoned in the newspaper. They knew such madness could come to Three Rivers and Smithville, as well; and it had, when it had taken Ray Newsome in its grasp.

There was plenty in the newspaper story that was not put there for Negroes to read. Or for Reuben. Things written not for them but sometimes about them. They had no way to bring their account to anyone—and to whom could it have been brought?

Reuben harkened for an answer to give—in his mind, at least— to the untruth of the occasional newspaper thrown out by travelers from Shreveport or Lufkin or Waco. At the least, the newspapers were telling him that it was a time to lie low and very out of sight from the enthusiastic vengeance of white people, a vengeance that imagined or invented offenses so as to have its thrilling occasions for torment and murder.

Mr. Grooms's wife had died childless of a cancer when she was forty, and he had lived now thirty-some years more without her, mourning her still, locked in grief of her some evenings, but also happy in memory of her. He was not sure that her ghost had not come into his bed again, breaking into this world with pity for him on a few occasions, and he had felt a mysterious slight comforting warmth, those nights.

He spoke often of his life in years past, of his slave days especially, of his masters, of holiday feasts, of old customs, and often of his legendary friend who had been flogged to death at about the age of Ray Newsome. The man who had owned Mr. Grooms had despised light-skinned slaves, so Mr. Grooms's friend had been marked for doom. (Mr. Grooms had had the luck, as defined by his sardonic time, to be born very dark, which had exempted him from the full rage, if not the daily anger, of the man who had owned him in his youth.)

What people like the Clarkes owned seemed to Reuben to answer every conceivable need of man, woman and child, and many needs he could not even try to guess. He did not think he coveted their possessions or envied the lives of others like them for whom he had worked; but he thought, yes, he did envy their having such choices and their happiness in one place. And he resented their ability to confer their luxury on Martha, a richness of things, a freedom from childhood work like what Francie had wanted for him and Frank and the girls, that he and the children he'd been a child with had never known, that Mr. Grooms, whose wife had not been able to bear a child, could not have provided. Now it was striking Reuben for the first time that he would have liked some such life as Martha's for children of his own, someday, and for his own wife, whoever she might turn out to be. He didn't see any way to accomplish that. He wanted only to go, and go far, from here, and take any work he could get, and not speak to anyone nor even meet anyone, if that was possible.

Mr. Corinthian Grooms had let Reuben his room at the back of the house when first they met. As a matter of course, after getting hired on at the mill, Reuben had walked to the Negro part of town to find a room. There, having noted the first house, which stood out from the poorer shacks that followed it down the dirt road toward the center of the village, Reuben had walked up to the elderly man sitting on the porch and asked him for lodging. Mr. Grooms had said straight off, without even a hello, and as if he were speaking to somebody next to him, that he hadn't seen a finer-looking man since he had slaved on the Felicity Plantation with the friend of his young life, slave-named Copper, a great strong young man who had died very young.

Reuben wasn't a man who had received compliments, and he had answered the old man's praise with an embarrassed smile. Mr. Grooms let Reuben the room without cash payment, in exchange for his working the heavy chores, keeping Mr. Grooms's horse, which the old man used no longer but would not sell to the knacker, and generally seeing to the house repairs. And although the mill claimed almost all of Reuben's days and strength, Mr. Grooms's chores had turned out to be very few. The horse—an old pet now, past saddling or harnessing—was easily fed and watered.

Reuben had settled happily into the house and the village. He liked the sound of voices in the evening in the nearby houses and in the road, and on Sundays, of children playing. The old man's unstinting welcome and encouragement of Reuben had diminished when he learned of Martha, and his mood had grown somber and anxious. He was horrified. After he had asked Reuben if what some of the colored were saying about him and a white girl was true, he began reading his Bible more often. But did not evict Reuben nor, after his shock, remonstrate with him much.

The house occupied an ambiguous position—it was out of Three Rivers proper, like all houses inhabited by dark-skinned persons, but although as unpainted as any of the houses in Smithville, was larger and better-kept than most. Mr. Grooms's industry and his respectful manners with whites had made him in his prime a chief carpenter on many white houses. Like a character in a drama that white folks viewed but did not live or even feel, Mr. Grooms had been given by them an epithet which in their speech followed his name like a part of his name, *Corinthian a good nigger.*

In Smithville itself he was also respected by most people, especially the women, for his uprightness and service to the church; and was admired for his generosity. He never gave satisfaction to white people by speaking ill of any person of color, as much as the general run of them frequently courted his agreement in their disparagement; and to his own, he defended some of the white folks, who he said were not entirely like the rest. Among his own, also, he could speak harshly, although some said with justice, and he had several times tried to arbitrate quarrels when they were brought to him, before they had reached a violent turn. He had a knack for finding the point of compromise that left each man feeling he had saved at least some face. Several women, widows and deserted, over the years since Mr. Grooms's wife had died, had made an effort at gaining his good will and had entertained the hope of moving into that house of his; and there were a few women who still gave this a thought once in a while. Faithful to the memory of his wife, he could not feel much interest in any woman who had not shared his experience at Felicity as she had, who had not risen with him by hard work after Emancipation, as she had, and who could not give him her particular sort of strength to continue through all the expected hardships of working for white people, as she had done. He could talk to her in his mind and she understood everything of which he spoke.

So he politely discouraged the occasional Sunday afternoon woman caller, when, still wearing her church clothes, she brought him some delicious dish she had cooked for him; he might visit on his front porch a while, but he did not invite her into his house. Mr. Grooms was aware that other young men in Smithville did not understand his generosity to Reuben, and after their mothers' overtures to Mr. Grooms, even resented it. But the young women, the girls—several of them would look at Reuben openly, offering him smiles and invitations, to which he had not responded.

Reuben did not have even a cardboard suitcase. He recalled two baskets, one large and one small. They had long, long ago broken or rotted and had been left behind. The old carpet bag he'd carried when he'd arrived in Three Rivers had torn through, and even Mr. Grooms with his skills hadn't been able to patch it. But Mr. Grooms did have a nice tight wooden box he had gotten from a white grocer in Three Rivers. In it had come a shipment of tea from England all the way to Three Rivers over months of transport to answer the special order of a white spinster woman who lived in a great frame house beside the little squat town bank building made of brick and stone. Ten years' worth of tea, Mr. Grooms and Reuben figured.

Into this box Reuben methodically packed his extra pair of trousers, two pairs of short stockings from Mr. Grooms, a square yard of good tanned leather he had been given in payment for helping dig a well and had not yet used for anything, his blue shirt, two undershirts, his long underwear, with holes at elbows and knees but still warm, his thin winter jacket, two proper pairs of under-drawers, not the ones he had worn that day at the river, his one pair of moccasins, gift of Adalia Mullaney, scarcely worn, a little scuffed black Bible that Mr. Grooms had given him when he'd learned that Reuben could read it, his old straight razor with mother-of-pearl handle, broken at the tip of the blade, the tin cup, the fishhooks. . . .

He fitted the snug lid onto the top, then rose and took the oil lantern and went to the back door. The night was cloudy and damp. Hanging between two nails on the wall of the back porch, the axe glinted when his lamplight hit the bright sharp edge. Odd to think he wouldn't use it again, or sharpen it again.

He went to the shed and rummaging by lamplight he found a half dozen small nails, which he put in his pocket. The horse woke and Reuben ran a hand down its back. He gathered one armful of split stove wood. He dropped it at the back door. Mr. Grooms met him in the kitchen. Softly he said, "You goan off, now—ain't good weather fo it, but . . . I understan. It's a hard break you got. But I'm tell you, much as I *hate* to see you go—it leaves me low—you smart to leave. You shoulda got out before now." He lowered his voice to a whisper. "You know dis time is bad. *Bad.* (Though I *wish* I could say dat I've seen a time dat was good, once in dis long life.) And it smart and it right to get away from that white girl."

Reuben did not answer.

"I see now, now dat I know whass goin on, how much you ain't even been your own good sef fo a while. Lord I couldn't bear it this time if somethin happen to *you*, now."

"It won't. What I'm worried about is somebody comes callin here after me."

"No, no, doan worry bout dat," Mr. Grooms said, "doan worry none. I know all de white folks and dey knows me. Dey got deir blood, for now." He looked at the floor. "But I *sorely* do wish all dis hadn't happened, Reuben. Was thinking you'd *stay* here wit me a *good* while, a good *long* while. You know, I could've hepped you. You a good worker. You always give yo share. But it jest ditn't work out for you, here. I see dat. Might be you made a mistake or two; and this world—white man's world, surely—certainly ain't very forgivin."

Reuben did not try to explain himself.

"Well, wit that Injin blood a yours, I guess you know yo way, Reuben, to wherever you goin."

Reuben smiled. "Can't inherit knowin how to live in the woods," he said. "You think I know the woods by bein part Chactaw? You doan think I had to learn?"

"Well, I doan know about dat," the old man said. "Anyway, you ain't got so much of Injin blood dat you couldn't have passed, somewhere, I doan doubt. But even a little bit is way too much for them that owns. Now, you does stay away from whiskey, which's good and Christian. Cause you know the Injin blood cain't hold they liquor."

Mr. Grooms gathered his thin frame with a sigh, and turned. "You set down and wait here jes a minute," he said over his shoulder. He went through the parlor into his bedroom. Reuben put the lamp on the kitchen table.

When Mr. Grooms came back he carefully unfolded a very small quilt across the kitchen table; he also laid down a knife sheathed in worn black leather. "This's old," he said, "but it's good steel dat keeps a fine edge. I noticed you ditn't have nothin like it," he added, looking up from under his eyebrows. Reuben pulled the knife from the sheath; the blade was mottled with tarnish and a thin powder of rust, the edge keen.

Outside, it had finally begun to rain. "Here's a little sharpnin stone, you take it. And thisyere's powful good luck, you keep it wichyou *all* the time—I'll git you a piece of soft twine to put thoo it, to wear it roun you neck." He laid an angular broken piece of whetstone on the quilt and beside it a silver coin like none Reuben had ever seen, with a hole pierced in its center.

"You got earnins left?" Mr. Grooms asked.

"Yessir," Reuben said.

"Thass good, thass good money, you put it inside hyere." He

handed Reuben a little leather pouch with a drawstring. It was heavy, and when Reuben pulled it open and looked inside he saw a glitter of silver and here and there of gold. He had never seen so much money, had never owned a gold coin of any kind. He looked up, open-mouthed.

"I got plenty a money, don't worry bout *dat*," Mr. Grooms said. "What I'm use it fo?" He laughed.

He took the money bag back from Reuben and said, "Go get your earnins, now, and bring it here." Reuben brought six dollars in coin from his room and the old man added it to the pouch. "Dat *all* you saved, fom de mill?"

Reuben grinned at him. He knew he should be feeling sad, but for this moment there was something happy in this leaving, it was the right thing, it lifted the burden from him, and now he knew what a burden it had been. "Six dollars's all I come to town with, when I started," he said.

Mr. Grooms shook his head. "I don't know what you bought wif it, I doan see nothin to show." He wrapped everything up for the younger man in the little quilt, and rolled it tight on itself.

"Pack dat and the knife where you keep it close to you," he said.

"You want me to take that quilt?" Reuben asked.

"Dis quilt's nearly's old as dat gold coin," Mr. Grooms said. "Twas to be quilt for a baby chile, chile we never did have; come to my wife as a gif when she thought she was goan have the baby. But didn't have it. Baby was bone dead. You take de lil quilt, it's got a good prayer in it for you and for yo children someday."

Mr. Grooms was looking at it thoughtfully. "You finish yo packin," he said, "and I'm goan put a prayer in this quilt fo you, and you'll be all right out dere."

Reuben went to his room and in the darkness sat on his bed. He waited a few moments, then returned to the kitchen, where the old man was sitting at the table with his eyes closed, his knobby hands palms down on the small rolled-up quilt, his lips moving. He opened his eyes and looked at Reuben with a grim expression on his face.

"Dey got very hard feelins about like what you done. If dey take it hard, though, if the man ain't black, I kin hope not. I think you the only Injin we had roun yere. And I know you rose the highess that any Injin did, if we did have one." He added: "But dat *girl*."

Mr. Grooms studied Reuben. "I'm told you befo, de color you skin put me in mind of Copper Griff—dat why dey called him dat, because he looked Injin. An like I tole you, he probly *was* some Injin, maybe same people as you, I doan know. Lots a black folks was and is. Dat was on Felicity Plantation, they callt it, long way back from here. Long bitter way back, befo I come to Texis."

He looked up past the dark ceiling of the room. "Things I seen, turrble things dat I have never forgot. Dere was a while when seem like things might could get better. But dey has got appreciable wuss instead. I doan know. Dese is dark days, Bible says we have em." He cleared his throat; his voice had gotten raspy. Then he went on. "Things I ain't never forgit, an doan want see again. . . . Dere's evil in a lot a folks, and a powful evil kin come out of even a good man sometime—maybe even a good white man is the one dass leass resistin to it, sometime. But dey's good and bad men, black and white and red and ever color between, we know dat, we seen dat." He lifted his hands from the bundle and nodded at it, and Reuben took it from the table. With his head tilted back a little and his hands clasped on the table, Mr. Grooms closed his eyes again, praying in silence, and Reuben lit a second lamp and carried it with him back to his room. He laid the tightly rolled-up quilt at the center of his box, replaced more clothes over it, and with an old hammer that had only half a handle he tapped the little lid down with the nails from his pocket. He tied a length of rope around the box, two ways, for a handle. When he went, early tomorrow morning, if the rain stopped, he would tie his boots one on each side, and would wear his moccasins. He had walked the roads before, and not so long ago, and he would walk them again—or even run them, for a few days. For now, he sat down on his bed, looking at that box on the floor. His eyes traveled to the stack of newspapers. He returned to the kitchen.

Earlier in the day, worried about rain, Alice, who cleaned and cooked for Mr. Grooms, for paid wages, had hung the clean wet clothes across the parlor on heavy twine that Mr. Grooms simply left strung up all the time from wall to wall, for such occasions. It made the parlor uncomfortably small. Even in the kitchen the space around Reuben felt too narrow.

Reuben put wood in the stove. He had not said good-bye to Alice—another thing finished in the wrong way. When the water in the kettle was warm enough for soaping his chin he set the lamp beside him where he stood in front of the dark pane of the kitchen window and watched himself shave his soft scanty beard.

When he finished he found Mr. Grooms reading his Bible in the parlor, half hidden among the heavy hanging clothes, which his lamp illumined weirdly. Recent events had disturbed his faith but had not destroyed it. The rain was lighter now, a steady pattering on the roof. Reuben said to Mr. Grooms, "I'm going outside for a few minutes." He went out the back door to walk past their shed down the dirt alley toward Smithville a little way, to breathe. Under the trees, he would not get very wet.

Maybe he had no need to leave so suddenly. Maybe no one but Mr. Grooms knew anything. Maybe his alarm was needless, or exaggerated. But to not see Martha he had to leave the town. And if he saw her, what was it for? Nothing was possible; nothing was permitted. Now he felt like if he could get over the first big hump of it, he could live, he could live without her if he set his mind to, it would be better for her, too, that was certain. But his chin was on his chest, tears on his cheeks.

When he was alone, rambling, living as he cared, he was only who he took himself to be, who he felt he was. But as soon as he met another person then he was something, some *thing*, made apparent only by the fact that he was different from the other person—darker, or lighter, of skin, and in so many other ways different. And so was permitted this and not that, was denied this and this, was made into someone he did not feel he was.

In a town named Slocum—he wasn't sure if he'd been there, or not, at some time—no one like him or darker of skin could be out walking in the night, even a rainy night when he wouldn't be seen.

30

Ciphers

He remembered being alone in his riverbank hiding place. Marking with a twig in the sand. Games of counting. Designs. Had passed a lot of time like that. And would go back to join the others for a meal or talking, and not tell them of his discoveries. Discovered the scribing of fives, for his five fingers and toes, and made patterns of five circles, five squares, five circles around squares, five squares within circles within squares. Discovered sums pretty much by himself. His mother had taught him to count. She. Who had learned it and even taught it for one year, just before the Indian School was closed.

When she saw him playing at his scribing in the dust near their cabin she taught him to write numbers instead of marks. Then at his private slate in the river-sand he discovered games of numbers, which occupied him for more than a year. Then she taught him how to multiply and his old games were surpassed by new ones.

He laughed now to think of himself then. A little boy who didn't know that what seemed unchanging was changing.

And who was it who remembered? And who was it who was remembered?

31

Away

Alone in her room, Martha looked abstractedly through her exercise book, her written notes on Reuben, but she did not find anything in what she had recorded that identified him, that secured him to her, that was of him specifically, that would serve to mark him out as himself and as hers. She tried to read a ladies' magazine but could not follow the sentences. She picked up her needlework and ruined the stitching she tried. Then she left her room and wandered about the house. It seemed small. Then she went back to her room but did not undress for bed. She could not quite believe she would not see him again. As if he were dead.

Even before she heard Reuben's hard words, there had been an air of strain around the Clarkes' supper table. James was absent, as often (and always excused, while Anne and Martha would never be). Anne had seemed out of sorts; Martha had not felt hungry. Mr. Clarke had made a few of his typical pronouncements regarding commerce and politics, for the edification of the women in his family. Martha felt like saying what she was thinking, for once, and she disagreed with him sharply, angrily. Her mother and Anne looked astonished. Her father only shook his head, acting like he wasn't sure of what he'd heard, or was too slow to follow her. Or wouldn't allow her to engage him as she was trying to do. He was not angry. He forked another portion of his meat without even answering her. She might as well not have spoken.

After her abrupt sally, Martha withdrew into her thoughts again. When it became clear that she would spare them this unwonted ferocity, her sister and mother released their held breath. Martha stood up and excused herself perfunctorily from the table. She could feel her parents staring after her and then confronting each other with their usual troubled eyes that seemed to search for blame. The night was hot and thick with damp.

She hid from the clearing of the table and the washing up. Pilgrim was still preparing supper six days a week but no longer stayed to serve and clean up. She had pled for time for her children, and Martha's mother had agreed to try the new hours for two weeks, but had cut Pilgrim's pay. When Anne began washing dishes, Martha had closed herself in her room. No one came looking for her. It was almost dark when she had slipped out for her brief unbearable rendezvous and had returned trying not to cry or scream. She was unable either to sit or to stand; she felt she would burst out of her body. How could it be that she had said good-bye already, without even touching him, to the only person she loved? She stayed in her room with the door shut, pacing, lying across her bed, pacing—so distracted by her own sudden plunge into uncertainty that she gave no thought to sounds from the other rooms or to anyone else. Someone came to the front door and left again. There was quiet talking somewhere. For days on end her father and mother had been stifling an argument they could neither settle nor speak of openly, because it centered on one of the subjects they had made taboo around their children—money. But all three children knew, anyway, that their father was being importuned to come into the oil business, which some said would be the great thing in a short while, and was already booming to the south. It was his main chance, they told him; he had some money to invest, and he had his good sense of the law and deals. He wanted to make the money, as other men were doing. Yet even as he argued to Caroline that they might think of leaving Three Rivers and settling close to the new fields of oil, he found himself—as all three children knew—giving in to her vehement refusal to leave the town where she had lived so long, where her dead children were buried. At late hours or quiet ones when the children were asleep or out, the muted unintelligible sound of this emphatic disagreement found its way through the house.

This night it must have been worse even than usual; the sound of voices, stripped of their words, had reached into every corner and recess. Anne, in her room, could hear the bitter tones, the rising of momentary advantage or frustration, the falling of momentary weariness or defeat. Martha scarcely noticed, for the noise in her own head was much louder.

Martha's door swung open and her mother, instead of saying good night, or that it was late for Martha to be still dressed, said, "Martha, come with me for a moment, please." Her voice was odd, as unmodulated as a gong. She led the way to the kitchen and sat Martha down there and stood facing her. It was odd, too, to be in the kitchen this late at night. An iciness rushed into Martha's chest; already more had been set in motion than she was ready to meet, more was about to happen. Her mother seemed able to get the words out only with the greatest labor, she tried two, three times, to speak, but did not say one word, and with great agitation stood, almost shaking, in front of Martha, who waited, not patiently but caught in the motionlessness of fear.

"People are sayin," her mother began again. "Some people are *sayin*, that you have bin *seen* with—that *Injin* boy! That one that works at the mill—whoever he could be—I can't even see how you could've ever *met* such a person or even *know* of im!"

(Thus was Reuben stabbingly dismissed.)

Martha's mother said, "Was't you? Could that've bin you? It couldn't have bin. Wasn't that—" (the hope, for several hours already—this had been the desperate argument with her husband) "—someb'dy else? It wouldn't be *inny* white girl atall in this town, but one of those pale nigger girls." But her face was distorted by anxiousness. "Your Father—" (introducing the yardstick, the plumb line, the precise weight against which both women must be measured) "—he refuses to believe it. He says it *cain't* be true, that tis absolutely impossible that yew of all people'd ever *do* innytheng of the kind." Please say it isn't true, her eyes added.

The walls had rushed outward away from Martha and she would fall; her chest felt pinched and dry inside; her breath was coming short. They would not comprehend it, they would banish her, she was not ready to be banished from her world. (Was there another one beyond it, really?) And if she wished not to be banished from it, she would have to tell them; but if she told them, she would lose him for certain, and she could not imagine what punishment or humiliation she herself would suffer. Her florid domineering father, her sister too slow of wit to understand Martha, her mother of set routine and unmovable opinion—what outrage that these would remain her judges for the rest of her life. (And what would be done to Reuben?)

She had already lost him, he was leaving, and now everything was crushing her. She, she and he, would have to be known of without her even having him. And men would go looking for him. She would not again be with him, and within his physical strength; not again rest in that ease he had in his own place in this world— he who had no place! He was always ready to do the next thing, whatever that was. He wasn't afraid. Yet he had come to her to tell her that he was leaving and thus had told her, if not in so many words, that he was afraid. He wasn't afraid. Yet he had every right to be afraid after what had just happened in the town and all over the county was happening.

"Martha? Martha?" Her mother had lowered her voice. "Martha, you *say* somethin t' me!" she croaked. Martha quaked when she heard a newspaper rattling in the next room, the living room; her father was still up, he had come out from *in there;* he was waiting for his wife—of twenty-eight years—to come to him, her assigned mission for him now accomplished, and reassure him that their daughter was a fine upstanding decent young Christian woman of quality who was herself quite taken aback at the very thought of what they were asking her.

Martha's gaze fell slowly down the length of her mother's figure—the woman's softness and vulnerability were revealed more
sharply under the pressures of fear and hope—till she felt she must
avert her eyes, she shouldn't see her mother in such extremity of
anxiousness, and she looked at her own feet. But before the silence
could incriminate her more resoundingly than any lie she herself
might unconvincingly tell, she gathered enough strength to raise
her eyes once more to her mother's. "He is a very fine man, he's
not what you think, and we want to be married," she said softly.
This is what it came into her head to say.

"Oh!" her mother said in a choked voice. "Oh no!" her mother
moaned. As if she'd been pushed from behind, she lurched into
Martha, clutching her daughter's dress at the shoulders, and her
head fell back, her eyes wide and staring up toward the ceiling.
"Oh!" she said in a fiercely contained whisper, "Oh Jesus Lord it
can't be, not my daughter, oh Lord," she whimpered, hanging on
Martha's shoulders. Then she let go and jerked backward, away
from Martha, and lifted the hem of her apron up to her bowed
head and covered her face with the soft cloth, hand-washed count-
less times by Pilgrim. Looking at her, Martha thought, She has to
save herself before she can save me. Martha braced herself for an
attack.

"Oh Lord, this will kill your Father," her mother said from inside the cloth. Then she dropped it and although her head was at a
submissive angle to one side as she looked at her daughter, a little
angry flame began to flicker in her eyes. In a steadier but still soft
voice now she said, "This will *kill* your Father!

"This'll *kill* im!" she whispered angrily. "Do you want that
man's mizry on your conscience, if you haven't got inny *shame* for
your own sake? He's waitin in the other room now for you to *come*
to him and tell im tisn't *true!* If you tell him—Martha!—he will
die, he'll *die* of the shame of it! The shame!" She was recovering
her fiber; Martha could see it coming back into her, starting at her
hips and straightening her back and pushing up through her spine
into her neck. And as anger was restoring her mother's strength,

195

Martha felt her own capability sink.

"*How* could you *do* this to *us!*" her mother hissed. She set her lower jaw with a mean determination and grabbed Martha's arm and yanked her up and farther away from the door to the living room where Martha's father was pretending to read the newspaper, every word of which he must have read twice already. He would be getting impatient, uneasy. He was not used to waiting. Martha's mother pulled her and Martha followed without much resisting to the other side of the kitchen, away from the parlor and into the dining room. Her mother shut that door behind them, too. Martha could feel tears coming, here they were rising up over the rim of herself and beginning to spill down her cheeks. Her mother was right; how could she have done it; for what? for a man's paltry love?—when she had not insisted he prove that love to her before she. . . . This *would* shame her father to death, he would never get over it, she would lose him and her mother and everything she knew, her life would be ended. Her body heaved with the effort of stifling a sob.

"Oh," her mother said. Then sharply to Martha: "He hasn't *touched* you, has he?" Martha flinched and closed her eyes, and tucked her chin into her right shoulder. "Oh my God," her mother said, "Oh no, no, no, no. That . . . *half-breed* boy? Oh my Lord in Heaven." Abruptly the woman turned her back to Martha. "Touched by *inny* man, I couldn't bear it," she said to the wall, softly. "I just couldn't. But by that . . . *dirt?*" Her body shook and trembled as she struggled with herself. She turned around again to Martha, very slowly and deliberately.

"Now you listen t' me," she said. Martha could do nothing else. "You are *not* goin to let your Father know bout *that*. All that's happened is that y'*spoke* with this *person* once or twice, d'y'understand? Thass all. Thass *all*. And you goan *go* in that parlor and *tell* your Father what y'done and *swear* to im on the Holy Bible on the Word of God swear on Holy Jesus *promise* im that you will *never* even think of such a thing again or ever look at that—" she really could not say the word "man"—"*person* again, you goan *beg* his forgiveness. Beg his forgiveness. D'y'hear me?" Martha wept silently, avoiding her mother's eyes. "You hear me?" Her mother shook Martha's arm. "We goan do it right now, we cain't wait another *minute*. D'y'understand?" Her face was close to Martha's. "And evertheng else you and I'll straighten out ourselves, between *us*. Martha, answer me. Are you lissnen to me?"

"What's goan on in there?" came Martha's father's hollow voice through the house. It sounded as if he had just looked into the kitchen from the other side and must have heard them talking.

"We're comin, we'll be right there," Martha's mother called to him with false brightness. "Martha?" she whispered sharply.

With docile soft tread Martha turned and went before her mother, who without touching her even slightly was there pushing her implacably from behind. Back through the door into the kitchen, back across that familiar room, the horizontal wood planking of the walls a dull white, above the side table a blue plate that had been hanging there since before Martha could remember, and on the ribbed porcelain side-counter of the sink the stack of dishes that Anne had washed and that Martha was supposed to have dried and put away, the evening chore she had neglected—would she ever have the privilege of performing it again?—and against the opposite wall the wood stove squatting low and dark in the perpetual uncomplaining readiness of its servitude. A room that Reuben himself had been in! Martha stopped at the next door and only barely put her hand against it, feeling drained of blood, cold, too weak to stand. Her mother reached past her and pushed it open and they entered the living room where on the striped horsehair sofa with the disarrayed newspaper in one hand her father sat, leaning back from his own bulk, blinking at them with an expression of peeved incomprehension. He had never let the newspaper pages get so disorderly.

"What is it?" he said—his introduction to a conversation which he thought he already understood the shape of, like a courtroom questioning of known witnesses. Women should keep their daughters properly advised in social matters, on right behavior, and control them fully if need be. But he had been pushed a little off balance by their having kept him waiting so long. Martha saw that his face was filled with a great desire to be relieved of his anxiety; this was the job of women in his life. He who was scarcely ever readily cheerful was forcing a hideously false half-smile. She knew she would now plunge him into shock, and then mortification; then she would feel his rage aimed at her—he who'd once carried her on his shoulders, who'd promised her every toy and trinket and candy he could afford to buy! She felt condemned to death; she felt about to die; if she could have died before she had to speak, she would have welcomed it. Why couldn't one just decide to die and do it? Like deciding to cough.

They could have all gone on as before, on the strength of her false assurances, if only she had lied to her mother. But what of her? If Reuben hadn't just told her they must part, if he wasn't her heart's blood.... She was changed now, anyway; they might as well be changed, too. The thought of his absence, the thought that *already* she had seen him for the last time, made her feel as numb as a board, she could not exist without the promise of him, the life that only six weeks ago she had begun to discover she might live.

Her father pushed himself up with his arms, stood up with work-weariness, still holding the newspaper. "What is it?" he said again, this time almost querulously, almost but not quite fearfully. The little delay had given him time to realize there seemed to be something he had not foreseen and could not control. But he rejected this. "Martha?" he said calmly. Turning his head: "Caroline?"

"Martha has somethin to tell you."

"Martha?" he said again. She couldn't bear to hear him ask again.

Not looking at him, but at the cuffs of his trousers, she said, "I promise—" and then the sob she had held back, before, returned and rushed up out of her, shaking her body, and she felt her mother's hand at her back, though whether to comfort her or to force her onward she had no time to tell. Her head fell down and to her own belly she said, "It *was* me, I was the one who was with Reuben."

Her father was for this last late short instant of the unfolding of things still puzzled, before the truth would break in on him. "Reuben? Who is Reuben? Reuben who?" Then he looked at Caroline's face and his own expression melted, the muscles in his cheeks sagged and his mouth fell open. "Is that the name of that *boy? That* was you? Cain't have been," he said, his voice hoarse. "That's impossible. We didn't raise you that way, you know better'n that, twas some other girl," he said, and added, "if it was inny white girl atall, which I doubt very much. You wouldn't have the reputation of a *cat* if innytheng like that happened in your own famly."

Martha started to turn around but her mother took her by the shoulders from behind and heavily pushed her down to her knees. She dropped under this force and then leaned sideways against his legs.

How had they raised her?

Her thoughts of independence had vanished; she had no strength to carry through her proud secret scheme for herself.

She spoke from within her crying, from under her hair, which had come unpinned and was surrounding her, hiding her. "Please, Daddy, please," she wept. She would do anything for them. "Please, I promise I won't see im again, I promise."

"You won't *see* im? *Again?*" he said, and he pushed, he removed her from himself, he stepped back and his calves were against the sofa, he couldn't get farther away. Slowly with each word, his evident disgust rising, he said, "*You* will never live in this *house* again!" His eyes opened wider. "*You* will never live in this *town* again," he shouted at her, waving his arms, the newspaper rustling and flapping. "And that boy will be a lesson—yet *another* lesson, although I didn't *approve* of that other theng—that boy will be a lesson to others I kin guarantee you *that*.

"*Dammit* Caroline I told you and I was *right* that we should *move* from this town! Damn *both* of you!"

199

"No!" Martha said, "No!" She took a step on her knees and put her arms around his calves and held him tightly, her head against his rigid legs. He could not get away from her, she looked up at him and her absurd hair that Goddamned hair half like niggerhair *where* in the hell had she got *that* fell away from her face and her face crumpled into a soundless mask, her mouth open and pulled down at the corners, her eyes clamped shut, she was repugnant to him but he could not escape, he couldn't think what this meant, he looked up at the ceiling but what he saw there, too, was his God-damned daughter, he imagined a dark boy, he could see it in his mind, the man was touching her, was pulling at her clothes, and she was letting him, the sight of it made him feel the greatest disgust and alarm of his life.

"No, please, I promise, I promise," she said. "Mama, Mama," she called while clinging to her father.

"Charles," her mother said. "Charles, *listen* to er, she wants to be good!"

"This is too *Gotdamn late* for lissnin," he spat out, and Caroline cried again, "Charles!" Then she whimpered, "Oh, don't blaspheme, even in anger." Futilely he looked down to each side of him, about to break away entirely, to bolt from the room, but Martha was still clinging to him, crying, saying "Daddy, please."

"*What* have you *done* with this girl?" he shouted at his wife.

"Please," Martha wept, as he dragged her a step sideways toward the front door. He succeeded in drawing one leg out of her grasp and he shook the other one violently. She fell away from him and he hurled the flapping newspaper at his wife. He looked down at Martha and his face contorted. "Did this boy *touch* you?" he shouted. He reached down and caught the shoulder of her dress and with a sudden convulsion of his own rage he ripped it down. She shrieked; her naked shoulder was exposed to him, and the side of her breast. "*Did* he?" he shouted. Martha collapsed on herself, curling up on her side and crying. It seemed for a moment that he was gathering himself to kick her. To put his heavy shoe into her. He thought his shoe might have hit Martha somewhere already when he threw her off his leg, it had felt like it but he wasn't sure. He didn't want to think about it.

In a struggle with himself that was clearly visible to his wife he only just resisted doing it, then he turned and went out the door as fast as he could go without actually trying to do something he had not done in twenty years, which was to run.

Martha crossed her arms to put her hands on opposite shoulders, hugging herself, and Caroline guided her to her feet and back to the horsehair sofa and hovered over her as if she had a fever, talking steadily, coaching her on how best to beg his forgiveness.

Then suddenly he was back, damp with rain and looking angry and frightened and dangerous. He stalked stiff-legged straight to Martha and said to her, "Who's *seen* you with im, who *knows* about this?" And to his wife, "I'm goan talk to that boy from the mill that came in here to see you, I'm goan talk to im mysef this time, I'm goan git to the bottom of this!" But he didn't wait for her to answer, since he knew that no one at all had to know and there would still be the obligation on him, as Martha's father, to do something like what was done in such matters. Anyway there must be dozens who knew, and himself virtually the last to hear of it. There would be talk of it all over the Goddamned mill, and *he* hadn't known. He had to make out it was an attack on his daughter, he had to *correct* the false impression, in the whole Goddamned town, it might be, that she had been in any way whatsoever willing. He drew back a hand to strike his wife in the face. But he managed to keep from doing it.

He crossed to the other side of the room. He was not eager to take up his obligation. It was something that happened once in a great while, and he did not want to participate in it, and would have avoided it if any other white man had come to him to ask, and had indeed managed to avoid it, without anyone thinking much the worse of him, only—this was the irony—a few nights before. But this was *his* daughter. His *daughter.*

So he began to say the same things over again, ranting at Martha and her mother, who hurriedly got the family Bible and was trying to interrupt him to show him Martha would swear on it that she was pure and that it all meant nothing and nothing like it would ever happen again. She reached down and grasped Martha's limp hand and held it on the Bible and tried to get him to stop and listen and to get Martha to wake from her trance of shock and sit up and swear on the Holy Bible that she was sorry for what she had done and she had done *nothing* and she would never see the boy again. But Martha was without strength, collapsed on the floor, her eyes shut, sobbing. And he would not listen as Caroline grew more and more shrill. On and on, till slowly Martha got herself up, her torn dress hanging from her, and left the room and with leaden movements pulled her pretty linen-covered valise that her mother had given her from under her bed and began to walk back and forth to her dresser, packing the valise with clothes; she had lost everything, she had lost Reuben, she had no idea where he was going, she would never find him again, and she had lost her own home, her own family and her own town, while her father and mother were still in the living room, shaking it with his bitter anger and her pleading. "Look, Charles, look!" her mother had tried to say to him over his rage, "She's swearin it on the Holy Bible, Charles. Look!" And then to Martha, "C'mon, honey, do like I told you, Marthie?" And now Anne was behind Martha in the doorway, wide-eyed in her nightgown, her mouth open.

Then it died down, and Martha's mother came into her room, pushing Anne to one side and shooing her out, and silently she took clothes from Martha's hand and put them back in the drawer and began emptying the valise and saying in a quiet, soothing voice, "It's goan be all right, honey, he's not goan send you *away*, this's where you b'long, here in your own room, sweetheart," and she put the empty valise back under the bed and led Martha to lie down, and sent Anne, who was still in the doorway, for a cool wet cloth for Martha's forehead. After Anne brought it her mother ordered her out and shut the door. She sat on the edge of Martha's bed and pulled Martha's dress together to cover her shoulder and breast, and stroked Martha's limp hand. "It's goan be all right, he'll be a good deal calmer in thc mornin, although his mind, whatever he's decided, will be set, for certain. And we'll talk about it then, you *did* the most important theng: you tole the truth and you said you were sorry. Somehow with God's great help we're goan git through this." Her face was sweating.

The house had grown almost instantly quiet after Martha's mother left her. With feverish energy Martha leapt up and dressed silently, much too warmly, in clothes for an outing or gardening or some such robust outdoor activity, and packed the valise with as many clothes as she was able to crush into it, and her exercise books of notes on Reuben and two novels she had gotten from Clara and would not return. She sneaked out the back door and ran and walked and ran, as fast as she could make herself go, to the place she had always called nigger town, two desperate miles of night and rain, it was so dreadfully dark she almost couldn't see, running and stumbling in the streets, past the shapes of houses, this street and then this street and then this, rushing. She arrived with burning lungs and trembling legs and muddy feet and hem at the house of Mr. Grooms, where she burst in, soaked by the rain, without knocking.

And the old man woke with a start and came out of his room carrying a cudgel, and in the dark he saw the white girl fall to the floor of his parlor, her valise thudding down with her. She was saying, or moaning and weeping, "They know. They know." Mr. Grooms stood, imprisoned by a lifetime of enforced habit, debating with himself in fear, before he could resolve to close the door behind her and most carefully, most tactfully and gently, help her to her feet, necessarily and most unfortunately having to touch her in order to do it. Reuben was not even around, he must have gone out again, he had been coming in and going out, he was very restless.

She wanted to wait in Reuben's room. Mr. Grooms asked her please to leave his house right away. They were standing in the dark among the still-damp ghostly hanging laundry. She said no, she said she had run away. "Yes ma'am, I'm sure you have, but you ain't run very far." They didn't know where she was, she said. "No ma'am, I'm sure they don't yet," he said, "but no matter where you go, they kin find you. And people know where Reuben lives." No, they wouldn't find her, she said, and she sat down in a rickety chair, exhausted but resolute, her eyes glowing. He asked her please to let him move the chair away from the window, and he did not offer to light a lamp. There they sat together, scarcely able to see each other, waiting for Reuben, while in his mind Mr. Grooms ran over all the places on the route from her house to his where even in these late dark hours and under the dark clouds and rain someone had most certainly seen her pass and was even now knocking at her father's door in the middle of the night, rousing him and others to come after her.

Reuben entered softly, rain-wet as well, and Martha leapt up and threw herself to him, saying, "They know, they know," and held herself to him, he could not deny himself, and he saw that the decision had been made already for them both, and again by her. He had only an instant to get his things from his room, to shake Mr. Grooms's hand and embrace the old man and say good-bye to him and to lead Martha back out into the soft rain, carrying her valise and his box.

There were two roads westward from Three Rivers. One was wide and went by the entrance of the sawmill. The other was small and went behind it. Both of them were bounded by tangled second growth where the forests had been logged years before. Reuben and Martha had to go that way to get started, because to the east there were only open fields, and the main roads north and south offered no hiding place for miles, that Reuben knew of. Without speaking, treading carefully and as quickly as she could go, she was excited and terrified to go, to be escaping together, Reuben took them the long way around the town through scruffy woods and black streets, away from white houses. It cost them some time. He wondered if there might be someone at the mill, which they had to pass close by, but it was as empty as if neither man nor beast had ever stood within or near it—the hulk of it, with piles of logs and lumber around it, with towers and poles sticking up from it, an unlit grim immensity in the dim night, a maw that was waiting to begin again eating the forests being brought to it daily by little men. Silently Reuben and Martha went past it toward where he hoped her father would never find them, without Reuben even having found out from her yet what had happened. He did not feel he was himself. He felt he was betraying her by not being as happy as she was to be fleeing. But who was he, now that all this was happening? She clung tight with her beautiful hand to his arm as he led.

Epilogue

"As Confederate veterans and law-abiding citizens of Texas and of the United States we are violently, vehemently and eternally opposed to the practice of burning a human being for any crime whatsoever. We appeal to all Confederate veterans, their wives and daughters, and to that great and glorious organization the Daughters of the Confederacy, one and all, to arise in their might and by precept and example, voice and pen, moral force and influence, help put a stop to this diabolical, barbaric, unlawful, inhuman and ungodly crime of burning human beings. We are inalterably opposed to the lynching of a human being, except perhaps for the one unmentionable crime."

—The L. W. Dickerson Camp of
Confederate Veterans of Texas

Part Three: Still 1910

32

Tea

A shouting mob of men (just like the one she had seen from her window when it went out with Ray Newsome on a rope to brandish his fate at the Negroes) seething with raised arms and open mouths, crowded up against her house, and her father stood in the doorway yelling at them, *"You can't have her!"*

The doctor was looking at her over his eyeglasses, his lips set in a toothy, threatening smile.

An automobile came careening at the buggy and Antonio shied and half-reared and she lost the reins and he was running toward the river.

They were walking. Reuben was leading her fast, too fast, pulling her by her left hand while she groped and flailed with her right to steady herself. The trees around them were moving, too, the near ones edging past them quickly backwards, and the circle of trunks beyond them more slowly, and the far ones standing almost still, but watching her.

On the hanging vines she had to brush away in front of her, there were shiny white unopened buds that looked like large eye-teeth.

A crescent moon rose before her, leaning back on its curve, making a tipped bowl big enough to hold a town. And then another, after it. And another. Three moons, or many.

Reuben was looking at her, looking into her eyes, his face inches from her face, his eyes brown, deep brown, black, tunnels, openings she was falling through.

In her kitchen, on the floor, a snake came out of a knothole in the floor, all the way out, and was in the room, and its head began to rise and fall, to bob, and Pilgrim was screaming, "It's quiled up! Look out Miss Martha! He's goan strike you!"

Following tomorrow's explosion and fire in the law offices of Mr. Clarke, the widow will announce that a memorial to her husband will be built in the town cemetery, she will say that he did not die in the fire, but of his deep heartache over his daughter, who was turned by witchcraft into a snake.

—How *long* since that Clarke girl was kidnapped by that half-breed Indian?

—A month?

—Oh no, it's been several years, if it's been a day.

—Was in September, wadn't it?

—Her pa would have paid any ransom to have her back, that girl could do no wrong, in his eyes.

—Don't say what'd happen to that degenerate mongrel.

—That's for certain.

—It's a tragedy.

—The poor thing was probably murdered and her body left in the wilderness, that's what they say.

—Oh, certain of it. It's just horrifying.

—You can't say what would be enough of a punishment for a filthy creature like that nigger that carried her off.

Sobs racking her, and unable to catch her breath, under green water, which way is up? Up she swims, her lungs blistering inside, her heavy, heavy thick clothes, layers and layers and layers of them heavy under the water, she can't even raise her arms, and she wants to wake, she's desperate to wake, please wake me.

A rooster cawed its first two notes in her ear and then stopped dead as if someone had caught it by its stretched-out scrawny neck.

"Martha?" He was here, he really was looking into her face. She looked down at herself, half-dressed, disheveled. Her clothes heavy with the damp. "Here's a tea I made for you. From leaves I know," he said.

He handed her a little tin cup and stood up and retreated from her a few steps. She realized she must be staring at him starkly.

"Martha?" he said.

"I'm all right," she said. And drank a sip of the hot pale bitter liquid.

She reached to him with her free hand, to bring him back to her.

He knelt down near her. She let the cup drop, spilling. She put her arm around his neck and pulled him sharply to her. Off balance, pulled down, he tumbled onto her, and then recovered himself and sat next to her, holding her inside his arms while she seemed to be trying to make herself smaller, smaller, pulling her knees up, tucking her head down, grappling herself as close to him as she could.

33

Together

The palm of Martha's hand lay on Reuben's bare back; he was sitting beside her where she lay clothed only in her chemise and underdrawers, in a sunny hidden spot he had found for them. Through a band of pines near the road, at the end of night, in intermittent showers of chilling rain and wind, he had seen a different darkness which revealed itself to be an extensive wood of beech and magnolia trees, through which he and she had moved easily while the sky was lightening to wet gray. The tree tops were like a ceiling over them, and their feet trod on a thickness of brown curled leaves. There had seemed no need for silence or caution. It felt as if no one had ever walked under those trees before. Then they had come on the sheltered hidden place, and stopped. And removed their clothes to dry out. The weather had been rainy, without cease, till this morning.

The first night they had walked roads, crossed ditches, waded up creeks, picked their way through thickets, taken new roads, backtracked and jumped off their own trail, till she could scarcely stand. The second night they had heard dogs, but distant, moving away. They went long ways through thick brush and gnarled trees, forcing their way along narrow deer paths, scratched and torn by dead twig-ends and thorns. The third night they came out onto dirt roads and walked them in the darkness, breathing more freely, struggling only with the air instead of branches and uneven ground. The fourth night, hungry and thirsty, back in woods, they skirted clearings, they waded in water, got out, backtracked again to water, waded a distance again, her shoes almost ruined long since, her feet blistered. He went barefoot. They came out on other roads, walked them a while, then struck off through more woods and thicket.

Now it was sweet to have arrived at this tiny open space within walls of trees and brush. Here they had laid their blanket down on soft weeds; but could not sleep in their state of exhaustion, rashness, fear, excitement; and had held each other in silence, had rested in each other's arms, and then had warmed to each other and taken half their clothes off, and for the first time in these four days and nights together, scared and heedless, they had made love.

(He thought it through again: he had made a pile of leaves and laid their blanket over it and they had taken off their shoes and then their outer clothes, but then while she kept the back of her chemise beneath her she had lifted the front to her waist, and reached and pulled her drawers down and off one leg, and looked at him, and slowly, he was almost afraid to look at her, afraid to see her watching him, he had pulled down his underdrawers and awkwardly knelt before her, in the arch of her legs.)

They fitted their bodies to each other as they did fit with a perfection, and moved and shuddered, first she, then he, and their muscles softened and again they were two, lying against each other. She sat up and studied herself and him, their naked shapes— she looked closely at the semen on his thigh, she put her fingertip to a drop of it and tasted it. And lay back down against him.

Their legs were aching. Leaves overhead were whispering in a humid breeze. Martha's dress was torn, she had small welts and scabs as narrow as threads on her ankles and arms, and he did too. Hazy sunlight was coming through the clouds. Lying on her back, shading her eyes with her right forearm, Martha was absently smoothing Reuben's back with her free hand. She was so sore and tired she could barely move, now.

How could he not be patient with her, and loving, since she seemed a miraculous presence accompanying him. To look at her made him happy. Several times, in the midst of their worst fatigue, as he insisted and coaxed her and chided her to keep moving, he had laughed out loud with happiness and had acknowledged to himself that he was certainly crazy.

Their clothes were heavy on them, and their burdens—her valise, his box, a water jug and a sodden rolled blanket—seemed too heavy to be worth carrying. He carried everything, and was content if she could come along unburdened. Her precious things were precious to him.

They walked when it rained and kept walking after it stopped raining, to dry their clothes on them as they moved. Rain was good. Rain washed away tracks and scent and slowed their pursuers, too. At every approach of wagon or horse they hid quickly, till the road was empty again. Only once were they completely surprised, when just after dawn at a sharp turn in the sandy road they had come upon a black family on foot, all standing still beside the road; waiting for someone or something—a neighbor, an apocalypse. Martha had lowered her head and hurried past them; Reuben had mumbled hello and put himself in front of her again. He led them on dirt wagon trails, small roads, woodland paths. After that encounter they had gotten off the roads even before dawn. They avoided open fields at all hours. Thus their toil by night, and only fitful, frightened bug-tormented sleep by day.

She moved her hand up and down his back gently, absent-mindedly, comforted by the warmth and smoothness of his skin as she lay on her back, in her own thoughts, her eyes closed under her forearm. She felt not pain now, not aching and soreness but a kind of buzzing and trembling in her limbs.

When they were inside that moment, sometimes, she didn't feel anymore like the Martha she had been, but around the edges of herself somewhere, somehow, she let go, she let herself go into him, and she let him come into her and it was like a moment of being as large, as open, as airy as the day around them, all the way to the edge of sight, it was all her and she was all of it. Sometimes.

There were other moments, she turned away from them. Who was he, then? Where was she? What was she doing? Like she was up in a tree overhead or slowly flying past in the air, some bird with big black wings, she looked down at herself, she saw herself lying on her back with her drawers down, some dirty woman lying there who was herself, she didn't feel what he was doing, it wasn't her down there, it was him, and she was doing it for him, he wanted her to do it, he liked it.

She could see, she could count, the very folds in the curtains of her room at home. It would be quiet there. Now. It was quiet here, too. Reuben's skin cool under her palm.

The woods were still except for the cooing of a dove, and a mockingbird singing from a treetop farther off, loud and saucy and inventive. The daylight would not fade for a long while yet, and when it did, they would have to strike out yet again. Reuben had said that this night there would be nearly a full moon to light the way. Wouldn't there be people on the lookout for them wherever they went, wouldn't word of them be in the telephone wires and the ink of the newspapers?

That she touched him at all was a bodily revelation to him; that anyone touched him as she did. He had shaken hands, hands felt no different for their color. The palm of the hand couldn't see. Whosoever's it was.

But no one had touched him. Francie had hugged him to her big body. He remembered times when he had been with a woman, and she had touched him—his cheek, his chest, his cock; his body had registered the sensation of touch, but as if he himself had not been in it: it was like some other thing that they had touched. No one he could remember had made him feel that she was touching him, himself, the person he was. He wanted to do everything in the world he could do, for her. What she wanted.

His mother must have touched him, as mothers touch their children, protectively and tenderly; to keep something inside them that is escaping, leaking out, as they grow older. He had seen that, hc had thought about it, but he could not remember it. When he'd run from Francie's house he had gone back toward his mother's grave. But had not found it. The roads hadn't looked at all the way he'd been sure he remembered them so clearly. Then he had thrown himself into life with others, or life alone, into his wanderings from town to town, and made out for himself as well as he could. But had not been touched. Mr. Grooms had been fatherly to him; but had not touched him.

The warmth of Martha's hand went into him a little way; he yielded to a shudder—of chill, of edginess, of wonder at the sensation of her hand on his back. Her hand rose up to his nape, to his hair, and he could only look up or away, not at her.

She had said to him with a sidelong look in her eyes that she didn't have any experience of love, yet when she had kissed him he felt that it was he who was unprepared, although he had more than once followed a woman to a room or a hayloft or a summer field, where sometimes for love of him, once for a coin, women had taken him and, sometimes amused, or sometimes impatient, with his ignorance, had given him instruction in his pleasure and his obligations. But what he'd learned had to do with the body only and now it was all of him that was taken and mixed with her and then released again back into just himself, changed.

They were going west, mostly. As he had gone with his mother, but much farther along the westering roads than she had ever walked. However, toward no Nations. There was no such Nation for him and her. There were creeks too deep and rivers too wide and baygalls they could not struggle through and open land where they would be easily seen, and Reuben had to make turns and detours, had to confuse their trackers, all the while keeping the town of Three Rivers at their backs.

They had not gone very far compared to how much distance men on horseback could travel, and men in automobiles. If they knew which direction to take. Stopping by day in deep thicket to rest, to eat (at first, the food Mr. Grooms had given to Reuben in haste; now, only what Reuben could find or steal; and they were very hungry), to drink from the small water jug he had given them, too, which they refilled at streams, they lay hidden wondering at what hour that first night Martha's absence had been discovered, not knowing who might be in pursuit and how close the pursuers might have come. Martha said over and over to him that she just wanted to endure sufficient distance for them to hide more comfortably—for them to take a train—and he always said back to her that she was strong, they were doing fine, they would make it. He considered that taking any train was impossible even with the subterfuge of boarding and traveling separately; he believed no distance was going to be great enough; but he did not tell her this.

Like the deer, they came out of hiding at dusk. But without the graceful strength of the deer. Still tired. Hungry. Bitten and scratched and sore. During the day they even hid where deer had hidden, where grass and weeds inside a thicket had been flattened, where a doe had lain. And they scratched the bites they got from the fleas the deer had left behind in the grass, and the mosquitoes that fed on deer, too.

There would come times when they could not hide so well; there would come a time to find a place to live, and where would that be? Some city in the North or the West. Maybe finally they would find a town from which to travel on, by train; maybe she was right, they could spend Mr. Grooms's money on good clothes, and get on separately, and go all the way to Chicago.

The little world they had left behind did not resound any longer in their ears, except in moments of fright when she imagined it and he listened hard for it. There might as well have been no one at all looking for them, so well did Reuben choose their path and conceal them from others. She would say it seemed like now they could walk out on the open road. But he said no.

They saw not one soul.

At some moments she thought it would almost have been a relief to have heard men ride close by them, looking for them—as long as they were not discovered.

She had nightmares.

As they were walking she would sometimes talk softly but not to him, only to herself, and he could not hear what she said.

She would stop him sometimes, reach ahead to grab his blue shirt and pull him back to her, and he would set down his box and her suitcase and put his arms around her waist, and she would put her arms around his neck and they would hold each other tightly for a moment. She didn't dare say she couldn't walk any further; she didn't want him to be mad at her.

Beside a deep-woods clear-running creek they made a real kind of camp on the sixth morning, and he said he must go out again to find them something to eat. She was aching with hunger. To him, she looked haggard, but perhaps a little calmer. Dirty and weary and lovely.

He looked smaller, to her.

Out of her suitcase she took two dresses and clean underclothes and another pair of black shoes that laced up over her ankle and one pair of slippers and a tiny leather kit snapped shut, and other things he had never seen before. She laid her clean things on a few tall springy weeds in a patch of sun, and while he watched her, she took off all her dirty clothes and stood naked in the air and rose up on her toes and stretched her arms up. The first time she had un-dressed completely in their flight. She smiled at him when she saw he was looking at her with something like wonder mixed with his appetite for her.

"You've got a bruise!" he said, when he saw the purple blotch on her breast. "How did y'get it?" He moved close to her. But she turned away from him with her arms folded over her breasts.

"It's nothin," she said. She wouldn't tell him any more about it. But his seeing it sent her back into her anger at her mother, at her father. Which she did not tell him, either.

She rinsed her body in the creek. Water like hands of angels.

He saw sadness come into her face as she turned to her things and studied her clean clothes, which would only become filthy, and then she looked for a while at what was left on the ground—her torn dress, and the now filthy one she had been wearing, and her dirty underclothes and her other small things. And two books—which surprised him. If she wore the good shoes now and threw the muddy split ones out, then the good ones too would be ruined in a few days. The inventory of their possessions, and even of their passions, was small.

He wanted to cheer her. He went to his box and slowly pulled the lid off, did it carefully and evenly to keep the little nails straight, and then brought out the leather pouch and handed it to her. Her eyes grew large, she expected to see the coins inside; but the gold ones surprised her. "Where'd you git it?" she said.

"Mr. Grooms give it to me," he said. "It might be all that he had saved up."

He went on, "When we git to wherever we're headed, we kin buy you new thengs."

Her eyebrows turned up in the middle of her brow: this thought had not cheered but rather sorrowed her. She handed the pouch back to him and he returned it to the box. He picked up a stone from the bank of the shallow creek and set it beside the box, for tapping the lid back on with, later. He put the good luck charm around her neck. "That's from Mr. Grooms, too. For luck," he said. She studied it. The string on which the old coin was threaded was awful. She didn't want it against her skin.

He figured they needed to rest an extra night, if he was to keep her moving at all. A few feet into the woods, where sunlight reached but she was sheltered from sight, he made her a thick bed of pine straw under the blanket. She lay down on it, with the early sun coming in to her at an angle. He went off carrying Mr. Grooms's knife and a throwing stick he'd already made.

"Reuben!" she called after him; he turned and saw she had leapt up again.

He rushed back to her whispering loudly, "What is it? You mustn't yell with all your voice like that, somebody could hear."

His hands firmly grasping her shoulders failed to stop her from shaking.

"I'm afraid," she said. Naked, still.

"Don't be afraid," he said. She hugged herself to him, into him, and he waited, holding her. Silent and motionless they stood till he separated himself from her, and looking at her he sought a reassurance. She smiled precariously and bowed her head, and he released her—to see if, like a balanced pole, she would stand by herself. She did, and again he walked away, noiselessly and more slowly this time, looking back at her several times, his eyebrows raised in a question which she answered yes by not calling to him again. Or perhaps reassuring himself that she was still there, that when he left her side she would not, out of anxiousness, simply disappear into thin air.

When he was gone, she sat down at the center of their small circle of things and pulled her knees up to her chest and hid her head between them and began to shiver. Despite the heat. She wanted to put her knees over her ears and shut out the silence of the woods. She wanted to be hidden from it. It was so naked to be outdoors, to have no shelter, there was no hiding, no protection from anything, not the wind and rain and sun and bugs, not even a falling leaf, a twig, a spider. So naked. But she did not dress. She put the insides of her knees against her ears and wrapped her arms around her head and knees and was afraid even to move, and began to imagine that something had sneaked up and was standing behind her, watching her, ready to leap on her if she moved the tiniest bit and she would be killed, a wolf, a panther, some men. It was there, it was right there, it was right behind her neck, it was behind her right at her naked back. She had chills and could not help from shivering and then, she couldn't help herself, involuntarily she hunched her shoulders in anticipation of teeth in her nape and then she had to go the rest of the way, she stood up all at once and was swaying on her feet, dizzy and there was nothing, nothing was near her, only the sun coming down into their hiding place and a bird chirping on a branch and the tops of the trees swaying a little. She stood with her shoulders still hunched up protecting her neck, she couldn't quite let go and when finally she did they ached and she had to force herself to lower them, let her shoulders down, let them fall, till she was standing in a normal way alone in the woods lost somewhere alone.

And still did not dress herself again, but arranged her things on the ground, slowly, setting them in order, putting herself at the center of them, curling up on the cloth of the blanket and lying with her eyes open and not seeing, her ears unstopped and not hearing.

He came back some time later, disappointed in his hunt because he had nothing to use but the throwing stick, something for a boy, he could not likely bring in anything with it more than one squirrel at a time, as he had done now, yet again, and because all the time he was gone he was worrying about her. When she saw the squirrel she shrank from it, from him. As he'd known she would. She told him she had been frightened—after an hour or so she had decided, she couldn't help it, that he was gone, that he had left her and was not coming back. She hadn't known what to do, and thought for a minute about leaving everything where it was—"everything," she said again, meaning how little she had—and going back in the direction where she thought the road lay.

But—he thought—I won't leave her, ever. "Oh no, don't ever do that!" he said. "Don't even think that! Don't go nowhere without me, because I'm takin care of you, I'm not goin to leave you."

"Aren't you?" she said.

"No!" He didn't ever want to feel sorry for her, he was afraid to feel that, he wanted her to be strong—strong as he'd thought she was at the beginning.

He looked at their little camp. She had made something of a nest for them. She had defined all the wild space that was not their small space by its contrast to the neat placement of his box and her valise, her dirty dress and underclothes, wet from her having rinsed them in the stream, and now drying on branches, and the blanket on which she had lain with the rolled-up torn dress for a pillow.

"Why do you keep that dress that's torn?" he asked her.

"I'll mend it," she said. "I can mend your thengs, too, for you." Beautiful and naked, standing in the warm sun; it would be a little while yet before cold days came. He felt odd that he was clothed.

He was holding the little gutted carcass by the tail. She didn't like the look of his hands, which were bloody and dirty. She turned away. He put the squirrel down on a rock and gathered wood for a fire. Their hunger made the risk of smoke unavoidable. He skinned the squirrel and spitted it on a green stick and when the flames died down to steady heat he stuck the end of the green stick in the ground so that it leaned over the flames, and he went down to the water and washed his hands and took off his shirt and washed his arms and neck and face. He came back shirtless and turned the meat every so often. Till it was blackened. The rock where he had skinned it was stained with blood.

He brought the meat to her where she was kneeling on the blanket, white except for the thick dark hair on her head and the patch of hair between her legs. He squatted down next to her, on the ground. He tore off a small piece of the flesh and held it up and she looked at him, in his eyes, and at the meat, and then she opened her mouth to be fed. Cautiously she accepted it but her gorge rose, as it had every time she'd eaten the squirrels he killed and cooked. She felt she would choke. He was watching and she forced herself to chew it and swallow.

"We'll git somethin to eat tomorrow that you'll like. You'd like some rabbit."

"I've had rabbit. At home," she said, pulling her mouth into a brief smile. She felt sunken, having disappointed him.

She chewed several bites more, and swallowed each hard. She would eat it for him. Then she stopped. She tucked her legs under her to one side. She avoided his eyes.

He waited a few moments, and neither of them spoke. He ate the rest of the squirrel.

"If I could kill a deer, we'd be eatin like home," he said. "When we stop somewhere, for a while, I might could find a way to kill one."

"I'm thirsty," she said. He jumped up and went to the creek with the tin cup and brought it to her dripping. Despite the water's clarity it tasted brown and ferny to her but she drank it down, chasing the taste of the gamey meat that lingered at the sides of her mouth.

She lay down, looking at him as he sat cross-legged in his trousers, shirtless and barefoot, by the fire. Its light was invisible in the splinters and shafts of sunlight that came down through the trees, and the swath of light from the side, from open ground; its warmth was superfluous now.

He roused himself again to heat a little water in the cup and make his tea for her. He liked doing that. It was easier than talking.

But they did talk, in the hours when they lay waiting for night, fully clothed again, side by side, not touching, as if, at this moment, they had never yet touched. Waiting for night, when they should sleep, so they could walk instead, so they could keep running away.

"Since we've known each other," she said to him, "I've told you a lot about me. Haven't I." They could talk to each other while looking up into the clouds that were moving into their portion of sky, from beyond the treetops, and then moving away from them.

"You didn't tell me so much," he said.

"You haven't told me so much about you as I'd like, either." She could regain her strength if he would give her some of his.

"And with all your questions that you ask?" He smiled.

"Seems like you're still alone some way," she said, "even now that we're together."

"I do?"

"I feel sometimes like you're somewhere inside somewhere, where I can't be close to you. Come over here, with me."

He was astonished: to himself he felt so transparent, it hadn't occurred to him that he might be as opaque to her as she was to him, now that they had time to try to know each other more deeply. He turned his head to look at her. He could tell she knew he was looking.

"I thenk we're just about the same mystery to each other. Don't you?" he said.

She said, "Tell me somethin more bout your mama."

In the still woods around them there was not even the sound of the creek.

"I will. I will," he said, his voice softer. He turned his head back to the sky. They were quiet a little while.

Fragments of memories appeared and disappeared in his mind. There was no connecting them into something he could tell her; they were images.

Martha searched for his hand and took it in hers.

"I saw a scissortail," he said, "that time I got bit by the snake, before we met, you remember I told you."

She nodded. "And I was thinkin bout that," she said. "When I was little, Mama told me, too, people said scissortail'd fly down and cut off your nose, nose of a child, if you were bad. But I could tell she didn't believe it, so I didn't believe it. I can see her pointin to the bird."

"It's a pretty bird," he said.

In her mind's eye Martha saw her mother—that irritating manner and expression, those hands that had soothed her when she was small.

"What did she look like?" she said.

He pondered. The tattered checked dress. Her bare feet, her hands—small, dark, callused and cracked with work—they seemed much older than the rest of her. "She looked something like me, I guess. Don't know *what* she looked like to other people. She got sick, she got weak in her body, and couldn't walk like she had, and we stopped where we was. Where we just happened to be."

Martha waited.

"I think she was a beautiful woman," Reuben said. "She had big pretty eyes." He could see those eyes looking into him—tearful eyes but proud of him and he could feel her trying to put strength into him with her pride.

"Same color as yours? A kind of greeny brown?"

"Could be."

The awful taste of the squirrel meat was still in her mouth. She wanted to clean her teeth. The creek, despite its own unpleasant taste, was right there. But she didn't want to let go of his hand.

The world outside her life was moving in a way more comprehensible to him than to her; he always knew what to do next and she had no idea. But now that they were also free, she wanted him to stop for a minute always thinking ahead and behind, to bring himself back from the road they were traveling, to be with her completely sometimes. There was some of his attention she wanted that she hadn't gotten.

"It's hard for me to thenk that you came out of *your* mama and daddy," he said. So he was thinking of something else entirely.

She didn't want to talk about them right now. She was afraid to be as angry at them as she wanted to be.

"It's hard for *me*," she said, "to thenk I don't know where in the world *you* came from, Reuben. Like you might'z well've had no mother, nor father, no famly innywhere, nor even had a house to live in when you were growin up. Like you might jest disappear all over again, back to somewhere else. I don't know where."

"I won't disappear. Nobody ast me bout my mother since I'z a boy but you. I been thinkin for years bout what'd happen next, today, tomorrow, that's all." He wanted her to feel better. "I got her back, a little bit, when I met you, though—cause you wanted to know bout her."

"I hope you did get her back, some."

(They were standing still, his mother and he, waiting. Her hair was matted, her clothes dirty, but something in her face was still her patient self. Sweet to him. He could feel how she focused her remaining power of life around him. And two knobs with uncanny slits in them, knobs the size of his fists he was clenching as he stood next to his mother, lay on the water beside the levee road where they were waiting for a white man and his wife up in their wagon to decide whether to hire on these two Indians and carry them home. The knobs rose up as eyes that widened on a long gnarled head and an alligator smiled wickedly at Reuben with a thousand pointed teeth.)

34

Behind Them

It was the quiet middle of the day, quieter because of the silence of children who might have been playing.

Inside Mr. Corinthian Grooms's parlor there was a jumble of furniture, much of it broken. Clothes and linens that had been hanging to dry on thick twine strung crisscross through the room, an eccentric old man's notion of drying clothes, indeed, lay on the floor trampled and torn. There were muddy footprints and even marks of horses' hooves on these clothes.

A glass-framed picture from the wall, some keepsakes and other things from tabletop or shelf—all were broken on the floor. A kerosene lamp lay shattered among them; the kerosene had leaked into cloth and wood.

In one bedroom, a thin pine-wood bureau had been ransacked and its contents were everywhere, also trampled and torn; the bed was on its side; the window shattered. The windows all around the house were broken. In the other bedroom, smaller, the same had been done and the walls scribed by charcoaled stick-ends with a string of large K's. Newspapers lay scattered, open, torn, around the room.

In the kitchen everything was destroyed, smashed, thrown down; food had been poured out and lay spoiled with all the other ruination on the floor.

Out the back door in the yard, a wash cauldron had been overturned and shot through with bullet holes; sticking out of the open door of the tiny shed or stable were the legs of a dead horse.

At the front of the house, the door had been broken in. Drooping like a flag of surrender from a post of the front porch where it had been nailed was a man's white shirt.

In the bright daylight, no one was in the road before the house, nor in it farther down, in the village, either. All was deserted.

35

Farther

In the years before Reuben had returned to Three Rivers—
when he had lived out in the open by avoiding any situation in
which other people had occasion to suspect him or be cautious
around him, when he had made a kind of life between white and
black, accepting his few possibilities and contenting himself with
what work he could find, willing to take food and lodging almost
anyplace he had found it—he had been wandering without freedom but he had avoided obligation and stayed out of danger. Now
he was still wandering unfree, and every sound wakened him and
he listened hard and turned his head slowly, and looked at Martha
while he listened, and then lay back again in his restless sleep,
where another unnatural dream picked him up and flung him
across visions and torments.

They walked on. With jays screeching overhead they were a
man and woman crossing the leafless gray barren of a chestnut
grove killed by the blight. The tangled shadows of the bare limbs
lay on the ground like webbing they must step through, two small
figures inching across the unprotecting expanse at dawn. Under
late hot sun they lay in thin shade where mosquitoes sought them
out, where red ants were crawling over the ground, and where in
the dead leaves Reuben first beat about with a stick to make sure
no copperhead was sleeping. Shielded from all view but a sparrow's if he could hide them that well each day, they slept in short
spells while around them heavy wasps hovered to test the scent of

their sweat and then swooped away. They rose from hiding in a dry gully at dusk and walked through piney woods, where in the night one sort of owl hooted and another sort screamed. (These were sounds of the night world that had been messages, when he'd been a boy in Grandfather's house.) Through clouds sliding across the slick blackness in which the narrowing moon was submerged Reuben looked for a star known to him. He put his hand to the trunks of trees, he listened to the whistle of a distant train, he calculated distances by the portion of night during which they walked whether on sandy or woodland paths, or down clear roads, or through heavy scrub.

They crossed water and walked in water. He collected roots and nuts and leaves and she ate them. He killed more squirrels. Once again, in hiding, they heard in the distance the unnatural daytime baying of hounds. They were a man and woman who did not move, who scarcely breathed; if dogs struck their trail they would not escape. They escaped.

Once in moonlight Reuben stunned a possum with his throwing stick and then clubbed it several times, but she could not bear for him even to touch it again, much less eat of it; and he left the carcass where he had killed it, unhappy at the waste, and hungry. They were both considerably thinner.

Up a low rise heading through woods at daybreak they came upon an immense leafless fantastic skeletal tree, all as white as bone, where in the high branches sat dozens of buzzards with raw heads, the tree and the ground underneath them crusted and stinking of their feces and vomit. At the appearance of the man and woman half of the birds took to the air, beating laboriously up into the hot sky. And others merely watched the invaders of their precinct, who hurried on past them, the pale woman tripping and catching herself, holding the crook of her elbow against her nose and mouth, the darker man grim-faced but unhurried as she rushed ahead of him with muffled cries.

They walked without sound on pale dirt roads and scuffed through pine needles in an accumulated depth of centuries; they walked over smooth bare stone and under low ancient bluffs; they picked a path slowly through nettles and burrs and sharp-edged weeds; their feet sank in wet mossy soil as soft as flesh under the shade of cedars. On hard sun-baked mud and on rock their feet struck the ground like blocks of wood. Martha pulled her legs forward numbly, she climbed without being able to draw a full breath, and when they rested by day she was so tired she could not settle herself comfortably on the ground. Reuben too was exhausted, but what defeated her—the ceaseless movement, the lack of food—hardened him despite his fatigue. Not because his body was stronger than hers, although it was, but because he had made such fugitive journeys before and nothing they encountered, for all its dispiriting hardship, was not some difficulty he had known already and had gotten through.

He kept thinking about how far they must go. But Martha was at the end of her physical endurance. And what weakened Reuben was her weakness. He felt that he must protect her, that while he could have escaped without difficulty alone, he must ensure that both of them escaped, and this seemed less and less likely. He saw only threats behind them; but when she looked back it refreshed her, for she felt anger. She made herself get up and go on by thinking of that night with her parents, of her father, of James.

In open country where there was no shelter they toiled ahead in dangerous light of stars and a waning moon across pastures and fields ploughed under. They walked till past dawn for several days from island to island of trees to get to full cover again, through fields not yet harvested, their heads floating just at the top of an infinite squared lake of dry rattling corn through which they pushed themselves. And in a hayfield eaten down to stubble they slowly and warily circled a sleepy bull that watched them through half-closed eyes from its chosen post beside a lone oak, whose bark it had rubbed away with its horns and head. The sun rose fast and burned hard even though the season was beginning to cool. They smelled of their animal exertions and their nerves.

They came out of woods at night to a small fenced pasture, and on the other side of it a few deer raised their heads at them at once, with long ears pricked forward, and then turned and bounded over the far fence into trees, their white tails like dim lamps arcing for an instant in the curves of their effortless high leaps. Reuben and Martha crossed the pasture and followed the deer, but for them every fence meant a bending and balancing, just so, between the sharply barbed strands of wire.

Webs of spiders and beards of moss touched their faces in the woods, the welts of poison oak rose on the backs of Martha's hands, and Reuben bound them with wet strips torn from her hem, soaked in an infusion of leaves he prepared with muddy creek water over a tiny angry fire. And he bade her not reach down or up for fear she would bring such poison back to her face.

One day as they made a pitiful camp Reuben nearly stepped on a rattlesnake before it shook its rattles furiously, and after a moment when he stood motionless and Martha watched from behind him, the snake relaxed its striking pose and slid away. His heart was thudding.

That night they walked up a long slope that turned to hummocks of limestone in a meadow of weeds and late burnt wildflowers, and they picked their way among these stones that were like the exposed backs of creatures half-buried where they had collapsed. At the top they could see dim lights of two towns. Reuben led them instead toward the darkness where there were no lights. Martha lingered at the view of the towns. The next day they slept inside the mouth of a damp cave, stale and close. At dusk, before they took to the road again, Martha cried out at a strange and frightening low noise and they fell to the powdery floor of their chamber as a cloud of bats beat its way out over them, choking the whole space, fanning Reuben and Martha with the ancient dead air of the depths of the cave. Reuben and Martha ran out hand in hand and then he went back inside for their things.

Walking beside a deep narrow river they saw a small log turn into a thick cottonmouth snake that contracted double and straightened like a whip and dropped soundlessly into the fast muddy current. Each night they traveled a lesser distance, each day they rested with less regaining of strength. Martha was haggard and going gaunt. Reuben's body had shrunk to an unaccustomed, weakened hardness. Listlessly as she walked Martha asked him how much farther, and pitying her he began to stop when she asked, and watch over her while she rested.

She sat with her back to him, untangling her hair with the precious brush she had brought with her. Her bandaged hands rising and falling. Once, she had wanted nothing more than for him to look at her, but now she would not permit him to. She let her chin fall to her chest; tears ran down her face. Tentatively he touched her shoulder, spoke to her gently, tried to reassure her with imagining out loud how soon they would settle. They would live in a place where there was no danger. He had heard it said that in Oklahoma white and Indian married each other without drawing any trouble on themselves. But that was somewhere northward a considerable distance. They needed a place where they could eat now and sleep now and now heal their fatigue and fear.

In the morning light he made a balm of wet pounded leaves and anointed her bites and scratches and unbound her hands, which were no longer so swollen. She undressed and gave her body to the sunlight. She looked away sharply, gritting her teeth, when he pulled two ticks slowly from her skin. He felt tender pity for her, and he bathed her with a rag torn from her underskirt. This intimacy did not lead them to desire.

They went on. They walked another few nights. Martha kept her nearly ruined second pair of shoes in her valise; her bare feet had toughened. But she had waking frights as something else in her grew weaker.

They were following the flat sandy bottom of a gully through scrubby woods above them on each side where there was no track except the narrowest threads of winding deer paths through brush too thick for a man and woman to penetrate. The gully was completely dry. In winds far overhead clouds were rushing past the last crescent of the moon, covering and uncovering it. And the gully bottom, although it was cracked and rutted here and there by water long since swallowed by the earth, was as clear a road as they could hope to find, where there were no roads.

Each time they came to another of its turns Martha acted like someone was hiding in ambush to leap out at them. Reuben's ears had already reassured him that they were as alone as anyone could be. But the night noises from the woods unsettled her. When she cringed at a sound of rustling to one side, he would reassure her, "There's an armadilla or a possum in the leaves." But she hung back. The first several times this happened he went ahead quietly and found nothing and whispered her forward. She ought not to be so skittish, he told her, after all the days and nights they had traveled, and she was doing fine, she had done so well.

She had, after all, become capable and even courageous. She had lost weight, the roundness was gone from her arms; under her breasts, when he looked at her naked, her ribs could be numbered at a glance. But she had not sickened; when they lay down at dawn to sleep she could even muster her spirits and say, for hope's sake, that she was glad they had run off to a life they couldn't as yet imagine.

But this night she held back, she slowed them down. His fear for her returned: whatever happened, he could never abandon her now, he must carry her through everything. What if they were found because it was unthinkable for him to leave her and it was impossible to escape with her?

"Martha," he called back to her softly. "'S nothin atall, come on this way."

But she leaned away from him, looking past him, ahead.

"Come listen," he said. "Just some little creature."

"They came from home," she said.

"Who did?" he asked her.

"You say little creatures," she whispered. "I know em."

She had left him behind again, as she always did when in her mind she moved away.

"You know em?" he said. He looked ahead, saw nothing, heard nothing, the night was quieter now that the heat of summer had passed. Tree frogs and crickets. Distant thunder.

"They knew we'd come this way," she said.

"*No* one knows where we are. Even I don't know, for certain," he said to her, braving it with a smile. "I know we're safe right now."

"*They* knew," she said. Her face was not as he had seen it before. "I must sit *down*," she said, "and wait for a while, for em to go by."

"You can't do that," he said. "We have to be walkin. There's no one but us. Martha? It's dark now, it's good time for walkin, just a little moonlight, just folla me. Will you?"

She stepped very deliberately to one side and put down the little clay water jug, and sat down on the sand. She pulled her knees up and rested her chin on them, staring straight ahead. "All right," she said, "I won't wait."

The weather was gathering, threatening rain. A thunderstorm had been building, far off to the west, and now it was going to fill the quiet night with its threats. A sizzling bolt of lightning burst out sideways above them, searing its thick knotted length on the dark sky for a long instant like an engorged vein on the very arm of God. She was blinking up at where the flash had been. The immense darkness of the woods around them had turned in the moment of the bolt into a frightening innumerableness of detail and in that lit instant every leaf and twig, every thread of their clothes and hair on their heads, was counted and recorded. Then came the blasting thunder, pushing through their bodies as if they were nothing, and beyond them echoing away over half the world.

The sky was windblown and huge. It seemed to be receding, growing larger, as if the earth were falling away from it. Trees, dim against the restored blackness of the night, were reaching down over the two of them.

Nothing he said brought forth any further comment or response from her. At length, he looked about them carefully to see if the spot she had chosen might invite a snake, and when he was satisfied that it probably wouldn't—but in any case she wouldn't move—he put down his box and her valise and the rolled-up blanket and he sat down cross-legged beside her. When he studied her as she sat still in her trance, resting from something beyond any physical fatigue, he was struck by the evident truth that he had never guessed till now—rather than being more capable than he, knowing more of that promenading world that ruled and only suffered him at its edge, she was an innocent with no experience of being alone or providing for herself, of wandering without need of the familiar. And beyond even this vulnerability: at the mercy of others— whether it was her father's power or even Reuben's own loving mercy. She was not his guide into that world to which she had belonged, but his follower in this one that was only half his—night trails and wilds and a hand-to-mouth survival. Beyond both their worlds must lie some new life he could not yet make out in the hazy imaginings he tried to throw forward into the future.

He breathed shallowly as his thoughts accelerated. He waited with her, cat-napping from time to time, while she remained awake, lost somewhere in a crowding progress of her own thoughts, not aware of him. The storm flew heavily over them without releasing its rain, holding its furious pent-up deluge for a farther place. Steadily, silently, sheet lightning ricocheted around the heavens and finally at dawn was adding its light to the eerie daylight, so filtered and dimmed by the clouded sky that in coming to Reuben and Martha and the gully and the woods it seemed to be trying to find its way to a place it had never been before. Martha stirred and said, "I'm tired, Reuben. Can we sleep here for a while?"

He could scarcely hold his own head up, and he said yes but they must move a little bit, and he led them up the bank of the gully into a circle of brush roofed by thicket and vine. As soon as he made a place for her and laid her down, she was asleep, breathing like a child.

In the afternoon she woke with hunger, said she wanted meat, and would even have eaten squirrel greedily if he could have provided it. Cautiously he went off only a little way, afraid to let her out of his hearing, and found past the brush a grove of pecans, and then saw something beyond that and hurriedly went to look. He brought back his shirt full of new-fallen pecans shaken down by the storm, and he cracked them for her noisily, heedlessly, while he told her he thought that nearby was a place for them to stay a while. She was almost too tired to stand again, and after eating the nuts, terribly thirsty. But she was Martha again, and he was not even sure what had happened in the night; perhaps it was less puzzling than it seemed. He led her out of the brush, through the pecan grove, into a meadow that once must have been a tilled field, now gone back to grasses and late yellow wildflowers. Beyond the flowers was a small abandoned house.

Black-eyed Susans, all the same height, made a yellow pond lapping the banks of trees, lapping the house itself with silent wind-stirred ripples. There was a meandering dark line through the yellow surface that was simply the absence of blossoms where an unhurried deer had grazed through, eating the petals and with small hooves trampling a few stems. Behind the house and on both sides stood thick forest of oak and sweet gum like what they had been walking through along the gully bottom. A grown-over wagon road went off through the trees to the left, under the pecan trees. Reuben said nearby must be a river big enough to have fish in it, he could feel it. Farther into the woods Martha could see here and there groups of trees and bushes lit by sun among the shadows. Thick bare vines hung down from high limbs to the ground. All was still, and the sun was lifting a warm weedy scent from the meadow.

Reuben led her hobbling toward the house across the pond of yellow, that washed against her long dress and his legs and made her smile weakly. They looked in.

This wreck of a cabin seemed a mansion after nights on the ground, and they could hide in it for a little while. Before the weather turned cold, when the hunt for them might have slackened or been called off, they could plan a real life and strike out for it. Maybe people would think they had gone farther than they had.

36

At Night

A small pale woman with very dark hair, a mane of it surrounding her face. But her mouth, very small, opened up and down, not smiling like a mouth but gaping, an aperture with fangs, and her eyes dead white but seeing. She hovered down over naked sleeping Reuben and with her fangs tore the flesh from his side, and he did not wake. Wake up, Reuben! Reuben! Wake up! But he sleeps and the blood leaks from his side, too much blood. And the creature hovers down his body and tears and eats away his... Reuben! Oh God please wake Reuben. Only it is too late, Reuben is bleeding and mutilated, if he wakes he will die of horror, and if he lives is not a man any longer. Oh Reuben. And the fiend hovers up and leaves him torn and still sleeping. Oh dear God please never let him wake. And Martha woke.

Out of breath, her heart lurching unevenly and her lungs quaking with thirst for air, and her body shuddering with her stifled sobbing as he lay beside her, truly asleep and unharmed, so undefended, such a creature—like her, like everyone—of tender softness and defenselessness against all that was hard and sharp and attacking.

She felt a pressure from outside herself that would crush her, she was hollow, her chest was hollow, her arms and legs were hollow, like a stiff empty shed skin of a locust, she would collapse and be crushed to a little flat figure of still paper, dry as a puff of dust, and be gone.

Peepers and crickets and who knows what were deafening her with their screaming shrilling that would not stop.

She sat very still for a while, thinking along wandering paths, and then when she thought to move she couldn't. She couldn't communicate to her legs and arms, that were solid and heavy again, that they were to move. They lay heavily where she had last had the sensation of them, but now numb, unresponding, paralyzed. The helplessness, the inexplicable catastrophe, was so thorough and convincing that she was astonished when some brusque impatient part of her animated her again, freed her limbs from their paralysis, lifting her, and the moment of collapse or defeat was over. Quickly she stood up on the wooden floor, stood far above Reuben, and fiercely looked about her.

37

The Half-fallen House

There were three rooms, and in all three the windows were
smashed and glass lay in sparkling ruin over the warped gray
floors. At one end of the main room spindly weeds were growing
up through holes where rotted floorboards had sagged and broken
and fallen to the dank earth below; the house had been built with
no ceiling, and the gaping holes at that end of the roof let in unwelcome sky. But at the other end of the room the roof was yet solid, and the floor, although springy, was sound. The kitchen and
small sleeping room had partly collapsed and were unsafe to tread.
A small rusted cookstove had fallen half through the failing floor
but looked as though it had been stilled in the act of crawling out
into the light from some hidden place in the lower world. But the
house would hold them up off the ground. (When Reuben had first
looked in he'd seen a snake coiled on the spavined floor of the
kitchen where sunlight came through the roof in a sharp patch. At
his first step in through the door it had convulsed and escaped
through the broken floorboards before he could see it clearly, and
he did not tell Martha of it.) In the good end of the main room a
small fireplace held up a narrow chimney; and there was one abandoned piece of furniture, a tall warped cabinet with no doors or
drawers, tilting toward an imminent fall.

With a branch of pine that Reuben broke for her, Martha made
an effort to sweep out some of the dust. She worked in a reverie of
memory, and saw in her mind's eye the horsehair sofa and book-

cases, the kitchen with the blue plate on the wall, and the cook-stove, every corner and space, every item and object; she could smell the scents of each room, each quite different. In the midst of this remembrance she abandoned it, raising the dust till she coughed, sweeping absently and ineffectually with the makeshift broom. Piece by piece she gathered all the broken glass with her fingertips, filling one cupped hand with the other, again and again, and held it out the open window and dropped it into the weeds. She swept again, and then she slowed her sweeping, and stopped, and the dust began to settle again where it had been, on the grainy rough boards. From outside came a soothing sound of leaves rustling in the freshening wind. The hot weather would break and soon a delicious cool would come. There was a crow a way off, cawing insistently.

She sat down on the floor and leaned back against a wall. In the full daylight Reuben went in and out surreptitiously several times, bringing armfuls of pine straw to pile in a corner. She got up again and smoothed and evened the pile and laid their blanket over it and then took out all her clothes and hung them here and there on the walls, on nails or splayed splinters. She leaned the pine bough in a corner as if it were a real broom. She lay down on their hard lumpy new bed to rest, and breathed the sweet scent of the pine needles she crushed under her. When Reuben came in again—she did not know from what—she raised her hand to him in a plea, and he lay down beside her in the obstructed but insistent daylight. Only then did a fatigue of days rather than of the one day reach through them fully, as if the floor, freeing them from the rough ground, made it impossible for them to deny any longer how tired and sore they were, how battered.

In each other's arms they slept, and woke again in the late afternoon. Reuben stirred himself and rose the full distance up from the floor to his standing height, and with a match from the precious store of them he had packed in his box, he lit a handful of pine straw and held it in the chimney where softly it crackled and went out. The smoke rose with evident response to the faint draft of a clear chimney, how miraculous, and he dropped the crackling pine straw into the fireplace and added a bit more, and went out the back of the house into tall weeds there to look up at the chimney top. From the outside there was no sign that the ruined cabin was occupied; from the chimney rose the infinitesimal trace of the last of the smoke he had created. He gathered dead brushwood and broke it as quietly as he could by standing and stamping on it, and carried it in and laid a fire for later, and piled more wood on the floor. He went out to try to hunt.

Martha lay with her face to the wall, and brought her knees to her chest, and closed her eyes again and listened to the wind in the leaves.

He brought back yet another minuscule squirrel carcass an hour or so later, already skinned and gutted. She watched him as he spitted it on a green stick and leaned it against the wall near the fireplace. He lit a small fire that crackled merrily and burned too fast, and he propped the spitted squirrel over it. The smell of the roasting meat overcame her disgust. Even she could have eaten three of the squirrels. The stick fell, and he picked it up, the raw squirrel now gray on one side with ash, and leaned it over the fire again.

She ate bits of the flesh that still, by habit now, he tore off for her with his fingers and handed to her lips. The taste would always make her throat rebel, but she would swallow it. Reuben had also gathered certain leaves, as he was always doing, to make the bitter tea she drank for lack of anything more or better. She sat close to him on the floor, in the cheering fluttering light from the fire, in the shadow of his being.

"This won't be a long spell, that we're here," he said. The fullness of night reached the cabin and surrounded it.

Behind the house was a well, but it had fallen in. By himself he went looking for a river and found one, just like he had wished it into being. They went down to it slowly by starlight. Partly hidden by overhanging trees and by one great fallen one in the water, with leaves still on it, they undressed and bathed. It was a cool, slow, muddy little river. They soaked and scrubbed their dirty clothes, and wrung them out and washed them again in the miraculous water. The night was warm enough. On her body the black water was some foretaste of the heaven promised in church, and in the deep dark she laved it over her shoulders with her cupped hands, and under her arms, and over and under her breasts, and down her legs and onto her private parts. She poured it again and again over the itching bites on her legs and arms and neck. Reuben washed her back and she his, and they went in deeper, standing side by side neck-deep in the water, not wanting to get out. She dipped her head back into the water and massaged her scalp. The cool water sent a pleasant chill down her arms; she felt goosebumps rise. Reuben was peering hard up and down the water—not at her, now, as he had when she had been washing herself. He said something about fish, and stepping carefully he moved to the riverbank and upstream a little and bent down and reached slowly with his arm under water into holes and cavities in the clay bank. She could barely see him, and she shuddered thinking of what he might touch. She fended the mosquitoes off her face. The water felt immensely soothing. She massaged her head and scrubbed her unruly hair again. Reuben suddenly gave a suppressed but excited cry and naked he came splashing noisily back over the fallen tree smiling and holding a writhing fish almost as long as his forearm and fatter. His face was gleeful. She waded out and wrung water from her hair, holding her head to one side and then the other, twisting her hair tightly in both tired hands, and then she whipped her hair back and wrung it again at her nape, and the chilly water ran down her spine.

They gathered their wet, somewhat less filthy clothes and hurriedly crossed back to the half-fallen house naked. They dressed again, their clothes unpleasantly wet and dirty on their clean bodies, and Reuben took the fish and the squirrel bones out behind the house and spitted the cleaned fish on another green stick and wrapped it around with a long green vine to keep the flesh from dropping off into the fire. He built the fire up again and they cooked the feast and ate it, burning their fingertips as they pulled off hunks of the hot fish; Martha taking her own share with her own hands. They drank more of the bitter tea from his tin cup. Then they lay down on the pine-straw bed as the fire died out quickly. The charred crumbling catfish was the most exquisitely delicious thing Martha had ever eaten in her life. She crossed her forearms over her face, and mosquitoes sang her to sleep.

"I sure didn't expect to see you in Mr. Grooms's house that night," he said. An almost admonitory image of Mr. Grooms had leapt into his head. His body had only just stopped trembling. "Didn't know you knew where it was."

An exhaustion, as if she had breathed out too much and couldn't get enough air back inside her, made Martha feel weak and languid: she did not answer him. Lovemaking had taken her away from her accustomed discomforts and thoughts.

Reuben had built the fire and cooked a fish for them at midday; fish was their main diet now. (He had set a three-hook trot line in the river—keeping the fourth hook in case a floating branch swept the line away.)

Food; then their bodies. He was still naked; Martha had wrapped her shoulders in her dress, and it fell its full length and covered her where open-legged she sat on their blanket facing the fire. What she would have given for a bed, or even for a chair.

Reuben bent closer to her—there were red welts on her arms and face where at night the mosquitoes were biting her. He stood up, restless, and paced with soft tread. Without looking she followed his movement by the shaking of the floor.

He had reconnoitered a good distance in all directions—it seemed that no one had come near their abandoned house for a long time; the nearest fields in use were far across the woods. He did not know where they were, it was no place he had been before, and he thought they were safe for a while. He had told her all this; she had said that in the mornings the room smelled of cold ash and the old musty walls.

"You give up more to be with me, than I ever had to give, didn't you."

"We'll get married. The way people do," she said. "I know we will. Everbody will get used to the idea somehow." The thought of their not being married sometimes came barging into her, knocking things down.

He did not meet her gaze. He could not say, "Yes, we will," because he did not believe it would be possible. He could not say "No, we won't," because he wanted her, he did want her, he did want to live with her and make a life, if they could.

But she spoke more—to the fire, so that the flame leapt with her words, and it was the flame that spoke to him for her, and he watched it instead of her, and listened to it instead of to her. The flame said that she believed that everyone *would* be reconciled. That she and Reuben might even go back to Three Rivers someday, with their own children.

He had begun to feel that there was something he had come to know about her—he could not have said what it was, for it appeared to him only once in a while, as on that night on the trail—that she herself did not know, and that he must not tell her, that he must actually keep her from knowing, something about herself that he must shelter her from. He sat down beside her.

"We will. You'll see," the flame said in her voice, and she inched closer to lean against him. "I love you," the flame said. Then it was silent again, although it leapt and played.

At such a moment, when she was so comfortably *with* him, when she seemed to admire him and love him, when the insufficiency of their life meant not nearly as much as the sufficiency of their feelings, he let go of his doubts, he put away his unavoidable knowledge, his morose clairvoyance, even his still-surprised resentment that this flight had begun with Martha's impulse; and he could not contain his happiness. She was a miraculous presence, a visitation that could last.

But her love had also disadjusted him to the familiarities of his life. It made him sometimes unaware of what he had been aware of, so that he might catch himself suddenly with a chill of fright realizing that he had not been paying attention to anything, that he must be more alert, readier, warier of everything and everyone, especially of all that with which they no longer had any contact.

But at some point they must have contact with it. With that other life. They were living, but they were outside of that life, which was for Martha the only life. Even if he could live nearly alone, and had done so, she could not.

"We'll have children," she said. She looked at her left arm. "Remember Clara?" she said. Martha touched the muscle of her upper arm. "She's so . . . *round,*" she said. And absently Martha looked off, and her hand moved like a blind stranger's hand gingerly touching her face. Then she laid her palm flat against her cheek, as if hiding it from Reuben. "I've got so thin," she said.

He took her hand away and held it in his own, so that their arms were side by side, and she followed his gaze to their own two hands. She found nothing lovelier, nor he, than her pale skin reddened by sun and chafed by weather next to his darker skin with welts and scratches from breaking through brush as they walked. The dress fell from her shoulders and she was as naked as he. Her nipples dark and smooth. She spoke to him, her eyes ablaze, and a dark tone in her voice made the hair rise on his neck. They twined arms to touch from shoulder to fingertip and looked at what they were.

Often they sat thus in the daytime luxury of a relative absence of mosquitoes. And freed from the hardship of walking all night and failing to sleep all day their bodies began to repair themselves on a diet of fish, and their thoughts were released into the realm of speculation, of some unknown and for now unknowable future. Thoughts seemed always to lead nowhere except to a rather small hope that had grown thin and tenuous. But bodies, at least, led to touch and self-forgetting.

She had had friends: other young women. Or at least one true friend, Clara. She desperately wished she could talk to someone. Her friends would have their babies, too; and now she could talk to none of them about that, either. She had had things: clothes and food and—all sorts of things. They must make a real life in some place where they would not be known and where—even harder to find—they would not be in new danger, she of contempt and abuse, he of worse, merely for being that two-colored creature they were together.

He looked at his hands. His forearms were strong; his wrists a little narrow—he had envied some men their thicker wrists. His hands were not large. The thought of stopping and settling felt very wrong. He was almost angry at her—at himself, too—for such an absurd idea. But he was also a little frightened, and this was why sometimes she grew angry at him. She didn't want *him* to be worried; her scheme for balancing their fate was for her to worry, even excessively, while she counted on him to remain steady and reassuring. Yet it was he who worried and she who dreamed.

She was leaning toward the fire, which had nearly died out— more to look into it than to feel its warmth. The weather was still warm enough, but a little precariously so. Her black hair—the same color as his, but of a warmer tone, falling in tight wisps, not straight like his; her white shoulders and arms, her narrowing back, with a dark mole on her right shoulder blade; her round breasts, dark nipples; her beautiful legs with such delicate knees; the hypnotizing curve of her hips, her buttocks; the deepening, below her navel, of her narrow V of dark hair. All of her but her sun-darkened face and arms white, white—could skin be so white? But she startled him by saying, "Are we so different?" as if she had read his thoughts. She touched the smooth skin of his chest, as smooth as hers. She studied his arm over hers, her leg over his.

He came rushing in at night and scared her, but it was only because on his ramble he'd found in a barn a trove of thrown-away newspapers only a few days old. Six of them, all from Dallas. He wondered if they were close to Dallas—maybe they'd gone farther than he'd thought. By the light of candle-stubs he had stolen from a back porch, they sat side by side on the floor and pored over the newsprint.

It made her suddenly glad to see him so absorbed in reading the reports—they looked together for any mention of themselves, their names, what had happened. But there was nothing. Only the news of Dallas, small odd events, including murder, in nearby towns, a flood along the Brazos River, affairs of business and the state capital, even of Washington D.C. She felt deep companionship in their equally avid reading.

Then the unwanted images of home crowded into her—her father reading the newspapers he too collected from elsewhere. She hated newspapers. She discovered she was staring at the far wall, flickering with dim candlelight and shadow, while Reuben was hunched over the papers beside her. She did not want to read any more. She longed for her room, it nearly overwhelmed her, it was a sob caught inside her that she could not release.

One cool night he left her sleeping and went out into the meadow around the house. A thousand miles of black sky sprinkled with stars. A noise, a crackling, in the dark woods made him start—the daily strain of walking ahead where he'd never been before, toward where he couldn't imagine, and of waiting now in the house, with the feeling that danger must inevitably draw near them if they did not keep moving, all this was not only a sharpening of his nerves to the point of rawness but also an intoxication of alertness. He remembered, before they had found a way to cross to the west bank, in an old man's boat, sitting with his mother on a wharf on the bank of the Mississippi River, afraid and excited. He looked back toward the house. Deer might graze in the clearing around the house at this time of night; he knew their ways well enough to hunt them, if he had the chance. But Reuben had never hunted with a gun; nor did he sit a horse well; he had walked on foot and lived by his hands all his life.

Many deer, perhaps two dozen doe, at twilight, grazing at the edge of a wood. He and his mother had come unnoticed on them, up close, around a twist of sandy road. As the deer fed always one head was rising up to look around and listen with large pricked ears, and then dipping again to the grass, and another after it rising, and another. His mother—some figure next to him in the dreamlike memory who must be his mother—nods slowly and he sees a buck with great red shoulders, only his antlerless summer head fully visible, watchful, his body hidden in the shadow at the edge of the woods: not moving. The figure next to him must be his mother, but when he tries to turn inside his memory and look at her then the memory isn't as real, he can't turn far enough to see her, she keeps withdrawing just beyond his memory-vision, so he can't see what she looks like, he wants to see what she looks like. By the time the very first doe moves, breaking for the woods in bounding leaps, the buck is already gone.

38

Days and Nights

She did not know what his _living_ was like; only his loving. Sitting in the empty door frame of the house, he pared a torn callus from his thumb with Mr. Grooms's knife. She watched him. The day was passing very slowly. He was not discontented with such days, however. Had she known the depth of his willingness to live so, she would have been frightened.

He came in at dawn, when she was reluctant to wake, with his shirt off and filled like a sack with hard small apples from an old orchard he had found, roaming restless in the first light. They were too tart and hard for her, but he ate some of them, elaborately cutting them with his knife, as if to sweeten them by treating them as if they'd been big and red instead of little knuckles mostly green. He boiled little pieces of them for her in the cup, but she didn't eat them; too sour. The promise of sugar would have made her do anything.

Alone, he was close to a farm, watching it from hiding. His senses were wide for sign or alarm; he was excited to be in danger that was clear rather than hidden. His eyes chased a fast skittering along the ground and caught up with it and paced it and then let it go. (Only a leaf.) The weather was turning.

Mornings, after they woke, not ready to rise yet, and with no pressing reason to rise, they lay against each other. Till first Reuben, then Martha, would sit up and then stand, and retreat through the broken wall to the shadow behind the house, to relieve the pressure of urine—Reuben to one side, where the weeds hissed under his stream, and Martha to the other, where he had pulled up the weeds to clear an area for her and like a cat she turned and kicked a little dirt over what she left there.

(Martha had been stricken with embarrassment the first time her bodily needs had forced her to ask Reuben, who had been leading them all night through thicknesses and darkness and rain, to stop for a moment. And even more so, in full daylight, when for fear of discovery she could scarcely move more than a few yards from where he had hidden them. She had had to pretend that no sound, no movement, nothing bodily, had happened. He too was embarrassed. Because of his woodcraft he could move farther away from their daytime lairs—to look around, as well. She had hoped to be needful of her privacy only at night, while they were walking. Now their bodies, fully known to each other, provoked no embarrassment, although Martha, not inured like Reuben to the use of leaves, and without even newspaper, must clean herself with a rag torn from a chemise, that she washed out in the river.)

Each returned to the morning pallet, which he refreshed every day with new layers of pine straw. Each took pleasure in the other's appetite. When he looked at the delicious spreading of her limbs— her arms flung out from her shoulders, her legs canted open—he had to shudder. He would put one hand on her thigh, near her hip, and smooth her leg downward, just to feel her skin. She grasped him about the waist, tugging at his solidity; tugging at him, her teeth clenched, laughing happily at the sheer reality of him; she looked down his narrow hips, put her palm against his wide flat chest. They often made love in the morning.

And sometimes rose without making love—when the touching and closeness, not only of hands but also of side and shoulder and leg, was an intense pleasure sufficient to itself. He was, she was, completely bodily, there was no thought in them, no thought of the future, not even any feeling except an animal contentment, a stopped time of happiness in the body, a horizon no further than their own limbs, a life that had no plans or fears, no future and no past.

Reuben lost himself in her body when they made love, he fell down a delirious whirlpool that made him lightheaded, light-chested; in his gut, in the sacred spot he had never forgotten from Grandfather's teaching, just below his breastbone, was an airy emptiness that thrilled him and pushed down into his belly narrowing and intensifying and made him rise up and pulled him toward her and into her. It almost seemed he was holding her completely in his hands, holding her in the air with his touch, her whole body resting in his hands, not on the blanket.

She luxuriated on the edge of a fall, the roots of her hair tingled, she pushed her feet against the tops of his as if standing on them. Till she must take his hand and hold it against her, pressing it hard to her; till she must turn to him or from him; till she must have him inside her, filling her; till she must be filled and filled, his hands on her breasts, hard, and her hands on him and on them together, seeing with her fingertips how they fit together, the coming and going, the fit of it; till she must have him more; till opening her eyes she could look into him, his face near hers, close, and her hips clenched and her belly squeezed down with the waves of it, harder, hard; till spent.

Sometimes, perhaps it was most times, when she rose to wipe herself with a towel made also from the panel of the chemise that had been all torn to rags for this and for that, she felt a shame burn through her. It was a guilt like a stain of blood, an accusing from some inaccessible place where she was not allowed to plead for herself, where someone always stopped her pleading and shamed her, someplace that sent a voice at her whispering words she could never make out but which she always knew the meaning of.

She could not explain this to him; she could not speak of it to herself. She lay down again on the blanket with Reuben, she tried to be small enough to shelter entirely in the crook of his arm, she tried to sleep in order to enter some sweet dream, to hide from the day, to hide from memory, in the shadow of him.

39

None Other Has Ever Known

I come to the garden alone and the dew is still on the roses.
The hymn was stuck in her head.

Behind the livery in Three Rivers, that had not yet suffered a decline since the dealer in automobiles had opened his garage, the blacksmith kept a little mangy fox in a wire cage.

From somewhere, she remembered, when she had been sitting in the buggy, off the road at a place where he might walk by on his way home from the mill, she heard repeated drawn-out cries of "No!" from a child, the small voice hoarse and weak.

A kind of elixir and tonic for their lungs, the air damp and scented with oak leaves and herbs; air as if it had never been breathed by anyone. In the early shade, in a lovely stillness after the birds have ceased singing but before the cicadas of noon; and under one sagging eave of the half-fallen house, an abandoned papery dome of last year's imperious hornets, silent. At last the mood of such a day seems not hasty or frightened, but a beforeness.

Once, in his life alone when he was a boy, on a back road in thick woods, Reuben was suddenly confronted by two Indian men on small scrawny ponies who came into the road before him, near him, from the right. They halted and looked at him where he was standing, surprised. They were barefoot, as he was, and wore overalls or trousers, as he did, and worn shirts with here and there a hole, as he did. One of them had on a suit jacket. His hair was much longer than Reuben's. The hair of the other was like Reuben's. The dark color of the irises of their eyes had spilled into the whites and their gaze was unreadable, their eyes were like holes burning with a small spark, a gaze piercing, almost crazed; but their demeanor was calm, their faces neither smiling nor frowning. They looked even poorer than Reuben, except for the ponies. Perhaps they expected Reuben to say something, to declare himself in some way. Perhaps they were going to take him with them. The two men and Reuben stared at each other in the silence. When they were satisfied, or disappointed, or changed their minds, or lost interest in him, he did not know which, they touched their ponies' flanks with their bare heels and went off the road to the left, disappearing into the woods.

When Reuben lifted Martha's hair from the nape of her neck, pushing up with gentle palms, and put his face there, at her nape, behind her ears, he could smell the sweetish, thick genital scent of that skin hidden under her hair.

All their possibles added up to a pitiful small pile of things, and no prospects.

At their evening bath, they watched two ducks come in for the night, shooting the stiff breeze with their wings cocked back, their bodies held as motionless as those of the ducks carved in Martha's father's ivory cufflinks. At the last instant the ducks stood up on the air and slowed and put their webbed feet in, splashing water ahead of them as they tipped down into a full stop, and then were paddling calmly.

Sitting on the floor, crumpled into a small form much smaller than she was, she was weeping; and he stood apart from her, stood straight as a board, and he said nothing to her; tears in his eyes.

A marriage, yes, of a sort, although it had been made only in heaven; but apparently it was to be lived out in hell.

When he had stood at the edge of the woods, a day long ago, in his boyhood, with nothing before him and nothingness behind him, he had been so startled he had jumped when, spoken by another voice, not his own, words came into his head, was it *her* speaking?, "Go on, now, go on, you have to go on, everything is in the going on."

What had begun as a kind of fatal mistake—a decision as if made by someone else somewhere else, that he didn't think was good but which for some reason did not resist (*why* hadn't he said that night, No, you have to go back home, you *have* to) and which she seized and didn't want to think about, only to act upon—turned out to have not only fear but also rapture in it.

He walks with me and He talks with me, and He tells me I am His own. And the joy we share as we tarry there none other has ever known.

Blasphemy for her to think of those lines, with Reuben's mop of hair in her fist, and her eyes closed tight, and him rocking sweetly into her as she climbed toward the precipice she wanted to and would leap from.

40

Horse and Lion

It was that Martha was not sure what to tell Reuben. It was that what had happened, had happened to someone she no longer was. She was a different person, now, and it all occupied her no longer; she did not think of it; now it was even hidden from her, within herself. Where it was buried she no longer looked; she would have thought—if she could think about it—that because it was something that had happened, it belonged in the past, it had no bearing on the present. Yet it lay inside her, beside other memories not so damaging, behind memories of what was still raw—her father's words, her mother's pitiful accompaniment to those words. After she had opened herself to Reuben, after he had come into her, she dreamed of frightening pursuit, of danger.

Martha was no bad judge of men and boys, but did not always allow herself to understand what she knew she knew. She had taken the measure of her father—although, even seeing him for the man he was among other men, the man who cowed her mother, still she could not protect herself from his power over her feelings. She could see in a minute what was in any young man trying to impress her. Yet James she could not see clearly; when she felt horror of him, she felt guilty for her horror—he was her brother. In their household, everything was for him. Some part of her was able to shrill curses against the rest of her, charging her with blindness, with foolishness, with inexplicable weakness for him. But she shrank from that part of herself. It was true that she had feared James, had hated him, and he was her brother.

He was younger than she, but he was out in the world with her father, while she remained housebound. She had "loved" him, yes; that was one reason why she feared him.

Four years ago, it had been games of teasing charged with a pulse-rattling forbiddenness. Anne had known nothing of it. But James at thirteen and Martha at fifteen had carried their bantering, the innuendoes of their small talk, their once-in-a-while idle summer afternoons when Anne was away with Mama, and the house was too quiet, up a slope that had made her curiosity feverish, that had overcome her repugnance for him, that had made her pretend that he had bumped against her accidentally, that had made her, that had led her to, give in to him. And he had a temper, he would have his own way, she was afraid of him, afraid of thwarting him, and her fear made her more moody. So there had come an afternoon hour of pounding silence, when time had seemed a blade that would at any instant fall heavily on her and mutilate her and wound her beyond healing. But she did not think it fell.

Rough-housing, a kind of taunting, antagonizing physical contact; but he had pushed her down and unbuttoned her dress and under-blouse. Holding her still, pinned, he had put his hand on her breast; she felt the hardness, the repulsiveness, of his hand through her chemise. No one had ever touched her breasts. Not even the doctor. No one would again, but him, for two years more. She had flinched and looked away, past him, but she had not stopped him, had not screamed at him, had not fought him. Why? She called to herself afterward, over tea, *Why* had she not? She heard herself ask it, but could find no answer; and felt blame sink into her like a dye that reached through her flesh all the way to her bones, turning them from white to red.

With Reuben, in their pitiful shack, she still remembered a horrible dream she had dreamed repeatedly since she was a small girl, that frightened her when some man, a stranger, walked after her where she was dawdling alone, in the woods, and she hid, and he

brought his crashing steps near where she was hidden and he found
her suddenly; and something happened that she could not be sure
of, something that in the dream she strenuously looked away from,
but felt. Who had that man been? And she would wake herself
with her tossing, it would take half an hour of pressing her hands
hard, one on top of the other, on her breast, against her heart, to
slow the knocking inside her. Mercy. Something of that dream lay
close to her thoughts when she was at the mercy of her younger
brother's hands, that time. Those times.

James had sat her down on the short small bed with tall headboard and footboard in Anne's room, of all places, and looked her
in the eye with a frightening, eager, reckless look. He was younger,
she must stand up at once and stop this. But she didn't. Slowly he
pushed her back on the bed and gently picked up her legs and put
them on the bed, turning her so her head was on Anne's pillow.
Then he sat next to her, but the other way, so he could hold her
down with his eyes. His hand came slipping up along her trembling
leg slowly as if taming a wild horse, and by imperceptible pitiless
stages he patiently found his way. And with his other hand he captured her hand and pulled it toward him to clasp him where he had
freed himself.

She had said nothing. She was looking at herself from somewhere else. There was such intense stillness in the house that when
something, somewhere in the house, made a slight sound, her startled body had jerked with a spasm of fright. But it was nothing,
and he smiled at her in a way she hated yet did not cry out against.
He smiled; but his eyes were cold, unreadable.

It filled her hand. And his own hand was wrapped around hers,
holding her to him. Just holding, while he was pushing the heel of
his other hand against her and the touch numbed her thighs, made
her feel she would twitch violently.

Then he had let her up. He'd started to straighten Anne's bed,
and Martha had replaced him at the task, not speaking, smoothing
the bed expertly.

He interrupted her, taking her wrist roughly in his left hand and he dragged her back from the bed a few steps, to frighten her. Her panic was sudden and intense. He said to her in a fierce whisper, "You ever tell a livin soul bout inny a this, I'll stab you. I'll stab you in your eyes and in your titties." He attacked her eyes with his. "You don't do what I say, then *I'll* tell what you did." He cuffed her on the back of her head and she fell, and he left the room.

She lay on the floor like a rag doll, not crying, scarcely breathing, her eyes open wide. She crossed her arms over her breasts. She squeezed her thighs together but a width had been driven between them and they could never be as close together again as they had been. When she moved again, gathered herself and stood all the way up again, it seemed she was in someone else's body. She finished smoothing Anne's bed.

She had not even remembered this much in at least a year.

But it had happened several more times at long intervals over two years' time—more, and worse, and the worst. And he had pushed at her, held her down, pushed into her, degraded her, laughed at her, at her body, at her fear, at her silence. He had won. Something in her mind finally with sufficient strength against him recoiled with revulsion. She never let him find her at home again alone. She could not afford to; she must not be available to him or she could not resist him, although she could not reason out why not. She stayed longer at school, helping her favorite teachers, on weekends and in the summer she left the house frequently, she took to walking to the town square and back, sometimes to afternoon rides behind the silent black liveryman who was always waiting at the stable nearest the bank all day for her father's bidding, and who would drive her for hours in her father's buggy, where she wished, without saying anything to her.

She went out with her mother and sister to call on members of the church, to shop, and Anne with open mouth was forever expressing surprise at Martha's having joined them, when she had used to insist on staying home. Spinning in Martha's head was the unimaginable and before unimagined, inconceivable act she was avoiding, which, as soon as she saw in her mind's eye what she had stopped doing, she could not see, it shot away from her to some hidden place.

She felt like a horse caught and enslaved, bound in traces to some heavy load she must pull and pull.

But worse than fright or revulsion, she had felt the sour canker of guilt. She accused herself. She was the older one, yet what had she allowed? It had been up to her to forbid, to crush, any such game from the first moment it began. She had known very well what it was about. And he was only a precocious boy. Yet she had let him do what he wanted; and let him think that it was his power that made it possible for him to do it, when it had been hers. Hadn't it?

She turned seventeen. She avoided looking at herself naked in the mirror, as she had often liked doing in the years when she had turned from skinny girl into young woman of roundness and weight. She put James away from her thoughts as entirely as she could; if he occurred to her, then it was with perfect casualness and quickness; she replaced a predictable dislike of him, of sister for brother, with a calculated ignoring of him that made her feel safer.

She came to resent her father's lording it over everyone else. He seemed to think that his own life was entirely sufficient to him, and that she and everyone else in the family was to feel grateful for any of his time whatsoever. She was angry at her mother. But "Yes ma'am" and "No ma'am," she would probably say until her mother's dying day, and would no doubt attend her at her death-bed, having come from her own house somewhere in town, her own proper husband.

Why had James attacked her in that way? Why hadn't he at-tacked Anne, who was younger? Martha had to be thankful that it was she and not Anne who had borne the assault. A second thought came—what if he had done the same to Anne already, could he have done it to both of them? Anne would never say. Neither would Martha.

He continued to ambush her in the house, but she escaped him. He looked through Martha's clothes to her breasts, which she had let him see and touch. He kept on with his teasing threatening eyes at the supper table but she looked away and made small talk, difficult as that was to do, with the others. This was the way it had turned out that he would treat her forever, she supposed. Once he caught her eye and showed her, low against his thigh, an open shiny knife. She ran away from him. On the pretext of fetching more cool tea or whatever else was wanted by Daddy or Mama, she hastened away as soon as he sat near her on the front porch. Her mother, who sermonized frequently and with maddening obliqueness on the priceless purity of young women, did not notice the anxiety Martha thought was all too apparent in herself, all too much a problem without solution. Gradually James had let go of her. He turned elsewhere with his appetites. By his sixteenth year everyone but his mother and father knew of his reputation in nigger town.

She had wanted to open her body to Reuben; and wanted him to give her his. He reacted at first with disbelief that she was as hungry for him as he for her, when they began, in Three Rivers. And still in hiding, now, among trees and vines, on pine straw, on grass, and in the abandoned leaning house, they ate and drank of each other, they lashed each other with their need, they slaked a panther thirst, sated a wolf hunger. And she had never said a word to him of James nor of her earlier dream of some approaching man. She had not even thought of James except once in a while; that came after, when Reuben might be sleeping and she lay awake, and she might look at him naked and gaze at what she had first held in her hand when—she shuddered. . . . At such a moment she might suspicion her desire for Reuben even as she craved him; and she could distrust even him. Like a flash of light in a dark room, some image of James would startle her thoughts, would rush up the corridors of her memory at her and fly past.

"I'm goan *have* you," he'd yelled at her after that first time, and she got up from the floor and she ran through the empty house, ran from him out the front door and down the porch steps and into the street, away, on foot, his voice in her ears, in the air where everyone must have heard it. And so he had.

The third or fourth time he had forced her into his game—tearing her thoughts sideways and opposite each other, this man in a boy's body, with a boy's sweaty otherness, yet with older eyes and impulses she would have to learn to comprehend—he had yelled aloud when gripping her hand in his hand holding him, while she tried to pull away. He used her to bring himself to his uncontrolled release. Yelled into the forbiddenness of the silence of the house, conquered it, mocked it, laughed loud at it, while she remained silent. She remained as still as if paralyzed while he subsided. Yet that was as nothing to what he would do to her. Then he had curled nearer her and looked up at her from an odd angle, as if lifting his head to her, as if, with his yellow-eyed little lion's gaze, he expected her to lick the blood of a fresh kill from his mane, and she herself the kill.

41

Sundays

The days of flight and hiding had lost all distinction for Martha, each day's promise of difference smudged to a repetition of the day before. The half-fallen house relieved the discomfort and thirst of long daily imprisonment by sunlight or rather, thick shade (except for one terrible day when to remain unseen they had had to lie without food or even water in the middle of a field of standing corn, fodder corn drying on the stalk, and were hidden from everyone but the sun, she would always remember); it abated the hunger and exhaustion of nights walking; but it did nothing to break, for Martha, the sameness of the days.

Sundays had marked the week definitively, and never before in her life had she been exempt from them. For her father Sunday was only a routine of dressing as for other days, if at a later hour. But for her and for her younger sister there had been the peculiarly enervating slowness, whether of confinement in the house after church because of bad winter weather or summer storms, even September threat of tornado, or of afternoons out. Martha recalled, as if she were being told of life on an exotic island somewhere in the southern seas, the Sunday breakfasts in dressing gowns rather than their old houserobes, the irritating maternal supervision of the scrubbing of their faces to be presented if not directly to God then to other righteously scrubbed faces; the maternal talk on appropriate comportment among young men; the clean best clothes of a sober fashion; the various rituals of maternal inspection and criticism, especially of their hair (whether they had brushed it out to a sufficient gloss, whether they had put it up with sufficient neatness); the formality of leaving the house all in a group, as they never did otherwise, and the winter cold cutting at them, or the summer heat a stifling stricture at their buttoned throats that held them from breathing deeply.

And the sermons, the Sunday School lessons, the freely offered admonitions of church men and church women in a Sunday mood to children and youths within their grasp—all spoke of sin and hell, of Satan and backsliding, of the Commandments, of the evils of drink and gambling; and spoke also with fervor of whippings and hidings, of strictness and punishment, of God's authority vested in the hands of fathers, of the obedience by which the wives were judged in the eyes of God and of husbands.

She had sinned. She was sinning still. She had disliked church but it had never occurred to her that she would escape it, and escape the God whose local representative authority it housed and her own father who with measured deliberateness, although without any apparent deep conviction, took on his own role in the chain of religious command.

But here were *weeks* without church and she did not feel she had escaped. She did not know which day *was* Sunday, and while in certain moods she could have said she hated Sunday and everything about it, not to know which day was Sunday was so odd, so unnatural. It was upsetting.

When, one morning in their flight, a special stillness had enclosed them, it had reminded her of Sundays—the comfort, even, of clear hard judgment; and the fear of that judgment. If she were to be judged only by her father and other fathers, so be it. If there was a further judgment, if they were right and she was wrong to have harkened only casually to them. . . . Summer Sundays; winter Sundays when the unheated church remained drafty and cold through the interminable service unless the sun was strong; spring Sundays when wildflowers were blooming along the roadside before the summer sun burned them away; rainy Sundays when the road and churchyard and hitching grove became horrible mire and there was no place to get down without muddying their good shoes; autumn Sundays—brief autumn that one wished there were more of—when the air was clear and of a fresh coolness and during the sermon one could follow the repeated climbing of a wasp up a closed windowpane, and its falling down again and starting over. Once, sitting on damp earth with Reuben, at broad noon, she had looked at her ruined shoes, her aching ankle, and wept suddenly and softly for a moment. "What is it?" he had whispered to her.

"Sundays," she'd said, shaking her head, quenching it.

Reuben had told her a little of the Negro churches. He had said he was partly raised by black people, but she did not quite accept this. She did not like black people. Everyone said their churches were loud and too boisterous. Black people frightened her, they were unpredictable, they hated white people, even when they seemed to be most helpful, most friendly, most accommodating. But in her own intuitions, in her own thinking, which had always been more guarded till she was released from the town that had circumscribed it, in the hours of hidden daylight when she could not sleep and wandered through her thoughts, what Reuben told her, and what she remembered Pilgrim saying, made her wonder.

Reuben had no church; if he had a God, he did not speak of this God, and she did not know if it was a God like the one she had been taught to imagine and revere and obey. She would have liked him to speak to her of his God.

Reuben's Sundays were when he might not have to work for someone, when he might sleep by day or read a discarded newspaper, in autumn take to the woods for the test of tracking and his primitively equipped small-game hunting, in summer to fish if living near water, or to swim and laze. The ground over which he was leading Martha was a field of treachery—not just difficult trails and hiding places. The tracks they left behind them as they fled were like a writing on the surface of the earth, a betrayal of them if anyone had eyes to see. In that flight Reuben had spent time out-witting not only whoever was trying to follow him and Martha but also the earth itself. Above them the sky, into which they could not fly to escape, mocked them with its vastness, its endless passage to some other realm they would not be allowed to enter. And every day had forced on him as labor what had formerly been his Sunday recreation, if he and Martha were to survive.

At dusk, after more than a week in their abandoned house, she hummed a hymn-tune, and, half-dozing with his back against the wall, away from her a little, he woke and looked at her. She lifted the hymn from humming to soft singing, and he listened to the words. Jesus and prayer. The hordes of mosquitoes were beginning to stir. At the sound of the first one at his ear, infuriating him because of their helplessness against such numbers, he got up and worked at the fire, to light a green stick and diffuse the smoke in the air. She did not watch him; it was a familiar task, now, and did only a little good. She had seen, on other evenings, the tiny predatory specks of them clinging everywhere high on the walls, their upright tiny shapes hateful to her, her arms and face wearing new welts each day. Reuben was not so bitten by them as she, nor so bothered by the bites when he was. She raised her knees, and put her forearms across them, and laid her forehead on her arms, and then her shoulders shook as silently she cried. He looked down at her, unable to think of anything to say, feeling blame for her misery. As much so as not to have to speak as for the little good it would do, he began more vigorously to wave the guttering torch along the futile walls in what might have been the crepuscular hours of the sacred day of rest.

42

Harriet, Texas

The collapsing farmhouse was a prison.

Martha could not abide the openness, the ugliness, nor any more of the sparse horrible food. After ten interminable days, tallied with marks she made on a wall with a burnt twig, the weather was turning colder. Careful to guess if she could not remember, she marked off the increasing total of all their days of hiding, and before that, of flight, and before that, of love, on one of the walls with the blackened burnt end of her twig from the fireplace. Even in this abandoned wreck of a house she unsettled herself when she made a mark on the wall. Whenever she asked Reuben what they would do now, he no longer wanted to answer, since he could only say, in good conscience, "Go on from here."

Far-off clouds thickened and rose as high as the sky, and then approached till their low gray undersides darkened to a sinister green-black overhead, and the lightning announced punishing thunder that arrived and then echoed as if off walls of heaven. Nor could she stand much longer the absence of other people.

The raininess continued, whispering some nights and on others speaking louder against the roof and leaves, not friendly, then shouting, beating against the house and finding its way through open places as though it was hunting them, to chill them, to stain them when instead it should have been clear and clean. They had only their one blanket.

She wanted to cling to him some days. And on others was angry at him. He sat still and waited out the hours with her, scarcely speaking. There was only the one thing to speak of. And often they brooded, she and he, separately. He might catch himself in thoughts of other times, other places, and then feel guilty for not concentrating mind and soul on what they must do to live. When they imagined danger, Martha thought of her father, and brushed and brushed her hair. Reuben thought of James.

When Reuben went out on his often futile twilight rambles she tried by the last light to read in one of her pair of novels instead of letting herself think any more. Thinking alone was too frightening. But fugitive life was not made for reading—she fell into painful reverie of remembrance of interior light from lamps, of curtains, and in that place, not this one, an open book, a chair. In that place, a book spoke so clearly she could truly hear it. Here the book was mute, was stubbornly opaque; why so many words? The printed letters wobbled in her sight, did not relate to each other, were as mysterious to her as Indian marks and peckings on rock; and she shut the book hard and looked away to a farther spot in the open empty room. A swarming hive of incomprehensible letters could fly out from the pages ready to sting.

When Reuben would return, often she would embrace him and cling to him again; at that moment, he could be all she needed or wanted.

They did not have enough wraps against the increasing chill of the nights; she could no longer bathe as she wanted to, and could not urge him to. She felt as skinny as she had ever been in her life, and even he seemed less solid. They could grow nothing, they had neither seed nor season; they had nothing to eat but what he found them, which now included twice having stolen a chicken and some late garden produce from a distant farm. His night forays were dangerous. And she asked him if it wouldn't be, wouldn't it?, just as safe to push on and find a place to live, a *town*, a town far from Three Rivers.

He did not know where that might be.

Carrying their pitiful few things, at the edge of the woods from which they had first entered the high-grass meadow, he looked back at the house. It wore no sign that for a while they had brought it back to its purpose, had filled it again with breathing and eating and sleeping. Had safely hidden inside it. Cold and empty and unwelcoming now, it sagged in its ragged precinct, and if he were encountering it now for the first time, he had to admit, he would not suggest to her that she stay with him in it. For the first time, Martha was setting a steady pace ahead of him in the direction he had told her they would try.

In the village where they stopped, black women and men stared hard at both of them and said nothing. A tiny but unruined two-room shack provided her a place where all she could do at first was hide from life itself a little longer while Reuben hired out at day-wages on this white farm or that. She would settle for that, for a little while longer—they could return to day-life, could sleep through the night like other people, could rise rested in the morning and go about something, instead of hiding. Or at least Reuben could.

He ascertained that they had come a hundred and fifty miles from Three Rivers. Having wandered back and forth more than he had thought. They were not near any rail line or main road. And whites scarcely ever entered this black village. But how people stared: and they must speak of what they saw, surely. Word would spread. No one, no stranger, could warn them of pursuers. When he was most tired, emotionally, he almost resigned himself to being trapped; but would in other moments wish he could fly and carry her with him, fast, as far away as there were places to go.

Martha, who had never worn anything but good and clean, was tormented by wearing torn and dirty. Even her valise was gone, they traded it for food as soon as they entered the village. But there would be no more roasted squirrel, there was bread; and with his money from Mr. Grooms Reuben bought sweet potatoes and green beans and corn and peas, and chicken, from neighbors, and a ham and some jars of fruit preserves, proper things. From the black grocery man in his tiny unlit store that smelled of dust and staleness. What feasts they ate. They smiled to be eating together; real food.

In her whole life she had never spent even one full day and night alone, unlike Reuben with the unnumbered such nights of his nomadic solitude. And even when she and he had been together in the woods and fields and half-fallen house, she had missed so much the casual presence of others, even her parents and Anne. (Not James). And Clara. Other friends she had not realized she cared for so much till she could never see them again. People in Three Rivers. She was living in a horrible dirty gray place surrounded by niggers; living with them. She couldn't talk to them. She stayed inside all day, alone, listening to the sound of their lives. They did not speak to her. She wanted to be home. She wanted never to go home again.

In her moments alone a thought would creep in that opened a vertical fall of fright inside her from the top of her head down through her to her navel, and would make the hair on her arms rise and tingle: that in only a few days white men who had heard of Martha's presence would come, penetrating into the black village by their rule over all, and would discover everything, and she did not know what would happen, she was wrong about everything, she had always been wrong, she did not even know this Reuben, she did not know her own mind, she was not in her right mind. (And, most frightening, she almost felt relief in the thought of their coming, as it did seem—so long as she left Reuben completely out of it—a kind of rescue.) But gradually, as the shock released in her by this sudden panic subsided, she came back to thinking: Reuben, yes I do know him, and I just don't know so much of him as I'd like to, but his eyes, his face, his hands, his love of me, I do know.

Only six days after they had arrived, Reuben rushed back to her and said he had seen someone who looked like Paul O'Connor, and she said it wasn't possible and it wasn't likely, but he insisted they must go—just when she had clean things and had made herself offer friendly words to the neighboring women on both sides—they were women, weren't they?—and had decided she could endure a while longer if she had to. This time they left with good food—ham wrapped in a clean cloth, cornbread, one of the jars of preserves—and Reuben turned farther north, against the weather, telling her this would deceive her father and his men. Four more days they walked, now more brazenly, with a sense of haste, almost of desperation, keeping to smaller roads but briskly walking long colder nights and even part of the day, making faster time than they had since the very beginning. Not speaking, just trudging together, at her pace, Reuben holding himself back.

Walking in daylight, having walked desperately all the day long, after sleeping, for once, through the night because Martha hadn't the strength for another night journey, they came near a sizable town. Martha wanted to walk right in, and he said no, they couldn't, it would be giving away the weeks, the months, they had spent hiding, it would mean the end, he could not go, nor could she. What about his promises? He had promised. She sank down where they stood. It was a stretch of open road exposed to the expanse of the slowly toppling clouds in waves of dim gray overhead. A cheerless unsettled place, an open place of road and cleared fields that now seemed even to Reuben too wide to cross, with the town there before them, a mile away, perhaps; two church spires rising above large trees. The late afternoon was somehow defeating him. He felt a thorough passivity come into him; his arms hung heavily at his sides. He dropped their things and knelt by her and gently brought her forehead to his shoulder. Her tears wet his skin. He looked up at the sky, and ahead to where the first buildings were clustered.

Circuitously they went through low ground by another river, through the black town, and by a sawmill on the flood plain. Another river town. He held his arm around her. They climbed up a gentle rise and the road broadened and dried out under their feet.

After they passed through some small garden fields they entered streets of frame houses, and then, proceeding slowly (but Martha with her face mostly covered by her overhanging scarf and her hands tucked away out of sight was secretly smiling and walking faster and Reuben was no longer capable of arguing with her about their safety) they entered a dusty square with a sizable gazebo at the center, and around its sides the familiar sorts of buildings, a bank and three churches, one low and squat and made of brick, the other two white frame buildings with the spires he had seen from afar. They took one look, Reuben said they must not stroll together any farther, they had already been stared at by several whites, despite Martha's keeping her face covered. They were so obviously outcasts and strangers to the town. What insanity it was to appear this way and be talked of by everyone. At this end of the workday people were on the streets. But greedily, looking straight ahead in a manner almost insane, she walked once around the square while he waited in alleyway shadow for her. Then she yielded to him and, separated by a hundred paces, she behind him, they returned to look for lodging near or in the black town. They saw an empty three-room cabin—tin roof, rickety porch in front, outhouse in back—where there was open unshaded space for a garden in the spring. Speaking of the steady work he would get, certain, and showing her a coin, Reuben conquered the doubts of the black woman who owned it, a widow living with her daughter next door, and gave her the coin. Reuben and Martha gave their names as Richard and Mary Johnson.

The house had the widow's little bit of battered furniture in it; Reuben and Martha sat down gingerly in two leaning chairs at a three-legged table propped on a wooden crate. They were silent, stunned by their exploits and exhaustion. After a little while the woman knocked loudly on the door and came in from her daughter's, bringing them a sheet and blanket to use on the sagging bed, till they could get their own. Martha fingered the thin cotton with reverence. And the woman brought them a portion of her baked supper and a few forks and spoons and three cracked plates. She offered them a little stove wood. When she looked at them with frank sorrow they stared down like children who had stayed out in a storm against instructions and were wet and chilled and chastened.

Before the woman left them she paused beside Martha and bent down to her, and spoke in her ear, and Martha looked at her quickly, with a greedy gratitude in her eyes that pierced Reuben when he saw it. Shortly afterward, Martha made up the bed, and lay down on it, and slept as if knocked unconscious. Reuben stayed awake into the night, watching her sleep.

The next morning he went out. He was taken on in town at the building of a big shed for another of these new businesses in automobiles. He received pay in coin at the end of the day, and promise of perhaps a week's work, and he went back to Martha. She had been cleaning the cabin, although not very effectually, from lack of experience and from weakness. She said she would have to go out, now, in this town, said she could no longer live penned up, said she would shop a little on the next day for as much as he would let her buy with his money—bread and meat, certainly. Sugar. Did he want coffee? She regretted—angry at herself—that she had not been able to bring her own money with her; but told him nothing of that feeling.

He wanted to show his good will to her on a day when she was in such a state of hope. She could barely lift her eyes to him, for fear he would be angry at her. He emptied his wooden box and smashed it and laid the wood in the stove, and looked to her frequently with smiles of bravado. She managed a weak smile that took back more than it gave. *This* was not what she wanted in life, this shack, this nigger village; this was in itself no cause for celebration.

This was, in effect, the end. Reuben only wanted time to get away when men came for them; he hoped some soul would warn him. He began bringing her his coin each day and trying to hoard Mr. Grooms's money, and forcing himself not to think of what was going to happen.

According to the world he had left behind, he was a kidnapper, a rapist, and a thief. He had entirely deceived and confused the young white lady, to whom he had spoken brashly and impertinently on earlier occasions, when only her sweet nature had kept her from denouncing him as she should have. He had set his savage eyes on her and planned his shocking crime. He had crept into her house in the middle of the night, through a window that had not been closed, had pocketed many small valuables and jewelry, had gagged and bound her in her bed. One could scarcely imagine the horrific fright which this must have caused her. He had then carried the young white woman off into the night and ravished her in the foul rooms of a deceitful old Negro man who was known to be untrustworthy, and then, not content with the heinous crimes he had already committed, he had fled town with the captive white girl in bondage to him. His skills in covering his trail had made finding him and his captive almost impossible. But decent men would not rest till every road and trail had been scoured for traces and clues, in the hope that the bestial creature could be found and properly punished, and his defenseless victim released from his grasp, brought back into civilization and given the chance to recover from this searing experience some semblance of a normal life, however unlikely that was.

Martha's everyday cleaning and cooking and even her idleness, when she had it, began making their house seem safe, seem as if it belonged to them, as if they could simply live—if nowhere else but in the drafty dirty cabin, then so be it for now. For two weeks, she shopped in the morning twice each week. She did it quickly and hated, after waiting so many hours and days, the necessity for haste. At the main dry goods store in town, she twice bought herself a ladies' magazine or bought Reuben a newspaper. At a poor white grocery on the edge of town, nearer what was now her home, she bought food. She set her two books on a little leaning stand that their landlady gave her and which she put on her side of their sagging bed. After supper she lit their one kerosene lamp, loaned by their landlady, and for a little while she tried to read. She made stews of what to her and Reuben seemed extraordinary richness with beef bones and potatoes and carrots and green beans, the last of the year's harvest. They sat down to eat supper together, happy to have bread, and food that had been cooked in a pot, disbelieving they were together, they were safe. And got into a bed to sleep as other people did, up off the floor. And lay awake, wrapped together, fearful, dozing and waking, till, with the morning light, came parting and the unspoken apprehension of each for the other.

Two weeks of food and rest made Reuben look hale and admirable; confidence crept back into Martha's face, but it fought with anxiety and if it did not entirely win, it fueled moods of near exhilaration, with Reuben. Her hair shone again. She washed it in real soap, dried it in a real towel, brushed it out. In their bed under a roof that was complete, sheltered from winds, they found in each other's bodies their great belief, their faith, their sustenance. Sometimes she laughed with it, sometimes wept, and either way his eyes might fill with tears for them both. After making love they made a long time of remaining close, of caresses past the heights of delirium, of embraces after passion, of sleeping close to each other, like children lost and alone. And neither of them ever spoke of what would come crashing and clamoring to their door. Because this time together was their victory, they would always have this, have done this, have had this. The meagerly built cabin, the warped planks that let the colder air in to chill them, the roaches and mice that crawled out of the walls and the floor, the dim smoking lamp, the smell of age and sickness and impoverishment—at one moment this shook Martha with repugnance and at another it seemed a salvation and she drew a deep breath to get the very strength of such persistent life into herself.

She began lingering a while in the square before returning by way of the store she frequented at the edge of town. She began to find that—without her feeling for Reuben diminishing in the slightest—she was nonetheless glad that he was not with her. By herself, and despite her appearance, she did not feel so constrained about going in or near the places that were of a familiar sort to her, even if she could buy nothing. She might be worn and pitiful looking and when in a plate-glass window she saw the condition of her clothes and her hair, she was mortified and ashamed; but at least she was not afraid of being seen with Reuben. She was relieved not to feel she was forcing him to attend her in something that, although important to her—accustomed, reassuring—was not only unimportant to him but entirely foreign as well.

In her ambling in the town, delaying her return to their shack— by now certainly a figure recognized by shopkeepers and the postmistress (who spent most of the day sitting in a wooden chair at the door of the tiny post office)—she was standing at a shop window and heard herself addressed by her own name, a woman's voice. Her heart leapt into her throat and her ears rang and, dazed, she turned as slowly as in a nightmare, hoping not to be struck. "Don't you remember me?" she heard. She was looking at an older woman, well-dressed. Martha shook her head slowly. The woman put a hand on Martha's arm. "Goodness. Are you the one people have talked of? That appeared in town from nowhere like some kinda ghost?"

The woman introduced herself. She had not seen Martha for eleven years, she calculated, yet had recognized her immediately. Martha did not remember her. Talking of herself, Mrs. Hagerman took Martha to the town's one tea-shop, half a block off the square in what had been a small house; led her in quickly to the private back room, where Helena Jacks served them tea. Staying a little too long with them.

Ruth Hagerman stopped speaking and with a sharp glance sent Helena Jacks out of the room. "I had heard that—oh, my dear—a strange-looking young woman had appeared a few times in town, and caused some speculation. But you had everyone convinced that you were very trashy white, indeed, I'm sorry to say." The woman's face was grave; she was waiting for the explanation of how Martha had come to such a state.

Martha could not think of how to reply. The woman was making no effort to cheer her.

"But we'll correct *that* first impression. Sure will. If only we can explain how you've come to look so lost and abandoned, oh Martha." At this, Martha wept a few tears. The woman remained dry-eyed, looking at her.

Martha sipped her tea. But suddenly could not quite believe she was truly permitted to do so. With a wobbly hand she put the cup back on the saucer. The weight of her own courage, through the weeks and weeks, felt too heavy to bear now. Not yet having said more than three words to Mrs. Hagerman, she laid her hands in her lap, bowed her head. Her shoulders shook and no sound came from her.

"I'm sure," the woman said, "we can solve what*ever* problem has brought you to this, Martha sweet. You *look* like you've bin runnin from some *war. Are* you all right?"

Martha nodded without looking up.

"Has somethin terrible happened to your famly?"

Martha looked up and smiled at her wanly. "Yes," she said. "Me."

"Whatever can you mean?"

"I have left them. But it has been mighty hard."

"Left them? Run off from them?"

"Yes. With a man."

"You mean eloped?" And in a lower voice, ("You're certainly old enough to get married, after all").

"Sort of. I guess you could say we did."

"Oh my word. And then he abandoned you? Left you in this state?"

Martha had to smile. "No. Jest the opposite. He's been beside me day and night. To protect me, to take care of me. As we have tried to hide from them and get away."

"They were that angry?"

Martha looked into Ruth's eyes; said nothing more, yet.

"Had you no money? And could you not travel to the North or some other far place?"

Martha shook her head. "No, we haven't been able to. But even if we had had more money, we couldn't have."

"I don't understand," Ruth Hagerman said. "Where is he?" she whispered.

"He's workin." Not true, exactly; that is, not true on this particular day.

"Workin? You mean laborin?"

"Yes."

Here was the crux. She must face it sooner or later. Martha bit her lip.

"Listen," Ruth Hagerman said, "don't worry yourself about tellin me innytheng but what you want to tell. D'you want more tea?"

She got up and went out. Martha looked down at her horrifying clothes. At her hands. She wanted to hide. Before she could even have moved, to escape through some other door, Ruth was back. "Helena'll bring us some more tea, and a bite a cake. All right?"

"Yes."

"Good." Ruth settled herself in her chair and sipped the last of her cup of tea. "Let me tell you a little about myself," she said.

Mr. Hagerman had passed away; he had owned both timberland and several mills, and Mrs. Hagerman lived on these businesses; lived very well; she had managers. They had been married only six years; a late marriage, this one, for both of them. And she had no children from her first marriage. Helena Jacks came in with another pot of tea and two delicate plates with slices of a yellow cake on them. Helena Jacks stood a moment after placing the food and drink on the table. When no one spoke, she turned and left; obviously put out.

Mrs. Hagerman said she was not one ever to stand in the way of love. Martha looked up at her sharply. Mrs. Hagerman said her own parents had not wanted her to marry her first husband, either. She said Martha and her husband must come to her house that very night to have supper with her and talk of their plans. She would help them if she could. Harriet was a good town. They ate their cake in silence for a moment. Martha much faster to finish hers than Ruth.

Then after Martha had swallowed more tea, she said, "Mrs. Hagerman, he's not a white man."

The woman's expression was of avid surprise; but Martha could not tell if she was distressed.

"Oh my," she said. "That is difficult." She added, "For myself, I've lived in Houston and New Orleans. I don't think I'm quite as shocked by these thengs as your parents. But . . ." Martha felt studied more closely, now. As if she were being diagnosed by a doctor—the way doctors are, they see some condition in you that they won't tell you, won't tell you yourself who has it, whatever it is.

Mrs. Hagerman said, "How did this ever happen?"

"He's Injin. Part Injin. He's got light skin."

"Oh." Again she looked away. Martha could see thoughts moving in the woman's mind; thoughts and, already, plans. "That might be different," the woman said. "*How* light is he?"

Martha leaned back, away from Ruth Hagerman.

The woman added, low-voiced, fastidiously, glancing away at the last moment as she spoke, "No nigra blood?"

"Would he have to not have it, to be a man?" Martha replied.

And then panicked, thinking she had scared away her only chance of help.

But Ruth was not dissuaded from her project. "Don't worry bout it now," she said. "After all, this's *not* unheard of. There're families in every Texis town that'd admit to *some* Injin blood—so long as it was added to their line a long time ago and they're a chief's descendants or a princess's, as they figger it." She looked into the teapot. "Old Ransom Wethers has been married to a full-blood Cherokee woman—I say 'old' but he's only a few years older than I am—since he was about twenty-one years old. He was a cowhand, when he started out. But nobody ever bothers her, or him about it, now." She looked upward. "There certainly *are* those who—like your daddy maybe—who do brood and rile over these thengs."

Mrs. Hagerman straightened her shoulders. She looked into Martha's eyes. She had the bearing of a person who had just been asked to take on a very large task that would tax her greatly but which she would secretly relish. Maybe she had been asked.

43

Mrs. Hagerman

Out of work this day and alone in the cabin while Martha was in town, Reuben had waited for her restlessly. But when she began to tell him what had happened, his eyes, that were hungry for her, grew narrow. Angry. At himself, too, for having failed to make her see how treacherous all ground still was to them, especially the familiar ground of her old ways of life. If they could gather sufficient money and necessities in this town, before being noticed by the wrong people, he wanted to go west, past Texas to some place that must exist beyond the reach of Martha's parents or people like her parents or perhaps anyone. "*How* not noticed?" she nearly yelled at him. "*How* are people not goan know there's a white girl and an Injin man livin in this pitiful little nigger house? In the first *day* it must've bin in the ears of innyone who *listens*. Sounded like Ruth had heard all about me, innyway. We have to live just as we *are*, and not pretindin to somethin else."

Then what about Oklahoma, where whites and Indians could marry each other, and Indians and black people, too.

"No," she said. "I won't *go* there. I doan know *where* tis, I doan know a *theng* about it. I doan *want* t'live there."

The feelings held back for days for fear of saying what she knew he did not want to hear ruled her now. But he said they could not go to Mrs. Hagerman's at all. They *must* leave tonight. Put their things together again and go on.

Martha answered talking very fast. "Ruth Hagerman's the *only* hope we've got. She's a respected woman, and if she takes to us, and she already has taken to *me*, she doesn't hate us just because you're diffrent, because you and I're diffrent, then she can help us, we can live like other people. Like white people. There *has* to've bin two people like us before, that settled down in a real place, that lived a normal kind of life." She stared at him hard. And then softened. "I'm sorry, I'm sorry," she said and leaned into him and held on to him.

But how little she understood of her own place in the world, how often he had felt like an uncomfortable bystander when she committed some failure to see, some unwitting cruelty, when even she, without half-realizing it, had with glance or word delivered a blow to someone not like herself who understood her or her kind better than she or her kind understood the others. Hadn't she realized how she'd behaved toward their landlady?

Martha was shocked. What had she done wrong?

"You treated her like she's your maid. When she had to go against custom even to rent us this cabin. People like you aren't suppose to be rentin in this part a town."

"No, I'm *not* supposed to," she said. "For good reasons."

He could not say no to her when she was in her fury of despair, her fists clenched at her hips, her body small where she stood in their dank, dusty shack.

He looked down at the floor. She was waiting for him to answer her, not simply to go along with her but to take up and carry some of her hope.

He did not hope. He went into the other room and sat on the bed, which creaked loudly under him. She followed him to the doorway and questioned him with a look, and he answered her with an open face, neither angry nor passive, simply open to her. She read it as assent. And smiled. And began to rush about.

She spent a frantic half-hour washing her face and brushing her hair and trying to scrub out stains and spots on her dress. He could not watch her. He had to pretend to busy himself; and he almost wished he could take her to this woman and leave her there, before he carried her life further into the ruin of her familiar ways and the defeat of her dreams. Then they sat and waited in silence till what they guessed was about the right hour—the right hour for the white woman, the right hour (Reuben thought) for them to walk into town noticed by only about half the world instead of all of it.

Out from the bare Negro village, where almost all the trees had been cut for firewood, they followed the main road through a small grove and then out into the fields that lay between the two settlements, white and black, fields that had been cleared by an earlier generation: Martha limping unevenly but gamely, an expression of eagerness on her tired face, and the black-haired young Reuben following her by a step and with deference, his body in a solicitous but cautious attitude, his pace smooth. In the pastures stood a few isolated live-oak trees, spreading huge and alone over cattle lying in trodden dust. Here and there a last few hungry crows were waddling with cocked eyes through the desolation of the gray-brown stubble of the harvested corn before flying to their roosts. On one side of the dirt road, the fence had five running strands of barbed wire; on the other, three. Sparrows clinging to the top wires fluttered away when Reuben and Martha reached them. Farther ahead, a small hawk was edgily commanding the ground from a fence-post. As they approached, it leaned forward and pulled its head down; it shat a white stream and beat up into the air and flew off, its last mouse-hunting of the day interrupted. Reuben led Martha to the other side of the road, away from where the hawk had given such bleak sign of the powers of the upper world.

The first few white houses, plain and small and unshaded, lay before them, vulnerably exposed, their sides or backs to the open fields. Two horsemen appeared from among the houses, coming out of town. Then came an automobile, speeding up when clear of houses and horsemen, scattering dust and fumes. Reuben and Martha huddled to one side, standing in weeds, as it sped noisily by. And an ox-cart was ahead of them; Reuben would have matched their pace to it, so as not to catch up, but Martha was gaining on it. As the horsemen approached, Martha bowed her head, pulling her scarf low, hiding her pale hands in it. Coming against them also was foot-traffic—a few Negro maids and workmen returning home in the November gloom under a falling wind that was flattening and pushing down the smoke from the chimneys at the edge of town, ahead. Some of the women were carrying baskets, the men were empty-handed. The tired servants pretended not even to glance at the mixed couple.

Martha was walking with little awareness of anything around her, excitedly assigning to her new acquaintance the role of their savior. Reuben measured every step of their passage into town, imagining the unwelcome scrutiny they would suffer once they were on white streets, even in the early darkness. He thought there was something he must have forgotten to bring with him. Like a fast horse. A gun.

Their entrance into the town was along Third Street, as the dirt road was called once it reached the first buildings. They passed an ice house, a small feed store and next to it a dry goods store, both of them owned by white men but trading with black customers, and then some unpainted gray buildings evidently unoccupied by any enterprise of men. And then the railroad tracks, laid in a long perfect curve as if by the hand and eye of God. The open corridor of air over the rails smelled of creosote and wet rust.

After that, cross streets led away on each side to frame houses set up on blocks of stone or cement, painted white or pale yellow or green, with raw nearly treeless yards. Reuben and Martha came under a few trees again, and passed larger houses lit with electricity. Then through the square. Martha kept walking with her head down, leading him by a step, but she had awakened to the evening world, and without even looking up she was unable now to keep from thinking covetously of establishments and stores, all of which she knew from her morning outings. She ticked them off in her head as quickly they passed each one. She was shivering under her scarf.

She was a little piece of iron being pulled by a great magnet. He didn't feel it. What was he, then—wood? stone? Reuben did not know where she traded, or who had seen her, but he pictured her in white shops, and far less needy of his care and protection alone than when with him or when in the black village which he had hoped they would leave soon, anyway. He could imagine Martha more at home in the town, certainly: larger, more her old self. He caught up to her and they walked very closely, silently, toward the house where she had a right to enter and where he must feel suffered. He understood also that each of her trips to town must have made it harder for her to return to their shack, and now this walk to town looked different to him. Because he kept seeing things as he imagined she saw them.

And yet she had returned to him each time she had left for town, and until today she had not complained to him. From the first, he had seen her as though she was a place to which he had never yet traveled, an exciting place, sufficient to itself. He had loved the full completeness of her. She had been another world. Now love and excitement had settled into a wrestle with pity, in a mere county of life. What she needed, at least as much as she wanted him, he could not give her because it did not belong to him. He steeled himself against the unknown evening and hoped that something, he could not know what, might come of it for her, and that it would bring no trouble or danger. As he walked, the fleshy part of his body— around his torso, on his thighs—seemed to have grown heavier, as if it had loosened slightly. The sensation was uncanny; it made his own body odd, foreign to him.

How was he to present himself to this woman in town? In her fine house, what would she require him to explain, to justify?

Martha looked wretched—when he compared her appearance to his memory of her in her father's carriage, dressed in good clothes, her face bright, her hair shining—and lovely: for the pensive expression on her face, the hope when she met his glance and as quick as lightning looked down and ahead again, as if she couldn't quite bear to imagine yet what wonderful good might come of this meeting. Was he simply to be forever besotted by her eyes and her body? Was that all it was? The loveliness of huge hope disarmed his caution, even though he knew at the same time that he was mistaken, for both their sakes, if he let her lead them out of hiding before they were farther from Three Rivers than this. There was New Mexico, too. They could try that. But her spirit was rising, so Reuben fought his anxiousness, his caution, with preposterous invented hopes that were the opposite of hers, and which he knew were foolish, but which distracted him: they would be given money and a horse and a buggy (they could not hope to ride the train together) to put them on the road west. *That* would be help. The thought cheered him up.

The house had two stories.

Beside the large door at the center of the broad railed front porch there was an electric lamp. Exposed, they had to walk into the light it cast so steadily. Up the steps they went, displayed to anyone who might look. A horde of delicate mosquito hawks and hard noisy flying beetles were flinging themselves against the lamp and the wall on which it was mounted. Martha took hold of the heavy brass knocker, shaped like an oversize three-toed claw, and rapped it three times against the polished metal plate beneath it; it made a loud flat sound that echoed down the street, and in a few seconds the door swung open and Mrs. Hagerman said good evening to them and invited them in with her hand. Martha thanked her and they entered through the fateful door. "I sent Delora home already," Mrs. Hagerman said. "It's just the three of us." Reuben nodded but said nothing in reply, it not being his custom to answer statements from people like Mrs. Hagerman. She faced him and, looking at him with a gaze that spoke of habitual victory but was not hostile, held out her hand and said to him, "Welcome to you, Reuben."

Delicately he touched her hand for a brief instant with his fingertips and said, "Thank you ma'am."

Martha looked at him with a smile flashing happiness and a

touch of fear. (What if—it had not occurred to her before—he wouldn't, he couldn't, come in with her to what Mrs. Hagerman might do for them? What if his hands wouldn't, his shoulders? But what if he *could* come in and he *didn't?* Come in—to house, to haven, to safety. To meals on plates and to clothes bought new, to habit and her accustomed ways? Didn't he want that? Wouldn't any person want that? Martha shoved the fear away, shook her head.)

"Did you say somethin, dear?" Mrs. Hagerman asked her.

Martha looked up quickly and smiled at her, "No, not a sengle word," she answered meekly.

Mrs. Hagerman was dressed very impressively. Her smile came at them from a calm distance. She pointed the way through open double glass doors to her dining room and followed them in; and Reuben was aware of her behind him, studying him. He had asked Martha if Mrs. Hagerman had *understood,* and Martha had said again and again she was a wonderful woman, she would help them, she had nothing against him, she wasn't like other people.

Under Martha's eyes were gray patches and on her face and the backs of her hands were mosquito welts. Her hair, which she had painstakingly pinned up, looked dull. Mrs. Hagerman was not staring.

Reuben took his place behind the chair Mrs. Hagerman indicated with a nod. He did not know what to do with his hands; he held them at his waist, clasped in front of him most unnaturally. The four blades of Mrs. Hagerman's electric ceiling fan were twirling slowly in the tiny bowl of the silver spoon laid on the table above his plate. A very strange spoon with little teeth. A tiny distorted image of the fan was twirling in every one of the six pieces of silverware at his place.

The table had been set for three. White china plates, one large and one small for each of them, wore a painted twining of flowers and leaves on their faces, and had gold edges. The drinking glasses were faceted as if they had been carved from an ice that did not melt. There were two forks on the left of Reuben's plate, one small and one large. And a knife and an ordinary spoon and a bigger one on the right side, and that unfamiliar spoon at the top. All the silverware had intricate woven patterns of design in the handles. There were two small fluted columns of glass with silver heads, looking to Reuben just like the shape of unnaturally fat dicks of dogs, but holding salt and pepper. Two silver candlesticks, with four new white tall candles in each twisted nest of silver arms, stood in the middle of the table, but the candles had not been lit. Instead, electric lamps were glowing with that steady light—not the living flame of a lamp—on the walls.

Mrs. Hagerman sat Martha and Reuben down, and brought in serving dishes of soup and meat and vegetables from her kitchen through a door that swung both in and out, without a latch. Reuben waited to be certain he, too, should eat. Mrs. Hagerman sat down and lifted a cut-glass decanter of red-black wine, and removed a crystalline plug from its mouth. She laid the plug on the table; it took in the electric lamplight and worked it into pale colors, roiling them silently like a little creature of light, not a friendly creature, and shooting a reflected beam at Reuben when he stirred.

There was extraordinary complication in eating at this table. First this; then that. Only a little of this; more of that. It was not eating, exactly, but a ceremony in which eating played a role. Obstacles to eating outnumbered the foodstuffs. And while Mrs. Hagerman and Martha were long practitioners of this rite, Reuben was not yet even a novice. When Mrs. Hagerman, pausing in her conversation with Martha, held up the decanter of wine and offered it to Reuben, he shook his head, and she forgot about him again and returned to their womanly conversation.

"Reuben, no—not that way," Mrs. Hagerman was saying to him and he put down the dull-edged but shining knife.

"Yes ma'am," he said quickly—not the polite "yes ma'am" of acquaintances but that other "yes ma'am" of the servant.

"Oh, I'm sorry," she said, and the surprised harshness was gone from her voice, but the apology was more to Martha than to Reuben.

Martha looked down, but then met Reuben's eyes and said, "Reuben you eat as makes you comfortable, don't feel you can't." He wanted to, and with his eyes he tried to thank her for seeing him truly, as he would hope that she could, instead of as Mrs. Hagerman expected her to. (And now it was Mrs. Hagerman's turn to look down at her own plate.) But he felt like a seed in the mouth of the room; he would be spat out. And it was a room of such a multitude of things—surfaces reflecting the strong light, a thousand objects like teeth to pierce him—that he could not even breathe freely, much less eat. His wrist, against the white linen tablecloth, was dark as a ripe apple.

Mrs. Hagerman was generous and liberal-minded. One made these things right simply by doing the right thing. She turned to him. "Martha's tole me a little bit about you," she said.

"Yes ma'am." He laid the knife down carefully from where he had picked it up, and it stained the tablecloth with drops of gravy. He put his hands in his lap, where they clasped each other and waited. If he was to talk, he did not want to try to eat at the same time.

"Where're you from?" Mrs. Hagerman asked him in a softer voice. Her polite substitute, in this instance, for the usual "Tell me about your people."

Reuben looked to Martha—not for an answer on his behalf but because he had not expected Mrs. Hagerman to want to speak to him at all. But then he looked back at the older woman so as not to allow Martha to guide him, for he must remember himself to himself, as he was and always had been.

He felt this strongly now and nearly said it, although the hands in his lap did not feel much reassurance, and did not let go of each other. But at least his world of talking with Martha—of answering all *her* questions, even when she had wanted of all things to write his answers in her copy book, his talk with her which had been far more than ever he had talked with anyone else since childhood— had prepared him to answer this woman more readily than he might have.

"Ma'am, my mama and I come out here when I was a boy. And I can't tell you exactly where we left from. It was the house of my grandpa and my grannie, that lived, I see now when I remember it, sharecroppin."

"Your mama was Injin?"

"I am the same as what she was, yes ma'am."

"And your daddy—because you don't . . ."

"My daddy I didn't know. I believe he had died."

"He was—part white, then?"

"Ma'am—"

In her softest voice, as if this statement were not part of their conversation, but an interruption of it, Mrs. Hagerman said, "Reuben, please just call me Ruth, my Christian name."

"Yes ma'am," he said. "My daddy was a man I never saw. But I am what he was, too, just as of my mama. Who died when I was a boy, at that time when we were aimin t'cross this part of the country, as I b'lieve now, and go north to The Nations. Oklahoma."

Mrs. Hagerman wore an expression of expectation; waiting for the missing word.

"Ruth," he said.

She smiled. "Your mama, what happened to her?"

"As I b'lieve now, she was lost. She was off the trail, and we were I don't rightly know where, when she died. Of a sickness that she had."

Martha had been eating slowly, through this first of her lover's social trials in her own world. She had never before heard a conversation between Reuben and another person. She was ashamed of herself for feeling embarrassed.

"Are you of a particlar tribe of *Indians*, then, Reuben?" Mrs. Hagerman asked him.

"Yes ma'am," he said, "thengs I recall, ways we had back then, when I was a child, was all Chactaw. Other thengs, too, I've come across."

"What do you mean?"

Gathering for later recall the mannerisms of her speech, acclimating himself to this new country, Reuben went on: "I mean, that from time to time I have run across another Indian man or woman, and we might talk about—"

"About your people?"

"Yes ma'am."

"Ruth," she said.

"Ruth," he said.

I want to be let live as I want to live, please.

A year before, Reuben had encountered an old man who was driving a team of two mules, one of them blind.

It was behind a livery and blacksmith—such spots Reuben knew well—in the last true town Reuben had seen before Three Rivers. The old man, with long gray hair, was sitting on the bench of a buckboard, holding the reins, waiting at the great open doorway, motionless as stone, looking like he expected to be waiting a week, evidently for some item to be consigned to him for delivery back to his boss. The day was hot and oppressively bright and close. It was just past the noon hour. The old man spoke softly and quite deliberately as Reuben was passing down the muddy alleyway. His skin was of Reuben's hue but darker. From the corners of his eyes a fan of wrinkles radiated to his cheeks and temples, and he squinted at Reuben and said, "Where you goin?" and he grinned and showed three teeth that were of no use to each other.

Reuben stopped. The old man was the first Indian he had seen in a long while. He felt no urge to answer; he studied the bent-backed figure on the buckboard. The mud smelled of the acrid mule piss, and the dozing beasts were stamping and twitching to shake off the biting flies. The old man closed his mouth and grunted, as if to regret the gesture of his question, as if taking Reuben's silence for a dismissal.

So Reuben said, "Howdy."

The old man nodded.

"You live round yere?" Reuben asked.

"Did once," he said. Reuben waited. "Came a long way, this time," the old man said, "to haul a lil iron gate for the Missy. Told her to wrote the man, to buy him here." He spat weakly down into the mud. "Graves of my people, though, in these parts," he said. "If you want to know. Cherokee."

Two white men came talking out of the darkness of the stable to the back door on the alleyway, and saw the two Indians and shot looks of disgust at them, which Reuben and the old man pretended not to have seen. The white men turned back toward the front of the large building, through the long dark interior of which the carriage door onto the main street was a frame of hot white afternoon light.

"And I kin take my time with these ole mules."

Reuben was not sure he wanted to talk to the old man; not sure he liked being seen with him; it was not inevitable that he and this man were alike. It could sometimes be an advantage, when white men looked, not to be seen at all. Like black people.

"Where you from?" the man asked him. In a backyard nearby, the other side of the alley, a house servant was chopping wood and singing one of those spiritual songs.

"I live here," Reuben said.

"Where you from?" the old man repeated. He scratched his side.

"Back across the big river. When I'z a little boy."

"Who are you?"

Reuben searched for the right answer to this. There was an empire of unknowing, and here a little door was opened on it, and Reuben felt like shutting the door, but wanted also to dart through it, fast, for a quick look at it, once more.

Chahtah, Reuben said to himself. But why should I tell you?

The man grunted again, at Reuben's silence. Whether this was approval or scorn or neither, Reuben couldn't tell. A black housemaid went by, denying them the recognition of her glance, stepping carefully across and around the puddles but leaving deep clear beautiful imprints of her bare feet in the soft mud and sand. She was carrying a pair of worn high-button shoes. The two men waited till she was gone.

"Say what you know," the old man said.

"*Hatak,*" Reuben said. Gave him that much. "*Hashi,*" he added. And then other words.

The answer was another grunt. At each turn, the old man was not to be surprised.

"You know what that means?" Reuben said, testing him.

"Chactaw," he said.

Both men still; the flies buzzing around the mules' eyes and nostrils and flanks; the sun shimmering in the rainpools; the two men like fortuitous prophets to each other: in the young man's eyes, the sight of the feebleness of age and servitude; in the old man's eyes, the sight of loss of place, of ignorance. The Cherokee man leaned over and dribbled a curd of sputum down to the mud. "You wait here a while with me," he said.

It was not a request or a command but a statement of what would be. Reuben stepped nearer and sat down on the flat bed of the buckboard, which sagged and made the blind off-mule take one step forward and then stop against the dead weight.

The old man was silent, apparently thinking. Then he said to Reuben over his shoulder, "Say your name to me." As though it had been waiting to be used and would answer of its own, the name moved in him. "Go ahead—it's all right," the Cherokee man said. Reuben felt the name come up from his gut, a bubble of sound that rose through him and issued from his mouth, his first saying of it since he was a boy and his mother was still alive. The name rose out of him released from oppressive hiding.

The old man nodded to him.

"Gideon, git in here!" a white man called from inside the stable and smithy. Slowly the old man lowered himself to the ground and went into the fly-swarming shadowed interior. Reuben waited a while, then stood up and away to one side as two bare-chested, small-waisted, well-muscled black men came rushing out carrying a large wrought-iron garden gate and laid it flat on the bed of the wagon. Their skin sparkling with sweat, the tightly curled hair on their chests and heads half-gray. They returned into the gloom side by side and the old Cherokee man came out stuffing a piece of paper into his filthy shirt pocket, and proceeded to tie the gate down to the buckboard. He indicated to Reuben to get back on, up front on the bench, and with practiced deliberateness he hauled himself up, too. He picked up the lifeless reins and lashed the lead mule, which broke into two quick steps but settled, and the blind one began to pull, too. Out the alley they plodded through the close air and past the back doors of the establishments of the enfranchised.

On the road, where Gideon would not be overheard, he told Reuben of how the world was made, and of wars between the tribes, and of corn boys, the moon, animals. Reuben tested the stories against those he knew, and noted several ways they were nearly the same. He did not say much—the old man was a talker, not one to listen.

The broad daylight was still unbearably hot; vultures were wheeling in the unattainable sky.

Repeatedly the old man said to Reuben, "My people b'lieve . . ." It was a complicated mood Reuben was wrapped in when, at a distance of six or seven slow miles from town, he had to get down if he did not want to spend all the rest of daylight walking back. He thanked Gideon and said good-bye to him quickly and without warning he jumped down from the slow-rolling wagon.

The wagon did not stop. Gideon's brown eyes, with whites in which broken blood vessels made a crowded map of a world that no longer existed, did not turn to offer a good-bye to the young man. The old hunched figure drove on; Reuben turned stiffly back toward the town, glad to get his buttocks off the hard wooden seat.

The old man's stories of what he said were true ways, not the erroneous and forgotten Chactaw ones, had brought many of Reuben's own memories back into his mind, and amidst them the one word he had spoken from within himself. If memory is an echo of what was, it is also a sound that is different from the sound that started it. Reuben's memory was stirred by these tales only half-remembered by Gideon himself. But having disclosed—almost as much to himself as to Gideon—his name, he felt altered. The sudden change made him feel undefended, vulnerable; but also free.

Walking back toward the town, he had cut to a narrower road that would bring him closer to where he wanted, and buzzards flapped up ahead of him. He came from upwind upon the carcass of a horse on its side with a snapped front leg and a bullet hole in its head. The flesh left to rot by someone with callous and wasteful habits. The stench hit Reuben hard and he expelled it from his nostrils and quickened his stride.

"You have a *rill* nice enunciation, Reuben," Mrs. Hagerman was saying to him.

He was working on it. He wondered what he had just been saying. "Thank you," he said, and picked up the larger fork again. Mrs. Hagerman turned back to Martha.

The table talk between them ran like a long-anticipated visit between two families that had been out of touch. Martha spoke of all the outward events in her parents' lives, and not of what had happened over Reuben. She spoke of her mother's activities and her father's work and his health. She said nothing of her mother's cold heart or her father's rage; she did not say anything about the mood of Three Rivers after what had happened in Palestine, after what had been done to the Negro boy; about the obvious. Martha said nothing of their fugitive weeks; although with Reuben she had learned to be a little proud, at cheerful moments, of her survival and her strength, here she did not mention it, for fear of being held low by Mrs. Hagerman, for shame of her circumstances— circumstances which in Mrs. Hagerman's eyes surely proved her mistake.

Reuben spoke only when infrequently he was spoken to, and he tried to act as he guessed he should act. Mrs. Hagerman offered him the red wine, again. He said no, and lifted his glass of water to his mouth and drank from it, as if to prove it was sufficient. He

303

drank it all, tipping the exquisite glass up.

Martha held her glass for more wine, and sipped it with eager lips held cautiously in a constrained smile. In her parents' Methodist house all alcohol was forbidden; this was the first time she had ever drunk of it, and although the taste was not pleasant, it gave a comforting warmth to her belly.

Reuben watched her and Mrs. Hagerman and he did as they did—ate as they ate, and at their pace, hungrier than they but holding himself to their demonstrated proportions. He stopped eating when they did, having gotten only some of what he had an appetite for.

"Isn't he?" Martha was saying, smiling at Reuben. "I took to his speakin right away—it was diffrent from what I expected. He talks like—"

"As I'm sure he does," Mrs. Hagerman said, "and naturally enough, bein a man of some experience, after all." Smiling at him. She said to Martha, "I want you both to move into my carriage house, in back. Over the stable."

They had eaten her food with her beautiful silverware, and she had brought them coffee in her delicate china cups with patterns of flowers painted against the bone-white, and now she had spoken in a way that was as decisive as an act. Reuben's thoughts moved freely toward the problems he confronted; he was agile enough in mind—but now when he spoke, somewhat differently he knew from Mrs. Hagerman and from Martha, but suffered by them with good will, he could think of only one word at a time, he felt bound by tight words, slowly stumbling forward: it was simply crazy to think of living in the town, now they would have their old pursuers and these new white people, too, to hide from. In his glass tiny bubbles in the water were clinging to the inside. He touched the glass and they were freed and rose to the surface and disappeared. Well, the dangers were already there. He would still have to hope for at least a few hours' warning when it came time to face the end.

Mrs. Hagerman was saying to Martha, "At my age I've passed through a period, a few years ago now, of a mood of, well, it was a defeat, I could say. A kind of defeat, at least of bein young, of wantin to stay young as I could. There'z so much I did want t'do. But this kind a defeat, you win out agginst it almost like it's agginst your will, seems like, just by your own . . . maturity, I suppose tis. But you, Martha, you're just now ready to plan and work and make your famly and if you'll let me hep you, it'd make *me* so happy to do it."

Martha was laughing softly with a sound almost of crying. She was crying. She pulled from her sleeve his handkerchief, that he had given her and that she cherished. He had not heard her laugh or cry in exactly this way in all the time they had been fleeing. And while he was thinking, the two women had already decided the matter. Martha's shoulders were shaking and Mrs. Hagerman was smiling very sweetly at her, while she was holding the thin handle of her cup of black coffee. They did not even see him, he had vanished from them, where they were it was only they who existed. His bowels had begun to churn, and he needed a privy. But he would hold it.

The empty spaces of the dark enormous house lay all around him, to the sides and above. There came back to Reuben a vision of a room seen from the outside, through a window, and the memory of hands holding him up to see it: a room like this, his mother's hands. He felt a new resolution: as soon as he and Martha left this house, again they would *have* to strike right out in the night to get safely away. He wasn't sure which way would be best to go.

Upstairs in the carriage house there was real furniture. Mrs. Hagerman went before them climbing the steps, carrying a lamp. They had hurried out across the yard without any wraps against the chill. Reuben saw no privy in the yard. The two rooms and the dark little kitchen were cold too, and Mrs. Hagerman asked Reuben to lay a fire in the wood stove that served for heat and cooking. There was an old dry bucket with enough wood in it for a brief fire. And newspaper, which he tried to scan as he picked it up and began to make paper twists of it. As he set to it, impatient with all these fussings that would come to nothing, with this Mrs. Hagerman holding her lamp up so he could see, Martha stood beside him where he knelt, and whispered to him several times, almost choking, "We've been rescued." He laid the fire with the kindling and dusty stove wood from which a few soft spiders ran trying to escape. He looked about and found matches and struck two and set fire to the newspaper under the wood. When it caught, he rose up from his knees. Mrs. Hagerman lit two more lamps and the rooms shrank together in the light. They were like no place he had ever lived.

Standing in the small arena of the rooms, Martha took Reuben's mute hand. She said to Mrs. Hagerman that she loved him, that they were going to be very happy, and forever they would owe her a greater debt than they could ever pay. Mrs. Hagerman surprised Reuben by approaching him closer and taking his other hand, lifting it in hers, looking at it for a moment like it was lifeless. "Martha is a wonderful girl, I've known her since she was born, just about, and I want to do evertheng I can to hep the two of you," she said to him.

This was impossible. "Thank you," he said.

She began bustling about, touching and straightening things evidently not used in a long while. "You're thenking of how you'll get on, in this town," she went on. "We're not so benighted as you might expect." They watched her. "Dallas isn't that far, you know." It was still her authority to opine, to own, to dispose, not theirs yet. "You're a *fine*-looking young man, Reuben. People are not going to mark you out. It's not like you're cullud! You'll get long fine—y'have that air bout you. I want you to stop worryin bout all that. I can *make* life all right for you, here. I can. And I want you to move in here right now, I don't want you all livin where you're stayin now, that just won't *do.* You need to get settled and take care of some *very* important thengs, real quick."

In Martha's face he saw that everything was stopping here. "Do you thenk that's true, Martha?" he said. "D'y'think we're

306

safe here?" She didn't answer right away.

"*Ruth* says it's all right. It's *not* Three Rivers. You're worried bout my parents, but everyone isn't *like* that. Not about *you*."

He felt his skin tighten on him, as if by referring to it repeatedly they were doing something to it. He could not tear it off his body but sometimes he would rather have had no skin, he would rather be a raw man. Like meat. Who could disclaim him or claim him, then?

"This's a lot bigger town than we're used to," Martha said to him.

"'S one of the reasons I never did want stay in Three Rivers," Mrs. Hagerman said. "It's jest too small!" (Martha contracted with sudden but unspoken defensiveness.) "They're very *narrow*," Ruth said.

Again she took Reuben's hand. It was one time too many, for him. But it was to Martha she spoke while she held on to him. "They're a *little* narrow, here, too," she said. "But we'll get you settled, fine. You let me hep you make a good life, here. I want you t' try." There was a gleam in her eye. "Now let's hurry back into my house and get some thengs together that I can give you," she said. She was excited; she seemed to have been waiting years to give away her own possessions.

She went down first, carrying the lamp she had brought with her, and the rooms behind them remained lit and began to warm as they crossed the dark yard again and Mrs. Hagerman preceded them into her back door. The two women began raiding Mrs. Hagerman's own house by the light of the electric lamps, gathering second-best china and silverware, linens and even underclothes and nightclothes and dresses for Martha, for although Martha was slightly taller, Mrs. Hagerman was not shaped so very differently from her. They made piles of things on the kitchen table and on two of the chairs. Mrs. Hagerman went into a side room by herself and Reuben whispered to Martha, "I have to go outside." Martha was looking at a little stack of books and ladies' magazines. She was dreaming; she even said to Mrs. Hagerman she thought she could write something that could be published in one of these magazines, she had an idea. Mrs. Hagerman appeared from a side room with another stack of them and the expression on Martha's face turned to grinning appetite. She was like a child on her birthday, beside herself with gifts and the riches of attention Mrs. Hagerman was pouring over her. All was possibility again, not risk, not sacrifice. But he had interrupted her. "What?" she said. "No!" she whispered harshly. "Ruth has an *inside* privy with a toilet." Of these, Reuben had heard. He looked around. She said, "I used it already." She took him by the hand and led him out of the kitchen, down the hall toward the front door, and then opened a door under the staircase and pointed him in. He ducked his head a little as he entered, though to do so was needless. Martha shut the door on him.

It was a small chamber of confinement floored with small white tiles the same shape as the cells of a bee-hive. A white sink was fastened to the wall, pipes underneath, and beside it a large white oval porcelain bucket, with wide lip, fastened to the floor. Held over it on a pipe and fastened also to the wall at the height of his head was a wooden box with a small-linked brass chain hanging from it, and in the oval bucket was standing water and for some reason it did not run out of the hole in the bottom. This was evidently the toilet.

He looked back at the closed door. Then at the small window in the outside wall, propped a little open. An electrical bulb of clear glass illuminated the chamber. His thoughts and bowels were moving.

He pushed the mother-of-pearl-tipped button sticking out from the wall: it snapped flush with the wall as the light went out, and another button above it, which he felt with his fingertips, came out. Now the room lay in the glow of faint moonlight from outside the window. He unfastened his trousers and dropped them to his ankles, and gingerly sat on the white bucket and released his bowels, having reached the last moment he could have held them. His eyes watered.

Then he remained where he sat, addressing the next problem:

no leaves, no newspaper. In the half-dark he scanned the white floor, the white walls. He saw nothing familiar except, lying on a little three-legged stand, a small book. He reached out for that and retrieved it and looked at it, turning it this way and that to catch the little light there was. His fingers traced the embossed letters of the title stamped on the cover. But he could not make out what it was. He felt the pages—they were not thin, it wasn't a Bible, he felt that at least he would commit no sin as Francie would have understood sin; or Martha either. He held the book up to the window and turned to the end. The last two pages were blank. Silently and slowly he tore those out. He set the book back down on the little table, and cleaned himself with the pages, dropped them into the toilet, and stood up. The soiled paper lay floating on the water.

He pulled up his trousers and fastened them. The sweat on his brow cooled sharply in the air from the window. He turned on the light again. Over the sink was a small mirror in a dark wooden frame. He glanced at himself quickly but did not hold his own gaze. The room no longer smelled clean.

He carefully shut the door behind him and stood in the hall. The door was made of the same white-painted wood panelling that covered the side of the staircase, almost like no door at all. In the kitchen the two women were absorbed in building Martha's stockpile of new things.

They had been planning. Mrs. Hagerman said she would get Reuben a job at the mill, a good job there, not just laboring, for Martha had told her of his skills and experience. And also, Ruth's double-duty house-man and stableboy had left her, and lucky he had, she now said, for Reuben could do that work, it was hardly anything, in exchange for their lodging in the carriage house. Since Reuben would be working at the mill, Ruth would manage her weekly affairs without great need of the carriage; she lived so near the center of town and enjoyed walking. She was not going to buy a motor car. "Like Daddy," Martha said. And then seemed to repent of having mentioned him—as though she had violated a taboo. Mrs. Hagerman went on: Reuben would care for the horses morning and evening, and on Saturday afternoons when he came home from the mill after his short Saturday shift he would harness them and carry her to several stores and other places. He would drive her on Sundays to church and her afternoon visits. He would also take care of her house and outbuildings.

Reuben must return to their cabin tomorrow and bring their things. They must stay from this very night in the carriage house.

Silently, carefully, he had been burrowing through the earth. He had been confined to dark trails with thicket interwoven overhead, while out on the roads alongside, hunters were running back and forth, looking to kill the deer. He had intended to go far enough to be able to break into the open and run free and fast, breathing deeply again—he had hoped to walk the road like any other man, and neither hunted nor hunting.

It was not yet so late, and he said, "I'm goan out there now and git our belongins from where we been stayin."

"Not now," Martha said.

"Yes. Now," he insisted. She was startled. Mrs. Hagerman's head came upright sharply; she looked at Reuben. He said to Martha, "I have to be out workin when the sun's up tomorrow, we're roofin." A lie to match hers that he was working at all. "I'll jest go now." She only looked at him at first, a question in her eyes. Then she came over to him and kissed him gently on the cheek, and walked back to stand beside Mrs. Hagerman.

Mrs. Hagerman said, "Surely you kin rest for a *day,* can't you Reuben, while I get them to find you a place at the mill?"

"Rather keep my word," he said. "And bring the belongins now. If that's all right. Won't take but a short while."

"Would you do one theng for me before you go, then?" Ruth said. And to Martha: "I want you to enjoy a good bath." And to Reuben: "Would you fill this buckit at the tap there over the long senk, and set it on my stove for me, and then you'll find more buckits on the back porch, and do the same with those. I'll build up the fire myself."

It was a relief: to be occupied in what might have been an accustomed way in white people's houses, had he been a servant. He filled five great buckets, crowded them on the top of the big cook stove, carried in more stove wood, and looked and poked a bit around her back room of tools and implements. Every blade, from ax to hoe, was dull. He stood unnoticed watching them through the half-open back door, Martha whom he loved and the older woman, as they talked. Then he opened the door a little more, and said to them, "I'll be back pretty soon," and with so much already decided, he left.

44

The Bath

Mrs. Hagerman's hair, of a dark auburn hue, pulled back and bound and coiled at her nape, had fallen loose and now hung disarrayed. The hour was getting late—the pendulum clock in the parlor had already chimed ten o'clock. Despite the coolness of the night, her small bathing room off the kitchen was warm, for the kitchen stovepipe went sideways through it. The one window, of etched glass, held a fine layer of condensed vapor, here and there scribed downward by a heavy descending droplet. Her house was very quiet. The worn-out girl's talk had veered abruptly from one thing to another at dinner, while the taciturn young Indian would scarcely speak at all unless she drew it out of him, and under his deference and veneer of humility was there not something threatening?

Martha Clarke had been reduced to the point of a nervous collapse, it seemed; she was very near the edge. And had she not happened to be standing on one particular street of Harriet at one precise moment, when the one person in all this region who might recognize and rescue her had been passing, she might still be living in a filthy hovel in nigger town, the object of scorn among women and obscene humor among men, and prey to who knew what danger.

Her romance with the Indian boy seemed no shallow illusion; it had certainly been tested over the past weeks, which had been anything but romantic. Everything in Martha's manner gave sign of a deep dependence on him, and nothing in his demeanor toward her ruled against him as a human being, of course; except that he simply would not do, it was impossible.

Together Martha and Mrs. Hagerman carried the heavy hot buckets one at a time together and poured the water into the copper bathing tub. Ruth said her mother had brought it with her when she and her husband and Ruth herself, then eleven years old, had left Philadelphia in '72 and gone to New Orleans to live. Ruth's mother had died when Ruth was Martha's age, and Ruth had left home soon after, but the tub was one thing, she said, that she had kept with her ever since, despite all the moving she had done— including her time in Three Rivers—till she had met Mr. Hagerman and they had made their home in Harriet, where one of his mills was. In the middle of the small bathing room, the tub rested on its flat bottom, somewhat oval-shaped and squared off at the ends. If Delora, Ruth's black maid, had been present, she would have prepared the bath. But the two white women managed.

With a mixture of modesty and relief Martha yielded to the motherly presence of the older woman. Laboriously she un-buttoned and unwrapped and removed every article of her dirty, mortifying clothing. Mrs. Hagerman kept her eyes away from Martha's body as the young woman tentatively stepped into the deep water which was almost too hot but cleansing, soothing. She sat down in the water slowly, carefully, holding to the sides of the tub as she would have done if the tub had been a small boat that she must not rock as she settled in it. Then she was down, fully in the hot water. The edges of the tub were rolled over into a smooth bar, and from the high back, behind Martha's head, the sides angled down to the narrower, lower foot, so she could rest her arms and lean back against the tarnished satiny metal warmed by the water and smoothed by the soap. The feeling of the bath made tears roll down her face; unbearable ease and pleasure. "I'm sorry," she said. "I can't seem to do innytheng but either laugh or cry and nothin in between."

"You go ahead, however you feel," Mrs. Hagerman said.

Mrs. Hagerman was demonstratively busy—thinking as she often did of setting the example—at making a neat bundle of Martha's old clothes. She tied it round with the arms of Martha's dress and placed it in the corner on the floor. "Oh this does feel wonderful to me," Martha breathed out. Mrs. Hagerman turned and, keeping her eyes respectfully from Martha's breasts, handed her a new bar of soap, transparent reddish-brown colored, the perfection of which was like that of a new coin, but began to be smoothed and worn as soon as Martha dipped it into the water and, with one hand then the other, glided it down the length of her arms from shoulder to wrist, above and below, and then along her legs.

Then Mrs. Hagerman went to refill the buckets, not so full as Reuben had filled them or she wouldn't be able to lift them by herself. She set them on the stove again while Martha leaned back against the silken warm copper, alone in the little bathing room. The knob on the shut door was of faceted glass.

On her arms her dark hair lay thinly webbed against her wet skin. In her armpits it thickened to a wet swatch. On her unshaven legs it lay thicker than on her arms, and she did not like how dark it looked when wet. Her feet were callused and smudged with dirt; she scrubbed them in turn, vigorously, splashing a little water on the floor; but was discouraged by how little she whitened them, and she lowered them again into the water where she would not see them. The door opened a little, and Mrs. Hagerman looked in. "Is there somethin you need?" she asked.

Sinking lower in the water, Martha said to her over the side of the tub, "This'll take much too *long*. I'm so . . . dirty."

"But I'm heatin more water," Mrs. Hagerman said brightly. "Are you beginnin to feel some better?"

"Oh, yes. Lots better." Her voice, amplified by the close hard walls. Mrs. Hagerman wished to open the next stage of her private inquiry, although perhaps it was too soon; she could not resist her own power of influence—without having realized it till now she had perhaps been storing it for such a dilemma as this, and it was overflowing her, and she must not waste even the first, premature drop of it.

Wanting some excuse for having entered the bathing room, she knelt down to pick up the bundle of Martha's old clothes. She said over her shoulder, "*Tell* me more of your feelins for Reuben."

"Oh." The hand holding the soap stopped moving. Then slowly began again, sliding down arms and legs and on shoulders and neck and nape, again and again. "I do love im. We want t' be married now, quick as we can." She wanted to look over her bare wet shoulder at Mrs. Hagerman. But didn't. "Do you thenk you can hep us with *that?*"

"I very *much* want to hep you," the woman said emphatically. The girl's face, softened by the warm luxury of the bath, beaded with perspiration and wash water, formed a half-smile. Then her forehead wrinkled. "Are you—do you thenk badly of me that I—" She raised her eyebrows.

"Oh, Martha. I can understand why your mother never even mintioned me to you. I did scandalize Three Rivers some in my time—stories I'll tell you. Of course I don't thenk badly of you atall." She was standing near the door. She studied the dirty clothes she was holding—not out of modesty but so as not to have seen the defenselessness of the young woman, so as to protect Martha from the frankness Martha herself had invited. "I am *so* happy to've found you," she said. "Or that *you've* found *me.* Very *happy* to be able to do somethin for you."

Martha was motionless in the water. "My father and mother will be huntin us," she said softly.

"There's no rason why they *have* to know you're here, at least for a while. You know, people can't talk the same way about what's taken for granted as ordinary as when they perceive somethin scandalous. I mean, if you're livin here, why then how are people to treat you like you were some kinda gypsy?" Not mentioning Reuben. "And if Charles and Caroline do find out . . . I b'lieve we can try and talk with em, sort it out."

Martha returned to washing herself, dreamily. The water was

trickling musically from her hands back into the tub.

"Um," Mrs. Hagerman said. She laid the bundle back down on the floor and from a shelf she reached a sponge as big as two fists, shaped like a ragged round stone, and handed it to Martha, who drowned it in the tub, squeezing the breath from it till it stopped bubbling, and then lifted it dripping like a catch and wrung it dry over her shoulders. The warm water ran down her back.

Martha raised her feet one at a time above the soapy surface and looked at them closely. Again she washed them. The deep dirt on them was softening and had begun to wash away. The very first thing she had purchased in Harriet, with Reuben's money, had been a pair of nail scissors. Her toenails had grown long enough to make her shoes uncomfortable, even though her shoes were ruined. She had bitten her fingernails, as out of habit she had always done; Reuben pared his own with his teeth, also, except for the thumbnails and his toenails, which he pared with a very sharp knife. Martha pulled her right foot closer and studied the nails. This sent a sharp pain through her ankle, which had been aching for too many days to remember, and she hoped her having come to favor it was not already more custom than necessity. "Do you have a little piece of pumice-stone?" she asked.

Mrs. Hagerman drew a low three-legged stand to the edge of the tub and on it she laid the stone. She was now perspiring freely in the close warm air in which they were both confined. She also laid on the stand a tiny pair of curved steel scissors and a ladies' safety razor, and then she picked up the bundle of clothes yet again and carried them out. Colder air poured through the door as she opened it and whirled around to close it again firmly.

Now Martha began again but this time methodically the task of the whole bath, beginning at her toes. She scrubbed her feet gently. She cut the soft soaked toenails and trimmed what little was not bitten from her fingernails. She put down the scissors and took up the razor, its mother-of-pearl handle scored for secure grasp. She soaped her shins and thighs. She shaved away the hair from her knees to her ankles. She laid the razor back on the stand.

Abstractedly she soaped herself once more. Her breasts and back were tingling from the heat. She rose up on her knees and lathered her dark pubic hair, which in the soap and water turned as soft as the hair on her arms, and washed herself carefully. She lay back again and drew the soap across her belly and under her breasts. Her chin on her collarbone, she studied her breasts: blue veins branched across the translucent skin; her nipples were soft and the aureoles smooth and broad. In her legs, in her back, in her shoulders, she felt a loosening, a relaxing, almost too much. She studied her belly.

She soaped her armpits again, and her chest above her breasts, following her collarbone that crossed like a dipping bridge from one shoulder to the other. And her shoulders and her neck and with both hands her face and her ears. Her slipping hand swam the soap over her skin, flowed with effortlessness, not like—but delivering to her a vivid sudden thought of—Reuben's gentle hands that washed her with air, when instead of smoothing and widening as they had done in the bath water her nipples would pucker and tense and became too sensitive for his touch.

It had never felt so good to wash. It had never felt so good.

To wash away dirt and everything.

She leaned back against the smooth luxurious copper. She had only her hair left to wash, and then to rinse and dry and brush out.

Mrs. Hagerman returned, coming in as quickly as she had gone out, with two large white towels, which she laid on the broad windowsill.

"My Mama and Daddy—" Martha began, with a troubled face; but Mrs. Hagerman interrupted her amiably.

"Tell me more of you and Reuben," she said. "I'm sorry but I must ask you right out, dear, do you truly love im, do you truly want im for your husband?" Feigning an expectation of assent, but disappointed when she heard it.

"I mean, it wouldn't be the first time," she continued, "it wouldn't be the end of the world, however shockin it may be to

318

some people, that a girl lost her good sense over a man that—"

"Yes. I said I did," Martha replied. "Didn't I?"

Ruth Hagerman, talking faster: "—when you of all people could certainly have a very promisin young man to marry you." Martha did not speak.

Ruth went on, "Reuben may well *be* a nice *boy.* Despite everytheng. He's surely good lookin. And well-spoken, considerin. . . . And intelligent. But I wonder—"

"Yes, I said yes," Martha repeated. "He's not a boy, he's twenty-four years old." Wondering how to mark Reuben's age when he did not know his birthday and didn't even bother himself about it.

The tiny room was quiet, except that Martha moved her leg in the water, which burbled around her glowing skin. Lost in thoughts of him. She needed him, more than she would let him know; and she hoped he did not feel such need for her, it was too much, she didn't want such need focused on her, it smothered her, it made her feel like she couldn't be herself, she had to be for him. She felt this clearly now, sitting in the tub, for the first time since they had escaped Three Rivers. She needed him; but this wasn't the wilderness, this was town. It wasn't the same. He would learn, though; he would change.

"I'll warm your water," Mrs. Hagerman said. She went out quickly and came back struggling to carry one of the buckets, which she set down on the floor with a thud, so that she could pull the door shut again. Then she lifted the bucket with a groan and poured it in at the foot of the tub. When she set the bucket down it clanked. She bent backwards, her hands at the small of her back, a little pain in her face.

"You don't b'lieve I love im," Martha said. And then more softly: "Or do you not b'lieve he loves me?"

"No, no—I kin see how he's protected you and cared for you, as you've told me, for a good while now. Surely as well as he could. And for him, pretty as *you* are, you're certainly a power. I expect you're both all excited about each other." In a lower tone, friendly and confessing: "I do understand that."

"But you say, 'excited.'"

"Um. Perhaps real love is somethin that does not *happen*—the way excitement kin *happen* and is very. . . well . . . *excitin*."

"What do you mean?—about us?"

"You sure may grow to love one another. You may very well."

"But?"

"No 'but.' What you feel for each other now—and it has been tested, I kin see that, and he hasn't jest gotten what he wanted and then left you and run off like—"

"He'd never do that!"

"No, I see that he wouldn't. But what you feel now, I'd say, is more like . . . promise? Possibility? Somethin like that? The possibility that, with some good luck and a good place where you won't be . . . that you'll love each other and make a good life?"

"No, we love each other now, and we've made *our* decision. He would no more leave me than I would leave him. I'm sure of that." The water getting tepid now. "Did you love your husband?"

"Oh. Well. He wasn't a man who was especially interested in home life. He had his work. He was so *involved* in the mill and all his business. . . . We have got to warsh your hair," Mrs. Hagerman said.

Martha hesitated. Then sighed and sat forward like a good daughter, with her head tilted back, her eyes closed, waiting—even eager despite the turmoil of her feelings—for the sensation of the water.

Mrs. Hagerman picked up a pitcher from the floor and dipped it full and very considerately poured it through Martha's hair, damp and massed and tangled. "Want me to do it for you?" she said.

"Sure do," Martha said. Her arms lay along the satiny edges of the tub.

Over Martha's hair Ruth rubbed the bar of soap, the molded manufacturer's name now melted away. Slowly a thin lather began to form and Mrs. Hagerman worked it through Martha's hair.

Mrs. Hagerman's massaging hands swept Martha toward sublime drowsiness, till too soon, much too soon, they stopped.

Mrs. Hagerman stood over her. On the water lay a scum of dirt and spent soap and floating hair. Mrs. Hagerman dipped two pitchers of clean water from the bucket and poured them through Martha's hair, and then began to rub more soap into it.

Martha was clasping her knees to her chest. Her head was still tilted back; she had not opened her eyes. She sat motionless, waiting, trusting. Again the soothing and stimulating massage of her head as the soap prickled, and her hair, that had been painful at the roots, began to feel clean.

The hands stopped again. Mrs. Hagerman picked up the empty bucket. "Goin for more clean water," she said, and went out quickly, leaving the door standing open this time. The colder air raised goosebumps on Martha's upper arms and chilled her neck. Mrs. Hagerman came back heavily with the nearly full bucket. "Close your eyes!" she said as she swept into the bathroom, leaving the door standing open, and lifted up the bucket with a laughing groan and poured half of it over Martha's head and set it down again. With a wet bedraggled sleeve she wiped perspiration from her forehead and tears of pain from her eyes and then with tired hands on her hips she said, "Keep your eyes closed good and tight now." Then she picked up the bucket.

Leaning her head back, holding the sides of the tub with both hands, her knees almost touching her breasts and her bitten ankles under the water, Martha kept her eyes tightly shut and held her breath as the water poured over her.

Ruth reached back to shut the door again. The room was much cooler for its having stood open for a moment. Both times she had lifted the bucket, it had been too heavy for her to hoist it safely as high as she needed. But impulsively, even recklessly, she had heaved it up, she almost could not hold it from falling from her grasp and injuring the girl, but she had tipped it empty at last. The streaming water had smoothed Martha's hair to her skull, chased the soap down her face and her shoulders and back and breasts, polishing her to solidity and immobility. Then as the empty bucket

321

clanked on the floor Martha gasped and breathed, but did not at first open her eyes. Like a child she rubbed the water from her eyes with her knuckles, and then opened them and smiled up at her friend.

But she could not catch the older woman's gaze; it was all inner.

Ruth had only just realized how her lifting the heavy buckets, an act out of her own character, dangerous had they fallen, had unsettled her, both physically and emotionally, for now the act shot into her an understanding of how upset she herself was. If Martha was to recover her wits fully, and get out of this trouble and return to a proper life, Ruth admonished herself, then she had need of a very stable, unflappable ally who was not going to be over-alarmed by the girl's meandering state of mind and uncertain feelings and appallingly bad judgment.

"Stand up, now, and we'll rinch you out from under all that soap," the woman said, and she went out for the last bucket, leaving the door open on purpose. Martha stood up and shivered in the unfriendly air.

Mrs. Hagerman came lumbering back. This time she first tipped a third of the bucket out into the bath, to lighten the weight, and then managed to lift it steadily as high as Martha's shoulders and pour it down her, first back then front.

She set that bucket down, the last one, next to the others, and said, "I've got clean clothes for you," and went out again. Through the open door Martha could see the wide kitchen, and it felt liberating to be standing naked in the house without worry of being seen. She leaned to one side and wrung out her hair over the water in which she was still standing. She reached to the windowsill and picked up one towel and wrapped it around her head, enclosing her wet hair. With the other towel she dried her shoulders and her arms and her chest, and stepped out of the tub onto the braided throw rug, red and green, and dried her back and her legs. She was still shivering. When she bent forward to look at her legs the turban fell off her head. She wound it back more tightly.

Mrs. Hagerman came in with an armful of clean clothes, and dressed Martha as she would have dressed a child, handing her one at a time a clean pair of white drawers, then a summer vest, then a pretty muslin night dress with embroidered collar and cuffs and a V-neck with a lace yoke. And over this, a warm robe, rose-colored thin wool. Disturbing that the Indian boy would see all this intimate clothing. Shocking.

"This feels so *good*," Martha said. "These are nicer than my thengs at home."

"Let's brush your hair out by the stove," Mrs. Hagerman said.

Martha sat in a kitchen chair and Mrs. Hagerman toweled her hair vigorously with the unwrapped turban and then began to pull the stiff-bristled hairbrush—so like Martha's own—through Martha's wet dark hair fiercely, beginning near the tangled ends and working back toward Martha's crown. Martha winced. But it was their custom as women that this pain was necessary.

It seemed like it had not been brushed for years. Martha had not had the heart to confront her own hair when she and Reuben were in flight, in hiding; it could make her see instantly, inescapably, her dressing table, all her things, and she might cry out not in physical pain but in despair. And she didn't want Reuben to hear her do that.

Each stroke of Mrs. Hagerman's strong arm pulled Martha's head back. Martha looked as though she might be a woman trying desperately to keep some word from being uttered through her—again and again the word rose, straightening her throat, throwing her head a little back, then battering unsuccessfully at her teeth, which were clenched against it. The word might have been "No!" But this was only the brushing of her hair.

How delicious the pain was, this time. Everything was different.

Reuben came into her mind, too, and with her eyes still closed she smiled.

When Mrs. Hagerman finished and stood back to admire the untangled cleanliness of Martha's hair, Martha said, without looking at her, "I've missed my monthly now two times, I b'lieve—I haven't been able to keep a clear count of the days, though heaven knows I tried."

Mrs. Hagerman drew her breath in sharply.

"So," Martha went on calmly, "I'm pritty sure I'm goin to have a baby. Reuben's and my first baby."

The brush clattered on the cold floor. Martha turned her head and over her shoulder said, "I haven't told Reuben yet. But now I want to tell im."

45

Night Journey

So he went out into the autumn air, refreshed by the chilly night. Freed from the house where the two women were talking, planning. There was almost no one about at this dark hour; the steam of his breath whitened the air in front of him and blew off, as, looking around, looking up at the sky that had partly cleared, he walked. He had forgotten many of the names he'd known, once upon a time, for some patterns of the stars. But he could make out stars here and there that he remembered he remembered; and he also remembered names for stars that he didn't remember where to look for. This occupied his thoughts as he walked. The light of the moon was dim gray, leaking down from behind moving clouds that had thickened in the east, even as the west was clearing. Once in a while the moon itself burst out into view in a fast clearing of cloud, and then was covered again. He had no trouble seeing his way back.

This time, through the town cautiously, invisibly, and then out past the commercial buildings and through the open reach of cultivated fields and pasture, and then into the Negro village, he moved much faster than he had when they had walked in together. He almost felt accompanied; perhaps it was by his mother's spirit. He felt again that he was on a long road alone, again to leave someone behind—Martha this time, as that time it had been his mother. Who had a true name. He could not leave Martha. Perched in the black village somewhere, as he entered, a mockingbird was singing and chattering without reason, in the night.

Martha was already very changed, after only a few hours, by being in the white woman's house. It was going to be very hard on her to leave this town and move on. It was like she was balanced, right now, on one foot on a narrow board, always close to falling off toward one side or the other into the same thing she had fallen into that night on the trail, and other times, when he would find her crying. She needed to get both feet down on the wide solid ground, and walk on.

But in this Mrs. Hagerman's house, while Martha seemed to feel more solidity underfoot, she was not really herself as she was with him. Not even as she had been, before they had run from Three Rivers. She went back beyond her old self, into something not her but rather a kind of likeness of herself; but it was, just as much, a likeness of other white girls like her. Or so he had to figure, not having known other white girls, like her or not. Not her own individual self, but the self she had in common with other young white women, it seemed like. Anyway, her white-world self. Whereas with him, in their time together, for all its hardships and frights, she was more a self that was her own and all her own. And where they had lived, the two of them alone together, had been a place that did not have any color of skin in it. It may have been no place to stay, but it had been their own place. Hadn't it?

He gathered their belongings in a single minute. He wished he still had that box, or her bag. He tied his things up in his other shirt, and hers in her other dress, which was tattered at the hem and cuffs, and torn still, at the place where it had been torn when he first saw it, taken from her bag beside a stream. He had thought that bringing their paltry few possessions tonight, in the dark, and putting them into those upstairs rooms, would soften for Martha the shame she would feel if the white woman saw by daylight how little was left to them and of what sort it was.

But also he needed to get away from both of them, so as to think. It was going to be hard on Martha to move on again, yes; he might not even be able to persuade her to go. Not now. And if he couldn't—if she couldn't see the danger in staying and pretending they could live like a white couple, without fear of her family in Three Rivers and her father's friends and white people in this town, too, no matter how different they were supposed to be—if he couldn't persuade of that. . . . A person like this Mrs. Hagerman could not know what life was like except in houses like her own. She could do favors but she couldn't change the way things were.

He had had to stiffen his back and by an effort of will not turn and look at her as he had gone out the door. Every time he left her, even to go to work in the mornings, had been harder for him to bear in this town. What was happening to her all day when she was alone? Where did she go when she went out? What if he went back to her at the end of the workday and she was gone, and men were waiting for him? What was she thinking? He could not understand her thinking; he also was afraid that he would come home and find her strange, altered. Almost part broken. Even at that moment of leaving her to her bath—had he wondered if he would ever see her again, without realizing that that was what he was wondering?

It would be a terrible thing if he decided to disappear; not to return tonight, while they were waiting, waiting till late, and then later. Worrying about him, at first. Then understanding he was not hurt, he was not wounded by someone else, or worse; he was gone of his own will, not to be seen again. Ever. That would be a terrible thing for her; for tonight, for days. For weeks and months would she feel it, for years? Did her bond to him really reach so deep in her, as in him the need for her reached through him downward, down to the soles of his feet? Did it? The white woman would be happy. She'd say if he left Martha that it was only what Martha should have expected of him. Given *what* he was.

But finally, sometime, Martha would be happier, if he left her now.

He was sitting on their sagging bed. A bed they would not again lie in together. As if his neck had been hatcheted, his chin lay on his chest, his head was inert, his body slouched into a position of sitting lifelessness. His bundle lay on the floor; hers on the bed next to him. Nothing in hers did she truly need. He roused himself, turned and untied hers once more, and looked at her things. Her precious hair brush. He lifted a gray but clean chemise from the soft pile and put it to his face, and breathed in through it. And dropped it to his lap, and tipped his head back and looked at the knotholes and warped planks of the underside of the roof, the black nail-tips poking through everywhere.

The half-fallen house in the abandoned place had been a ruin; but scoured clean by time and winds. This cabin smelled of grease and smoke, was cluttered with rags, scraps of old paper, broken things, broken furniture and windows and doors, the walls blackened by soot, the wide cracks between the floorboards inviting spiders up from the dark space underneath, from a whole world of other creatures below this world. An old calendar hung at an angle on a nail, the roof leaked, the mattress smelled of sweat and rank fatigue. But he would rather have stayed here a while than become part of that woman's household.

Martha would not find another good place like Mrs. Hagerman's, with a friend to care for her till she felt like going back home. Harriet was her place, her kind of place. She could not tolerate hidden life, dirty life, poor life. As she saw it. She must have her familiar way of doing things. She thought they could both have that. He was not certain he could want it.

He tied up her things again, and carrying one bundle under each arm he went next door. There was no light. He knocked softly, so as not to frighten or threaten. After a moment he heard a stirring. "Who there?" the timorous widow called. He spoke his false name. The door opened a bit. She had not lit a lamp.

"I'm leave you, now, leave your house," he said.

"You leavin? You and the white girl both?" She was frowzy with sleep and the surprise of dealing with him. But then, more warily, she said, "Cause I cain't be takin keer her, now, fer you. Ain't got power nor money for that." She was afraid.

"No," he said, and was going to explain, but she interrupted him, waking fully now, "That girl need her own people," she said emphatically.

"She's in a good place now, she's in town with white folks."

That brought the landlady to abrupt silence. "She all right?" she whispered.

"She's good, she's all right," he said.

The landlady looked at him from an angle. "And you," she said, her voice lower in pitch. "You fixin to light out?"

"I b'lieve I am," he said softly. "I'm studyin it now. Jest wanted to thank you for heppin us like you did." He put his bundles down on the porch and pulled out his coin purse, and she opened the door wider and leaned forward to watch his hand. He took out a coin and handed it to her. The moon was behind the moving clouds again as she tried to look at it and not having expected it couldn't yet make it out. She rubbed her thumb hard against it and smelled it and looked up at him again. She said, "This's moren you owe me." She had it in the center of her fist, and he remembered Francie holding the coin he'd retrieved for her from under the house.

"You keep well," he said, and he went down off the soft wood of her porch with his coin purse and his bundles and he heard the door close quietly and carefully behind him as he walked. He started off toward town. He would have to leave Martha's bundle for her where she would find it and understand its meaning.

He moved out into the night where to all he was invisible, and he felt, if not happy, then at least accustomed, and perhaps this custom of solitude was happiness. Perhaps it was all he was fit to feel, but "Oh Lord," he said out loud as he thought of her, of her mouth, her voice, her hand in his hand, her body held tight to his, his time with her when he was complete, not *having* to be alone, her shoulders, her hair, her eyes looking into him, her talking to him. Thank God, if there was one, and thank all powers, that he had had this much. This much had come to him and left him a different man. It did not seem possible that all this had happened in the space of three months or so.

At the edge of the black village he turned off the dirt road and ducked into the woods. He sat down on a fallen tree and put his burdens down. The moving clouds rushed overhead and as they uncovered the moon and covered it again they raised and lowered the mood of the still woods around him, exposing then dimming the contours of the trunks, the thick shadow. Reuben picked up a stick and although he couldn't see anything in the dark he drew absent imaginary sketches with the point of it through the pine straw, feeling the way his hand and wrist moved to form lines this way and that, an R, an S, another S. He remembered an old black man he'd encountered at the crossing of a muddy small river. It was a ford across a sandy rocky bottom, green water of a slow current arriving out of muddy bends and proceeding on toward more, but at this one place slipping over a higher stream-bed that would hold up the laden wheels of wagons. The man was at the back of his own wagon, pulled to one side of the road, his mule stamping off flies. He was hanging to a cross-board, by a heavy home-made wire hook, a soft-shell turtle, his fourth catch. One small, three medium-sized, they hung front legs down, their limp necks and heads dangling down from the shells at full length like the cocks of men.

He must get up, he must move, one way or the other.

Slowly he rose and picked up his things and entered the road again. He did not sense the presence of his mother's ghost any more. He studied the stars again on the way back as the clouds retreated from more of the sky. Remembered the ball game: two sticks Grandfather had made for him and the hard little ball of leather, and he'd carried them around with no place to play, no one to play with; only, once in a while he could get Grandfather to come out of his bad moods and tell him again about the great games, the villages assembled to play and yell, and cook and sing, and the wild game, the men running full speed and swirling this way and that like a herd, the dust rising, the doctors working their medicine, the women screaming, the injuries, the long day of running and fighting for the ball till the men were exhausted and finally it was over, the bets lost or won, the one village feasting and tending wounds and the other scattering into the night empty-handed and beaten. "Still play a game," Grandfather wondered aloud, "over at Bogue Homa?" Reuben had left those sticks hanging from a thong on the wall that day he and his mother had left. Long ago. Could still remember that day, the road had seemed so long, the bridge over the river—the first river—so high. They would be gone, those sticks; that hut would be gone, all those people gone, wherever that had been. Maybe he should go back that way sometime, and see was there anyone he might find that knew of his people. Maybe he should have gone back a long time ago. Maybe it wasn't so far as he'd always told himself it was. And he might have lived there all right. He hadn't been so curious about it before Martha had stirred it up in him again, asking him everything he could tell her; even writing things that he said to her.

He went back toward town and then through it; he took an alley rather than the street to Mrs. Hagerman's house. All the houses but hers were dark now. Her kitchen and upstairs were lit. And the carriage house still lit with the lamps they had left burning. Quietly he approached the back door, hoping not to be seen by a neighbor and shot for a thief, with his suspicious bundles under his arms. He had better not go up the outside stairs to the carriage house after all.

So, up the four back steps of Mrs. Hagerman's house silently he went, through the little porch room of garden tools and old shoes, and to the door. There was no one in the kitchen; they must be upstairs. Stuffing one bundle with the other under his left arm, he tried the door handle and it turned, and he pushed the door open soundlessly, and put Martha's bundle down on the floor and backed out again and pulled the door shut. The latch clicked, but not loudly. He stood motionless for a moment, waiting, and heard nothing.

He hung his head and closed his eyes. His feet seemed unable to respond to his decision.

A bright light flooded him and startled him into the moment, which rushed past him before he could catch it. The door was open and Martha was standing in it, looking at him, smiling, and the white woman behind her. Above him an electric lamp was burning, pouring itself angrily down on him. Martha stepped out to him, down the half-step from kitchen to porch, to meet him, dressed in a fine and lovely robe, her hair pulled back severely from her face and shining—she seemed older, even stoic, and more beautiful. The shape of her was dizzying. He did not know anymore if she was a beautiful young woman, only that he could not look at her without feeling she had been sent to him, for him; without wanting to say a prayer to life; without wanting to thank her for being.

The heat of the bath had reddened the mosquito welts on her forehead, but in her long sleeves and the long fall of the robe, with a scent of perfume about her, she was as commanding as when he had first seen her, first been drawn into her, into the heady risk of their being together.

Reuben set his own bundle down and she embraced him, pressing her cheek against his dirty shirt, against his breathing. He felt he was staining her cleanliness. She was not saying anything; her eyes were closed.

Over her, behind her, the white woman was looking at him and he looked back at her. He did not say anything to her, even with his eyes, but only looked back at her.

He could hear his heart beating in Martha's ear. His arms were still hanging at his sides, and tentatively he put them around Martha, reclaiming her despite himself.

But without some permission that he now lacked. That he had had before, when they had been fleeing and desperate and dependent only on each other. He bowed his head over Martha's shoulder, his face in her hair.

There were too many worlds. He had entered and left so many, even tonight he had gone to another: the black village; and on his return stopped in another: the woods; and another: his memory; and now stood stunned in yet another: her presence.

She leaned back from him and looked into his eyes. "I have some news for you," she said. She was pulling at him. "Come inside with us," she said, "somethin I want to tell you."

Part Four: 1916

46

Clothes: One View

The Choctaws state that, at a remote period, the earth was a vast plain, destitute of hills, and a mere quagmire. The word which they use to express this primitive state is applied to clotted blood, jelly, etc., which will serve to explain what their ideas were. The earth in this chaotic state, some of them suppose, was produced by the immediate power of the Creator; but others, indeed the majority who have conversed relative to this subject, have no knowledge how the earth was produced in this state; nor do they appear ever to have extended their thoughts so far as to make a single inquiry with respect to it.

While the earth was in this situation, a superior being, who is represented to have been in appearance as a red man, came down from above, and alighting near the center of the Choctaw Nation, threw up a large mound, or hill, called in their language *nanih waya,* "stooping or sloping hill." When this was done, he caused the red people to come out of it, and when he supposed that a sufficient number had come out, he stamped on the ground with his foot. When this signal of his power was given, some were partly formed, others were just raising their heads above the mud, emerging into the light, and struggling into life, all of whom perished. The red people being thus formed from the earth, and seated on the area of the hill, their Creator told them that they should live forever. But not understanding him, they inquired what he said, upon which he took away the grant he had given them of immortality, and told them they would become subject to death.

After the formation of man from the ground, the hills were formed, the earth indurated and fitted to become a habitation for man. The hills, they suppose, were formed by the agitation of the waters. While the earth was in its chaotic state, the waters are represented as having been thrown into a state of great agitation, like that of a boiling liquid, and being driven by violent winds, the soft mud was carried in various directions, and being deposited in different places, formed the mountains and hills which now appear on the face of the earth.

When the Creator had formed the red people from the ground, and fitted the earth for their residence, he told them the earth would bring forth spontaneously the chestnut, hickory nut, and acorn for their subsistence. Accordingly, the Choctaws state that in ancient times they lived principally upon these productions of the earth. And they suppose it was not till sometime after they had been a people, that the corn, which now forms no inconsiderable part of their food, was discovered by means of a crow.

They state, that at their first creation, both males and females went entirely naked. After some time, though from what cause they do not know, they began to use some covering. At first, the long moss, which abounds in southern climates, tied round their waists, formed their only covering. At some later period, after the invention of the bow and arrow, when they had acquired skill in hunting wild beasts, they began to use the skins of animals for clothing.

47

Monday, July 3

Reuben was wearing a long-sleeved white shirt and a short black tie, dark trousers, and scuffed, dusty leather brogues with a pattern of foxing and perforations across the toe, and thick soles and sides that trod readily and unharmed over sharp stones and broken glass.

In the welcome shade of the porch of Reilly's dry goods store, which Martha favored, and holding a small paper bag containing ribbon and lace he had purchased as a present for her birthday on Wednesday, the day after the fourth, he watched the mail boy pass by. The skinny black youth, perhaps eighteen years old, was pushing the iron-wheeled post-office hand truck slowly in the July heat and with arms at full length, his head bowed down, trudging along the walk that, from store to store, building to building on this block, changed from wood to brick and back again, so that the cart rumbled and then rattled and then rumbled again. His shirt was soaked with sweat down his back and under his arms. Francie's Frank would be a man now, almost as old as me; hope he has done even as well as this boy, Reuben thought.

It had taken Reuben twenty minutes to walk into the center of the town and purchase his presents. He had more time than he needed. He looked out at the street; as if for signs. The sunlight was blinding; and it shoved at his headache, making his temples throb. An affliction he had never had when he was younger.

Two automobiles passed in succession, the first raising dust that the second one breathed, and then he stepped down into the wide dirt street and crossed it at an angle, heading toward the square. Although he now drove Ruth Hagerman's automobile for her on Sundays, habitually he kept well clear of automobiles when he was on foot. He preferred to walk. He accomplished a longer journey on foot than if he had gone by horse or wagon or automobile, if he measured distance by how far he went in his thoughts, and how fast. Very far and fast.

He too had sweated into the armpits of his shirt and in a patch that he could feel sticking to his back. His hair was short and parted in the middle. He reached the other side of the street and without breaking his fluid stride he stepped up onto the walk. Pasted sloppily and unevenly on the boarded-up door of the old livery was a recruitment poster for the War. Since the spring, Mr. Clapham, the postmaster, had been zealously agitating among the young men for them to sign up. Reuben was past the age. From antipathy to Clapham—who always cut him when they met, not speaking to him, upholding his satisfied outrage when at least some others, not only Ruth, were willing to let their anger go—Reuben stayed out of the man's way. And anyway Reuben's interest remained in what was nearest at hand: his own children, his wife, not in realms of trouble farther off, of which he heard and read much, and from which he would be content for the rest of his life to stay clear, if he could.

"Mr. Sweet," someone called behind him and he turned. It was the little man from the dry goods store, limping after him, holding up an oblong of glaring white in the wearying noon sun. "Y'forgot yore newspaper," he said, coming near as Reuben waited. The skinny clerk, Reuben's age but seeming older, was evidently pleased to have a second look at Reuben in the daylight; unlike most whites he enjoyed prolonging his contact with the man from the mill who led a white life because he was the protégé of the wealthiest woman in town.

"Thanks," Reuben said. But said no more than that, as the clerk stood in front of him. He tucked the folded newspaper under his arm and resumed his trek. The clerk was the kind of person who would smile with contentment at being rebuffed. In the blinding heat Reuben heard doves cooing under the wooden eaves of one of the buildings. And a distressed clanking, squeaking, yelping, lowing sound, ahead.

In the square, where the sun beat hottest and the dust seemed to absorb it like a sponge and radiate it back through the soles of his shoes, the new municipal band—assembled by Henry Mooney, eager follower of Clapham, and, when performing on Sundays, outfitted in gathered uniforms, most of them stifling wool, that suggested a motley of firemen, Spanish-war corporals and a few Confederate veterans of the War of Northern Aggression—was tooting and blowing in the shade of an open-sided canvas tent-roof with a small American flag flying from the top of the protruding center pole. Mason's Fancy and Staple Goods, the blacksmith, the hotel, and many other establishments kept Confederate flags on their walls—the usual inherited bitterness here and there about the so-called Independence Day celebration. Some whites still grinned that word of emancipation had been kept from blacks in Texas long after it had been proclaimed in the North and other southern states, almost fifty years ago. And there had been men, too, to complete the job of exterminating and driving out the savages with equal satisfaction, by a few years after that. The pale white faces of the band, under red hair or blond hair or brown—shop clerks, office men, even some new immigrants—were flushed with heat and exertion.

They were evidently rehearsing for the parade the next afternoon. Henry Mooney wore his pale hair a little long in front and it was always falling in his eyes; Ruth had described him as a misfit who persisted in vague dreams of artistic talent, although he had lived long enough already to prove to all the world that he had none. He was very enthusiastic about his band. He even had a conductor's baton, ordered by mail from the music store in Dallas. Among the dozen players was Reuben's friend, or as much of a friend as he had, Tish Stangle, who, having only arrived in Texas a few years ago, from his old country, did not yet possess all the prejudices of his new compatriots.

But no point embarrassing Tish by signaling a hello. Reuben crossed the square on the diagonal. He was several blocks out the Mill Road when the band finally attacked, with a concerted, muffled, echoing blast of cornets, a military march. The blast and then the quieter, steady beat of the music, bass drum and cymbals, reached him less and less as he walked, quickly, till it became an unmusical wafted occasional murmur. Hot wind was rattling the leaves of the small new trees planted by the mayor along the barren streets of this poorer side. At the foot of each of the new poles carrying the telephone line out Mill Road, where people were only just beginning to get service, the raw red dirt had not yet settled. Then Reuben came to where waste scrub bordered Mill Road. A rising plume of black smoke, blown thin and dispersed by the wind, marked the mill up ahead. Reuben stepped off the road and in the shade of sapling pines perched the flat paper bag with his presents in a crotch of branches at eye level, and pulled from his trousers pocket a sandwich wrapped in butcher paper. He took two minutes to eat it; he balled up the brown butcher paper and dropped it onto the ground. Then from his shirt pocket he took a rolled cigarette, which he lit with a match. He stood, smoking, looking upward.

Last year it had been in hot still summer, also, when Reuben's second child, his son, had come into the shared, common existence of men and women. Now he was at the age when he would try to point at things, the infant hand becoming human. Reuben loved lying in bed with him in the crook of his arm. Littleruth favored her mother, but Joseph took after his father. Delora, seeing the two of them when she was helping Martha one day, had laughed and said, "You have plenty time to enjoy that, is what you think, and I'll tell you, he ain't *goan* be a little arm-baby for that long." She had leaned down to Joe and touched his cheek with a fingertip and cooed at him, far friendlier to the baby than she had ever been to Reuben. She resented Reuben's privileges and luck. Never where Ruth could hear her, she would say, where it seemed like she meant Reuben to hear her, "Only the dogs are treated worse than blacks." Her motto. But he liked her anyway; she wasn't a bad person, really. Only had made the wrong alliance, he believed, although he knew it was the only one she could make, and better than none.

Reuben had forgotten how tiny babies were, how tiny Littleruth had been, then Joseph came and reminded him. Those first few months of Joe's life—when he lay on his back with his bottom wrapped in soft cloth, his tiny hands in the air over his chest, pumping first one short leg and then the other, looking up, just up at whatever might be there that he could not yet see. His expression both wizened and perplexed. Entering him through the tiny shell of his ear, what sounds made sense to him? "Joe," Reuben would often whisper to him, as Joe grew, till Joe knew his father and when he heard the whisper would turn his outsized head at this sound, and arch his back, pushing off with his bare feet to roll sideways toward the spirit that wanted to surround and protect him. Then, stronger, pushing till he rolled up halfway, onto his side, staring wide-eyed at the great face near his, then following his roll onto his stomach and pushing himself up on his short arms to look at his father.

He would let himself down, then, in those days before he would crawl—was it from fatigue after a few seconds, those little arms unable yet to do more? And then would push himself up again, and a little backwards on the sheets; and again and again, concentrating hard on his movement, till the great hand brought him back. . . . And often in Joe's first year, Reuben had stretched out on the bed with his baby in the crook of his arm, that way he liked, to draw in the creaturely scent of infant. And would remember having smelled Littleruth, that way. And would regret that she had grown so much already. Already almost five years old, she might inch near Reuben and Joe, and he would pull her onto the bed, too. She wanted to be invited.

The little girl would lie with her father and brother, smiling at Joe and then at Reuben. Still almost as struck with wonder at her parents as they were at her.

When Martha uncovered her breast and gave it to Joe, he'd stare into her eyes as he sucked at her; his hands, opening and closing slowly, uncontrolled, softly beat at the air around her breast, and at her breast. Till his belly filled and his eyes half closed and he was finished, and would lie quietly in her arms, if she let him. Sleeping the most sheltered sleep he would know, life-long. He was a little darker than Littleruth.

On Sundays Martha dressed both children in beautiful clothes that Ruth had ordered sewn for them by a friend of Delora's, and which Martha herself embroidered with jolly figures, and the two women and two children went to the early services at the Episcopal Church. Reuben drove them and let them off at the door, and then took his time parking the automobile before he stepped into the church and sat down at the back in a corner. Before the service was over, he went out and brought the automobile to the church door and waited for them to come out. No one had told him—that is, Ruth had not—to take up this routine of self-effacement. After church let out, when he had left Martha and the children at home again, he drove Ruth to her visits, and parked the car under shade trees and read the newspaper while he waited. He might receive a wave and hello but he was not invited in. Not that he wanted to go in. He wanted to read the newspaper, if he had to give up being with his family. Ruth didn't seem to want him to spend that time with his own children, with his beloved and legal wife. And how could he say no to her? The census taker had come through town at the end of that year they had arrived in Harriet, just in time to put down Martha and him; somebody Ruth knew; and had marked him W in the column for race. And written down his new last name; Ruth's idea.

Reuben kicked a hole in the ground where he stood, and dropped into it the butt of his cigarette, and ground it out with his heel and kicked the ground over it again. Buried it, thus; like something dead. Stood on it. He reached down his presents, and folded the bag carefully and slid it into his trousers pocket where the sandwich had been.

Memory does not come down from the upper world; in the upper world there is no memory, only ceaseless being, unchanging images, bright birds forever the same in perfect plumage. When they come to the middle world and alight then their aspect begins to fray: their feathers molt, they scratch with their beaks at lice, they are hungry predators and eaten prey.

Memory does not rise from the lower world; in the lower world there is no memory, only ceaseless forgetting. Under the ground, under the water, things are absorbed and dissolved and there is no remembering.

Only in this middle world is there the ceaseless creation of memory out of what happens, and the ceaseless secret of it in the soul—where, if it does not wish to bring itself out, in its own time, unasked (as at times it does bring itself out), it can be found again only with effort. And where it is stored away, there is a ceaseless changing of the remembered from what it was to what it will be remembered as having been, what will be created anew and differently by the very act of remembering.

The white woman, sitting on the ground, took her baby from Reuben without a word and held him tightly to her breast. The water was pouring off Reuben, dripping from his long hair, from his dirty clothes, puddling on the ground at his feet, and he'd held the baby out to her, handed the baby down to her, after the two white men had pulled her, too, from the river. She was barefooted, she had left her shoes on the bank when she had turned up her dress and, laughing loud enough to waken Reuben, had carried her baby into the water so he could play in the shallows. Now she was scared and angry, sitting on the bank, one of the men holding her up. Her baby was unharmed and not even frightened. The water had meant nothing to him—when Reuben had lifted him up above the water and held him in the air with one hand while swimming back to the bank, the baby had laughed. The baby had not even swallowed any water; did not even choke; had laughed.

The woman was still gasping; the baby was cooing happily and had found her face with his eyes. On that face, which was looking at Reuben, was an expression of disgust.

Reuben backed away from her. The two white men were looking at him with something like sympathy; maybe it had struck even them that her anger was poor recompense for his having saved her baby's life. But they would not say or do anything for him.

Around them was the empty Sunday morning; this was a place deserted except for the three men, the woman and the baby—a chance meeting of three parties that had saved the woman, and her child, when so foolishly she had waded where she did not know the narrow green river. It was a new, somewhat remote place; the ground had been scraped clear and a few sheds had been laid down on it like toys. From one of them Reuben, having slept unauthorized through the night, had just come out, cautiously, to slip away—because he had heard the woman's voice as she cooed at her baby—when he saw her wading in the river with her baby and she went under. At the same moment the two white men, approaching from the other shore, saw her as well. All three men had leapt into the water and it was Reuben, his eyes open, already in the deeps, stroking hard to pull his body down, when always it wanted of its own accord to float up, who had caught hold of the baby suspended in the water. Holding its breath by instinct. Reuben who had rescued it from the realm of forgetting, rising up with it to push it first out of the water, above him, holding it up on one hand.

He backed away from the three whites, dripping river-water, turned and picked up his carpet bag and his shoes and walked on. It struck him that she might not be as safe as she assumed with those two white men. But it was not for him to do anything about that. He felt himself growing smaller to them as he got farther away; he knew they were still watching him. They would remember what he had done. He would remember what he had done.

346

Reuben had made up a game to distract Littleruth from her jealousy of Joe. He was with her on a Sunday when she found a penny that must have fallen from his trouser pocket to the floor near the big bed. She was very excited, so Reuben began now and then to leave a penny where she might find it. She knew it was he who had done this, but they pretended that the pennies were no one's, were something added to them from without by an unknown presence. Martha joined the game, too, and at any time one of them might find a penny in the house—on the floor, in the open, or under the edge of the hook rug, or in a shoe, or under a supper plate. Till all of them were puzzled because father, mother and daughter each said, "*I didn't put it there!*" and it began to seem that this wealth of pennies, which really was a kind of wealth if you saw what a penny was, was appearing by a kind of magic.

There seemed to have been some magic performed; some spell chanted. Here were two children in the world who were his own. He had the feeling they had come on their own decision. Littleruth, right away—to confirm him in his staying in Harriet, to be welcomed into a new life with her parents. And Joseph had waited and waited till Littleruth was nearly old enough to watch over him, and then he too jumped down into this world through his mother, last summer. Summer hot as this one.

Reuben continued toward the mill. He stepped over the tracks of the two rail lines into the yard. On the spur beside the loading docks were several empty flatcars to be loaded with orders for Dallas. The dust of the Harriet streets had whitened his trouser cuffs and he bent and slapped them a few times before approaching the mill office. Martha's presents were by far too little to make much of a difference to her, just a remembrance, to give her pleasure at the remembering. Her birthday was so important to her.

Since the birth of Littleruth, and far more so since Joe's birth, which had seemed to draw nearly all of Martha's strength out of her, she had dipped more frequently, more erratically, into her moods of—he did not know what it was. A kind of losing of her bearings, of her sense of direction not in the town or even in her feelings but in her connectedness to what was. She seemed to Reuben sometimes like a waking person who had been caught, and held back even after waking, in a dream place. Her eyes saw what was in the dream place, not what was in the waking world from which he and others were speaking, asking her if she was all right. And no one else could see what she saw; Reuben could only try to guess from what she said what it was that agitated or even terrified her there in that place she was seeing while he stood beside her, and Littleruth looked up at her quietly, and Joseph babbled in his crib. But Reuben could not guess.

Now she was sick, again, with a fever this time, and her digestion upset, and for three days Ruth Hagerman had been looking after her and watching Joe and sending Littleruth off to play with her friends, while Reuben worked his days at the mill. Martha had seemed better this morning. She had not looked so wan or damp when he first woke and turned to look at her. He had eaten his breakfast silently from a loaf of bread and a pot of jam. Joe was awake in his crib, but only watched his father with clear eyes, moving his head to one side and then the other to follow Reuben's quiet movement in the room. Reuben had dressed quickly, bent over and whispered a little farewell to Joe and kissed Littleruth as she slept. Martha was sleeping again, or pretending to. He had gone carefully down the creaking steps and then stopped at Mrs. Hagerman's back door to tell her he was leaving, and she, ready for him and waiting in her kitchen, had come out to replace him at Martha's side and to give the children their breakfast.

When he and she had had nothing, he had been everything to her, he was a man of the world of nothing. Now that they had something, he felt unneeded. What did she need him for in the world of something? He wanted, just as much as before, to do for her, but in the world of something he had not been able to do very much. In that brief time when they had tramped and camped through the woods and fields, till they had reached Harriet and stopped, she had needed him not only in order to survive but also to have a reason to survive; their love.

Just before the whistle blew to end the noon dinner hour Reuben stepped into the mill office where he worked with three other men. He took his chair and went back to copying from scrawled and idiosyncratically symbolized notes on scraps of paper— handwriting and marks that would have puzzled an outsider but which Reuben and the other clerks knew how to decipher; he had made such signs himself, for a while, of the reports of loads of timber brought in, the orders for lumber shipping out—onto triplicate bills of lading and invoices with carbon paper interleaved to make two extra copies, one of them yellow. He had a stack of the cryptic scraps like dry leaves picked up in a forest, bearing messages from gods or spirits, which as priest he could interpret and pass on in copy-script intelligible to ordinary persons who did not know how to read the secret signs. And he had a gray ledger book bound in canvas, and an inkwell and pen, and pencils sharpened not with a knife but in a hand-cranked little mill. And for the hours of the day, through the morning when the saws were screaming and the moving logs and planks clattering and rumbling and the men at work and in danger, and again through the afternoon that began with a blast as sudden as the band's, he wrote at the desk assigned to him.

The money he and Martha and the children lived on was only partly his own. Even though their rooms were modest, they had all the things that Ruth Hagerman provided—like the children's clothes—that were more properly the things of wealth than of the ordinary working man's life. Reuben had not come to feel that his family was living from his work, for Ruth added her own purchases so generously, and apart from Reuben's, to answer directly what Martha needed or wanted. Martha often showed him new clothes for the children or for herself, or something new in the kitchen, or a new piece of furniture for their crowded rooms; it was not his money, most of which he gave to her every pay day, that had bought these things. He had not even had to buy all his own clothes, for Ruth had had a large stock of her dead husband's things, which although unworn for years and so a little strange to wear at all, fit him so uncannily well he had not been able to refuse them, and which gave him such an air of civic solidity that he and Ruth Hagerman were both surprised. At the mill he could not help wearing expensive shirts and trousers, since he had no others. Martha, however, approved.

They owned now what seemed to Reuben a lot of Ruth Hagerman's knickknacks—castoffs, really, but she had conferred them on Martha at the beginning with enough kindness to keep them from seeming the worried attempt they had been (Reuben saw this) to enliven Martha with pretty things: statuettes and vases and a glass paperweight with a whorl of red color in it. And he had often caught Martha staring off, or at something, like the paperweight or a blue bottle she was fond of—but beyond it or into it at something he could not see with her. Time stopped for her for a moment, till she would wake back into life and resume her cooking or tending Joseph or reading to Littleruth.

His own money went for their food; and he bought things, himself, for the children—and then when he'd given Littleruth a new vest or some candy, or Joe a wooden toy, he felt he had . . . *provided* . . . beyond the necessities. Reuben's occasional household labor was still their nominal barter for rent, as well. But the rest of the money that Martha spent or that was spent on her and the children—he was not sure how much that was—came from someone else to whom it seemed he would always have to be grateful.

He could have lived with less. But it made him happy to see the children's things; their snug new clothes. They looked to him just like the kind of children he had once imagined Martha would have in her old way of life in Three Rivers (as her parents and her sister and the snaky James kept on in their ways). There seemed nothing that was not made for these children of hers, and his, even if he did feel that the gifts from Ruth Hagerman also seemed to remove the children a little from him. But who owned and who gave and who was grateful, all disappeared from his mind when he was with Littleruth and Joe in the evening—merely holding Joseph and laughing with him, or pacing and hugging him to his shoulder to stop his fussing, and talking with Littleruth as her smallness drew him back to his own childhood and he recovered stories and memories, which he told her in secret. He played at swearing Littleruth to secrecy, because the stories had power—and truly he did tell her things he had never told to Martha, despite all of Martha's insistent asking. For, from time to time she still returned to it, when she was in an industrious mood and planning the things she would yet do in her life.

Reuben told Littleruth what his mother had told him—about jaybirds and redbirds and crows, and leaves and roots that would cure a stomachache or a cough or a bad dream, about where people had come from in the beginning, about the different kinds of people. They would sneak away together and hide in the stable, and now garage, underneath. (Martha and Littleruth and Ruth had laughed as they had watched Reuben first learn to drive Ruth's car; it always made him smile to remember them laughing at him that afternoon.) Hidden in a dim corner they would spend a half an hour or more whispering and talking. Littleruth on Reuben's lap. Her hands playing with his collar and his shirt buttons, or with his hair. In those shadows, he told her a true name he had given her when she was born, in secret; and he was sure that at moments— no one else noticed—when he looked at her with that name in his mind and she knew he was thinking it, something deeper showed in her. Something understood but not said. How powerful that was.

But there always came a moment in their hidden time when she wanted, suddenly, to go back upstairs to Martha, and he let her run off, and he would stay by himself. Smoke a cigarette, alone.

When in the beginning times all the animals and plants could speak, they and the people lived together in harmonious friendship. But the people increased their numbers more rapidly than the animals and plants, till people were showing up everywhere, in all sorts of places where they had never been before; and where they were settled, they began to invent weapons and to kill the larger animals and take their skins from them for their own clothing, and to eat their bodies; they crushed the small animals underfoot without even noticing them. So the animals called councils among themselves.

It was proposed among the Bears that they go to war against the people, and make weapons, as the people had done, and use them in this war—bows and arrows. But the Bears could not shoot the arrows accurately and they gave up, and the people continued to hunt them and kill them, without remorse.

It was proposed among the Deer to send illness among the people whenever a hunter killed a Deer without asking the Deer's pardon for his offense. And a stiffness in the bones, a crippling, was duly sent on its way to punish unrepentant hunters.

It was proposed among the Fishes and Reptiles to send frightening dreams of Snakes, of eating rotten Fish, among people to repay their evil. And so they did, and people sickened and sometimes died of their terrible dreams.

And the Birds and smaller animals and the Insects and Worms all put their minds to work inventing diseases, which they began to send out among the pestiferous people.

The Plants, however, remained friendly to the people, and when they heard what the animals had done, they too held a council. Each tree and bush and shrub and flower and weed and herb offered itself as a remedy for one of the diseases invented by the animals, and each promised, "I shall appear to help Man when he calls upon me in his need."

Aunty Ruth, often spending half her day with the children, taking Littleruth with her into her house to play, helping Martha prepare supper, and spending all day with Martha when she was not well, was like a grandmother to them, on Martha's side; while behind Reuben, looking over his shoulder at the little ones, stood only ghosts. But it was to Reuben that Littleruth stole with that special look in her eye, and she would whisper in his ear, "Tell me something," and he would wink at her and lead her out the door and down the wooden steps to their hiding place.

He remembered moments of awe when Littleruth was smaller, moments when some resource as fiercely splendid as the sun seemed to open in him and could sustain him forever, because of the wonder of his child, wonder of the moment that contained him and Martha and his own children. As when Littleruth, she must have been about three, was sitting in Martha's lap one evening as Reuben at the table studying a newspaper; word had just come of his promotion from office assistant to clerk. Littleruth, held protectively in Martha's arms, with her pudgy hands was toying with her mother's face, talking with the fervor of a new talker into her mother's ear while Martha was trying to talk and listen to Reuben. Martha was absently hushing Littleruth again and again, sweetly, without even looking at her daughter, and Littleruth was talking on, smiling, teasing her mother perhaps, and touching Martha's cheeks, her eyebrows, her nose, her mouth, and then when Reuben was looking up at them Littleruth pressed her face into her mother's neck and put her arms around her mother's neck and clung tightly, tightly to her, and Reuben had got up and hurried to them and put his arms around both of them and in silence they all three rode a rushing almost dreadful intensity of feeling, that let them out of its grip after a moment and then they were all three quiet. So. He would always have that image. And others. That was the wealth that he had somehow earned, and which he could not lose.

Because of Ruth Hagerman, Reuben had worked quickly upward at the mill. Ruth had given him his new clothes and even his new name. With his head for figures, and his reading and writing, he did not doubt the justice of having been brought into the office, paid more money and freed of dangerous work; he had even almost expected it, if only because expectation was less tiring than

353

fear. And Ruth would promote him again, in time.

Reuben's officemates had started in their white-shirt jobs, and knew nothing first-hand of the life in the yard. When the whistle blew at Hagerman's Mill to signal the beginning of the noon dinner hour, Reuben would have liked to sit with the yard crews, but had to remain in the group of his officemates. He was close to none of them; but how could he be, no matter how cleansed and like them he looked and acted? He liked Tish. There was no Mr. Grooms for him now, nor any black friend.

He often walked to town at the noontime dinner hour. In and back again, past houses where wives were keeping and cooking and washing. Clothes on the lines in backyard. Children at play, like his children.

Martha dried their clothes on a line that ran out from her kitchen window, high above the ground, to a pecan tree, a line he had rigged for her with pulleys he'd found among the old and discarded tack in Mrs. Hagerman's stable. When Martha was well, as she was more of the time than not, she cooked supper; it was waiting for him when he returned from the deafening mill. And she had turned out to be good at the cooking and sewing which her mother—so long ago—had used to urge on her and which she had resisted. On Saturday after his half-day at work, Reuben came home for dinner, as well, and then drove Ruth on her errands, and afterward Martha heated water for his bath. He carried the washtub up from the storage underneath their rooms, and she washed his back and his hair, and he might hold Joseph in the tub with him to splash and laugh. Because Littleruth did not want to be left out, Reuben liked to pretend he was about to splash her. She had turned out to be especially sensitive about her clothes, and she would dash screaming and laughing away from him, and then return on tiptoe, both of them pretending he did not see her till he made a sudden movement and said to her "I'm goan *splash* you!" and again she retreated with a delighted screech. Then that game was over, and naked on his buttocks in the big galvanized washtub—nothing like the deep copper tub in Ruth Hagerman's house where he had bathed one time only, where Martha and the children took all their baths (and sometimes in good weather Reuben would look out the window and see Martha crossing back to their steps and coming up wearing a robe and slippers and with a towel wrapped around her hair, to dress in their own rooms)— Reuben would hold naked baby Joe in his wet arms and sit without speaking in the luxury of Martha's attention, living the minutes as if they were hours.

Sometimes Martha hummed a tune, a hymn tune da-da-da-da-da-da-da-dee, as she was about things, even as she washed Reuben's back for him. He might think to ask her what she was singing, but while she sang he didn't want to interrupt, and after she stopped, it could seem an intrusion to ask. As it often seemed when he would have wanted to know her thoughts. When Reuben stood up in the washtub he first reached out to pick up Mr. Grooms's baby quilt and wrap his son in it and hand him to his wife; then he dried himself and dressed. Littleruth would stand to one side—awed by the naked man and his tiny image, the naked baby boy.

And if the children were with their Aunty Ruth in her house, as on a Sunday afternoon they sometimes were, Reuben might look at Martha, might look into her hungrily, and for this moment, before the danger of their passion, she might look back into him as he led her to their bed.

In hot weather with an ancient rusted pick tied by a leather thong through its wooden handle to their battered ice box he would chip slivers from the bubbly crystalline block and drop them slippery into his old tin cup, which he kept on a high shelf and used only rarely, and carry the ice back to the bed to share as they lay together in the heat, in their afterward, dark arm over pale shoulder, white calf over darker thigh.

Their bed—they had come to call it the Big Bed, when speaking to Littleruth—was like the bed Ruth Hagerman slept in, like the bed Martha's parents slept in, wide and soft, and in it Martha herself seemed softer to him and her scent gathered like a perfume in the warm sheets; but at night he had trouble sleeping. He had never slept well in it, not since the very first night when despite the late hour Martha had been as excited as at dawn, after her bath, and she had made Reuben bathe also and Ruth Hagerman had given him the clothes of her husband in which to dress, those clothes of a dead man which had fit him so well. And the lovers had gotten into the freshly-made bed very late but he had not been able to sleep. Had watched her sleeping.

The Big Bed was a place of peaceful waking respite when on Sunday mornings Littleruth would lie between her parents. Reuben was reluctant to rise and dress for church. He would fetch Joe and cradle him in his arms, all four of them in the Big Bed. Reuben would listen with a kind of calm excitement of pleasure to Martha reading to Littleruth from books—great long passages and stories and adventures and Littleruth in the enchanted space of the bodies of her parents lay awake and daydreaming as she listened, as Reuben listened, as Joe slept, again.

He was tired, those nights of his first year at the mill when the work had been physically hard, and tired after he had been moved to the office and the work had remained hard because he would forever be on edge there. But no matter how far into sleep his fatigue took him, and no matter how close to blessed sleep their exertions of love carried him in the after-minutes when he was spent and she was rounded and sleepy beside him, holding herself close in to his side, he habitually woke in the night. Sometimes with aching head. Not suddenly with a start, but fully and completely and calmly, his eyes scanning the dark, and for a few minutes he would listen to the sound of her quiet breathing, then he would gently withdraw himself from the one warm sheltered creature they almost made by sleeping together, and he would sit up in the bed and swing his legs out from under the bedcovers, and stand; again a creature apart. The chair and dressing table for Martha, the washstand and wardrobe—he would study their familiar shadowy forms, and then sometimes in defeat simply lie back down awake, but the bed was not the same, the night was not. Or sometimes rise and tread quietly into their little kitchen, where the ashes were cold in the cook stove, the stovepipe cold to his touch, the oak icebox cool.

At times he woke from no cause he could determine; at times it was a noise, or the pain in his temples. The noise could be—it evidently always was—an ordinary sound of the night: a rafter creaking as it cooled, a raccoon in the garbage, rain on the roof, cold winds. Whatever the cause, it was not his reason but his instinct that sometimes got him up in stark wakefulness, and he was moving so slowly and noiselessly that his legs and feet nearly became numb. This happened often. Carefully he inched toward the sound he thought he had heard, imagining an intruder and knowing that he should do something else, not approach, but approaching anyway, expecting some presence, he could not guess who or what, after all these years, to break through the door—open to the screen on summer nights—and . . . what? Shoot him with a gun? He could hear the blood beating in his ears. Slowly he turned his head right then left—did he expect it to make a noise? to rattle if he had turned it quickly?—and listened with each ear in turn. He would move his left hand out toward the door-knob. Reaching toward it, yet not attaining it, not touching it, his hand motionless in the air.

But when he was awake, and sometimes even when he was back inside his hard-won sleep, he would hear Martha cry out. As happened in her dreaming sometimes. Then leaning over her he rocked her shoulders, and would speak to her softly at first so as not to startle her, and also not wanting to wake Littleruth, and then Joe. "Martha, wake," he'd say, "wake up, sugar, 's a dream, 's a bad dream, that's all." Which seemed to be more than enough. And might be such an exhausting ordeal that it could leave her groggy for half the next day, and ill-tempered and not aware when the children needed her.

Only now, through these hot summer days of Joseph's first

birthday—like Martha's, like Littleruth's, it was a summer birthday, and they had already celebrated all three with a cake that Littleruth had helped Martha to make—Martha did not seem to have even the energy to carry the residue of her dreams into the daylight hours; she simply lay on the bed and slept that sleep of illness that does not refresh, that is fitful and rent by aching half-wakefulness. She withdrew into herself when she was ill, and neither Reuben nor the children found in her any welcome. She was down inside herself, unaware of anyone else—as she had been after Littleruth was born, and again after Joseph was born.

Reuben tried to cheer her, to tell her—against his own lack of conviction, against his own foreboding, which had never left him—of how lucky they were, living just as she had wanted to live, the two little ones healthy and safe, with good food in the house, and good clothes, and his job at the mill, and all the help that was given to them. She did not always answer these speeches of his, even when she seemed quite well. If her mood was not tangled and irritable, it might be absent and unresponding.

When, once, he conquered his dislike of extra obligation of spirit to ask Ruth Hagerman to help Martha when these moods were on her, the woman told him it would pass, Martha's mother was the same, it was something that could run in a family, he should not worry so.

It was not only that if Martha wept there seemed to be nothing he could do to comfort her—it was also that he could not look ahead and tell her of more good things to come, of a better place, for they had found their good place and yet something remained as unresolved in her as in him. His desire to protect her, to put himself around her and shield her, not only could not guard against what was inside her, but had also failed to gain Ruth Hagerman's respect. He could feel how the older woman wanted to hold him away, to interpose herself between him and Martha. For all that she had given him, she had withheld some last, most vital, portion of acceptance. Reuben, who had huddled with Martha in cold rainy darkness and had warmed himself with her hope and her love and warmed her with his, saw himself in Ruth Hagerman's eyes as a stranger. There was some zone of being from which he was excluded, a zone to which he as much as anyone had a right, a zone that he and Martha occupied together in each other's lives and in life. A zone of Martha's being, yes, all right; but more than that, a zone in which all of them had their being, didn't they? But from which he felt he could be, might be, pushed.

Delora, too, stood with the white women, even if they would not have stood with her. He had become like a servant, then, and it could seem that Delora outranked him. She served wholly, and she had a kind of power drawn from, conferred by, the white woman. She gave up a good portion of her own life and in return the wealthy woman gave her this adjunct power of association with wealth and estate.

Reuben carried a neat pile of his papers to the office manager's desk and put it into the man's wooden box for approval. The manager did not look up from his work. Reuben sat down again and arranged the next sheets, took up a sharp pencil. He thought of taking Littleruth's perfect hand and leaning down over her. When she was perhaps three. The two of them walking in the road, out in front of Mrs. Hagerman's house, one of Littleruth's first real walks in the world. Her life reached so far in front of her, a different life from his; better. But having to skirt so much danger, the horses the carriages the wells the barn roofs the other children the boys the men.

Now she would enter school; he would not walk her there every morning, as he used to think to himself that he would. Martha was going to do it. (Would she?) Men didn't do such, anyway, he saw, although he didn't understand why not. And he had to leave for the mill too early each morning.

On that walk when she was only three a cricket was chirping in the dewy weeds near them, he had wanted to find it and show it to her, but she was making little sounds of happiness, watching her own feet—in white shoes she had been given by her Aunty—

appear in front of her, and then disappear again. He sat down next to her and pulled her onto his lap and took off her shoes and stockings and set her walking again with her toes in the cool soft dust of the road. They had gone three houses that way, and then they had turned and come back, and she was happy all the way. Then he had gotten down once more and brushed her feet off with his hands and put her white stockings and shoes back on her, before taking her into the house. A supreme triumph.

On a sunny afternoon Martha reeled in the clothesline and took from it their bed sheets, pulling each one taut with Reuben from opposite ends and then stepping close to fold it, then stepping back to pull taut the fold, and then closer again. He had done this with his mother when he was a small boy. He realized it was his smile that must have raised Martha's eyebrows, and he said, "I love to do this with you."

Mr. Grooms's money was still hidden in the stable; where was that old razor? He hadn't meant to throw it out. Mr. Grooms's knife was somewhere in a drawer, and the good luck charm on a string—where was that?

Approaching each other, naked, warmth calling to warmth, skin to skin. They had sought each other's eyes, that was part of the appetite, the thirst, and looking into each other was a great part of the slaking of the thirst, what went between them, what they were looking into each other's eyes to see. As they rode up toward and through their bodily destinations. But that seemed to be gone now. Maybe it would come back. Now, she kept her eyes closed; sometimes her head was turned sharply to one side and she was traveling without him through reaches only she saw. And he put his own face into the pillow and thought of her with his eyes shut. Her body. The very body he was holding, entering. Looked at her in his mind, where she was looking back at him, instead of looking at her next to him where she lay inside herself. Not that he, or she, drew no pleasure from what they did. They did.

The hands on the electric clock on the office wall lay in a straight vertical line. Reuben's office mates were standing and stretching, straightening their papers. One of them was closing the windows, although even open they failed to ventilate the stifling heat of the upstairs room. There was rarely any speaking inside this office; everyone worked and then at the noon hour and after work, when they got outside, they spewed talk. About the War, nowadays. Deciding whether to enlist, now that the U.S. was in it. Reuben had already arranged his pile of invoices, clipped to bills of lading, on his desk, and he exchanged silent nods of farewell with the other men, and was the first out the door. From the outside landing he looked out over the yard, where the laborers still toiled, then he ran quickly down the steps. He always left his collar buttoned all the way home.

He patted his trousers pocket, and reached inside. The paper bag was slightly damp from his own perspiration. He walked well to one side of the road, away from the dust raised by automobiles that often as not drove down the middle far too fast, swerving to miss each other when they met. When he drove Ruth Hagerman's car on Sundays he observed more caution.

Walking home, he followed the telephone wire and Mill Road back into the square. The shops were closed, and there were few people about. The shadow of the tent-roof under which the band played was elongated and huge and way off to one side of the canvas, like it had slipped loose from the object that cast it and then had grown. Down the alley he stepped more quickly, hoping to find Martha up from the Big Bed and even smiling. He would give her the little present now. Why wait till the day after tomorrow? Would catch Littleruth in his arms and hug her. Would snatch Joe up from his cradle. Would hold him at full arm's length overhead and Joe would laugh.

48

Tell Me Again

I'll tell you again about Kwanokasha.

Kwanokasha lives in a cave, remember? Lives deep down under big rocks, in a wild broken part of the country, with lots of hidden places. He's no bigger than a little child—he looks like he's only two or three years old!

But he's much much older than *everyone.*

And when a child is that age—the age that Kwanokasha looks— say two or three or four years old, you know how a little child gets sick once in a while? Well, the little child gets up from where the mother is, she's saying, "Now lie still and rest!", but when no one is looking the little child runs away from his home! (You know boys and girls can always find their way in the woods, they don't get lost.)

The little child runs away from home, and goes deep into the woods, way in among the trees, a *long* way from home. (You know how when you feel bad sometimes you just want to make some mischief?) But just when that little child is far from his home, *that's* when Kwanokasha *jumps* out and *grabs* the child and off they go. (Did I scare you?)

They travel a long way, long way, far.

When Kwanokasha and the child go down into that cave down in the hidden places in the wild and broken country, here come three more spirits, they're all very very *old,* they have long white hair.

The first spirit comes up to the boy—or it might be a little girl, just as well—and it holds out . . . a *knife.*

The second spirit comes up and holds out . . . a handful of leaves and berries—and all of them are *poison.*

And the third spirit comes up and holds out—what?—more leaves and berries. But these are all *good* medicine.

Now, if the child takes the knife—then that child is certain to grow up to be a bad person, who might even kill a friend!

If the child takes the plants that are poison—then that child will never be able to help anybody else.

But if the child takes the good plants, the good medicine plants, then that child will be a great *doctor,* a good *person.* And all the people will feel trust in him when he is a man. Or if the child is a little girl, then all the people will trust in her when she grows up to be a woman.

If it's the good plants that the child takes, then Kwanokasha and the three spirits show the child how to use them, they tell all the *secrets* of making medicine from roots and leaves and bark and berries, and how to cure fevers, and pains, and sickness, and snakebites, and how to make wounds and hurts get well.

The little child stays with Kwanokasha and the three spirits for three days. And then goes home again.

Does anybody find out where that little child has been? No! That little child doesn't tell *anyone* about Kwanokasha, or where Kwanokasha is or what happened there. And it's not till the child grows up that all of this *knowledge* of medicine can be used. To help people. So everything has to be *remembered.* (You think you could remember?) But even if the little child grows up and lives so long that white hair like the hair of the spirits grows on his head (or on her head!) no one will ever hear where this great knowledge came from!

But, you know, I'll tell you: it's only a few children that wait for the third spirit, and take those good plants. Yes, that's true, that's sad but it's true.

And that's why there aren't many doctors, and there aren't many great people, and a truly good person is pretty rare.

You don't remember right now, I can tell, but when you were littler, old Kwanokasha found you and took you to the spirits and you chose the good medicine of plants, I know. You don't remember right now but one day you're going to remember. Because you're one of the good persons in this world. You surely are. You believe me? Good. Now how many times I told you this story?

Tell me again.

———

49

Birth and Darkness

She had smiled at him that next morning, that first morning of their new life, as she left with Ruth. To go to shops, for clothes. To meet two of Ruth's friends.

The pastor had introduced himself to Reuben and shaken Reuben's hand, but when he talked about the wedding and things, he had looked only at Ruth and Martha.

She said Ruth had all the power to protect them, that people in Harriet did not take offense, it was only her father who would take offense, since after all Reuben was not a nigger, he had a good job and was accepted by white people, in Ruth's world. It was time to stop worrying, she said. Said she regretted now that they had endured such hardship while in flight from Three Rivers.

(To think that his caution may have been needless.)

Delora had used to serve the coffee after supper, if the three of them ate together, and then she would leave. Reuben had quickly got better with the silverware and china, the delicate chairs, the smells of cedar, wallpaper, furniture polish. At an interval in the evening's games of cards he used to go outside and smoke while Martha and Ruth continued to talk. He could win the card games, he found; but didn't try.

In the fourth month of her first pregnancy, Martha had bled. Ruth had moved her from the carriage house into one of her spare bedrooms. The doctor had called at the house every day for a week. Martha was confined to bed. The bleeding had been light, and it stopped. But on the doctor's orders she remained in bed. And that first year had changed from fall to winter while she had lain there.

Attended by Ruth and Delora.

He used to study everything out, step by step, and the only way he could conclude was to think that if he waited and worked and went along, then everything might be different when their baby was born and they were all three back in their own home, together, and this life they were still piecing together could take a more definite shape. He could practice it till he got it right, if only things wouldn't keep changing. Life would not feel so provisional, so temporary; as though it were only a preparation for further journeying, new trouble. In the small hours, through fall and winter and spring and into summer, he roamed the cramped space of the carriage house, up in their rooms, and down in the stable and garage, stepping silently and with blood beating in his throat. He used to move slowly through shadows, feeling the presence of threat, not yet encountering it.

So during Martha's first pregnancy Reuben came home from work to an empty dwelling, without her life in it. He was dirty, and after changing his clothes, washing his hands and face, wetting his hair and combing it back, he went down the outside steps and across the yard to Ruth's back door, and entered cautiously. Did he truly have the permission Ruth had emphatically given him? He proceeded quietly to the front hall, to the wide stairs leading upward.

Each time—end of workday or Saturday afternoon or Sunday—he must contend with all the possibilities.

If he happened to encounter Ruth, she might welcome him in with a smile, and even straighten the very shirt he was wearing; or she might hush him with an intense glance, her mouth pursed, her forefinger raised up and touching her lips. And forbid him.

If he was not forewarned by Ruth about Martha's waking or sleeping, on the upstairs landing he knocked very softly at Martha's new door and pushed it open.

If she was asleep, he sat in the small white chair beside the bed, looking at her, looking around the room at the repeated patterns of the floral wallpaper, at the furnishings. When she was at the end of her pregnancy, the weather was stultifyingly hot. Even in the last hours of full daylight the curtains remained closed, the dimness was murky. If she did not wake in a while, he left again softly, to eat and return again later.

If she was awake, and alerted by his knocking, she would turn her head to him as he entered and most times she would smile, and reach him her hand, and he would sit with her a little while in greeting. In the hot weather she most often lay on top of the sheets in a thin cotton nightdress, with only her feet covered by the counterpane. Her belly was very large, but not so much, Ruth said, as one might expect so close to the expected date of delivery.

Mourning doves roosting under the eaves of the upper story, or in the trees, were cooing steadily, the males puffing up their throats and gurgling and spreading their wings, bobbing their small heads, in display of their claim to mate. The air inside the house was still and hot, the room—even though it was on the north side of the house and did not receive directly either the unwanted warming of the morning sun or the blasting intensity of the sun after noon—was darkened against the heat. Something might clatter once, or clump far down in the house. Such quiet. In the stillness in which Reuben and Martha might sit for some hours, he once heard a drop of the sweat from his own forehead hit the bare wood floor as he sat in the little chair, leaning forward toward her, holding her hand.

How surprised he had used to feel when he heard from downstairs a sudden movement in the kitchen where Delora might be at work, or from below, the grinding ring of the telephone on the wall of the back hall. And footsteps rushing to pick up the receiver and then the overloud talk into it—Ruth giving some recipe or telling of the return of someone's cousin or a matter of town affairs or even the mill or simply gossip. The telephone made it possible to speak to someone distant, but it made it possible for everyone around each of the persons speaking to hear half of what was said and to put their powers to work at guessing the other half. There was no quietness in it, no privacy. Reuben felt he must stop talking with Martha and wait till the call was over, before he could speak again; he felt forced to listen against his will to the voice downstairs, he had to wait until that little piece of someone else's life was over, before his, theirs, could be taken up again.

Best was when, with near certainty that Ruth would not burst in on them, Martha smiled slyly at him, her spirits high instead of low. He went around to the other side and if he was in clean clothes he took off his shoes and stockings, and lay alongside her under the bedcovers, breathing the scent of her hair, holding her fair swollen breasts in his hands, carefully, anxiously, receiving through the palm of his hand the warmth of the life in her womb.

He had gone home one day after work and, from the alleyway, a good fifty yards before he reached their carriage house, he heard Martha scream. He raced to Ruth's back door and into the house and was startled to see a strange white woman Ruth's age in the kitchen, busy with towels. The woman, too, was startled and she shuddered backward at Reuben's entrance, she opened her mouth to yell, he realized she took him for thief or murderer, even though she had to have been *told*, so he said, "I'm Martha's husband." The mouth closed abruptly, and the features of her face flattened, and in an instant the woman scanned down the whole stature of him from his hair to his muddy boots—which he had not taken the trouble to scrape—and then with controlled but not fully concealed shock she returned to her towels. Another scream came from upstairs and Reuben ran to the foyer, past the little privy room that always, without fail, even this time, reminded him of his stupid ignorant use of the book that first night.

Ruth was on the stairs, halfway down to meet him; she stopped him from going up. "The doctor's with her, Reuben, you're going to have to wait now in the kitchen."

He didn't move.

"There's nothin you can do, nothin I can do, this's a time for the doctor, and for Martha. Evertheng'll be fine. But we have to wait."

She put her hands on his shoulders and turned him around like he was a boy and he started downstairs before her. She had touched him only seldom, and her hands on him unsettled him. He resisted Ruth, a little, with ungovernable reluctance—looking back over his shoulder up at the closed door. He did not want to hear that scream again.

But scream she did, as soon as they were in the kitchen, and it came down through the ceiling like a blade. Ruth sat him down and threw a somewhat angled glance, highly meaningful, at the other woman. One of those who had been alert over a lifetime for the slightest differences in human beings. The woman said, "I've got a good big pile a clean towels folded and ready. I'll take em up?" Talking to Ruth, looking at Reuben.

The elbow of God himself had been planted on Martha's belly and He was leaning His weight, the weight of all creation, on her and she expelled every atom of breath out of her lungs in one burst, and then she lifted the weight of her own chest to draw another breath in. The doctor was saying something in a low voice but she could not hear what he was saying, it made no sense what he was saying, it didn't matter what he was saying. The squeezing contorted her body and expelled a softer, gasping cry, and another, and yet another, and then it waned, but the baby would not come, it was stuck inside her, she would die with it inside her, they would both die, she and the baby. "Reuben," she whispered. Her gown was soaked through with her sweat, some of her hair was wet and limp, sticking to her temples and neck, her eyes were burning. Involuntarily she drew her mouth down and could see in her mind's eye her own strained, unchanging grimace of pain and exhaustion. The doctor was talking. She did not know of what. "Reuben," she whispered to herself with each exhaling, a feeble prayer she said to him, if only he were here. Where was he?

What other prayer could she speak? Who was God to put her

371

under such punishment? Who was God? Had any sin she had committed ever justified such punishment? Hadn't she been married in a Christian ceremony? Downstairs. Only two days after she and Reuben had arrived, with Ruth and those women attending, and the Episcopal pastor rushing through the ceremonial words with his odd pleasure, and Reuben not even knowing—what? It was not what she had imagined her wedding would be. "Reuben," she breathed.

Was God God? Or had Someone Else usurped God, tormenting instead of loving, and imprisoning God where He could do nothing, and no one knew of His imprisonment?

It slammed into her again, that elbow and she rattled out a cry and the doctor talked at her and with his hands did something under her gown, her raised knees. She opened her eyes wide when it hit and she stared so intensely at the ceiling, at that spot where two cracks in the plaster came running jaggedly in close to each other and then without touching parted again—so intensely that she thought she might bring the ceiling down on them with the weight of her own looking dragging at it. And the shriek that faded from her ears was her own. Everything was formed, like creation itself, her creation, from that shriek—it created the world of pain, and it separated the high stabbing pain from the low aching pain, and it formed the many different places of pain and all the creatures of pain. And then when the pain ended, finally, for a little while, the other creation, God's creation, stole quietly back into the room and again it constituted bed and walls and floor and ceiling and window and the sound of that doctor's incessant ceaseless talk, did he think that she was going to talk with him?

She lay in a kind of aching sleep for a while, and then it all began once more. The morning light had changed to noon glare and then after refusing to lessen one bit for hours and hours it finally grew yellower and began to dim, and darkened, and blackened, and the electric lamps burned on the wall and the black glass of the mirror reflected them back, and then—she couldn't believe it was possible—a horrible gray paleness began to appear, the whole night

*had passed and another day was beginning and the baby had not yet
been born.*

No better than a spy in that house, he stood on the upstairs
landing. On the green carpet. He saw her contorted face through
the half-open door. He went back downstairs.

The doctor came into the parlor and poured himself a glass of
bourbon and drank it down and looked at Reuben and said nothing. Put down the empty glass. Went upstairs again.

Then he had to move again. Again. He sneaked up the stairs
when the house was silent, he had to speak to her, why was she
silent now? When he approached the open door that other white
woman, standing inside, turned and saw him, and stepped toward
him and quietly, carefully shut the door in his face. He heard that
Martha was not in fact silent, but only moaning softly. He went
back down the stairs.

In the mill yard he was lucky not to have killed another man
instead of himself, or in addition to himself, with his wearied in-
attention and poor judgment. He lasted the morning and at the
noon whistle, for knowledge and food, he rushed all the way back,
as unsteady as a drunk in the street, running then walking. He
went into the kitchen and Delora, perhaps it was the first time,
smiled at him and said, "Yo baby girl's upstairs with her mama.
They both'll be all right now." He rushed past her.

The evidence of suffering was gone. Clean sheets smelling of
sunlight and air were on the bed. Martha in a fresh nightdress,
beads of sweat on her forehead, was under the counterpane to her
waist and the infant lay in her left arm, asleep like her mother.
Reuben stood on his knees beside the bed, his hands hovering over
and around them not knowing where to light, not daring to touch
them. Martha opened her eyes and looked at him from a long way
away, from beyond forests and lakes and rivers and roads and cities
of man, from beyond pain and weariness, from some quiet, ease-
ful but distant meadow at which finally she had arrived. "Little

Ruth," she breathed.

"Like you wanted," he whispered back, smiling at her hopefully and tenderly.

"Yes. Do you want to hold your daughter, Reuben Sweetbitter?"

He reached his hands under the creature, under head and body, and brought her to him, to his face, and beheld her and breathed in the scent of her. She did not wake. For a while she lay in his left arm against his chest, while with his other hand he held Martha's hand, their fingers interlaced as she lay with her eyes closed. Relieved, exhilarated, he and she.

Then Martha entered a kind of tunnel under and through life that separated her from it. Days, weeks, months, when she lay listless in bed back in the carriage house. She nursed Littleruth almost without feeling it. While Littleruth slept, Martha sat motionless in her chair near the crib, not seeing anything, not hearing anything, for hours. For weeks that seemed months. Ruth sent Delora over with meals, she brought new clothes, she brought flowers and arranged them, she came with Delora and they cleaned and dusted. While Martha was inert, mournful, distant; did not want to wear the new clothes or go out in them. She clung to Littleruth, the one passionate claim she seemed to hold on life.

A moment came when nearly a year had gone by and Reuben had been promoted to the mill office, and Mrs. Hagerman had given him suits and waistcoats and shirts and even new shoes, and it seemed that this way of life had become all of life, and Martha began to emerge like a tentative leaf from a buried bulb. When Reuben held lovely dark-eyed Littleruth in his arms, and she gazed into him, Martha was beginning to notice and to smile at them both. She wakened to her window, to the light outside it, and to Reuben. He came home one day and he felt ice in his throat and chest to see her packing things into boxes, to think that it was over, their attempt had failed, and she was returning to her old life, she was taking Littleruth with her and he would have lost them both.

All this, in his head, in the instant he saw her. And then she got up from where she had been kneeling, and came to him and embraced him without saying anything, and looked up into his face and said, "I'm goin to start all over again in these rooms and make them real pretty for us."

And again she took him close to her, took him into her, opened to the new summer.

Once she was back in life, God, it might have been, as if to answer one prayer to make her doubt once more her own doubts, brought her no more children for a longer while than she or Ruth could make sense of. When she consulted the doctor he told her he could find nothing wrong with her. It took a steeling of herself to undergo his examination; it was violation much worse than what her father and mother and everyone back there must have assumed she had suffered with her Indian man, and violation not only of her but also, in some way, even of Reuben. The horrible doctor, Ruth insisted on him, looking at her with his smug jowly face. Reuben at the mill working knew nothing of her appointments or of what doctors did with women and she would not tell him. But she submitted. And was told not to worry. This doctor—did all doctors?—said more often than anything else, "Don't worry." She had worried. And nothing happened. And anyway she wasn't sure she could bear to go through it again, and was almost grateful if something was wrong with her and she would not be able to produce another child.

Somehow there were years that went by. Somehow there was a life they had not decided to create but which was creating them, as they were turning out to be, Martha and Reuben Sweet, with a child called Littleruth. Workdays and church days and errands and cooking and sewing and cards with Ruth and her friends, outings in the car on Sunday with Ruth. Ordinary lives, like those she had scorned in Three Rivers.

There was a humble little deep-blue bottle, empty, stopperless, and without a label, that she had found in the alleyway behind the carriage house, before her confinement. She had asked Ruth to bring it to her in her sickroom, and now she kept it with her in her kitchen. It had returned with her, to life. When she was lying inside her own darkness, the blue glass bottle had been like a path she had followed, light that came through it came to her; and back along it, along a sweet blue ray, the light led her toward some goodness, some desire to remain in the world, to endure. Some kind of patent medicine had filled it once but had left not even an odor. Trapped in the thick glass were a few tiny white bubbles, and when the bottle, which stood on a windowsill, was struck by the sun in the afternoon, it sparkled and intensified in hue, and its blue ray reached and spread down to the floor and tinctured the wood like a faery beam, as magical to her, as inviting of her faraway thoughts, as the occasional dawn mist that had lain close to the ground over small meadows she had seen when she and Reuben had been walking westward, and she had wanted to step into that mist and stand in it, she felt invited to be taken into its power. On beautiful mornings. There had never been mornings more beautiful than those awful mornings.

But she had had him to lead her on through the hiding places and hidden paths. Now she must find her own way. He was alongside her, he was living into the days with her, but he was not leading her. No one was leading them, they were being led by life.

She had nightmares. He had worries that pushed into his waking mind. Or woke him to get at him directly.

Before she had been confined to her sickroom in Ruth's house, she had tried to make Reuben feel less apprehensive about—about everything. But then she would wake, after he had gotten up in the night—because his absence had detoured her dreaming to an unpleasant scene that had hemmed her in, crowding her, pushing her breathing to a faster pace, till she came out of her sleep and found him gone. She had gotten up and come into the kitchen space, had stopped short of approaching him, had said out loud, "Reuben? Is somethin wrong?"

That had sometimes broken the spell, if spell was what it had been. From that distance, not moving toward her, he would say,

"No." One time he asked her, "Did you have another bad dream?" His eyes were liquid, glittering in the dark. He was holding a cup towel in his hands; had knotted it up. Something in his posture— the self-protective hunch of his big shoulders, the angle of his head turned toward her—had kept her at a little distance from him. Not out of fear, but out of caution for him. Like he was a wild creature and would have bolted if she had gone any closer. They had stood silently for a moment.

"Dreamt I was being chased, again," she'd said. "Will you come back to bed?"

"Yes, I will," he'd said, but he hadn't moved. "Remember my hand print on the white wood?" he asked her.

Slowly she had backed away a step and returned to bed. But had lain awake, half propped up on pillows, watching the doorway to the kitchen, beyond which he must still be standing, although she heard nothing. Till she could stay awake no more. How could he stand motionless, silent, so long? She had fallen back toward her bad dream, dream from a repertoire of a half dozen that came to her repeatedly, that she feared enough not even to want to sleep, some nights, for not wanting to encounter what she knew was there waiting for her yet again; and from another such dream she had waked that night to find him sleeping beside her once more.

This scene was repeated many nights: she woke to discover he was not beside her, she reassured herself that he was still in the house, he had not gone away, she did not approach him closely, she retreated again to bed; and, if she could, to sleep.

She never asked him about his nights. His disturbance robbed him of his rest and carried him away from her. She wanted him always to come back. She wanted him back in her bed, back with her when, inside herself, she walked through the dream places. But pull hard as she might on his dream hand, he would not follow. While she slept and was hemmed in, was pursued, he might be awake and in the kitchen, or out on the landing of the outside steps, not even beside her in the bed where lying still she had to run so fast, holding to him with hands that reached out of the dream into the waking world and did not find him. And while he was restlessly pacing the corridors of his waking mind, she was unable to go with him, to comfort him, and might even be at the same moment running only a little ahead of a dream-pursuer. All this before she bled, with Littleruth inside her.

And Littleruth had come. Martha had gone into her own dark place, in that dark room, and not till she came out of it again did she think again of why she was in Harriet, why they had run. All that time Reuben had waked alone and watched alone. For both of them. She could cry over his protectiveness. And she could not get him to stop, though he seemed finally to accept that in Harriet they were home. This was their place. Much nearer to Three Rivers than they had ever imagined it would be. Yet different; letting them alone; with Ruth Hagerman.

When four years had passed after Littleruth's birth and Martha no longer thought of having another child, even though they often lost themselves in each other, she and he, in the dim night when they could not quite see each other, she became pregnant again. And she carried the baby this time without the ordeal of confinement to bed, for she did not bleed, as before. And the doctor seemed less excited by his own disapproval of her, this time.

She stayed in her own home. Grateful for the big shade trees over their carriage house, but, even so, chafed and fevered by the summer heat, wrung out by it. And frightened of labor. As it came closer to her she was caught between desperation to escape her heaviness and discomfort and isolation and immobility, and fear of the pain of birth. But Delora and Ruth attended her again, as well as the doctor. More jowly now, more repugnant to her, and she could not keep him from touching her and looking at her. He gave her no reassurance.

She got through it, it did not last so long the second time, although she screamed into an emptiness the size of the earth itself that held only her and her pain. The rest of them in the room, even Reuben, who now could insist with his eyes on staying near, were only ghosts who faded with each beat of her throbbing pulse.

And then Joseph, blood-red and puling, had been placed at her perspiring breast. She could have licked him. Somehow he looked like Reuben from the first moment. And became of Reuben's color: beautiful.

A fear which she had not permitted herself to feel, and which had more than anything else made her sometimes frantic with secret self-shaming all the while she carried Joe, grew to a monstrous fright that she could not outrun and it came after her and swallowed her. Again the tunnel, the gloom, the time of being locked away inside herself. But only half a year (only half a long year!) this time, and she had over and over steeled her will by some last effort and not walked away from them all to throw herself into the filthy stinking river. She had not done that. She had survived that thing; that lightlessness. But scarred and diminished when finally she emerged again—no one else could see the scars because no one else had seen the beast that had inflicted them; but she had seen it, and she saw the welts and bruises of its fists on her being. She could smile, she could play with Joe, she could read to Littleruth and teach her to cook and let her play with her baby brother and pretend to mother him like a child, she could rest contented beside Reuben at night. Some part of her felt cleaned out, destroyed, though; cauterized by that other thing. She went to sleep knowing that Reuben would wake and pace the room and check that the door was locked (although most people didn't lock their doors), and look out the windows on the watch for his own fears— she did not worry any longer; those people would leave her and all of her family (*her* family!) alone—and that he would watch over her, as well. Because he could see, he understood, he knew—she never spoke to him about this, to speak to him would be to lose ground in her nightmare of fleeing—that while she slept she was racing to escape her nightmare pursuers. While his did not chase, but simply stood silently, patiently across from him, wherever he looked at night. Waiting. Tireless.

When they made love she wanted to see his eyes, as she had used to do. But they kept the room dark and she didn't look, and she didn't let him look into her, because she was afraid of what was in his eyes now. She hadn't been, the first while; she wanted to be that free again, but she couldn't be. Afraid not because he meant her harm—that was unthinkable in Reuben. No one could love her more than he did. No one had loved her as much as he did. But because she was afraid of something in his eyes, in him, that could overpower her, that might erase her from herself. Not that he meant to. But he couldn't help it. He wanted too much. Of her being.

Frightened not by him but by this change in herself, that she didn't want to have happened, she tried to talk to Ruth about it but she could not find the words for it—out of loyalty to their secret life together, to their intimacy, out of not wanting to betray that by telling anyone of it. And she said, trying to say it, "It's simpler for him, seems like."

And Ruth, thinking she knew what Martha was trying to say, said, "Well, he's a man, isn't he?"

No more children.

50

While He Slept

Reuben's spirit left his body where it lay sleeping in the bed with Martha, left the rooms where Littleruth and Joseph were sleeping, whose new breath sweetened the air, and went out over the roads, eastward, looking for signs of what was to come.

Went through the tree tops and stood shoulder to shoulder with the owl on a high limb, watching the field below. Went low on the ground and with the snake crawled silently under the houses of men and coiled up its body and listened.

Went along the roads with fast horses and flew besides automobiles and was on the lookout for white men from Three Rivers. Listened all the way back in Three Rivers to what men and women said, talking of the trash white girl from good family that run away with the half-breed, don't matter what color his skin is it don't change what he is.

Saw the empty house, weeds growing through the porch, windows broken out, where Mr. Grooms had lived. Terrible.

Listened at the corner of the white church building in the small still hours of the night for echoes of what had been prayed there in the morning.

Turned to come westward again. Stopped to look at blue trees that rose from the low river banks and leaned out over the silver-gray water. Stopped to taste the wild grape. Paused to study the track of a bear and couldn't help following it against its own better judgment and so saw the bear standing up on its hind legs, tearing the bark off a hickory tree with its sharp claws. Got away from the sight of the bear.

Looked at the moonlight on the poor villages.

Brought all this back to Reuben in dreams, but everything it knew it could show him only in a different form—the blue trees were telephone-wire poles, the automobiles were deer, the houses of men were bushes, the words of men were noises in the palmetto swamp.

That is the only way the spirit can speak to the person it inhabits, and so it is never understood properly, or understood only a little. But that his spirit saw the bear, and the horses especially, was no good omen, and Reuben woke troubled.

51

Tuesday, July 4

A neighbor woman, Reuben didn't know her, had invited
Littleruth and her friends to join her own daughter in a summer
play school and they gathered every morning—even on July
Fourth morning. When Littleruth was ready to go, he gave her a
small drink of water from his tin cup, and went with her around to
the front of Aunty Ruth's house, and they talked as they went,
then he waited with her for a moment. Three girls were coming up
the street on their way to the play school, and dawdled a moment
while Littleruth joined them. The girls walked away; when Littleruth was not aware of Reuben, and he could watch her, he had a
sensation which he would have called happiness except that it was
something else, also, like an aching. Simply seeing Littleruth walking on with the other small girls, fully in her own life—it pleased
him; at the same time it saddened him not to be able to go with her.
Littleruth walked up on her toes; so much energy.

The smallest girl in the group—perhaps Littleruth's age but
shorter and thinner—tripped and fell forward on her hands. She
picked herself up with a stifled cry and caught up with the bigger
ones again, who had kept walking—Littleruth included—and
paid her no heed. The hurt girl looked back at Reuben with a
pleading expression. Reuben thought that, not watching where she
was going, she would fall again, and he took one step toward the
girls. But the small one rejoined her friends resolutely. Determined
not to hope for rescue, maybe. Anxious not to be left behind,

383

braving the pain of her scraped palms, she went on with them, her fists clenched at her sides. He returned to the backyard and went up their steps and inside.

Despite the heat, even in the morning, Martha was making tea, with Joe on her hip. She was feeling better. She picked up the kettle and held it over the teapot and boiling water gushed from the battered mouth. She put Joe down on his feet and held him by his hands. He took two tottering steps toward his father, with lightning smiles and frowns alternating on his face, and then he stopped. She let go of his hands and he windmilled his arms and smiled decisively and toppled forward. Reuben caught him and stood him up again and steadied him with his right hand flat against Joe's chest, so Joe could lean into it as he walked. Reuben's hand dark against Joe's clean white bib.

"Ready to walk some more, Joe? Less see you walk," he said, and Martha smiled down at them. The ribbon he had given her was lying in her open sewing basket near the window. A day to be grateful for.

Of all the clothes he had seen on her, the dress in which she had married him had been the most remarkable. Overnight Ruth Hagerman had fitted, with only small difficulty and Delora's help, her own white wedding dress to Martha's body. Her preacher had come to the house, and in the living room Ruth rarely used, with furniture pushed back to make a ceremonial space, the preacher had performed the marriage of Reuben and Martha, with himself and Ruth as witnesses. Afterward Delora served them a lavish supper at the dining room table where only two nights before Reuben had first encountered the accouterments of wealthy dining. Everything had happened very fast—a new house and new names, both of them. He did not know how Mrs. Hagerman arranged such things. But what satisfied her should satisfy any white person. When Littleruth and then Joseph were born, their birth certificates, like the census sheet, showed a mark of W for each of them, as it did for Martha; and for Reuben.

Before they had sat down to eat that wedding supper Ruth Hagerman had kept them in the living room where she also briefly admitted a photographer, a man who had a permanent studio for photography in town but whom Ruth had brought into the privacy of her house for this occasion. And with the knickknacks and pictures on Ruth's walls behind them, they were photographed in their wedding clothes: Martha's white dress and a filmy veil pulled back from her face, a silver tiara in her dark hair, and Reuben in the best of his dead man's clothes.

The photograph hung in a dark wooden frame on the wall over the headboard of the Big Bed, now. The wood of the frame matched the wood of the windows, and seemed another window, tiny and looking into a space where the two dressed dolls stood close beside each other, the Martha doll holding a bouquet of flowers, her cheeks wiped dry of her tears, and the Reuben doll stern-faced, braced against bewilderment. "Look at you, so handsome," she had said to him.

Dust lay across the top edge of the picture frame, and a dulling layer of grease from cooking so near in their kitchen had yellowed the light from that tiny window. Reuben had noticed this, but had not taken the framed photograph down to clean it, had not touched it. Martha in that dress, as beautiful a person as Reuben had ever seen in his life; shining into him like a lamp.

Restless, he left her and Joe and went out again, down the street in the other direction from Littleruth's play. At the corner he turned toward town and walked to the square. The streets and spaces had been turned to a parade route and roped-off areas for spectators. The band was practicing yet again. Reuben sat on a nearby bench and watched them. Mooney with his hair in his eyes and the baton. Exhorting. Tish saw Reuben and raised his red eyebrows, and winked. Glancing to each side, the men lined up more or less as Mooney instructed; he exploded at several of them as if they were children, dragging them by the arm to where he wanted them. He put himself at the head of his musical column, signaled, and they lifted their instruments smartly, like weapons. Then he got them going in a march, but was soon rushing around the group, yelling, correcting the formation. However, they could only keep themselves in good order when they weren't playing at the same time. They went around the square once. Reuben smiled; it was amusing.

Then they stopped and walked away from him in different directions home; where later they would don their various uniforms. Holding his clarinet, Tish loped over to Reuben in a funny-looking way—not like people usually run but some kind of old-country kind of running. He shook Reuben's hand as he sat down next to him. His palms were sweaty; the backs of his hands had red hair on them, too.

"What poor orchestra," he said, shaking his head.

"I guess you're good enough," Reuben said.

"Ach—you don't know," Tish said. "You've never seen *real* orchestra marching in the street, good playing."

"No, that's true," Reuben said. "I've jest seen East Texas, mostly, and mostly the back side of that."

"Are you going to worry to me on Fourtha July?" Tish said. "You have six years here, good job, it's like you live in beautiful big house . . ." Tish often teased Reuben. "You are coming to the parade, yes?"

"Yep, we'll all come to hear you play and see you march down the street and raise a lot a dust." Tish Stangel, improbable Texas feed-store clerk. His manner, the intensity of his cheer, always made Reuben feel better.

Reuben and his family had attended last year's parade; the first time they had done so. Ruth did not like the crowds. For Littleruth's sake, they would come again.

"But you must come because of great American holiday," Tish said.

"That, too."

"No, you don't believe, you don't believe," Tish taunted him. "You know why? Because you still believe in someting else—little gods and spirits. You are no better tan everybody else, who go to church!" Tish was not a believer.

Reuben did not answer.

"What are you in square for, you tink there is early performance?" Tish said, grinning. He tootled a few notes on the clarinet, surprisingly loud.

"Jest killin a little time. I guess I'll go back, see if I can do innytheng useful."

"Drive big lady's car? She should be in parade, you drive."

"Not this year, I don't think."

"Come around to back of store on Saturday, I teach you new card game," Tish said.

"I'll come, but probly bring Littleruth. She likes to see the saddles and barrels and everytheng—I suppose she'd have loved it even more if we still had a horse."

"Horses always there's going to be, don't you worry. Good, bring beautiful girl! I teach her card game, too." Tish got up, shook Reuben's hand again with a parting wink, and walked briskly away. Reuben went back home slowly; there was a lot to notice, on every block, at every step. He entered the stable-turned-garage under his family's rooms.

Cleaning and straightening, from time to time Martha discovered things that had been mislaid and forgotten—things just old enough to make her feel, happily, that some little history had accumulated in their lives, that there was some direction to their affairs that they had been pursuing all along as if it had been known to them. What prompted her greatest surprise, when she found it where she herself had abandoned it at least a year before, was her forgotten diary book, with lined pages, that Ruth had given her soon after their new life in the carriage house had begun. It was half-filled with her writing.

Martha was not sure she had ever had any true friend, besides Ruth. Not Clara, not really. The women she had met, Ruth's friends, either made too much of their own broadmindedness, never letting it out of sight, or presented an impeccable but cold politeness to Martha. Even when Reuben was not mentioned, he never seemed to be out of other women's minds. But at least, because Martha had found that her hands could embroider better than most, while her mind for months at a time was in a brown fog of unwanting and unwilling, she was asked by some women to produce finished pieces for them. She had a very small but steady income from that, and from fine hand sewing, an income of which Ruth emphatically approved.

The sight of the diary book made Martha glad; the encounter with what she had written disturbed her. At first there was her record of things that happened, beginning with her own account of the marriage—now, as she read it, she saw it was filled with forced hope. But then came pages in which, for hours at a time when she was alone in their rooms, she had tried to record her mind. Now she could see, and did not want to see, how scattered her thoughts had been, how unsettled and unsettling every memory of her old life had been, how her dark thoughts had crowded over her after Littleruth was born, how what she had expressed had been, really, a lack of connection with—with life? And drafts of a letter to her mother, never yet sent—although Ruth was still urging her to write, and she had finally decided she must; she would, soon. They had news of Three Rivers from time to time, but only of public matters. Reuben worried over her parents, over James, still. Also in her diary book was the beginning of her new attempt to set down what she could of Reuben—of Reuben not as his familiar self, but as the exotic being who had burst into her acquaintance one hot afternoon in Three Rivers.

Here were her notes, her careful categorizations. (*Where* were the old notebooks from Three Rivers? She hadn't been able to find them, and had started all over again with him.) Reuben had told her very little, the first time she had tried to gather from him the traces of his origins. And he seemed to have remembered, in fact, even less the second time—when they were in the home they had made for themselves and they knew each other far better. So almost all of the space she had marked off for her proudly remembered categories of "Material Culture" and "Social Culture" was blank. Under "Myths" she had recorded in note form without any connectedness a few sketchy tales or legends, she wasn't sure what to call them because she didn't know from Reuben's reluctant recitation of them whether they were stories his mama or grannie had made up or the residue of beliefs of his ancestors. And each time he had told them to her, the three of these tales that he had told, he'd said them differently.

Reuben was out, somewhere; Joe asleep. Martha's fever was gone. Sitting by the window with the blue glass bottle, her diary book in her lap, she was again in the mood that had already seized her twice and that made her feel she was attempting something useful with her mind. She wanted at least to make a record for the children, a kind of tribute to Reuben, who was always, who had always been, so steadfast for her. Who was, really, such an unusual person in ways that other people would never understand. Who else even knew him? But she had never succeeded in drawing him into a sense of purpose that matched her own. Martha had told a few of her women acquaintances whose attitudes like Ruth's were broad—Ruth believed, and some of her friends believed, that Harriet was a town of generous and progressive spirit—that she wanted to write a brief formal note for publication, something modest as befitted her small learning, about the history of Reuben's people. Someday, she said, this would be of interest to everyone. One of the women had brought Martha a maroon-bound issue of a journal of scientific study of primitive peoples; the woman's husband was a doctor, she had taken it from his study. All the articles were by men. Martha had smiled to think of repetitions everywhere of the surreptitious study of the books of husbands and fathers by their own wives and daughters. In the strong light slanting in the window even the steam from Martha's cup of medicinal tea cast a shadow, a swaying uprising veil wavering over the white windowsill when she set the cup down there next to the blue bottle and she pondered what to write down. She would try to produce her treatise, beginning at a new page in the elegant diary book in which she no longer wanted to record what happened to her and what didn't happen to her day by day, and what she thought, and what she felt. From now on she was going to pretend, if only for him and the children, that she didn't feel such twinges and bleaks. She finished drinking her tea.

Sounds of the band's clashing and booming interrupted the rustling and whispering of the trees in full summer leaf. The hot breeze was carrying the noise everywhere. Littleruth and Joseph heard it after their parents did, but it excited Littleruth more.

Reuben shepherded them all toward the parade. Littleruth in a bonnet ran ahead and back, ahead and back. He carried Joe in his arms. Martha held a parasol over her head; felt somewhat weak, still. The noise steadied and no longer came in bursts. They heard trombone and bass drum and what must have been Tish's clarinet. The last block was Polk Street, and they walked past more big houses like Ruth Hagerman's, on which here and there some residents were sitting in white wooden lawn chairs under shade oaks, attended by maids bringing glasses of cool tea.

At the corner of Polk and Main, they saw that Main was crowded with spectators on both sides for several blocks. The air was dusty and filled with the strong scent of horses and baked wood and brick and the dust itself. There were no trees along Main. At the far end where spectators thinned was a large cordoned section of Negro families.

There were those in Harriet who did not celebrate Independence Day. Others, like Mr. Clapham and plenty of commercial men, saw it as a proper occasion for enthusiasm and conviction; and with the European war burning and ravening, and so many young men and old in Harriet spoiling to enter it, impatient with the President's reluctance, the Fourth of July was an occasion for patriotic celebration of courage and battle glory. The town had only two elderly veterans of the War Between the States, who having thinned with age could again wear the Confederate uniforms preserved from their youth, and four other men who had fought in 1898 and who in middle life could no longer fit into theirs. The sunlight had sharpened the edges of the buildings, bright sides meeting shadowed sides at the corners like knife blades.

Reuben's own stories, learned and kept and going on now to Littleruth, had prophesied of these wars. Once the woods and forests extended from the land of the *chahtah* westward to the far edge of the world. The expanse of trees was inhabited by the *na hollo*, a race of giant people with white skin. It may be that the skin of the *na hollo* was white because they came from the invisible world, but when they arrived in the middle world, this world, they stayed.

The *chahtah* lived in full dread of them, because whenever the *na hollo* came upon the *chahtah*, the *na hollo* captured and tormented and killed and ate them.

The *na hollo* were divided into different bands and, although they were not numerous, they also warred savagely against their own kind. They could not abide the presence of any other creatures.

The whole vast stretch of woodland was destroyed by them—they would break off the lower branches and eat the leaves, and even gnaw off the bark, and the trees died. In this way the woods became great open and empty plains.

Because of the ceaseless battling of the bands of *na hollo* against each other, they became fewer and fewer. Finally, after many years, there were only two *na hollo* left, two huge males. Separate and alone, they wandered about, each confining himself to a last tract of forest. But at last they happened to confront each other, and on sight they leapt into struggle, fighting ferociously, until one was killed by the other. The last *na hollo*, ruler of the empty world of the plains and small groves, exulted in his triumph and his freedom and his independence and his solitude. He had won over all others. Then he died, and the race was extinct.

When the new white men first appeared in this world, the *chahtah* called them, too, because of their skin, *na hollo*, even though they were not giants.

But there were puzzles Reuben could not solve. The Indian peoples had warred against each other, too; before they killed whites, they had killed each other. As the white peoples were doing now, in distant Europe. Whites warred against other peoples, too, as in Slocum, Texas, the year he and Martha had run off from Three Rivers.

Mr. Mooney's band played and marched; now, however, in a true procession. The whole train of participants extended only two blocks, so, having staged the parade out Mill Road, they marched in and were to continue around the square three times. First came the mayor, riding in an open car at very slow speed, its motor rattling. Then a military corps of boys from the white High School, wearing baggy dark blue wool with gold braid and epaulettes and ill-fitting caps and marching raggedly to a cadence squeaked out by a boy wielding a chromium baton hung with more gold braid—a kind of decorated war cudgel. Then the ministers of the three white churches, walking together soberly. Then the small truck that Clayton Abernathy with undeniable but irritating ingenuity had converted to the town's first and only motorized fire engine, painted a dull red, carrying a small tank and two inadequate ladders, a few fire hoses and axes; it seemed scarcely able to move. Its engine was terribly loud, its klaxon horn croaked repeatedly; nearly a dozen white men were riding in it and hanging on to it, the H.V.F.D.

Littleruth clamored to be lifted up so she could see. Reuben handed Joe to his mother and picked up Littleruth under her arms and hoisted her onto his shoulders. A large wagon drawn by two horses had stopped. A special detachment of the band sat in the wagon bed—with trumpet and trombone, bass drum and accordion, each man wearing a straw hat. They played a popular patriotic tune. The wagon had been decorated with fresh paint and red, white, and blue cloth bunting, yards of it. When they finished the wagon moved on. The sunlight was stark and hot, that full heat that intensified and held everything in its grasp for hours every day, stilling most movement but that of listless leaves on the shaded streets, and perhaps a little dust devil racing a few yards before vanishing and dropping its scraps of paper and broken twigs and dust. This was not an hour when physical activity was normally undertaken except by laborers who had no choice. Sweating and lathering, the two horses drawing the band wagon, with nerves wracked by the blaring instruments, were quivering in harness, jerking their heads upward and blowing despite the calm attentions of a large placid man in a white shirt, black trousers, and polished boots.

Reuben was holding Littleruth's ankles. He reached up for a moment to her torso and through her thin summer dress he could feel the symmetry of her little ribs.

Underfoot the grass was beaten down, the dry dust coating everyone's shoes. The full band approached on foot in their ragged formation. Their repertoire had been so publicly rehearsed that everyone had already heard it several times and could expect no surprises. They struck up a familiar march and gamely moved past. Reuben pointed out Tish to Littleruth and she waved at him. After marching around the square with the rest of the parade, the band would sit down under the canvas tent-roof and wait while the mayor made a speech from the gazebo and then the sheriff and his two deputies fired off twenty-one rounds into the air from their hunting rifles. Then the band would play their concert. The light was immensely bright and hot; it seemed to be made even brighter by the great puffy white clouds that floated here and there high above them in the pale blue sky. At nine-thirty in the evening, when it was dark and a little cooler, a small display of specially ordered fireworks was to be set off by members of the H.V.F.D. Reuben had promised Littleruth she could stay up to watch.

Despite all the noise, Joe was asleep in Martha's arms, and she had arranged his pink bonnet and white blouse to shield him from the intense sun. Although Ruth Hagerman had not come with them, she had helped dress Littleruth, who was wearing a very fine short-sleeved pale green dress with white trim and black shoes

393

with white ankle socks. Littleruth was inadvertently pulling at Reuben's hair despite his asking her not to, and avidly looking down to each side on sunbonnets, straw hats, bald spots. Her arms and face were brown from her summer play. Her legs were longer than Reuben had realized; he held her by her ankles and shifted from time to time under her weight.

A voice said, "You!" Not loudly, and to Reuben's right. He could not see around Littleruth's legs without turning his body toward the voice and taking her away from the band and the horses. He did not know if the guttural angry word was addressed to him. "I'm talkin a you," the voice said, soft and closer and angry. "Stand off."

Reuben bent his head forward to see around Ruth's legs; the fabric of her dress smelled starched and clean. His head was aching.

A stout bareheaded white man with heavy black eyebrows and curly black hair, standing to Reuben's right with a little boy in front of him, was staring hard at Reuben, his face contorted. A shout went up from the other side of the street and farther down, where the Negro citizens were gathered in their designated area. It was a comic act—Macel Blake, who was said to have performed in a Wild West Show for years before he settled in Harriet, was stunting on and off his horse; he did it slowly, not as he must have done when young; but anyway it was more entertaining to see him do it at his age than it would have been to see it done by a youth of whom such feats might be expected.

"I said, stand off," the man said again, bitterly. Urgently he spat on the ground near Reuben's shoes. He had not looked at Martha, and she had not yet noticed him, nor had she even heard him yet, in the noise. The band, the fire truck, the voices.

"R'you talkin to me?" Reuben said evenly, with a practiced tone meant neither to give offense nor to offer acquiescence. The man had a wall-eyed gaze.

"Yore goddamn lil half-breed girl's shadduh is touchin my boy. Now stand off, nigger."

394

Men were raising an American flag on the new flagpole at the center of the parched square. There was a dizzying number of parasols raised over female shoulders. Littleruth said, "Daddy turn back around!" Reuben was facing the man. It wasn't defiance that kept him where he stood but disbelief. The man's face was red. His lower lip was caught tightly in his teeth. It was just when Martha stepped around Reuben to look up at Littleruth, to make sure her face was shaded by her bonnet, that the man exploded like a charge. In a blue fury he jerked his son behind him and squared himself to Reuben as Martha and Littleruth watched, too shocked even to breathe.

"Why do they want t'go fight a war overseas when we still haven't killed off all a you, yet," the man said. "You got no place here with us, git down the street with the rest a the niggers and take your whore of a wife with you." The short man hopped twice and kicked dust at Reuben. The band struck up a new march and over their noise the man's oaths rose like a song lyric of rage. People were standing away from this scene in their midst. Another man came up behind the short man and took his shoulders carefully and pulled at him and spoke to him in his ear. The little boy was staring at Reuben with an ugly look.

With deliberateness Reuben turned his back to this man, to them all, and guided Martha before him and they began to move away, Littleruth twisting on Reuben's shoulders looking back at the man, who was following them at a few paces, pulling his friend with him, shaking both his fists and yelling.

"Daddy, are we leavin?" Littleruth said, leaning down to speak in his ear. Her hands and arms were choking him. Other people were crowding behind him now, watching the family as they moved steadily away and the short man's arms waving in the air made it look like he was conducting the band playing out of sight behind the people.

They walked faster, Martha speechless, feeling very weak again. Reuben, shaking.

She walked in front of him, looking from behind quite calm, but he saw the storm in her mind. He must back away, back away and calm himself, he must never even react to such a display if he hoped to keep his family safe. He pulled Littleruth's hands from his throat and she began to fuss and yell, "Put me down, I want to get down." As if he were a stranger. He lowered her to the ground and she ran ahead to Martha in her beautiful clothes and new shoes.

No one was following them. They had only a few blocks to walk. No one else had spoken to them, either to condemn or defend. Or console. No one else had joined the short man in his diatribe; no one seemed to have told him to stop; or had argued with him. There had been many people around Reuben and Martha who knew who they were, but no one had said anything. People who knew Ruth. Everyone had watched. No one near them had been watching the parade at that moment. It would all be much talked of, surely. Reuben burned with anger; with humiliation, that Littleruth had had to hear it, see it. What would he say to Martha? What would they say to each other when they reached home? Only Joseph, sleeping through it all, had not been touched by it.

52

Clothes: Another View

The white people state that, at a remote period, the earth was fashioned out of nothingness by the Creator, first the heavens and then the land beneath them.

They have a holy book of considerable antiquity (much reprinted and widely distributed) in which this story is recounted, but as it was gathered in a remote time, has been altered and translated from more than one language by various hands and revised more than once, one cannot say that in any presently available version it is entirely authoritative, all the more so since the whites believe that the precise wording of the version in English was itself inspired by the Creator, who is thus counted most improbably as having intervened at the stage of translation more decisively than at the state of the initial composition of the text. When asked about these questions, and about the evidence that the tales in this book have been corrupted by legends of other peoples, most persons appear to have little interest in enquiry or answers. Indeed, they react with hostility to any question that endeavors to elucidate the contradictions and variations in their holy tales which they defend fiercely.

When the earth had been formed, the tales of the white people say, the Creator fashioned a man, and then he took a part of the man's body and from it fashioned a woman.

At the time of creating the first man and woman, the Creator had already constituted the entire aspect of the land and sea, and graced it with flora and populated it with fauna, over all of which he gave the man perfect power.

There was thus, the whites suppose, an extraordinary abundance of wild fruit and nuts on which to feast, and a complete harmony among all the creatures of the earth. The man and woman, like natural creatures themselves, lived freely in a mild clime that apparently required not even shelter against the weather.

The Creator, having invented life but not death, told the first man and woman that they would live forever. But when they disobeyed the Creator and at the suggestion of a wily serpent they ate of the fruit of a magical tree that would give them powers of intelligence, the Creator punished them and told them they would die. From this aboriginal pair the entire race of men is supposed to have descended, beginning with their two sons, one of whom murdered the other. Whence came the wives of these sons, the holy tales of the white people do not state, and they do not remember.

Over succeeding generations of death, the Creator followed with a jealous, demanding and ever-vigilant eye the people of his creation; he exacted tributes and sacrifices, sent them to war against other peoples (although how these other peoples came into being, and their own gods as well, again the holy tales say not, and the whites no longer have any knowledge), and delivered them from those enemies who from time to time gained power over the Creator's people and caused them suffering.

They state that at their creation, both males and females went entirely naked. After they had eaten the fruit of the magic tree and looked upon each other not as animals see but as men and women see, they covered their bodies at first with leaves. It was presumably after this that they began to kill the animals and fashion the first clothing from skins.

53

Martha's Book

She went looking for Reuben and found him downstairs, underneath their rooms, in the storage and stable, and when he saw she was carrying her diary book and a pencil, his eyebrows rose and his head turned a little to one side, cautiously, and he said, "You goin to start that yet another time? Now?"

"The two don't have innytheng to do with each other. That horrible man, that was somethin we never experienced before and probably won't ever happen aggin. It's Saturday, can't we feel like it never happened? Haven't we talked about it enough, now? . . . Aren't you goin to take Littleruth to see the store, and talk to Tish?"

"I don't much feel like it," he said.

"Ruby," she said, the nickname she used only when they were alone together. "Would you mind if I asked you some more of my old questions, like I used to?"

"You kin ask," he said. "Askin, writin, it does seem to make you happy, every so many years. But what you put down in your book you might as well write it yoursef. It's not goan make *inny* diffrunce to people. It's jest what you want. Like you set my birthday for me, that isn't even my birthday."

"That wasn't the same," she said.

"I don't know it wasn't."

"You didn't *know* your birthday. And everbody needs to have one. The children and I wouldn't be able to give you a *presint* if you didn't have a birthday. You wouldn't know how old you are."

"We only guessed innyway," he said. He had taken down some of the disused harness hanging on old nails, and was oiling the leather and polishing the metal.

"But now we keep good track," she said.

"What if I told you that you—you, and Ruth, and Littleruth and Joe and everone else in town, an everone in the whole state of Texis, didn't know their real name. And I gave you a name, I *made one up* f'you without your even askin for it or feelin that you needed it."

"But that proves my point—it *is* somethin you need, a birthday. And somethin more that maybe we need if we doan have it, a real name like the real name you had, when you were little."

"It's still my name," he said.

She hesitated. "You never told it to me, though," she said softly. Sadly.

He continued to rub the harness. The half-lit wooden space, in which he sat on an empty keg and she stood near him, still smelled of the horse and manure, and oats in a barrel.

"*I* could just'z easy write down notes about you, and your famly," he said to Martha.

She cocked her head. "So you could," she said. But that was not for now.

He shook his head. He did not intend to give her permission by adopting her reasons for himself.

She was holding the diary book. "No?" she said, softly.

"I doan want to," he said. Not looking at her.

She hoped she was hiding her disappointment in him. "I don't want you to let what happened make you feel this way."

"That's the way it really is, Martha, the way everbody is and you can't pretind they're not."

"I'm not pretindin. I'm not." She laid her notebook and pencil down. She wanted to touch him, to be touched by him, she did not want these words—icy or hot she couldn't say which, but freezing or searing her, not what she wanted.

"And I don't *want* you copyin in your book all my thengs I say."

"I'm tryin to keep for our *children* somethin about you before you forget it too."

"You started it long time ago, before it was for Joe and Littleruth, you started it f'*you*."

"I *did*. I was excited—to be able to write down thengs for you—"

"I'm not forgettin innytheng. But I don't like writin it down. Don't know why."

"But it's somethin that'll be lost."

"Lost to who?"

"To people that ought to know, to Littleruth and Joe. *Why* does it make you angry?"

"Not angry, exactly. I've thought more about tellin them than you have, only you don't realize it. And it's not addin much to them if people will hate them for it. And it feels like your takin away from me, too. Takin away from me when I haven't got hardly innytheng that's not taken away."

"That's not true—"

"*And* I can't tell it to you right, innyway, it doesn't come out right when I say it, what you write down, that's not it, what I *thenk*, what I *know*."

"Then *you* can hep me put it in my book the *right* way."

"I *can't*. Can't get it right for you, 's only right when I remember it, when I feel it, just me, inside of me. Not when I tell you."

She would have helped him if he'd let her.

She needed to *know*, she wanted to look back through him at the people in his line, she wanted to give her children a sense of themselves that way, she wanted to connect them to something more than an empty void, an unpeopled place where nobody was anymore, a lost grave and beyond that no one at all.

"You can thenk about it all you want, and tell me whenever you feel like it, and you can see how I write it down, and see that it's right, that it fits what you feel."

"It isn't like that. You askin me makes me say it to you a way

I don't—I don't say it to mysef. I don't *say* thengs to mysef, things I know. And then you're askin me to make mysef back into an Indian when evertheng I've done for years now . . . I can't be two kinds a man, all at the same time, I haven't bin able to do that."

"I never wanted you not to be your own sef. . . . I fell in love with you, remember, just the way I met you, a long time ago?"

He'd come from a world that, while it lay right beside her world, right underneath her world, she had never known about.

Who he'd been at that time—standing to one side of the white man's world and stepping up to take this job or that when it was offered, and standing back once more when he was done, and watching from the side: that had been someone else he had been, at that time. "Sweetbitter," some bossing white man would say, "Git holt t'other end a this, we'll carryit yonder and don't set it down till I say." And he'd done it and done it and done it. He was different now. He might show Joe how to make a throwing stick, and he might show Littleruth some plants in the woods that would soothe an itch or cure a stomachache; but he didn't do those things himself anymore. He went into Reilly's dry goods store and stood at the counter in his white shirt like any other man and paid coin for what he wanted, even medicine that Martha or Ruth Hagerman told him to buy and that he brought home and that Martha gave to the child who was ill.

Later, she was holding out her hands to him but he was not taking them. "Sweetheart," she said. "I'm sorry if you felt hurt by it, somehow. And please don't worry so much."

His head was bowed. Tired. She reached out and put her hand on his thick shoulder. He raised his head and looked at her just an instant, with an expression of truce, and then he moved and her hand fell away from him, and he walked slowly, with light step, through the kitchen and out the screen door, and stood on the landing outside in the hot late-afternoon air, and let the door close gently, holding it from being pulled heavily shut by its rusty coiled spring. She could see him through the tarnished slack screen—he was looking up into the sky, over the trees, into the scattered lonely song of a few daytime birds calling nearby: jay and redbird and dove.

54

The Coushattas

Once, this happened:

Into the gathering of huts, that looked as if they had been laid down carelessly by a giant hand, in haste, without care, came walking the young man some part Indian, some part white, carrying a carpetbag, wearing moccasins. It was a damp fall day, and a bitter smoke seeped out of doors and windows and rolled down from the mouths of mud chimneys. The young man's hair was cut short like a white man's. Dogs began barking. A fullblood woman, shorter than he, darker than he, with longer hair than his, came to a doorway and looked out at him. He returned her gaze frankly, without question or answer. She pulled her head back, as if disgusted with what she saw, and looked him up and down. He had slowed and was hesitating, and now his hesitation was a question aimed at her. But she snorted and her expression was of offended pity. He looked around the reservation village. A few other faces were staring at him. Three dogs were close around him, snarling and barking. No one said anything to him. He turned around slowly and with a measured pace walked away, with the dogs following at a cowardly distance but barking and growling angrily, till he had gone far enough down the yellow sand road through the dense thicket to lessen their craven anger, and they put their tails back up and trotted away, sniffing here and there, pissing on tree trunks and palmettos, as they moved lazily and already without memory of him back to their home.

55

On a Difference

Russet with henna tones; cinnamon; tawny; topaz; claret-tinged with cyan highlights; pale cinnabar or cochineal, with a luster of hazel; a blush of auburn; apricot, indigo, turquoise, magenta, taupe, pearly, gilded, blue or black—what color might the skin of man or woman not be? Color of bell-tones, color of apple-scent, color of salt-taste, color of warmth. Color of Phoenicia or Manila, of São Paolo or Natal, yes, admitted and even praised as God's inventiveness, in its place.

But what did it come from, this duskiness? What did it occult? What was concealed beneath it that would not show itself to be trusted, to be led, to be brought into the pale?

The white reaction—the dislike, distrust, disease—came not from the color or the colors themselves but from color as the sign of a different speaking, a different laughter, a different singing, a different gait. Expectations of God and of seed, of remembrance and eloquence, of supper and of nakedness together—these differed and diverged, and must never be merged or miscegenated, oh no.

For there was white belief that the old warring and savagery of these darker ones had suppurated from innate beastliness; there was the present sight of drunkenness, of feeble legs unable to raise a man from the clotted vomit in which he had slept, of inarticulate tongues too stuporous to apologize to man or even woman of substance, of decency, of whiteness. And all the tales of nobility and grace, of wisdom and courage, had been forgotten or turned to myths about a people who had disappeared long ago. For what did the white people tell now? That there had been unnatural stoicism. That there had been merciless torment and arrogant indifference to suffering. That there had been paint on faces. So people told, who had not seen it, but whose grandmothers were said to have been raped, whose grandfathers had raped.

Can the Ethiopian change his skin? No more than can the savage. And those whose black or red blood was mixed with white are most dangerous, these readily fall victim of a fatal arrogance to assume a place not theirs. But such as these can learn new ways, can be taught new customs, can be educated and rise to the higher plane of civilization, can take their place at the side of the white man and participate in a larger world, a more advanced society, a better way of life, a progress toward advantage and contentment of all kinds, with acknowledged and scientific limits. They must only be willing to learn.

56

In Cold Weather

It would be a strange time, that would be much talked of afterward, that day in late February when a fine snow fell for hours and lay on the new good green leaves and in the cups of early spring blossoms.

The snow fell lightly and the world was changed, brighter and harsher and more open. The snow defined each leaf and bud and killed some. The snow lay on each bare limb that was leafless, and outlined it sharply. The snow lay evenly on the ground.

On this cold overcast winter Saturday afternoon Reuben might go toward the door to answer the knocking. Littleruth might be walking ahead of him, curious, and might stand before him as he opened it. The icy air would be coming in and on the other side of the screen door would be a stranger, a white man about Reuben's age with a few days' growth of beard. He might be wearing a business suit, but it would look like he hadn't changed his clothes for several days. Little snow crystals in his hair and on his shoulders.

"Beggin yur pardon," the man might say. "I b'lieve I got the wrong *add*ress."

"Who you lookin for?" Reuben might answer him.

"Well," the man might say. He would look back over his shoulder down the stairs, toward the alley. "Well, I'm lookin for a Mr. Sweet."

"Thass my daddy," Littleruth would certainly say. The man

might look down at her, and then at Reuben again, with a studying kind of gaze.

"Is that right," he might say.

"What's your bidness?" Reuben would ask him. He would guide Littleruth by the shoulders to his side and part way behind him.

"I've got a friend with me that'd like to have a word with you," the man might say.

"Bout what."

"Well, he'd rather talk with you himsef. He's waitin in our automobile."

"Sent you up here lookin for me?"

"I come with im, yessir I did."

"From where?"

"I'd recommend that you come down with me, would be a lot better if you did."

"Who *is* your friend?"

"This is kindly confidential."

Littleruth would be behind Reuben now, looking around him at the man, whose tone of voice would have turned from the feigned mannerliness of strangers to a hard caution.

"Martha?" Reuben would call out, but not taking his eyes off the man. She would come holding Joseph and saying "Reuben, it's too cold for you to be standin there with the door open. Who is it?"

"Martha," he would say again. He might feel so precariously balanced that he was about to tip, for good or ill, for life or death, any instant. And who would take care of his babies? Reuben would shut the door hard and turn the latch.

"Reuben?" Martha would say quickly, puzzled.

Reuben might stand unmoving, his hand still on the latch, listening. He would hear the stranger go quickly down the steps and trot out of sight into the alley.

Martha would stand next to him. "Who *was* that?" she would say. She might pull aside the window curtain that covered the small glass pane set in the door, and look out. Reuben would be watching her face.

She would let the curtain fall back. "Reuben," she would say urgently.

"I don't know," he would say. "But I know what's happened."

She would be looking into his eyes. Her mouth would open. "They've come?" she would whisper.

"I b'lieve they have," he would say to her.

Again she might look out through the windowpane, this time trying not to move the curtain much. Then she would rush away to lay Joseph in his crib and rush back and take Littleruth by the hand and pull her away from the door. "I want you to get your coat on," she would say to the child. But Littleruth would say no and would hold on to Reuben's trousers with her free hand. "Doan want to," she might say.

Reuben might wish there was more than the simple latch on the door. He would look around the room but he wouldn't see any solutions.

"You can't take Littleruth and Joe out," he would say. "Can't git past em."

"But who *is* it?" she would ask him.

"I doan know yet," he would answer.

"I've got to git to Ruth's telephone and call for help. The *sheriff*'d come."

"He might. But we can't *git* out a here, Martha," he would say again. "And they must've figgered that out before they knocked on the door."

Reuben wouldn't want to get too far from the door, because he was the only thing besides the latch that could hold it. But he couldn't stand behind it forever.

Littleruth would be pulling at his trousers, and if she did that then he would pick her up but he'd still be in his thoughts.

Martha would probably run to the windows on the side facing Ruth's house and throw one of them open and yell for her friend, "Ruth! Ruth! Can you hear me? Ruth! Help us!"

There wouldn't be any response from the big empty-looking house. "Ruth! Ruth!" she would call again. And then she'd call, "Delora!" The cold damp air would chill her. She would be very afraid. She might pull the window down and go back to the door and peek out through the curtain again. A man would be sitting on the bottom step, his back to her, smoking a cigarette. Sitting right out in the snowfall.

Martha would turn the latch and jerk the door open. "What d'you want?" she'd yell at him. He might turn around and look up at her over his shoulder, exhaling smoke. "Like to talk to *Mr.* Sweet, ma'am, as I b'lieve he calls himsef now," he might say.

Reuben might be just about to push the door shut again when she would gasp and put her hand to her throat, and touch her collar, a little thing she always did when she was upset, and Reuben would look out over her shoulder and a man would be standing at the foot of the steps, wearing a new U.S. Army uniform and new boots.

"Hello, big sister," he might say, not so loud, because on a winter day like that the outside feels almost like the inside, it's quiet, and you can talk softly and be heard. He'd be looking up toward their door, squinting against the falling snow.

"You got no right to come here and bother us," she'd say to him, her voice quavering.

"Yore home town ain't bin the same since you up and left it," he might say. "Mama and Daddy moved away, to Beaumont, did you know that? And Annie got hersef married, has a couple babies."

"Go away," Martha would say. Still speaking in a loud voice.

"You oughta let me catch you up on thengs," he might say. The other man would have stood up and flicked his cigarette away. He would be standing behind James. "I ain't got a lotta time," James would say. "Catchin the train north, and then I'm goan ship out overseas. Whyn't you send *Mr. Sweet* down here so we kin talk with him a little bit, and then you an I kin have a kind of famly reunion."

Reuben would shove the door closed and turn the latch again.

"It's not goan be any use," he would say. "They got their minds on just one theng, that's all they want." How imponderably precious it had been even to suffer the worst of his sleepless nights in this place with his children and Martha.

Reuben might think for a few more minutes, pacing the room, picking up Littleruth and putting her down; she would keep running to the same window to look at the small snowflakes falling. He would say to Martha, "Call James and his friend up."

She wouldn't believe him.

"Yes, do it," he'd say. He would stand at the door, unlatch it, hold it open a little bit for her. "Martha, there's no time to be talkin, call them up and when I'm gone git the children into Ruth's house and lock the doors and telephone some help if you can find it."

Still looking over her shoulder at Reuben she would move slowly to the door and open it farther. "You all come up here now. We have to talk," she would call down. The snowflakes would be sparkling on the shoulders of the men, on their dark clothes.

"What?" James would say, looking up at her. Not believing. She would force herself to turn her head away from Reuben and toward the men down on the ground, and say it again.

James and his friend would look at each other, and then come up the stairs, cautiously, James first. He would be wearing a black holster on his uniform belt, with a large revolver in it. Reuben would reach for Martha, as the men were coming up, and hug her and touch Littleruth's hair and glance back at the crib where Joe lay wrapped in Mr. Grooms's quilt, he would push Martha gently away from the door and she would be saying, "Oh Reuben, oh sweetheart, no, no," and he would take the doorknob in his hand, watching them come, and when they were almost at the landing he would fly through the door.

Reuben would leap halfway down the stairs and bowl the two of them down and somehow recover his feet and keep going. In the alley he would race past a third man, who was in the automobile, running the engine to keep the heater on. After dodging through alleyways with James and the first man chasing him on foot and the car in sliding pursuit behind them, and not seeing a single other person, when usually there were people in their backyards and garages and stables, Reuben would reach the one stretch of woods that still provided an escape from Harriet through cover; woods like a last stream of life that fed the town from worlds as they used to be—and, farther off, still were—before the settlers came and warred and the trees were felled for the mill and the great crop fields were planted.

At first Reuben would hear James and the other man running after him in the alleyways; they only dropped away because Reuben sprinted ahead of them down routes he already knew, around corners they did not know, and was running with plans, while they in their predatory anger were following and guessing. By the time Reuben entered the woods, the two running men would have gotten into the automobile and it would be closing on him. He'd cut across a bushy unfenced lot and hear the automobile door slam as someone got out to chase him again on foot, and the automobile would spin away as the driver went on, trying the roads to keep abreast of the foot-chase.

For now, there would be no one to harm Martha if all three men were chasing Reuben.

Reuben would glance over his shoulder as he ran, knowing before he looked, but looking anyway, that he would see behind him the dark clear prints of his smooth-soled street shoes, one of his two original identical and identically-worn pairs, bought for him by Ruth. He had newer shoes for work now, and these old ones he wore on Saturdays. Not the shoes for running over the snow and across the expanse of the earth.

This was a narrow neck of woods, mixed oak and magnolia and beech and pine; like the opposite of a real river, it narrowed as it approached the town and only poured a little stream of trees into it. He would run as fast as he could, now, up into its widening and if he could have followed it for a day and a night it would have opened into a great ocean of woods. But the mills had taken most of the trees around here; and the snow lay on the ground, on the dead leaves, and with every step he left the sign of his passing.

He would veer to the left, tearing through thicker brush till he hit the gravel road and could move to the melted lanes left by automobile tires and then running along those, slipping from time to time on the loose wet gravel, but not leaving such visible prints now. No one would come out of the woods behind him.

The snow would have made all worlds quieter. There wouldn't be a single sound of bird. The air would be still under the cold overcast sky. He'd have to listen between the sounds of his own feet hitting the road, between the sounds of his own breath in his throat and mouth, for the automobile.

He would hope they were following him, for now. He would use his footprints to lead them just so far. He wouldn't want to go so fast they couldn't catch his direction. And he would hope he could get away from them.

To the right, the mixed woods and on the left a piney wood, the road running along the edge between the two.

Reuben would keep on for a few minutes and then move to the leftmost and then when nearest the verge, he'd leap off and into the ditch. And stumble. His stumbling would be marked by a darker area where he had shaken the light snow from the stems and leaves of the weeds and trampled the ground. He would stop and study it. It would be too full of sign that he had leapt to it. And now a motor car would be coming from the other direction and he'd have to crouch low and only half hidden behind the trunk of a pine as the vehicle sped past, spewing snow-melt and mud from its tires. A small truck moving very fast; a white man driving, looking straight ahead, preoccupied, with a cigarette in his mouth; on the door faded lettering naming a meat merchant.

He'd climb back onto the road and run on another few minutes.

By now they would be about to reach him on this road, if they had guessed anything like the right direction. For its size, Harriet had too few roads in and out.

He would stay to the left. He was going to enter that piney wood. There would be no sound but the sound he made, running and breathing. He'd feel the full weight of his body with each stride, his middle having thickened with the life of working at the mill and merely walking to and from it. But his legs would be fit, his heart untaxed as yet, his lungs strong.

He'd run and run. Past the trees that were watching him and unable either to aid or harm him. Past an old snakeskin sparkling fantastically with crystals of snow along its dry contorted length. Past weeds nodding their heads under caps of white.

A little farther up where the ditch was shallower, there would be a low long pile of sand and dirt, the kind the steam grader left when it scraped the road. A long low ridge parallel to the road. He'd run past it twenty yards, stop, pick his way back along the melted tire lane, and then leap out again, landing just past the peak of the piled dirt on the other side, where his track couldn't be seen from the road. Then through the patchy weeds he'd get up onto the floor of the thick piney woods. Now, trotting, he would pick his way with more deliberateness; not so much snow would have sifted down through the pine tops to show his tracks on the slippery ground covered with an uncountable infinitude of pine needles. The whistled chord of a freight train would come through the quiet cold air.

The only other sound would be his running. He would avoid open sand and open ground where snow lay. He only had to outwit three white men used to town life. If the car didn't catch them up to him so fast that they could actually see or hear him ahead of them through the open pine forest, he'd have a good chance of getting away. And could hope that by the time they gave up, Martha and the children would have some safety.

Men like these had buried his mother and it had been scarcely bearable for them to touch her poor body.

He would be breathing very hard now, but still moving steadily. He'd come to a shallow gully, where water had not run for a dozen years already, and young trees were growing along the bottom. He would stop at the edge and turn and listen behind him. He'd hear the faint complicated sound of the automobile and voices out on the road. They would have seen his track. Even a little snow on the pine needles, no friend, was false to him, it told them everything.

He would scramble to the bottom of the little draw and turn up it, running among the small trees.

He could run from them and keep going, and never come back, and give it all up.

It might be that there was help for him, too, coming in response to Martha's telephone call. But not so likely, and no help could reach him in time, now.

He could hide a while—perhaps a few weeks, and return secretly to Martha and leave with her and the children. But how would they sort it out? Traveling and hiding with the children would be impossible; impossible also was the choice to stay in Harriet. Martha could not do it again, and the children could not. If they had an automobile of their own and cash, they could go as far as California; but they had never had enough from his earnings to save or buy an automobile, and Ruth would have laughed if he had ever suggested it. Would she give them her automobile now?

He could try to kill James and the other men. If he drew them far enough into the woods and had a chance to confront them one at a time, he might be able to do that. Then he could never go back; but at least Martha would never have to think of James again. James had a gun, though. And anyway, what good would it do if he could fight them? If he killed even one of them then other men would hang him.

They might catch him and he could do nothing; they might kill him. They were going to kill him.

There might be no way back—to that kitchen, those rooms,

those children, that home, all of it that had been his—his children, his place. His lungs were burning, his heart was burning, his sides were aching, his being was cracked through, like a plate that has not yet quite fallen into the pieces into which a crack has divided it.

So why not turn and face them. What difference did it make now, no matter what he did. They had the power to do what they wanted, and although they might be prevented if someone tried to stop them beforehand, if they succeeded they did not have to fear great consequences.

He would try to imagine what Martha was doing. What Little-ruth was feeling. All the king's horses and all the king's men couldn't put Humpty Dumpty together again: that's what that was about. He understood it now.

It might be that they catch him alone, and he doesn't yell or call. The hour is quiet, and not so far away in the woods someone living on the outskirts of the town is hammering—that would be Clement Morgan's new roof being put on by three black hired men.

It might be that they tear from his hand the wedding ring that Martha bought for him.

Or it might be that alone in the woods, to try to annihilate his own illusions, to punish himself for them, he pulls the ring off and places it on a rock and lifts another stone with both hands and brings it down hard. The impact shoots stone-chips to right and left. He is still, kneeling with both hands holding the stone, breathing heavily. Then he picks up the smashed ring wearily and tosses it to one side without looking after it.

It might be that a blow catches him in the face and he doesn't feel pain so much as the sudden disorientation of his head banged to one side, his eyes instinctively closed. But what he can see when he opens them is cloudy, he opens them after the shutting reflex passes and he thinks I need to open my eyes, and then he realizes he has opened them and there is still only darkness. Give me a few seconds back, he's thinking, I wasn't ready. He has to wrench himself out of a sickening cold fall merely in order to remind himself to crouch, to cover his head, to defend himself as well as he can. But something else in him is pushing him up again, pushing him to stand up and he gets his eyes open and he can see again and he's standing, and in front of him is the first man with a heavy stick in his fists. He pulls it back and brings it down at an angle aimed again at the side of Reuben's head but Reuben fends it off this time with one arm, it bruises and tears his forearm, but his eyes are clearing a little more and he's standing up to his full height, looking at the man, not moving toward him. Behind the man James is standing, watching.

"He's not goin anywhere, Frank, he's got nowhere to go," one of them might say. James would put his revolver back into the black holster, and look around for a good-sized tree limb, and say over the first man's shoulder something like, "You about t'be a shovel full of shit now, you Injin bastard."

It might be that he tries to fight them when they catch him but a huge blow lifts him from underneath, in his belly, and drops him again, a kick or a bullet, he doesn't know which, he's on his side now, and there is a stunning, through-moving pain in his body, he has no breath; he thinks, he thinks he is calling, "Martha!" and "Littleruth!" and "Joe!"

With sounds of the men behind him he comes to a small ravine rushing with winter rains and melting snow, and around him the snow has whitened everything to a sharp contrast. Across the narrow gully someone has laid a long trimmed pine trunk for a bridge but it will require considerable balance to keep a sure footing on it and cross it and not fall. And now it has a layer of snow on top. Snow has capped the limestone rocks on the ground and in the water, the exposed knuckles of tree roots, the eroded protrusions of the banks. It might be he could cross over on the pine trunk and then throw it down into the gully water. Crossing water was always a moment of vulnerability for the spirit of a man.

Now Reuben might throw off his shoes and stockings and take the first step out onto the freezing log and then the second, he would feel in good balance, his feet would not slip. He would take a third step and a fourth. He would hear faintly the sound of men running behind him. Still too far away to shoot him. He would be halfway across. Under him the water would be muddy and rushing—scarcely deep enough to swim in but far enough down, maybe eighteen or twenty feet, and the bed muddy enough, to trap him, no doubt, if he falls. More steps and he would be nearly to the other side where if he would glance up for an instant he would see that the snow has scarcely fallen and the floor of the woods under the pines is green, and there would be miles and miles of clear running, deep hiding, plentiful hunting; and for a journey he has always been a good one when forced.

57

Reuben's Voice

Ya kut unta le ma
ohoyo ut akiania

yo me kia ne ne
isa kanimi

Ya kut unta le ma
ohoyo ut akiania

yo me kia ne ne
isa kanimi

Ya kut unta le ma
ohoyo ut akiania

yo me kia ne ne
isa kanimi

About the Author

Reginald Gibbons was born in Houston, Texas, and was raised in the then semirural area called Spring Branch. His maternal grandparents, Maurice Lubowski and Sophie Frederick Lubowski, emigrated from Poland in 1900 and settled in Houston around 1915. His paternal grandfather, William Frank Gibbons, was of Irish descent, and his paternal grandmother, Ruby Harrell Gibbons, was half Choctaw.

Gibbons' father left the family farm in Mississippi and went to Texas around 1926, where he settled.

Gibbons is an award-winning poet and the long-time editor of *TriQuarterly*, one of the premier literary magazines in the United States. His previous works include *Five Pears or Peaches* (Broken Moon, 1991), *Maybe It Was So* (University of Chicago Press, 1991), and *Saints* (Persea Books, 1986). His work has also appeared in *Harper's* and other magazines. *Sweetbitter* is his first novel. He makes his home in Evanston, Illinois.

Design by Laura Joyce Shaw.

Text set in Stempel Garamond
by Blue Fescue Typography and Design,
Seattle, Washington.